Highlander's Rebellious Love

By

Donna Fletcher

Donna Fletcher

This is a work of fiction. Names, characters, places, and incidents are either the product of the author's imagination or are used fictitiously, and any resemblance to actual persons, living or dead, business establishments, events or locales is entirely coincidental.

Highlander's Rebellious Love

All rights reserved.
Copyright November 2014 by Donna Fletcher

Cover art
Kim Killion Group

Ebook Design
A Thirsty Mind Book Design

Visit Donna's Web site
http://www.donnafletcher.com
http://www.facebook.com/donna.fletcher.author

Donna Fletcher

Table of Contents

Chapter 1
Chapter 2
Chapter 3
Chapter 4
Chapter 5
Chapter 6
Chapter 7
Chapter 8
Chapter 9
Chapter 10
Chapter 11
Chapter 12
Chapter 13
Chapter 14
Chapter 15
Chapter 16
Chapter 17
Chapter 18
Chapter 19
Chapter 20
Chapter 21
Chapter 22
Chapter 23
Chapter 24
Chapter 25
Chapter 26
Chapter 27
Chapter 28
Chapter 29
Chapter 30

Donna Fletcher

Chapter 31
Chapter 32
Chapter 33
Chapter 34

Titles by Donna Fletcher
About the Author

Chapter One

"You cannot be serious, Father."

Anytime his middle daughter Patience called him Father, Donald Macinnes knew he was in trouble. Unlike his eldest daughter Heather who was sweet and kind, or his youngest daughter Emma who was too interested in learning all she could about everything she could, Patience was nothing like her name.

"I have not been home a full day. I have yet to see my sister Emma who I have learned is wed to Rogan MacClennan and who had been Heather's intended. I also have not yet found my sister Heather who has been abducted by the vile Dark Dragon." Patience threw her arms up in the air. "And what does my father want of me? He wants me to go settle a squabble for a clan that claims us kin, but we have not heard from since," —she threw her hands up into the air again— "since when, Father? Heather is my priority, not some distant, inconsequential squabble between two insignificant clans."

Donald Macinnes pulled himself away from the pillows that supported his back in the bed and glared at his daughter. "The last time I looked, I was still laird of this clan and your father, and that means you will obey whatever order I give you."

"Why would you think that would work now, Father, when it has not worked since I was young."

"Because you are not only the finest warrior I have, but you are the most capable to see this matter settled without a war ensuing."

"You think to ply me with compliments, so I will do as you ask?" Patience said, planting her hands on her slim hips while a glint of fire surged in her bold green eyes.

"I ply you with the truth," Donald snapped. "You are an exceptionally skilled and capable warrior and as your laird I am sending you where your talents are most needed. I am in correspondence with the King to see what can be done to have Heather returned home to us."

"King James do something?" Patience laughed. "He is too afraid of the Dark Dragon to do anything. We must rescue Heather ourselves."

"Enough!" Donald demanded. "Whether I speak to you as my daughter or one of my loyal warriors, you have no choice but to obey me on this, and do not think it insignificant. You know full well that the McFarden clan is necessary to our clan's safety and we to theirs. Their land borders McLaud land. They are fierce and mighty Highlanders that will not be ignored and they are claiming that a portion of McFarden land belongs to them. If we allow them to stake claim to it, then they will not stop there and soon McFarden land—our land—will belong to the McLauds."

Patience understood the importance of what her father was telling her, but what mattered more to her was finding her sister Heather. If it had been herself who had been captured, Heather would not rest until Patience was returned home. And Patience intended to do the same for her sister. She would not rest, would not relent in her pursuit to find Heather.

"Let Rogan MacClennan send a troop of warriors to settle this dispute, since our clans have now been joined by marriage." Patience's eyes flared a fiery green once again. "Did you even bother to ask Emma if she wanted to wed Rogan MacClennan?"

Donald dropped back against the pillow, worn out from arguing with his daughter. Ever since she had been young, it had not been easy getting her to obey. She had a mind of her own and a sharp mind at that, and she was full of confidence. She had all the requisites of a fine laird, which made her exasperating to deal with.

"Emma and Rogan happen to love each other," he said.

"You are sure of that?" Patience asked. "Rogan had not wanted Emma and now he claims to love her?"

"I understand your misgivings, but their love is there for all to see and your sister is happy. And I am happy and relieved that the arranged marriage turned out so well for her."

"You will not marry me off to anyone without my consent," Patience warned with a shake of her finger.

"I would not dare, Patience. Your husband is yours to choose."

A fit of coughing gripped Donald and Patience hurried to his side to help him sit up and drink some of the brew kept on the chest by his bed. Her father had appeared much improved since last she saw him over a month ago, but that did not mean he had completely recovered from his illness. She had failed to keep that in mind when he had summoned her to his bedchamber. She had assumed he wanted to speak with her about formulating a plan to rescue Heather. To learn that his only intention where Heather was concerned was to keep in correspondence with the King had infuriated her, and that she was to be sent off to deal with witless warriors infuriated her even more.

Donald took hold of his daughter's hand as she helped him to lie back on his pillows. "I know what I ask of you makes you angry, but sometimes a laird has no choice but to do what must be done even if he does not like it himself. And if you dare to think that I am giving up on your sister, then you should be ashamed of yourself. I love all three of my daughters with all my heart and I would give my life to keep you all safe and see you all happy."

The anger drained from Patience like a receding wave, leaving a heavy dose of guilt in its wake. Her da was right. No one could ever doubt his love for his daughters.

"I am truly sorry, Da," she said and hugged him.

He patted her back. "It has been a difficult time for all of us, but fear not, I will see that all turns out well."

His reassuring words lightened her heart a bit and reminded her of what she should have realized, that her da would not rest until Heather was rescued.

Donald patted the bed for Patience to sit, and she did. "It is a most unwelcoming area, mountainous range and barren land, another reason the McFarden joined with us. We provide them with much needed staples. They in turn keep watch over that area and let us know of any unrest."

"There is always unrest in the Highlands, all of Scotland for that matter. I sometimes wonder if Scotland will ever be at peace."

"A feeling felt by all," Donald said, "which is why we must make certain we do all we can to keep our clan and holdings as strong as possible."

Patience had no choice but to agree. "You are right, Da, but I hate delaying my search for Heather over nothing but a—"

"A matter that can be settled with relative haste," Donald said, "thus avoiding a major conflict that if left unattended could cause far worse delays in finding your sister. And need I remind you again that I do not sit idle when it comes to your sister's abduction. You must trust that I am doing more than you realize to see everything ends well."

Her da was a man of his word and he was a wise and courageous laird. He had taught her much and she continued to learn from him. She could see to this matter and return home in no time. Another thought struck her that made this mission more appealing. It would give her a chance to extend her search for the Dark Dragon's lair. The trail she had followed had gotten her nowhere. It seemed the Dark Dragon's warriors lived up to their name—ghost warriors. Their tracks were there one moment and gone the next. The only thing she had learned was that the Dark Dragon's army was vast and would not be easy to battle against. It had made her reach the conclusion that it would take a much wiser plan to defeat the evil beast.

"I will ready my warriors and leave in the

morning," Patience said.

"Take a new batch of warriors with you. Your faithful group needs a rest."

"They go where I go," Patience insisted, knowing her men would not take kindly to being left behind.

"Think, Patience," her da said. "Your men are worn out. Fresh warriors will serve you better and help keep your mission brief."

If anything, she wanted this mission to be as brief as possible. "Another point conceded, Da, though my men will not be happy about it."

"Nonetheless, they will obey you as you do your laird," Donald said. "Now listen well, for you need to know about the McLauds. Greer is the oldest of three sons and laird since his da's passing a few months ago. He is a fierce one and short-tempered, so tread carefully around him. Rona, his wife, is as short-tempered as her husband. Rab is the middle son, skilled in weapons and battle, and it is he who leads the McLaud warriors when it comes to conflict. He recently wed, her name is Saundra. She is the eldest daughter of Hew McDolan, laird of the McDolan clan and you know well that we have almost come to conflict with them several times. So, it is easy to assume that he is behind this attempt to confiscate some of our land. And there is no need for me to tell you that land is power here in the Highlands."

Patience hated to admit it, but her da was right in seeing to this matter immediately. Left unattended the McLauds would seek to encroach and lay claim to more Macinnes land. "From the little I recall about the McLauds, they are a more brute than intelligent lot. Do you think Hew McDolan is behind this encroachment?"

"Craig MacFarden will know if there has been interference from the McDolans."

"And if there has been?" Patience asked and grew upset watching her da take a deep breath, as if trying to lift a heavy weight off himself. She spoke up before he could answer, wanting to lighten his burden. "I will see to it, Da."

"With little or no bloodshed," he said, though more commanded. "Now about the youngest McLaud, though there is not much to tell. From what I hear, Hunter keeps himself busy entertaining the lassies. His father, Kevin, when he was alive, spoke poorly of him. And it is well known he came to blows with Hunter on more than one occasion. I do not think you have much to worry about when it comes to him."

"Men are men, Da, I can handle them," Patience said with confidence.

Donald shook his head. "And what happens when there comes a day you cannot handle one?"

Patience laughed. "I will marry him."

Chapter Two

Patience was looking forward to a bath and a decent meal after two grueling weeks on the road. How anyone lived in this desolate area of Scotland was a mystery to her. She wanted to get this matter settled and be on her way home.

Her bold green eyes widened with each step her stallion took into the village, though it resembled anything but a village. There was a cluster of buildings, each in desperate need of repair and a longhouse for communal meetings that needed attention as well. The villagers themselves eyed her suspiciously, though that was not surprising. She did not dress like most women. She wore a man's shirt made to fit her slim size and she wrapped her plaid around her body like a warrior. Leather strips crisscrossed her chest and back, leaving no doubt she was a woman and that she carried weapons; a sword in her back sheath and one at her side. Leather boots rode up mid-thigh and leather leggings covered the rest of her legs. She wore her dark hair pulled back taut and tied with a leather strip.

She had been told numerous times that she possessed a stark beauty that caught men's eyes, though her intense green eyes intimidated, which was fine with her.

When Patience saw a lanky man about her height step out of the longhouse, she directed her horse toward him. Her father had described Craig McFarden to her, though he had warned her to add several years to his description, since it had been some time since he had last seen the man. And he had been right, though the years or perhaps the harsh land had not been kind to Craig McFarden.

Gray hairs dominated his long dark hair and deep lines accented his eyes and mouth, though his dark eyes were sharp. And though his body was slim, he stood straight and tall and looked fit enough. He wore no smile when he saw her, but then she had not expected a warm welcome.

"Macinnes sends me a woman to deal with our problem?" Craig McFarden called out as she and her warriors approached him.

"Do I need to teach you manners, McFarden?" she asked, though it sounded more like a warning as she stopped her stallion in front of him.

McFarden laughed, a robust laugh that echoed in the late spring air. "You can try, lassie."

Patience slipped off her horse with ease and walked over to McFarden. She stopped almost face to face with him. "Apologize loud enough for all to hear," she ordered.

"Or what?" he asked with a mocking smile. "You will tear up and cry?" He laughed again.

She leaned in close and whispered, "No, I will cut off your balls."

McFarden froze and his laughter died instantly when he felt her blade slip between his legs.

"Now!" she warned, pressing the blade to his skin, probably nicking it a bit, but then he would know she was a woman of her word. "And make sure all know that I am Patience Macinnes, daughter of Donald Macinnes here to settle the dispute."

"I am truly sorry for my unmannerly welcome," McFarden called out. "The clan is most pleased to welcome you, Patience Macinnes, daughter of Donald Macinnes, and more than pleased that you are here to settle the dispute with the McLaud clan. I invite you and your men to join me and mine in the longhouse for food and drink."

"Much better," Patience said and returned her dagger to the sheath at her waist. With the scowl that crossed McFarden's face, she knew she had made no friend, but she was not here to make friends.

They were soon ensconced in the longhouse, a structure that held a few tables, benches, and a fire pit in the middle. The smoke went out a hole in the roof, though a portion of it lingered in the confined space, creating a hazy cloud that settled overhead.

A group of women came and went with food and drink, their worried expressions obvious, and Patience wondered if the situation had grown worse here. Craig McFarden minded his manners and spoke not a word about the problem while the meal was eaten. But Patience, wanting this done with, broached the matter.

"Tell me what goes on here," she said to McFarden as she dunked a stale piece of bread into the thin stew broth to soften it.

McFarden took a swig of ale before answering her, as if needing to fortify himself. "The McLauds want our land, plain and simple. Several McLaud warriors have set up camp a good distance from where our land borders theirs to the north and are refusing to leave. Greer McLaud claims the area belongs to him, and I fear he will be moving more warriors in any time now."

"Why, after all this time of peace between the two clans, has it changed?" she asked.

"Greer's father, Kevin could be an uncompromising man, but he respected your father, since they had fought beside each other on several occasions. So, he made no move on our land. Greer holds no such respect. He is a greedy man who cares naught but for himself and with his brother Rab marrying Hew McDolan's daughter, Greer has grown brazen."

"Has McDolan showed any signs of helping Greer McLaud?"

"None that I can see, but I know he is at least whispering in Greer's ear and urging him to make a claim."

"And start a battle he cannot win," Patience said.

"Are you so sure?" McFarden asked with concern. "The daughter of Donald Macinnes arrives with only forty men. Greer will find that laughable, as would most warriors."

"My forty warriors are worth a hundred of his and I have far many more that will come if needed and you can add to that the MacClennan warriors as well, since my sister Emma recently wed Rogan MacClennan."

That news actually brought a smile to McFarden. "Then you should be sending for them, for I have no doubt you will be needing them."

"Perhaps, we will see," Patience said, "but first I will see if I can persuade the McLaud warriors to leave our land."

McFarden's smile disappeared. "I mean no disrespect, Lady Patience—"

"Patience, call me Patience," she said, cringing at being called Lady Patience. She was far from what was expected of the title Lady and had no want to be addressed as such.

McFarden bobbed his head. "As you wish, Patience. The McLauds are going to laugh at you."

"Like you did?"

McFarden's face burned red with embarrassment.

"My father would never have sent me if he did not think me capable of seeing this matter settled. I will have it done soon enough and you will have nothing to fear from the McLauds. Now tell me why your village is in such disrepair?" She banged a hard chunk of bread on the table. "And your food stale."

"This is harsh and unforgiven land and what little we can grow has not done well. And this situation has not helped, since the people fear hunting and fishing the stream with the McLaud warriors lurking about."

"Have they harmed any of you?" Patience was quick to ask.

"One lad took a beating from a couple of them for protecting one of our lassies, and I complained bitterly about it to Greer. He assured me he would see the warriors punished, but he never had any intentions of doing anything. He knows his warriors outnumber ours and it would take weeks for the Macinnes warriors to reach us, and by then," —he shrugged— "most, if not all, of us would be dead."

Patience's anger grew and though she was tired from her long journey, it was still early in the day, enough time for things to be seen to. And since she was not one to wait, she said, "Take me to these McLaud warriors who encroach on our land."

~~~

"How much farther?" Patience asked McFarden after they had traveled about an hour.

"Not long now, just over that rise," he said, pointing not far in the distance. "We will stop at Lyall's croft to rest the horses a bit and quench our thirsts. She is a bit of an odd one, though harmless. Many believe her a witch, but she is just a bit different and a good soul."

Patience nodded, glad they would be stopping briefly before she dealt with the McLaud warriors. She had already instructed her warriors at what might need to be done, but it was always good to go over the plans again.

It was not long before they came upon the small croft. To Patience's surprise it was better maintained than the places in the McFarden village. She did wonder how the woman could live here alone in such barren surroundings, empty land stretching as far as the eye could see. But then McFarden had remarked about her being a bit odd.

McFarden rode ahead and had already dismounted when Patience and her warriors reached him. He was not far from the cottage door when a woman and a man, both half-dressed, stumbled laughing out of the cottage in each other's arms.

The woman was attractive and had a robust figure. Her flaming red hair was a mass of curls that looked as if they refused to be tamed, and she was quick to pull up her blouse to cover her plump breasts when she caught sight of her visitors.

The man on the other hand made no move to hide the fact that he was aroused beneath his plaid or cover his naked chest with the shirt he held in his hand. His strong features caught the eye. He was a good-looking man, but there was something more about him that appealed than just his attractive features. Maybe it was his muscles that rippled over his lean frame or his dark hair that just about touched his shoulders or the brash look from his alluring blue eyes. Whatever it was, it was obvious that he was a man confident with himself... and women.

Patience noticed that McFarden was hesitant to speak and when he did, she understood why.

"Hunter," McFarden said, acknowledging the youngest of the McLauds with a nod. "Have we interrupted you?"

"Yes, you have," he said, turning to give Lyall a hungry kiss while squeezing her backside. "I promised to take this beautiful woman to the stream for a swim."

"There is still a chill to the spring air," McFarden said.

"Hunter will not let me get chilled," Lyall said, running her hand over his naked chest.

Patience watched as passion soared in Hunter's blue eyes for the woman. He looked ready to devour her with unrelenting lust. He seemed like a stallion after a mare in heat. And curiosity had her wondering just how powerfully he would ride the woman. And damn if her own body did not flare to life. She silently scolded herself for such a foolish reaction.

"Do not let us delay you," McFarden said, then turned to Lyall. "I just stopped to see if you were faring well."

Lyall's smile widened. "I fare quite well thank you, Craig McFarden."

"Then we will be on our way," McFarden said with a nod.

"What? Leave without introducing us to your friends," Hunter said, his stark blue eyes turning to Patience. "That is not mannerly."

"Nor is it any of your concern, Hunter McLaud," McFarden said tersely.

Hunter shrugged. "It matters not to me, though the McLaud warriors over the rise will find your small troop amusing, especially the scrawny woman."

Patience refused to lash out at the arrogant warrior, since he was obviously baiting her. He was insignificant when it came to the problem. Let him go poke the willing woman while true warriors settled the issue.

She signaled her men, then turned and rode off without a word or a backward glance at the one McLaud who was not worth sparing her breath on.

McFarden joined her after a few moments, echoing her thoughts. "Hunter McLaud is a worthless warrior and will give us no trouble."

"Still, you did not want him to know who I was."

"Blood ties run deep. There is no point in taking a chance he would alert McLaud warriors to our arrival."

"I surmised as much. Are you sure he will not hurry to warn them?"

McFarden laughed, shaking his head. "That fool is only interested in one thing." His cheeks heated red. "Excuse my ill-manners once again."

"There is no need for an apology when you speak the truth."

Patience signaled her men to be on alert as they approached the rise. Once they reached the top, one glance told her she could disperse the motley group without a problem. There seemed to be no leadership. The warriors, if they could be called that, roamed or lazed around with no purpose and the camp itself had been poorly established.

McFarden rode up beside her. "As I feared, Greer has moved more men here. They have twice the men you have."

"And not a warrior among them," she said and signaled her men to follow. Her warriors were trained well and would take these men down without much effort.

Patience led the group as they entered the camp, some of the men getting to their feet, others remaining as they were, and most all of them snickering.

"Who leads this poor excuse for warriors?" Patience called out.

A barrel-chested man lacking height stepped forward. "What foolish woman dares to enter my camp and dares to make a demand?"

"The woman who is going to throw your sorry arses off Macinnes land."

"This is McLaud land," the man shouted his face flushing red.

"This is, always has been, and always will be

Macinnes land," Patience said her voice raised loud enough for all to hear.

The man went to speak.

"Spare me your ignorance," she snapped. "I have no patience for it. Now gather your men and get off my land."

Another warrior who stood at least two heads over the barrel-chested one approached, laughing.

"Make us," he challenged.

Patience dismounted and approached the big warrior. Snickers, laughter, and rude remarks followed every step she took. "I will give you one last chance to leave with your honor intact. If you do not take my offer, then I will send you home defeated by not only fewer warriors than yourselves, but a woman as well."

The warrior threw back his head and laughed. Patience did not wait. She lowered her head and rammed it with such force in the man's stomach that he went flying back off his feet, landing on his back with a heavy thud, grasping for breath. She then let loose with a battle cry and her warriors descended on the unprepared group and had them rounded up with hardly a weapon being drawn.

"Your name," Patience demanded of the barrel-chested man, so red in the face with anger that she thought he would explode.

"Dunn," he spit out as he got to his feet. "And you are going to pay for this."

She took a quick step at him and he stumbled away from her almost falling to his knees. "You dare threaten me?" She turned to McFarden who had not moved off his horse, so stunned was he by what had happened. "How far to their home by horse?"

"And hour or more."

Patience turned back to Dunn. "You will be walking home."

"You cannot steal our horses?" Dunn said and his men began to grumble.

"I will return them when I come to speak to Greer McLaud tomorrow. And let him know that I expect a warm welcome, for if any harm befalls me or my warriors, the Macinnes and MacClennan wrath will fall upon the McLauds."

Brows furrowed and eyes turned wide at the mention of the two strong clans being united.

"Now douse the fires and clean your mess before you take your leave," Patience ordered.

"Do it yourself," Dunn snapped.

Patience was on him in an instant, her dagger drawn and at his throat. Color drained from the man's face and sweat sprang from his brow.

"You learn much too slowly, Dunn. Shall I leave you with a small reminder of what happens when you disobey my command and treat me rudely?"

"You would not be so brave if your men were not here to protect you," Dunn challenged in an attempt to save face in front of his men.

"And did her men help her get that dagger to your throat?"

Patience did not turn to see who had spoken, she recognized that mocking voice.

"Her troop surprised us," Dunn said.

"A liar as well as a slow learner," Patience said and went to prick his skin with the tip of her dagger. Her wrist was grabbed quick, a band of steel feeling as if it coiled around it.

"I cannot let you harm one of my clansmen, though useless as they may be," Hunter said and yanked her hand away from Dunn's neck.

Patience glared at him. "Let go of me."

"You promise to be nice?" Hunter said with a grin that warned and titillated at the same time.

"I promise that if you do not release me, you will be sorry," Patience threatened.

Hunter lowered his head so that his nose almost touched hers. "And I promise you that when I have hold of a beautiful woman, I am never sorry... and either is she."

He released her so quickly that she stumbled.

Hunter turned to Dunn. "Do as she told you. Douse the fires and clean your mess, then start walking. Let Greer know to prepare for an important guest tomorrow."

Hunter turned back to Patience after Dunn angrily nodded and walked off grumbling. His blue eyes seemed to capture her in a soft caress and for a mere moment she felt a flutter in her stomach.

Annoyed at herself for letting a rogue like him affect her, she said, "This is Macinnes land and you McLauds will do well to remember it."

"My brother seems to think differently, though I daresay there is an easy solution to the problem."

"And what might that be?"

"Marry me and unite the clans."

Chapter Three

Patience stared at Hunter in disbelief. He was insane. He had to be to suggest that she wed him. "I would keep better control of that tongue of yours and stop speaking nonsense."

His eyes heated to a fiery blue. "Trust me, Patience, I have absolute control over my tongue and there are many who would attest to that."

"Women no doubt."

"Jealous?" Hunter whispered.

Patience took a step back, her imagination suddenly wondering exactly what his wicked tongue could do. "You are insane."

Hunter took a step closer, his expression turning serious. He kept his voice low when he said, "What I propose is far from insane and after you meet my family you may very well realize that and think again about my proposal."

Patience gave him a quick jab in the chest. "Let me be clear about this, Hunter McLaud. There is no way in heaven or hell that I would ever wed you."

"Careful," he said with a smug grin, "you may wind up having to eat those words."

"I would starve first."

"You would not last long. You are too skinny."

Her green eyes blazed with fury. "Go along with your men, McLaud, with your tail tucked between your legs and tell your brother I will be settling this matter tomorrow with him."

A low rumble of laughter echoed deep from his chest. "Oh, *mo chridhe*, you got the length of what is tucked between my legs right, and if you are lucky I may just show you how proficient I am with it." He walked off, his laughter growing louder.

Patience had all she could do to stop from going after him and leaving a mark on him he would never forget. How dare he speak so rudely to her and how dare he call her *my love*. She was not his love and never would be.

She was glad when she finally watched the motley group leave the area, Hunter having ridden off before they had finished with their task. She wondered what he would tell his brothers. From his remark about his family, she surmised that perhaps he did not get along well with them. But then she could see why. His family probably had no use for his cavorting ways.

When the McLaud men could no longer be seen, she took her leave, a few of her men lagging behind to make certain no one followed them.

Patience wondered why McFarden made no mention of stopping at Lyall's cottage on their return, but realized why when they passed the place. Hunter's horse was in the lean-to, appearing as if it had been bedded down for the remainder of day. She had assumed Hunter would rush home to warn his family of her impending visit, evidently McFarden knew better.

Of what she saw today of the McLauds, they would prove little trouble, though she would still use caution. She never took any enemy for granted, for it could prove a fatal move.

When they arrived back at the McFarden village, her warriors were quick to let her know that they intended to hunt for their supper and prepare it themselves. She called them all cowards and they laughed, knowing she wished that she could join them. But it would be an insult not to join Craig McFarden for supper, though she made the men promise to save her some of their food.

Patience walked through the small village, thinking of how Emma would be appalled by it. The thought of her sister had her missing her home and feeling guilty that she was here dealing with this mess while she should be searching for Heather. She missed her sisters terribly. They had been inseparable and going so long without seeing either of them left her feeling terribly lonely. There was no one to share, or more importantly, to trust with her concerns. The three of them had always shared their worries with each other, and it had made all concerns less worrisome.

She had been relentless in her pursuit of Heather and had followed so closely behind her abductors that she had thought for sure she would have caught up with them. But Heather's abductors had been talented in eluding Patience, splitting in two different directions, misdirecting tracks, and more. Their one failure had been not to realize the strength of her resolve. There had been no way she would stop searching for her sister. She had remained dogged on their trail until the trail had suddenly disappeared. What she learned after that had upset her badly and only turned her more determined.

Patience still could not believe that the Dark Dragon had been responsible for abducting Heather. She could not understand what he wanted from her or perhaps she did not want to admit what he wanted from her.

She kicked at a small stone in the dirt as she kept walking. She did not know how she was going to do it. She only knew that nothing, and no one, would stop her from rescuing Heather from the Dark Dragon's lair. And she knew there was one person she could count on to help her... her sister Emma. Together they would get their sister Heather back. And God help the dark Dragon if he had hurt her.

"My lady."

Patience stopped and turned so abruptly that the soft-spoken woman who had annoyed her by referring to her as my lady, took a quick step back. "Patience. Please call me Patience."

The rail-thin woman with pure white, plaited hair nodded. "Forgive me for not being here to greet you earlier, Patience. I am Edna, Craig's wife, and I wish to welcome you to our meager home."

Guilt fell heavily on Patience's shoulder for having been snappish with the woman. She looked as worn as Craig and Patience reminded herself that these people were part of the Clan Macinnes and she owed them the respect they showed her.

"Thank you, Edna, I am pleased to be here to help."

Edna sighed. "We can use all the help you can give us. My husband is a proud man and proud to be part of the Clan Macinnes."

"Too proud," Patience asked, "to let my father

know that you need more help here than just this skirmish with the McLauds?"

Edna smiled and Patience could see the beautiful woman she had once been.

"Edna, hurry and see that all is ready for the meal. Our guest must be starving," McFarden called out as he approached.

Edna leaned in close to Patience and whispered, "He worries what I will say to you, for he knows I do not mind my tongue like I should."

"Then we share something in common," Patience said with a smile.

"What are you two whispering about?" McFarden asked anxiously when he reached them.

"Women stuff," Patience said, which was what she and her sisters would say to their father when he caught them whispering.

"Well, it can wait," McFarden said and turned to his wife. "Is our cottage ready for Patience?"

Patience spoke up. "I will sleep where my men camp."

McFarden went to protest.

Patience raised her hand. "Please take no offense to my sleeping arrangements. It is a rule that is strictly followed when on a mission."

"Then come and at least let us give you a fine meal and good drink before you retire for the night," McFarden said.

Patience smiled and walked with the couple to the longhouse.

~~~

Patience woke before dawn and impatiently waited for the sun to rise. She had not slept well. She did not know if it had been the tasteless food that had not settled well in her stomach or her concern for this small village. The people were kind and generous and in need of help in more ways than just this problem with the McLauds. She intended to speak with her father on her return home to see what could be done.

When she had returned to camp last night, her warriors had complained bitterly about the poor conditions of the McLaud horses they had brought along with them. Her warriors had insisted that the horses not be returned to them, at least until their conditions improved. As much as Patience agreed with them, keeping their horses could start a much bigger problem for all concerned.

Patience stretched the soreness out of her lean body before getting to her feet and watching the sun rise. Her warriors had been stirring and were quick to get to their feet and see this task done.

McFarden came to collect her for breakfast, but her stomach had finally felt better and she did not want to chance upsetting it with another poorly cooked meal. She thanked him and explained she was not hungry, but eager to get to the McLauds.

They reached the McLaud keep by mid-morning. The village preceding the keep was a slovenly place. The odor permeating the air around it wrinkled the nose and stung the eyes, though she had seen and smelled worse, which always made her more grateful for the home she had.

When they got closer to the keep, Patience noticed one small cottage that sat off from the others and looked far different. It was neat and well-cared for, with a small garden on the side. She wondered who occupied the place.

McLaud warriors began to gather near the steps of the keep, fanning out on both sides of the unimpressive structure. If they thought to intimidate, they were fools. They had situated themselves badly, for her warriors would easily be able to take them down quickly with a flow of arrows.

The tall narrow doors to the keep opened as Patience brought her horse to a halt, her men spreading out behind her and McFarden at her side. A big man, thick all over and with features that did not attract much attention stepped out along with a thick-boned, attractive woman. At least, she would have been attractive if she did not wear such a deep scowl. Another man appeared, stepping to the big man's left. He was a bit shorter, with more defined features and whereas the big man's dark hair fell in scraggily strands to his shoulders, this man's light brown hair was cropped short. A woman followed him out to stand at his side. She was short in comparison to the others and had plain features, though beautiful, long blond hair. She kept her head bowed and her shoulders were slumped as if she carried to much weight upon them.

Patience was not surprised that Hunter made no appearance, though she had noticed that his horse had not been at Lyall's when they had passed by her cottage. She remained on her horse, waiting to be greeted properly.

The big man stepped forward. "Did you bring my horses?"

Patient glared at him, but spoke not a word. She assumed he was Greer, the new laird of the Clan McLaud and oldest brother.

"Are you deaf, woman? Answer me," the man shouted.

Patience kept a steady glare on him.

The man walked down the steps, his face contorted in anger and approached Patience, stopping beside her horse. "Are you too fearful to speak to me?"

Patience looked down at the red-cheeked man. "Not now since you are where you belong, looking up at me." She did not think his face could grow any redder, but it did.

"I am Greer McLaud, laird of the Clan McLaud. How dare you insult me!"

"I am Patience Macinnes, daughter of Donald Macinnes, laird of the Clan Macinnes, and how dare you encroach on Macinnes land."

"Macinnes sent his daughter to tend to this dispute?" Greer threw back his head and laughed.

Patience smiled. "Need I remind you that it was a woman who bested your men and sent them back to you without their horses?" That wiped the grin off Greer's face, though Patience retained her smile.

"You caught them unaware," Greer accused.

"You admit that your own warriors were caught unaware?" This time Patience laughed. "That does not say much for your leadership." Before Greer could continue arguing, Patience held up her hand. "I did not come here to discuss your warriors' lack of skills and laziness. I am here to settle this dispute."

"Then come inside and let us get this done," Greer

said and turned to walk away from her, then stopped and turned back. "Your warriors wait outside."

"As do yours," she said.

His dark eyes narrowed and he looked ready to bark orders at her, when he stopped and said, "They will be keeping an eye on your warriors."

"Then they better have eyes in the back of their heads," Patience warned and Greer's nostrils flared.

McFarden went with Patience into the keep, reminding her in a whisper that she should not trust Greer that he was not a man of his word. She did not need the reminder. She remembered well what McFarden had told her about him.

She and McFarden both wrinkled their noses at the disturbing odor upon entering the Great Hall. With one glance Patience could tell the stench came from the rushes that looked as if they had not been cleaned out in not just days but weeks. Emma would be appalled and would refuse to remain here, but Patience wanted to see this done quickly so that she could return home and at least get to be reunited with her one sister.

Patience, however, was annoyed that Greer along with the other man and two women went to the small dais and took seats there and left her and McFarden to stand in front of it. No seat was offered to them nor drink or food.

"Have your say," Greer ordered.

Patience could tell from the man's tone and demeanor that he would be stubborn about laying claim to the land. From what she could see for herself, the McLauds did not have a large contingent of warriors. It did not seem likely that he had intentions of going to war over this... unless. Could the McLauds have joined forces with another clan or two? If that was so, then it could prove a bloody and harsh outcome for all concerned.

She decided to be blunt. "What is it you want, Greer?"

"Land that rightfully belongs to the McLauds, and I will settle for nothing less."

"That land has never belonged to the McLauds."

Patience turned to see a petite woman with honey-colored hair streaked with white enter the room. She had soft, pretty features and looked worn, though not from age.

"I ordered you to stay out of this, woman," Greer shouted, shaking his fist at her.

Rab stood. "Greer is right. This is no concern of yours. Leave us."

Greer turned to the woman beside him. "Rona, see her back to her cottage."

Rona's scowl deepened. "Why must I always tend the hag, let Saundra do it."

Saundra stood as if anxious to leave. "I will see to her."

The older woman stepped closer to the dais. "I am not going anywhere. I am here to make certain you do not sully the McLaud's name. Your father may have been mean-tempered like you, but he was a man of his word and expected the same of his sons."

Greer roared, grabbed a tankard and threw it at the woman.

Patience stuck her hand out, knocking the tankard to the ground before it could hit the woman. She ignored the sting to her hand and glared at Greer.

"Are you insane? You could have killed her."

"Then she would be no more trouble to me," Greer spat and picked up another tankard.

Patience did not hesitate; she jumped in front of the woman. Her arm went up as she did, the tankard smashing against it. She paid no heed to the stinging blow. She was too busy retrieving her dagger from her sheath and throwing it to land at the edge of the table right near Greer's crotch.

Greer's eyes turned wide and he turned pale.

Rona gasped. "You could have severed his manhood."

"Believe me, if I wanted his pathetic excuse for a manhood severed, it would be on the floor right now."

Hunter stumbled into the room with a woman under one arm and a tankard of ale in his hand. He stopped and grinned, taking in the scene. His smile vanished and he dropped the tankard and shoved the woman away from him, then hurried to the older woman's side.

"Have you been harmed?" he asked his arm going around her.

Patience was shocked by the concern in his voice and the way he so tenderly held the woman.

"Patience Macinnes came to my aid," the woman said softly.

Patience felt a punch to her stomach when he turned grateful blue eyes on her. Never had she seen sentiment expressed so vividly in a man's eyes. No wonder women found him so appealing.

"I owe you for that," Hunter said, then turned to the woman. "Wait here by Patience a moment and I will see you home." He gave a nod to Patience and she bobbed her head, letting him know she would watch over the woman.

He walked over to the dais. "I warned you Greer."

"And I warned her to hold her tongue. She obeys me or she suffers for it," Greer said with an angry snarl. "As will you if you do not obey your laird."

Patience was shocked to see how fast Hunter snatched her dagger out of the table and held it to his brother's throat. She was even more shocked at what he said next.

"It will be you who will be obeying me, Greer. Patience has agreed to become my wife, which will make me the laird of the Clan Macinnes, joining our clans."

Chapter Four

Greer pounded the table. "You lie!"

Hunter moved the dagger away from Greer's throat as he turned to Patience. "Tell him you accepted my proposal."

His blue eyes were heated with a combination of fury and concern. She was not sure what Hunter was up to, but something told her to go along with him. They could settle it later, for he surely had to know that she had no intentions of marrying him.

"Aye, I agreed," Patience said. "It is the best solution to the situation."

Greer exploded with rage. "I did not condone this union and I forbid you to wed her."

"You cannot forbid me to wed her," Hunter said. "The choice is mine and the other clans in the region will be happy to hear of such a union between our clans."

Greer's anger turned to a snide smile. "Then we will celebrate and invite the surrounding clans to your nuptials and wedding feast in a week's time."

Patience stepped forward. "No! I want my family present at my wedding. We will wed at my home."

Greer placed his meaty fists on the table and glared at her, a snarl on his lips as he said, "You can wed here and wed again when you return home. But I will see you properly joined before you leave here."

Patience wanted to put a stop to this farce but

until she could speak to Hunter and see what this was all about, she decided to continue the charade. She did not know why that for the moment she was trusting Hunter, except that instinct advised her to do so. Though she would be damned if she would eat her words about marrying him. Never, ever would she wed Hunter McLaud.

McFarden spoke up. "It will be good to have the McLauds not only as neighbors but as allies as well."

Greer scowled, but before he could respond, Patience said, "Boundaries continue to be respected, even more so, once clans are joined in marriage."

Greer folded his arms across his wide chest. "So, a Macinnes takes the cowardly way out of settling a dispute by marrying a warrior who does nothing but poke women all day."

Patience stepped next to Hunter. "A Macinnes knows when to sacrifice for the good of her clan and also to expand Macinnes holdings. Macinnes land and reputation stretches far and wide and its reach holds no bounds. You should be grateful you will be part of such a powerful clan, although the wedding has yet to take place. I might find it more prudent to call the wrath of my clan and its allies down upon you."

Greer grinned, appearing appeased. "I would welcome the challenge of battling the Macinnes."

Patience realized then that Greer had aligned himself with either one or more clans and clans he assumed could possibly beat the Macinnes clan. If that was so, then he had planned for this confrontation and what seemed even more plausible... to go to war with the Clan Macinnes.

The thought disturbed her. She could not allow a

war to happen. Countless lives would be lost and the search for her sister would be brought to an abrupt halt. This situation was far worse than she had believed, but there was one person who could provide the information she needed... Hunter. She had to talk with him and the sooner the better.

Patience nodded at Greer. "Aye, you would, since foolish and selfish men think that war is the only answer."

"Be careful, woman, or you will feel the mighty wrath of a McLaud," Greer said, striking the table once again with his fist.

Hunter spoke up. "There is no changing the fact that Patience will be my wife. So it is time that you show her the respect she deserves."

Patience did not need him speaking up for her, and she certainly did not need him as a husband. The problem was... how did she resolve this issue without being forced to wed Hunter? She kept her silence, at least for the moment.

Greer turned to Saundra, Rab's wife. "See that a room is prepared for Lady Macinnes."

"I will not have my future wife staying in this filth. She will reside with our mother until the wedding."

The woman Patience had protected stepped forward. "I would be honored to have Lady Patience stay with me."

Patience found herself speechless. To think that Greer would harm his own mother was unthinkable, and it made her realize just what kind of man she was dealing with. If he could harm his own mother, then there was not anything he would not do to get what he wanted.

Greer's wife Rona sprang out of her seat. "We cannot have Lady Patience stay in a mere cottage. What will others think?"

"I do not care what others think," Hunter said tersely. "Patience will reside with Mum."

"That has always been your problem, Hunter," Rona accused, shaking her finger at him. "You do not care about anyone but your own selfish needs."

"That seems to be a recurring trait among the McLaud men," Hunter shot back.

"My husband does what is best for the clan," Rona shouted her face turning bright red.

"Throwing things at his mother, gripping her arms so tight he leaves bruises, telling her he would be better off if she was dead, is doing what is best for the clan?"

"She interferes when it is not her concern," Greer bellowed.

Patience could not believe her ears, though it was difficult not to since it seemed the McLauds could not converse without shouting. How could a son treat his mother so badly? She was relieved to see that Hunter was not like his brother in that respect.

"Our mother will not trouble you any longer," Hunter said with such an evil sneer that Greer actually took a step back. "As soon as Patience and I exchange vows, Mum will be leaving with us."

"Take the hag with you," Greer said with an abrupt wave of his hand. "But you and your bride will not leave until I am sure that your vows have been consummated."

Hunter not only laughed, but the servants did as

well. "You truly are a fool. Knowing that I do not go a day without a woman, do you actually believe I would not bed my own wife?"

"He does have a point," Rab said, "and perhaps the sooner they take their leave the better." Geer turned a vicious sneer on his brother, but Rab was quick to continue. "The sooner they wed the better. Why waste a celebration on them? Let us see them wed and be gone."

Patience watched the expressions of the two brothers. It was obvious some silent message had been exchanged and she wondered over it. The two brothers had plotted and with their original plot foiled by Hunter's announcement, they would be looking to regroup and plot again. Something was very wrong here and Patience wondered how her father had not been made aware of it. Besides the McFarden clan, her father was on good terms with many of the clans in the area. Surely one of them would have apprised him of a troubling situation in the making.

Greer turned to Hunter. "I want the lot of you gone once the ceremony is done."

"It will not be soon enough for me," Hunter said.

"The cleric is at a neighboring clan," Rab said. "I will send a message for him to return. It should take two days at the most for him to arrive."

"Enough time for mother and me to pack our belongings and be ready to be on our way," Hunter said.

"And it will be good riddance to both of you," Rona screamed.

From the furious anger in the woman's eyes, Patience could not help but think that Rona protested too much and was truly unhappy that Hunter was leaving, and she wondered why.

Hunter turned to Patience and with a hand on her arm, he whispered, "Come with me, we need to talk." He also turned to his mother and took her hand, walking both women to the door.

McFarden followed along with the trio, having been struck silent by the whole bizarre exchange.

"This is not done between us," Greer shouted.

Hunter stopped and stepped away from the two women to turn around. "You are right. It is not over between us. There is much you have to answer for and I will make certain you answer for every evil deed you have done."

"You do not have the skill or the balls to raise a sword against me," Greer called out with a laugh.

"I would look to your own balls, since you have failed to get your wife with child. Whereas my wife will quickly get with child and you know what that means Greer." Hunter smiled. "My child will be the firstborn McLaud and rightful heir to the clan with you having sired no heir."

Greer's thunderous roar could be heard outside the keep and had Hunter smiling as he guided the two women down the steps.

Edward, Patience's lead warrior, approached her and she stepped away from Hunter and his mother to speak with him. McFarden joined her.

She kept her voice low. "Find a place to camp on the outskirts of the castle's outer walls."

"What walls?" Edward said with disgust. "The decaying walls crumble from lack of attention as does much in this pathetic village."

"We will be here a couple of days. I want the men on alert at all times and to be prepared to leave at a moment's notice. Also," —she shook her head— "you will hear that I am going to wed Hunter McLaud to keep the peace between our clans. It is a ruse, but no one must know that. Something goes on here that I am not aware of and it worries me. We have been led into some kind of trap and I fear what may happen when the trap is sprung."

"I do not understand," McFarden said. "You think the McLauds encroaching on our land was a ruse to lure you here?"

"I do," Patience admitted, "though I believe Hunter foiled the plan by announcing that he and I would wed."

"Will you wed him?" McFarden asked as if worried over her reply.

"Do you truly believe me a fool?" she snapped and did not give him a chance to respond. "I need to talk with Hunter and see what he knows, for there is surely more to this whole matter than we are seeing."

"What can I do to help?" McFarden asked.

"Be ready to ride to your village and be ready to send some of your men to my father's allies in the area if the need should arise."

Both men gave her a nod and walked off while she turned and rejoined Hunter and his mother. She was not surprised when Hunter led them to the only well-tended cottage in the village. One look and Patience knew she could not stay here. It was small, the single bed barely big enough to hold one person. Fresh rushes dotted with sprigs of heather covered the dirt floor, providing a pleasant scent that permeated the room.

Hunter's mother smiled as Patience turned to her. "I would be pleased if you would call me Una, Lady Patience."

Patience cringed. "Only if you call me Patience, since I cannot abide being referred to as Lady Patience."

"Welcome to my home, Patience," Una said. "I am honored to have you stay here."

Patience looked from her to the bed.

Una spoke up before Patience could protest. "I will sleep by the hearth. My old bones could use the warmth."

Patience shook her head. "I will not permit that. I will sleep on the floor or I will not sleep here at all."

"Patience gives orders, Mum, she does not take them," Hunter said and turned with a grin to Patience, "which is why I will make you a good husband. I will not dictate to you."

"We need to talk," Patience said irritated by his assumption that they were actually going to wed.

Una hurried to snatch up a basket filled with heather by the door. "I will leave you two to talk. I promised Morag I would bring her some heather." Tears filled her eyes, though she fought valiantly to keep them from falling. "I also want to let her know that I will be leaving here." A tear slipped out and down her cheek.

Hunter was at her side in an instant, slipping his arm around her. "I know this is not easy for you, Mum, but I will not leave you behind to be abused. You will be safe and have a good life with the Macinnes clan." He turned to Patience. "Will she not?"

Damn him for asking her to confirm it. It was as if he was asking her to reaffirm that they would wed. And the more she confirmed it, the more it took root, until she feared she would have no choice but to honor her words. Had that been his plan all along? At the moment, it did not matter since Una's tears were breaking her heart, though Hunter's kindness and concern for his mum touched her heart differently.

What choice did she have but to answer, "You will be most welcomed at my home and find it quite a pleasing place. Food is plentiful and delicious, the keep is as clean as your cottage, the people are friendly, and heather covers the hills, so you can gather as much as you want."

"You are most gracious, Patience," Una said with a gentle nod. "And my son is lucky to have you as his wife. Now I will leave you two to talk."

Hunter turned to Patience after the door closed behind his mother.

"Explain yourself," Patience ordered curtly.

Hunter threw his arms wide. "What? No loving embrace for your future husband."

Irritated, Patience snapped at him. "Just because you keep saying it, does not make it so."

Hunter dropped his arms and walked over to her.

Patience stood her ground, though she had thought to back away from him as he approached. He held his shoulders wide and walked with a confident gate. Then there were those blue eyes of his that seemed to always be filled with heated passion. And his slim lips that looked ever hungry to kiss a woman. Even his long, slim fingers were appealing, especially since she had seen how tender he had been with his mother. And yet the strength she had felt when he had gripped her wrist showed another side of him.

"I believe in the power of words," he said as if he challenged her.

He was about to take a step much too close to her and she raised her arm to stop him. The sleeve of her shirt slipped down, and she was startled by the sudden anger that raged in his eyes, turning them a startling blue.

His hand reached out and took tender hold of her arm, his finger running lightly along her flesh, and she flinched. She realized then what had angered him.

"You got this bruise protecting my mother." He bent her arm so that her hand brushed her face and ran his fingers ever so lightly over the purplish spot. "Does it pain you?"

Not any longer. Not with the way he was stroking her arm and sending tingles rushing all over her. The exquisite sensation almost had her body shuddering, but she caught herself and snatched her arm away from him.

"It is a bruise, nothing more. It will heal," she said annoyed that she sounded a bit breathless.

"What did he throw at her?" Hunter asked anger still evident in his eyes.

"Two tankards."

"*Twice* you defended her?"

"I was not going to stand there and do nothing," she said as if he should know that.

His brow scrunched and he spoke as if he was just realizing something. "You are an honorable woman."

"I am, and now it is time for you to tell me what is

going on, for I have been brought here falsely."

"Honorable and intelligent," Hunter said with a smile. "My mum is right, I am lucky to have you as a wife."

"We are not going to wed," Patience said with a firmness that could not be ignored.

"After you hear what I have to say, I believe you will be eager to wed me."

Chapter Five

"Never would I be eager to wed you," Patience informed him in a tone that left no doubt that she meant it.

"How about bed me?" he asked and left her no room to respond. His hand shot out, gripping her neck and yanking her toward him. He settled his lips on hers and kissed her.

Patience was too stunned to react. And, of course, his kiss had to turn her senseless... damn him. She had been kissed before, at least she had thought she had, but Hunter's kiss made her realize that she had never known a true kiss. His lips were in full control and his tongue, good lord, but his tongue worked magic. He had brought her whole body alive with a kiss, and it was responding like never before. Her nipples perked up, her stomach fluttered, and a tingle settled between her legs, turning her wet.

As fast as he had captured her lips in a kiss was how fast he ended it, leaving her wanting so much more.

He grabbed her face in his hands. "I have been aching to do that since I first laid eyes on you. I knew you would taste exquisite. You are a warrior woman whose passion runs deep in everything that she does, and there are not many men who could satisfy you. But I will." He brushed his lips over hers. "I will always satisfy you, always be there for you, and always protect you when you cannot protect yourself."

Patience's breath caught and she feared for a moment she would not be able to breathe. He had released something in her that she worried she would never be able to tame, or did she worry that only he would be able to tame it?

She stepped away from him and that he let her was not lost on her. She had felt his strength and knew if he had wanted to stop her he could, though her blade would have objected. And she supposed that was what made her curious. Here was a man who possibly had the strength to best her and yet he made no effort to do so.

She shook her head, trying to regain her senses and asked, "Tell me what goes on here."

The heated passion in his eyes faded, though lingered, but then Patience did not think there was a time passion did not shine bright in Hunter's eyes.

Hunter responded to her demand without hesitation. "The Clan McDolan, Saundra's father, has encouraged Greer to challenge the Clan Macinnes and its claim on the land around here. Hew McDolan has also encouraged him to engage other clans who are less than favorable to your father. He has amassed quite an army and while it is doubtful he could win completely, he could cost you loss of life and land. And believe me when I tell you that Greer will sacrifice endless men, women, and children to get what he wants."

"My father has allies in the area that could stop him," Patience said but not with as much confidence as she would have liked.

"You are too beautiful to die," Hunter said.

For a moment Patience thought him sincere, then she shook her head at the insane thought and said, "Do not bother to spew your nonsense on me."

"I speak the truth," Hunter insisted. "You and your men would be slaughtered before help could reach you. Greer has warriors waiting to attack you and he is growing ever more impatient to give the signal."

Patience turned away from him, taking a moment to think. Her father had at least one strong ally nearby who she could count on to help. He could be here before Greer was aware she had summoned him. And while Greer was a mean-tempered man, he did not strike her as foolish when it came to battle. He fought to win and he would not be so eager to enter a melee that could prove disastrous for him.

She turned quickly. "What are you not telling me?"

"You are perceptive," Hunter said with a hint of admiration.

"I am also impatient."

"So you do not live up to your lovely name?"

"No, but I do live up to my reputation with a dagger, which you will find out shortly if you do not answer me," she warned.

"*Mo chridhe*, you not only threaten me, but your own pleasure if you think to cut off my—"

"Enough of you prattling that serves only to distract from my question," she said, shoving a shaking finger in his face. "Now answer me."

"Damn if your anger does not turn me hard," he said his eyes lighting with a sensuous fire. "I cannot wait to bed you."

"You have a long wait in front of you." Her dagger was out of her sheath so fast and at his throat that Hunter actually startled, taking a few stumbling steps back away from her. "I will have my answer."

Hunter answered without delay. "Greer believes he has an ally in the Dark Dragon."

Patience was unable to do anything but stare at him for a moment, so shocked was she by his words. The implications and possibilities startled her and had her mind stirring and questions mounting.

She started with one. "Why would your brother think that?"

"Greer knows the Dark Dragon's uncle."

"The Dark Dragon's uncle resides in this area?"

"He once did," Hunter confirmed.

"And Greer and he were friends?"

"He was more friends with my father, but where you found my father, you also found Greer. My father wanted him prepared to take the reins of the clan when the time came. So, he had Greer trail him like a faithful hound."

"Then he is counting on the uncle to persuade the Dark Dragon to help him?"

Hunter nodded. "That is his plan and hope. Of course Hew McDolan encouraged him to do so."

Patience did not want to show her excitement to Hunter, but it was difficult to keep it contained. This news was an unexpected gift. She asked with as much calm as she could muster, "Greer is in touch with the uncle and knows where he lives?"

"Ewan, the uncle, has a family croft about a day's ride south from here. Most of the clans and folks in the area know his relationship to the Dark Dragon and leave the family alone. Ewan can be found there now and again, visiting."

That news changed her plans. As soon as she finished here, she knew where she would be going. So, the sooner she settled this mess, the sooner she could take a step closer to finding her sister.

"If Greer has clans already willing to help him take McFarden land, why does he want help from the Dark Dragon?" It struck her then and she turned glaring eyes on Hunter. "He is power hungry and wants to lay claim to all Macinnes land, and he would need a powerful army of warriors to accomplish that."

"You have a warrior's mind," Hunter complimented. "And perhaps now you see why a marriage between us would foil all his plans."

"Yet your brother Rab encourages our immediate departure after we are wed." Patience thought a moment, and then shook her head. "Please tell me that your brothers would not attempt to take our lives." She shoved her dagger back in its sheath.

"Not yours, mine and my mother's."

"Of course," she said annoyed at not having thought of it. "Greer will claim that I never wanted a union with the Clan McLaud and that I rid myself of the problem."

"And end his worry that he could also lose his claim on McLaud land once you get with child."

"That is one concern of his that will never happen," she assured him or was she assuring herself? It was difficult to ignore his fine features and sensual blue eyes. The more she was around him the more she realized that he simply oozed lust. She doubted that one woman would be able to please him. He would probably wear her out, and then be off chasing after other women. That was not what she wanted in a husband. She would never be able to trust him. And she wanted a husband—no— she wanted a partner who she could always rely on no matter what.

"Do you not want children?" he asked.

His concern surprised her, and she said, "Do you?"

"Aye, a keep full," he said with a smile and a nod.

She would not have thought that of him and she shook her head. "That is a large brood to tend to and a lot to ask of a woman. Or do you believe that is what a wife is for... to bear child after child and be a slave to her husband's whims and desires."

Hunter laughed. "A slave you would never be, though..." His eyes filled with such lust that they turned a deeper blue. "I could show you how enjoyable playing at being a love slave could be."

Between the lust in his eyes and his sensually suggestive tone, she felt herself growing wet yet again. She was quick to grab her dagger and point it at him, though she did not take a step near him. "I will never be a slave to you or any man and especially no love slave."

"Never say never, *mo chridhe*, you do not know what the future may hold."

"My future will not be me being enslaved by my husband, and do not call me my love. I am not your love."

"You will be my wife, so you are *mo chridhe*."

"I am not going to be your wife," she insisted while slipping her dagger back, once again, into the sheath at her waist, fearing if she did not she just might use it on him.

"How else do you propose this matter be settled?" he asked, folding his arms across his chest.

Of course, her eyes could not help being drawn to the way his shirt suddenly hugged the muscles in his arms or grew taut against his defined chest. The man was all lean, hard muscle and it only added to his appeal.

"Greer is intent on claiming Macinnes land one way or another. Our marriage can, at least for a time, delay his plans until we can finally put an end to his power-thirsty intentions. This marriage could save thousands of lives from being lost in a senseless battle. It could unite clans and give some people who have felt down-trodden some hope. It would gain other clans' respect by seeing that an unnecessary battle was prevented. And it would strengthen the north against invaders."

Damn, why did he have to make sense? Patience was all for preventing unnecessary battle. Raising swords against other clans only served to create more animosity. In the last few years, she had been able to settle disputes without drawing her sword. Well, at least without drawing it in battle. There were times a well-placed sword served a good purpose and prevented major bloodshed.

The problem was being shackled to this man for the rest of her life. He would not even have made it on her list of possible men to wed.

"What is it that you object about me being your husband?" he asked.

Patience was about to tell him how selfish she

thought he was, but stopped herself. A selfish man would not care about his mother and take her with him when he wed. He would also not care about lives lost in battle or that it was a senseless battle to begin with. No, in certain respects, Hunter McLaud was not selfish.

So, what then did she object to about him?

She stared at his fine features and his blue eyes so boldly lustful and knew. "You will not be a faithful husband."

"Why do you think that?"

"You admitted it yourself when you laughed at your brother and told him that you did not go a day without poking a woman. What if your wife does not favor coupling every day? Will you find your pleasure elsewhere?"

He rubbed at his smooth chin. "That is a reasonable question and one that troubles me. I would more than please my wife when we make love, so I do not know why she would not want to couple with me every day. And I certainly would not want her making love with me out of sheer duty."

"Then what would you do if she denied you? Find another woman to satisfy your insatiable appetite?"

Hunter dropped his arms away from his chest as he laughed. "My wife would enjoy coupling far too much to ever deny me."

"You are—"

"Confident and extremely skilled at making love."

"Making Love? You cannot love every woman you poke," she insisted frustrated with his arrogant demeanor.

He scrunched his brow. "But of course I have

loved every woman I have poked. Only when a man loves the woman he couples with can either of them find true pleasure."

"So then love means nothing to you, since you can love every woman you have rutted with."

"I do not *rut*. Animals *rut*," Hunter said with tempered anger. "And as far as love, *mo chridhe*, it would take you many years, perhaps your whole life to understand love as I do and to cherish it as I do. We may be strangers to each other now, but once we are wed you will become my whole life and I will love you with every beat of my heart. I will be there to comfort you, to listen when you need me to, to wipe away your tears, to share your laughter and joy, to soothe your troubles, and to keep you safe. We will be husband and wife and I will honor our union and you until the day I die."

Patience stood staring at him speechless. Never had she expected such heartfelt words from him. And never would she have thought that he could flutter her insides and ignite her passion simultaneously. And never would she have thought that his words could actually make her consider marrying him.

She had to ask, "You do not know me. How could you love me?"

"I think that is a question you are going to have to find the answer to yourself."

It was Patience's turn to scrunch her brow. "I do not like riddles."

"Give yourself time, have patience, and you will see for yourself that it is no riddle," he said. "Now do you agree to marry me?"

"Let me think—"

"There is no time and you know it. It is why I announced it as I did. If I had taken the time to speak with you about it, you would have objected and precious time would have been lost. Even now time may be against us. Once we wed, we will need to go straight to Ewan's croft and have a message sent to the Dark Dragon that we have wed and no threat exists between our clans."

He had given her many sound reasons why their marriage would prove beneficial, but this one sent her over the edge. If Hunter could provide a link to the Dark Dragon, then nothing could stop her from finding her sister. And if she had to sacrifice and wed Hunter to find her sister, then so be it. It was better than leaving Heather in the clutches of such an evil man.

"I will wed you, but there will be certain conditions and I will have witnesses to it; your mother, Craig McFarden, and Edward, my lead warrior will hear them."

"You are a wise warrior, I would expect nothing less, but I would like to discuss these conditions with you first."

"They are not negotiable," she assured him.

"Still, I would prefer you shared them with me before we speak of them to others."

Patience did just that. "You will lay no claim to the title of Chieftain of the Clan Macinnes, even if my father offers it to you. You will not dictate or expect obedience from me. Your word will not usurp mine. And between you and me, you will never cheat on me... even if I deny you pleasure."

Hunter grinned and grabbed himself between his

legs. "Ouch! You may not have taken a dagger to me, but you have deprived me of my balls nonetheless."

She turned a huge grin on him. "That is only fair, since I will be shackled to you for the rest of my life. And again these conditions are not negotiable. Now do you agree to marry me?"

"Since you asked so nicely, how could I refuse?" he said with a quick bob of his head. "I will marry you."

Patience thought about her words to McFarden when he asked her if she would wed Hunter. *I am no fool*. But was she being a fool by agreeing to this? She could not think of it that way if she was going to save Heather or prevent an unnecessary battle. Her father had told her often that being a chieftain of a clan called for much sacrifice, and he asked her if she could sacrifice. She had not hesitated when she had answered, '*aye I would.*'

"Then let us gather those people and see it done, so we will be ready to wed." She turned and suddenly found an arm around her neck and another around her waist with Hunter's hand on the hilt of her dagger.

"One thing more, *mo chridhe*," he whispered in her ear, "*never, ever* pull your dagger on me again or you will suffer the consequences."

He released her and walked to the door.

"What are the consequences?" she asked, annoyed that she had not even realized he had moved until it was too late.

Hunter opened the door and turned back around to her with his blue eyes as lusty as could be. "Not something you would favor." His eyes suddenly flared with passion and his grin turned wicked. "Or perhaps you would favor it... to my great delight." He turned and walked out the door.

Naturally, Patience could think of only one thing and the image was quite clear... her tied naked to his bed.

"*Never. Ever*," she whispered, but then she had been just as adamant about not marrying Hunter McLaud.

Chapter Six

Hunter was not surprised that his mother was pleased by the news that Patience and he would actually wed, though she was the only one. Patience's warrior, Edward, and Craig McFarden stood staring in disbelief at her.

Curious to see how she responded to their stunned expressions and stone-cold silence, Hunter watched and waited. She was a beauty and was probably even more beautiful when she let her long dark hair loose from the leather strip that kept the thick, silky strands tightly confined at the nape of her neck. Her bold green eyes reflected her nature as well as the color. She was not one to hold her tongue, but rather spoke as she pleased, whether it pleased others or not. And while she wore a shirt and her plaid like a man, there was no mistaken a woman's body lay beneath. Her plump breasts sat high and firm and her waist narrowed onto nicely curved hips, and her legs were long and slender. She was a prize that would soon be his.

"It is the sensible thing to do," Patience finally said.

Edward spoke before thinking. "Since when are you sensible?"

Patience shot him a murderous scowl that had him lowering his head and mumbling an apology.

Hunter spoke up then. "Patience is a true leader.

She sacrifices for her clan, saving many lives and avoiding bloodshed by this union."

"I do not need you to defend me," Patience snapped and Edward raised his head, smiling. She realized then that he, and probably her other warriors, would worry that Hunter would become Laird of the Clan Macinnes. She wore a smile when she finally related the terms of their marriage, and Edward and McFarden smiled as she finished. Hunter's mother's smile remained, the additional news not at all disturbing her.

Hunter turned to his mother. "Mum, see to getting your things together so that you will be ready to leave as soon as this is done."

Una nodded and turned to Patience, reaching out and giving her hand a squeeze. "I am so proud that you will be my daughter. Hunter will be a good husband to you."

"I am sure he will," Patience said, doing her best to sound like she meant it.

Once Una walked away, Patience turned to Edward and kept her voice low as she said, "Greer is not happy with this union, though I do not believe he will prevent it. I also believe he will not allow it to last long. We will need to be cautious on our return journey." She did not advise Edward of the detour they would take first, that news she would relate later when they were no longer on McLaud land. "I will not have the men hearing of this from anyone but me. We go speak with them now."

She turned to Hunter and was about to dismiss him when he took a step closer to her, and then said to the other two men, "I will have a private word with

Patience."

Edward looked to Patience, and she was quick to assure him. "Get the men together. I will join you in a moment."

Edward bobbed his head respectfully and turned and walked off. McFarden followed, though at a slower pace.

Patience was accustomed to being taller than most women and some men, so it surprised her that Hunter stood almost a full head over her. She did not have to crane her neck to look at him, though she had to tilt it a bit, which she did, staring him straight in the eyes. Too late, she realized her mistake. His blue eyes seemed to grab hold of her or was it the heated passion that seemed to forever lurk in them that had taken hold of her? Whatever it was, she was too captivated by it to turn away.

"Be careful what you share with your men. There is no telling who can be trusted," Hunter warned with a whisper that drifted over her and set her skin tingling.

"I need no advice from you," she snapped annoyed at her body's unexpected response.

"No need to take offense, *mo chridhe*," he said with a gentle stroke beneath her chin. "Greer has ears everywhere. Now that I have done my duty by making you aware of the reach of my brother's control, I will take myself off to enjoy a poke."

"You will not," she ordered with a jab to his chest.

He laughed softly. "Jealous?"

"You are insufferable."

"I have been called worse."

"And rightfully so," she said with another jab. "You will not poke another woman now that we are to wed."

"But we are not wed yet," he said, his smile much too disarming. "And somehow I doubt you would grace my bed before we wed."

"I may not grace your bed after we wed."

He grabbed her hand, stopping her from poking him again and leaned his face close to hers. "Our vows will be sealed immediately. I will not give anyone any reason to challenge our union."

"And I will not be humiliated and disrespected by my intended. No pokes or no marriage." That he actually paused to consider her ultimatum frustrated her all the more.

"I have your word that you will not deny me on our wedding night?"

Why did a tiny tingle settle between her legs? Could she possibly want to bed this man? The thought irritated her, and she answered gruffly. "You have my word."

"You sound as if it will be more penance than pleasure for you."

She turned an astute grin on him. "And which one will you make me suffer?"

His own grin was just as cunning. "Both."

The tiny tingle between her legs erupted into shooting sparks and damn if she was not riddled with a burning need. How could she let a man, a stranger to boot, affect her so intimately? And how had she ever agreed to marry such a rogue?

"I have important things to see to," she said, taking a step away from him. "Be off with you and try to behave."

"*Behave*," he asked with feigned surprise. "I have not behaved since I was a very young lad, and my family will attest to that."

Patience rolled her eyes, groaned, and turned to hurry away from him, worried that if she remained in his presence she would strangle him.

~~~

"Patience," McFarden said, falling into step with her. "Can we talk before you address your men?"

She slowed her pace, looked around, and tired of being the center of village gossip with villagers having kept curious eyes on her and her group since arriving here, pointed to a cropping of large flat stones.

McFarden nodded and followed her over to sit on the smooth stones.

"Let me guess," Patience said before McFarden could speak. "You think I am a fool for marrying Hunter McLaud."

"I cannot say that for sure, for perhaps your union with him could change things here for the better, not to mention prevent a useless war. No," —he shook his head— "that is for you to decide. Besides, Hunter is a harmless one, not so his brothers. I fear what they may plan, though I fear more your father's retaliation if anything should happen to you. Several clans in the area would be only more than happy to accompany you on your journey home to make certain you remain safe."

"I appreciate your offer and your concern, but it is

not necessary," she said, her mind already strategizing what she would do.

McFarden nodded and kept his lips closed tight, a sure sign to Patience that he had more to say.

"Speak what you will, McFarden," she ordered sharply.

"There are rumors spreading that Greer will pledge allegiance to the Dark Dragon and soon all the north will belong to the infamous warrior."

His words followed what Hunter had told her about Greer and the Dark Dragon.

"No one defeats the Dark Dragon," McFarden said with a shudder. "He devours whatever he claims and soon he would devour us all."

Was that what the Dark Dragon was doing right now... devouring her sister? The thought turned her livid.

"That will not happen—I will not let it," she stated with such resolve that it actually brought a smile of relief to McFarden's face. "Now I must speak with my men."

McFarden nodded and followed along with her.

~~~

Patience was not surprised to see that her warriors were not happy with the news that she would wed Hunter McLaud. She made it clear that she would continue to lead them and that Hunter would hold no authority over them. That seemed to mollify them and their heads began to nod in agreement when she explained that uniting the clans would give the Clan Macinnes a stronger foothold in the north.

She finished with, "I will have more to say once we leave McLaud land."

Her warriors exchanged glances, knowing there was more to tell them, though not at the moment.

She walked amongst her warriors, having a word with each one, reassuring them and encouraging them and each one letting her know that she had their full allegiance. After that was done, she walked off to find a private spot. She needed time alone, time to think and sort through things, time to plan, and mostly time to pray that this whole ordeal would prove beneficial in finding her sister.

The land around here stretched on endlessly and was dotted with more large rocks than trees. A narrow stream cut a path several feet passed the village and that was where she wandered off to. The clear water gurgled along the rocky bottom and Patience stooped down to scoop up a handful and drink, then she found a small cropping of rocks to sit down by and rest her back against.

She dropped her head back for a moment and closed her eyes, though not for long and when she opened them, she was struck by how the brilliant blue sky reminded her of the color of Hunter's eyes. With a sigh, she turned her gaze on the stream. She had been impetus when she was young, but learned to curb it when she realized it was not a good trait when it came to settling skirmishes. She wondered now if she had been too impetus in agreeing to marry Hunter. If she had given herself time to think on the situation, could she have arrived at a better solution? But time was not on her side, especially not for Heather.

Prayer was her only recourse at the moment, and she was glad for it. If she did not have that, she would feel as if she failed her sister completely. Heather would not lose hope. She would know that she and Emma would be coming for her, that they would not abandon her.

It seemed like years since Heather had been captured, but it had been only months, and that was too long. She desperately missed her sisters and longed to be reunited with them, though nothing would be as it once was. Life had changed for all three of them.

Rarely, did Patience cry. She preferred action to sobbing, so the tears that threatened her were quickly dispersed. She had no time to surrender to such nonsense. But try as she might, she could not stop a single tear from lurking in the corner of her eye.

Annoyed at letting it creep past her defenses, she brushed it away harshly.

"Sometimes tears help."

Patience jumped startled to see Hunter walk around from behind her. She had trained herself to always be alert to her surroundings and to always pay attention to sounds, so it disturbed her not to have heard his approach.

"Go away," she demanded, shooing him with her hand.

"You are upset and I daresay exhausted," he said and dropped down to sit beside her, his shoulder nudging against hers.

Patience glanced over at his shoulder, ready to order him to move away and be gone when she realized how nice it would be to drop her head upon it and rest, if only for a short time. Instead, she rested her head back on the rock.

She tried chasing him away once again. "Go away."

Ignoring her demand, he said, "Come back to my mother's cottage and rest before we are wed tonight."

That brought her head up fast and she glared at him, waiting for him to explain.

"The cleric completed his task sooner than expected and has just arrived home. He is going to rest for a few hours, and then he will marry us. Today, Patience Macinnes, you become my wife."

Chapter Seven

A cloud of haze hung heavy in the stale air, dogs dug for scrapes of rotting food in the smelly rushes, and the tables where covered with the remnants of a meal yet to be cleaned away. Patience could not believe this was where she had gotten wed, but glancing down at her left hand and the gold band that circled her finger proved it was all too true.

Hunter took her hand in his and tapped her ring, and then the one he wore. "They belonged to my parents. My mother wished us to have them. She loved my da and he loved her. Though he had a mean streak, it was never directed at her. He treated her good, never raised a hand to her, and always protected her. She hopes that by us wearing the rings we will find the love they shared."

"Thoughtful of her," Patience said and realized that the gold bands represented so much more. This had not been just a handfasting that could be dismissed easily. With the cleric performing the ceremony, it meant their vows bound them solidly together for as long as they lived. Sudden realization of what she had done struck her, and her legs turned weak.

Without thinking, she grabbed Hunter's arm and felt solid muscle, thick and strong.

Hunter's arm coiled around her waist and he eased her to rest against him. He leaned his face down close to hers and whispered, "One breathe at a time, *mo chridhe*."

Patience had not realized that she had been holding her breathe, and she was quick to do as he said and take one breathe at a time.

"I would like to believe it is this stinking hovel we were married in that upset you so much that it stole your breathe and not that we are husband and wife," he said, giving her waist a gentle squeeze.

"A bit of both," she confessed with a labored whisper.

He smiled. "You do speak your mind."

"I speak the truth."

"I can ask for no more."

"See that you do not," she warned, though her tone was tender.

"I will take only what you wish to give and I believe you are a *very* giving person."

A smile tickled at the corners of her mouth. "Working your charm on me will not get you the results you desire."

"But it has... it brought color back to your cheeks and a smile to your face."

She did feel much better and she let her smile grow as she said, "Thank you."

"Never do you need to thank me, *mo chridhe*, I am your husband and it is—"

"Your duty," she said, wondering why it should disappoint her. After all, they did not love each other. They barely knew each other.

He stroked her chin and corrected, "My privilege."

"Married but minutes and already he seduces you

with his lying words," Rona said with angry belligerence as she approached them. "You will regret the day you agreed to marry him. He will promise you everything and give you nothing and take his pleasure where he will. He ruts like an animal and cares not who he harms."

"How would you know he ruts like an animal?" Patience asked, raising her brow and a smile.

Rona's anger mounted, flushing her cheeks bright red, and she stumbled over her words. "He is th-the talk of th-the women in the village."

"So I married a man that *every* woman in your village desires." Patience nodded. "That would make me believe that for so many women to want him, his rutting must be exceptional."

Rona looked ready to spew fire from her mouth, and she raised her hand to shake a finger at Patience. "Mark my words, you will be sorry."

Patience took a quick step toward her and Rona stumbled. Patience grabbed her arm to stop her from falling, then whispered close for only her to hear. "Does your husband know you desire his brother?"

Rona gasped and the heat in her face drained away, leaving her ghastly pale. "I will see you suffer for speaking so sinfully to me."

"And how will you do that?" Patience challenged.

Confidence along with color returned to Rona's face as fast as it had vanished, and it was with a smug smile that she said, "I will see that you are made a slave of the Dark Dragon just like your sister."

Patience did not hesitate. She let her fist fly and knocked the woman out cold with one punch to her jaw.

Hunter jumped in front of Patience as Greer came charging at her. "I will kill you before I let you lay a hand on my wife."

"She laid a hand on mine," Greer screamed with such rage that the veins in his neck bulged near to exploding.

"Do you truly want to know why?" Hunter challenged.

Patience wondered over the unspoken message between the two. And she wondered if Greer actually believed that Hunter had coupled with his wife. From the way Greer growled and muttered beneath his breath, it seemed like a logic conclusion, but from Rona's angry reaction and insulting words, Patience did not believe it to be so. She also could not believe that Greer, nor anyone else had bothered to come to the aid of the unconscious woman. She laid there like a discarded sack no one wished to touch.

Greer shook a beefy fist at Hunter. "It is done; you are wed. Leave at first light, and I promise you that you will never lay claim to McLaud land."

"McFarden," Hunter called out and the man who had stood witness to their union stepped forward. "Take my wife and mother and wait outside for me."

Patience was about to step around her husband and tell him that she was not going anywhere. Then she thought better of it. She did not want him interfering with her and her sisters. So, she would not interfere with him and his brothers... unless they left her no choice.

Hunter was glad his wife respected his stance and went without a word with McFarden. As soon as the doors to the Great Hall closed behind them, he looked from Greer to Rab, and said, "Hear me well, brothers, you both will rue the day I return."

Rab shuddered, but Greer let out a hardy laugh.

Hunter's blue eyes darkened and his brow narrowed as he glared at each man. "You have my word on it."

Greer's laughter died instantly. "And you, the fool that you are, have just given me what I need to start a war that will give the McLauds more power than anyone thought possible."

Hunter's smile was slight and so ominous that Greer drew back away from him. "Be careful, Greer, you were never wise enough to see what was right in front of you."

"What is that supposed to mean?" Greer demanded.

"Time to take my leave," Hunter said and turned and walked to the door, though called out, "Until next time, Greer, when I finally make you pay for what you did."

A loud, vicious string of oaths followed Hunter out the door and he hurried down the keep steps to the three people waiting for him.

Patience stepped toward him. "I do not think we should remain here another moment. If we leave now we can make it to the McFarden village before it retires for the night."

"I thought the same myself," Hunter said.

"I will go alert my warriors," Patience said.

Hunter nodded and turned to his mother. "Come, mum, we will gather our belongings and be on our way."

Una went to her son's side and he wrapped his

arm around her. "Do not worry, all will be well."

Patience and McFarden hurried to where the Macinnes warriors were camped. She spoke with Edward, instructing him to have the men ready to leave upon her return.

"Where do you go?" Edward asked.

Patience did not object to Edward questioning her. It was, after all, by her instructions that he did. She had made it clear that she was to know where her warriors were at all times when on a mission, and they were to know the same of her. It was a way to make sure that all remained protected.

So, she did not hesitate to answer him. "I intend to speak to Rona McLaud. She may know something about Heather's whereabouts."

"I could go with you," Edward said, stepping forward.

"No, it is best I go alone. If I do not return shortly, then come look for me." With that she took off for the keep, determined to get answers from the angry woman.

~~~

"Hunter."

The soft, familiar voice had Hunter turning with a smile. "Saundra."

The beautiful, though delicate woman stepped out of the shadows beside Una's cottage with tears in her eyes. "You must do me a favor. You must take Beast with you. You cannot deny me this, Hunter. You know what will happen if you leave him without you to come to his defense. Greer will kill him and my heart breaks enough as it is. I would die, knowing I failed to save my best friend. And perhaps you can find him a more fitting name than the one Greer bestowed on him." Saundra turned to the shadows behind her. "Come, Beast."

A good-sized, black dog stepped out of the shadows to stand at her side. She bent down to hug the animal and he licked her face. "I love you, Beast, but now you must go with Hunter. He will always protect you." She looked up at Hunter, tears streaming down her pale cheeks.

Hunter wanted to reach out and insist she come with him, but he knew that was not possible. She would not go with him, for she knew her departure could start a war. Instead, he did the only thing he could for her.

"Come here, Beast, you are going with me," he ordered.

Beast looked to Saundra and she threw her arms around his neck, hugged him tight, kissed his head, and commanded, "Go, and stay with Hunter."

The dog went to Hunter's side and when the animal turned to look to his master, she was gone, a soft, sobbing thank you drifting through the night air.

Hunter looked down at the animal, who whined softly for the person who loved him as much as he loved her. "I will see that you are returned to her, but for now you must stay with me."

The dog seemed to understand and he followed Hunter into the cottage.

~~~

Patience could not recall the last time she apologized to someone. It was something she barely did, since she rarely had reason to do so. She was not, however, averse to apologizing on those rare occasions if it served a higher purpose. This was one of those uncommon occasions.

"Where are you going?"

Patience turned at the top step of the keep, her hand on the hilt of her dagger to see Saundra staring wide-eyed at her. "To apologize to Rona."

Saundra grabbed the sides of her gown and lifted it so that she could hurry up the stairs to Patience. "Though I may seem too delicate to most, I am no fool. You are not sorry you struck Rona. So, why apologize?"

Patience was prepared in case that question was asked, but before she could respond the door to the keep flew open and Rab walked out. When he caught sight of his wife, he hurried toward her.

He grabbed her wrist and twisted it back. "Where have you been?"

Patience saw panic and fear fill Saundra's eyes and she had no doubt that Rab was a husband who raised his hand probably all too frequently to his wife.

"Answer me," Rab demanded, giving her wrist a twist and causing his wife to wince in pain.

"She came to get me," Patience said, fighting to contain the urge to stick her dagger in the vile man.

Rab turned dark, angry eyes on her, and snapped, "Why?"

"She reminded me that I was a guest here and had been treated with respect," —she paused a moment, worried that she would betray her false words— "and in return I had been ill-mannered and disrespectful to Rona and that was not what was expected of a Macinnes. She insisted that I owed Rona an apology. And after a bit of a debate, I agreed. I am here to apologize to Rona."

Rab released his wife's wrist and grinned at her. "You are not as useless as I thought."

Patience moved her hand off the hilt of her dagger, the temptation to use it on him too great.

Rab turned to Patience. "My wife will show you to Rona's room. She required rest after your vicious assault." He turned back to Saundra. "See her out of the keep as soon as she is done." With that he walked down the steps without another word to either woman.

"Whatever reason you returned here, hurry and be done with it," Saundra said, rushing ahead of Patience.

The Great Hall was empty, not even servants lingered about, though the room could use tending. Patience's stomach roiled at the disgusting sight and she shook her head.

"When Kevin McLaud was alive and Una in charge of the keep, it was a lovely place," Saundra said. "Not so since Greer has become chieftain."

Patience followed her up a narrow, curving staircase, the wooden steps creaking with each footfall that fell upon the worn boards. "Is Greer with his wife?"

Saundra laughed softly. "Rona cannot get with child because Greer barely touches her. He is too busy finding his pleasure elsewhere. Faithfulness was one trait the McLaud men did not inherit from their father, but then I never saw a man love a woman as Kevin McLaud loved Una. I had hoped that Rab and I would love at least half as much as his parents, but that is not possible."

"Why?" Patience asked curious.

"He loves another. He always has and he always will. I feel terrible for him, stuck with me when he wants to be with her, which is where he probably is right now." Saundra wiped at the tear that trickled down her cheek. "Come and be done with this so you can take your leave from this hideous place."

Patience grabbed her arm, stopping her. "How do you know we leave?"

"It would be the wise thing to do and I believe you are a very wise woman." Saundra tugged at Patience's arm, pulling her along.

They stopped at a closed door and before Saundra knocked, she said, "Do you wish privacy?"

Patience nodded.

"Then I will wait out here for you." With that Saundra knocked on the door and opened it once Rona bid her to enter. Saundra was quick to tell a startled Rona that Patience was there to apologize, then she took her leave to wait outside the closed door.

Rona sat in bed, pillows piled behind her back and her chin tilted up as if purposely displaying the dark purple bruise along her jaw. "I never expected a woman who was more like an uncivilized brute to apologize for her crude manners."

"You would be right about the apologizing part."

Rona's eyes widened and not with anger, but with fear.

Patience walked over to the side of the bed.

Rona drew back away, gripping at the blanket. "I will call out for my husband."

"He is too busy poking another woman."

"How dare—"

Patience drew her dagger and pointed it at Rona. "I dare anything when someone suggests that they will have me enslaved like they did my sister. What do you know of my sister's abduction?"

Rona paled and was quick to explain. "I know not why the Dark Dragon took your sister or what he does with her."

"Then why threaten me as you did?" Patience moved closer, the point of her dagger not far from Rona's face to make certain the woman understood she would have no trouble using it.

"I will not say, since I fear Greer more than I fear your blade. You may leave me with a scar or two, but Greer will see me dead."

"There is no one here but you and me."

"Fear has given Greer ears everywhere," Rona said with a shudder. "You will learn nothing from me." Her chin went up a notch higher.

Patience shrugged and slipped her dagger in its sheath. "You already have."

"I have done no such thing," Rona argued.

"You confirmed what I just heard, that your husband has allied with the Dark Dragon."

"Then word has finally come," Rona said joyfully.

"So, you still wait for word from the infamous warrior," Patience confirmed.

Rona glared at Patience with fury. "You tricked

me."

"As you did me, claiming you were acquainted with the Dark Dragon. Did you truly believe I would not seek the truth?"

"Seek all you want, but in the end it is my husband you will deal with, for he is friends with the Dark Dragon and the infamous warrior will ally with the McLauds. Then it will be my husband who will decide if you ever see your sister again."

Patience's dagger was in her hand and at Rona's throat in an instant while her other hand gripped a handful of hair on the top of the woman's head. "If you ever threaten my sister's return or safety, I will show you why you should fear me far more than your useless husband."

"You do not frighten me," Rona said, though she trembled.

Patience swung her blade and Rona shut her eyes tight and yelped.

After a moment of feeling no pain, Rona opened her eyes and let out a scream.

Patience stood over her, holding long strands of hair she had chopped off Rona's head.

Rona's hand went to the top of her head and rage sparked in her eyes along with tears. "I will see you pay for this."

"And I will see you pay for the havoc the McLauds have brought upon my family and this whole area." Patience walked to the door, though turned before opening it. "I will return here and see this finished once and for all. On that you have my word."

Saundra jumped out of the shadows when

Patience walked out of the room.

"Poor woman is pulling her hair out of her head from worry," Patience said and handed Saundra the thatch of hair. "You best see to her. I will see myself out."

"And take your leave quickly," Saundra warned.

"My plans exactly," Patience said, hurrying down the corridor, to the stairs, and out of the keep.

Chapter Eight

The Macinnes warriors were mounted and ready to leave when Hunter, his mum, and Beast arrived at the dismantled campsite. He glanced around and grew concerned when he did not see his wife. He was about to ask Edward where she was when she suddenly appeared.

"Time to leave," Patience announced and without help from anyone mounted her horse.

He was not surprised by her strength. Though tall and slender, her body was well-defined and he imagined it was from strenuous training. Her warrior skills were well-known and she could have only achieved such talent by constant practice.

She took the lead, Edward following alongside her, though not for long. He cut away from her and he joined with another warrior and they took over the lead, several feet in front of her. Hunter had taken count of her warriors and two were missing, which meant she had sent them to scout ahead.

He rode up beside her and though he knew she would not like him questioning where she had been, he had every intention of finding out.

"Is the dog yours?" she asked, nodding done at the big black dog trotting alongside his horse.

"For now," Hunter said and seeing her brow knit he explained. "I am keeping him for a friend until such a time I can return him to her."

"Friend or lover?" Patience asked, not liking the annoyance she heard in her own voice.

"He belongs to Saundra. She fears for his safety with me gone, since Greer has a habit of abusing the animal and I have a habit of protecting him. He was the runt of the litter and Greer wanted strong dogs, so he ordered him destroyed. Somehow Saundra managed to save the weak pup and care for him, and she and the animal became inseparable much to Greer and Rab's dismay. He will grow into a fine dog soon."

"Grow into?" Patience asked. "He is not fully grown yet?"

Hunter laughed. "Beast is a pup, only six months old."

"Beast?" She laughed. "A fitting name since he is already a size."

"Where did you go off to?"

Patience glared at him. "If you think by abruptly changing the subject you would catch me off guard and I would answer without thinking, you are sorely mistaken."

"It does not matter if you smile or scowl, you are still beautiful."

She laughed. "Flattery or that sinfully delicious smile will not get you an answer to your question."

"Sinfully delicious?" he repeated. "I am pleased you find me so tasty. It will certainly make for a delightful union between us and no doubt many children."

His teasing remark reminded her that they were husband and wife and that they would be sleeping together tonight. Unless there was some way she could prevent it, at least for a little while. He was, after all, a stranger to her and the thought of sharing such intimacy with him unnerved her. She could not delay long in joining with him for their vows had to be sealed, but it would not hurt to wait a day or two, though she had given her word, so what choice did she have?

"I look forward to tonight and discovering how delicious you will taste."

His words had her stomach clenching tight and a rush of gooseflesh rushing over her. She immediately employed his tactic of changing the subject. "I went to talk to Rona."

It worked. His blue eyes fired a deeper blue, his nostrils flared as he sucked in a breath and she could not help but think how devilishly handsome he was when he looked about to explode.

Hunter fought to contain his abrupt fury. He could have a terrible temper much like his father, though he had learned to control it as he matured. He had hated when his father ranted and raved and struck out at people. He had sworn to himself he would never be like him, never lose his temper, be mean-spirited, and he had done a fine job of it. But his wife was tempting his control.

"That was foolish," he admonished, keeping a tight rein on his words and forcing his anger to subside.

Patience's temper flared, though she did not conceal it. "More foolish if I had not taken the opportunity to find out what Rona knew about my sister. She made a remark about Heather being enslaved by the Dark Dragon, and I was not about to dismiss it as irrelevant without finding out if she actually had information that could help me."

"Rona is a foolish woman, who more surmises than speaks the truth."

"So I learned, but I also know that somewhere, somehow she had heard something regarding my sister and any bit of information may just be the piece I need to find her."

Hunter glanced at one, then the other warrior who had suddenly appeared to either side of him and Patience. She settled his curiosity without him having to ask.

"My warriors have been made aware that there could be an attempt on your life by your family and your death blamed on the Clan Macinnes."

"Like you, I can look after myself," — he leaned over to whisper— "but I must say I would not want anything to happen to me before I had the chance to make love to you."

She did not respond, since she was at a loss as to what to say.

"You must admit there is an attraction between us."

Patience signaled the two warriors to ride ahead. This was a conversation meant only for her and her husband, and she intended to keep it private. She turned to Hunter as soon as the warriors took a position a few feet in front of them. "You are attracted to every woman you see."

He laughed. "Not true, though most women are quite lovely and unique in their own way. That can make a woman even more attractive. But that is the past and you are my future, and I have thoughts only for you."

"Your tongue charms much too easily," she accused.

"But truthfully," he was quick to add. And just as quick to ask, "Do you fear making love with me?"

"Do you always change the subject so abruptly?"

"Do you always avoid responding?"

"Do not worry, husband, I will do my duty."

Hunter laughed. "Oh, *mo chridhe*, it is not duty that will bring you repeatedly to our bed."

"So you think you can please every woman?" she snapped.

"I do not think I can, I *know* I can, but I am only interested in pleasing one... my wife."

"And what if you do not please me?"

Hunter laughed again, harder this time. "That will never happen."

Patience's hand fisted and she had all she could do to stop herself from throwing a punch that would surely knock him off his horse. "What if I find that particular wifely duty not to my liking no matter how much you boast about your exceptional skills?"

His smile faded, though it didn't disappear entirely. "If you truly disliked sharing the intimacy part of our marriage with me, then I would only seek your bed when we decided on another child. Otherwise, I would find my pleasure elsewhere."

Why did that disturb her? She knew of some women who were pleased that their husbands found their pleasures elsewhere and only troubled them on occasion. The idea, however, did not sit well with her.

His devilish grin returned in full force, along with his cocky confidence. "But believe me, *mo chridhe*, you will not be able to get enough of me."

One punch, just one punch, and she would send him flying off his horse and that would make her feel so much better.

"I can see the passion stirring in your eyes now for me."

"Something is stirring," she mumbled.

Hunter kept a sharp eye on her tightly fisted hand, prepared to duck if she should throw the punch she obviously struggled to contain. He could not help but tease her, though there was truth to his words. It was easy to see that his wife was a passionate woman. It was evident in all she did and would be even more so when he introduced her to the pleasures of the flesh. And he planned on making the introduction memorable.

"You will be glad you wed me," he said with certainty.

She turned a huge grin on him. "But will you be glad you wed me?"

~~~

They arrived at the McFarden village just as it was settling down for the night. Edna McFarden took charge of seeing to Hunter's mother and as soon as she learned that Patience and Hunter were wed, she insisted on having a cottage prepared for them.

It was pointless to argue with her, so Patience smiled as if pleased by her generosity and hurried off to instruct her warriors. They were setting up camp on the outskirts of the village and guards had already been posted, though no one could see them.

She truly did not expect Greer and his warriors to openly attack the McFarden village. He would wait until they were a distance away, and then make it seem as if a Macinnes warrior killed Hunter and they came to his defense. And the only way to stop that was for her to stick close to Hunter and prevent it from happening.

Edward spoke to her briefly, assuring her that all was well in hand. He thought the same as she did, though precaution would still be taken, since one never truly knew what to expect of an enemy.

Her warriors were so well-trained that there was little left for her to do, and she wished she could simply bed down in the camp with them for the night. She was tired and the pain in her arm from warding off the blows of the tankards thrown at Una had begun to hurt or perhaps it was that she finally had time to notice the pain.

Edward approached her. "All is seen to here. We will be ready to leave at dawn. I will see you then."

Patience felt as if he was dismissing her, then she realized that he was letting her know that she need not linger there since it was her wedding night. She left the camp reluctantly, wishing she had given more thought to marrying Hunter. Her thoughts dragged along with her steps. Had there been a way to avoid marrying him? Had she been foolish to rush into what she had believed was the only solution? She was responsible for her clansmen and life could be difficult enough in the Highlands without adding another battle to it that could possibly prove to turn into a raging war.

No matter how she looked at it, her only

alternative had been to wed Hunter, and her father had advised her that he was the least harmless of the McLaud brothers. And she had set rules down to him, instead of a husband setting rules on her. She supposed she should be grateful that he would be an easy one to handle. He was also easy to look upon, had a generous smile, and seemed to have a pleasant nature, unlike his brothers. Why then did she still have reservations?

Edna hurried over to her. "Your husband has declined my offer of our cottage for the night, though graciously thanked me for my generosity. He confided in me that he has something special planned."

With Edna's smile and eyes so wide, Patience could only imagine the charm her husband had worked on the woman.

"You are a lucky woman," Edna said her smile growing. "He seems so intent on pleasing you and claims you stole his heart when he first looked upon you."

McFarden approached, slipping his arm around his wife. "Una McLaud asks for you."

Edna hurried off after a nod and a smile to Patience.

"My wife is as gullible to Hunter's charm as are most women, though not you," McFarden said, "and I am glad to see that. You sacrificed and married out of duty to your clan and I admire you for that, for you prevented certain war and have saved the lives of my clansmen."

Her doubts vanished with his words, though she reminded, "My sacrifice will matter little if I do not get my husband home alive. And you must keep watch over the McLauds, since they cannot be trusted even more so now that our clans are joined. Greer truly wants no part of us, so send word if he does anything that disturbs you."

"I will keep a watchful eye," McFarden assured her.

"And I will send needed supplies to you with a few of my warriors who will visit for a while."

McFarden nodded slowly. "Your father should be proud. You are truly a fine leader and warrior. It would be my honor to serve you."

Patience rarely was startled by anything said to her, but his words gave her a start, her eyes widening, though not that he could detect the difference. She had trained herself to contain her response to any and all things. It made it that much harder for any foes to deal with her.

"And it would be an honor to serve in any battle with you," Patience said, for the man had proven himself worthy, "though I hope that does not prove necessary."

"A prayer to the heavens that it be so."

They exchanged a few more words, and then not being able to delay the inevitable any longer, she went in search of her husband. She walked slowly through the village, realizing once again how needy the people and dwellings were and she was eager to see that they got what they needed.

She spotted Beast, sitting to the side of a door to a small cottage. She assumed Hunter was inside and approached the door cautiously, since Beast kept a steady eye on her. She loved animals, though it was her sister Heather who had a fine way with them. It was as if they sensed her loving and caring heart and sought her out.

Patience stopped before reaching the door. If this dog was going to be a steady companion to Hunter, it was best she made friends with him. She approached slowly, her hands down at her sides so that he saw that she posed no threat to him. He was big, his chest broad, his rigid stance intimidating, and his large ears flopped over, softening him a bit. His paws were a size and he had yet to finish growing.

"Good evening, Beast, I am Patience, and I am pleased to meet you." She extended her hand out slowly to him and his nose reached out to sniff it. She gave him a minute to accept her, and then rubbed behind his ear. When he turned his head for her to scratch behind his other ear, she knew she had won him over.

She crouched down beside him and gave him a good rub. "I hear you will be staying with us until you can go home to Saundra."

His head shot up and he licked her face, as if understanding and happy to hear the news.

The door to the cottage opened and Patience was surprised when Una stepped out. Beast went immediately to her side.

"So, you have made friends with Patience," she said, rubbing the dog's neck. "He is a good dog. Saundra trained him well and he is a good and faithful companion to the lonely lass."

"She does not fit with the McLauds," Patience said what she had surmised upon meeting the lot of them.

"I fear she never will," Una said sadly. "But one must endure for that is the way of arranged marriages," —she smiled— "unless you are lucky to wed a man like Hunter. You will not regret marrying my son. He is a good man as I remind you repeatedly."

"You are prejudice, Mum," Hunter said from behind Patience.

"Of course I am." His mum laughed and Patience could see where he got his amiable smile. "Now then, Beast and I are going to settle down for a good night's sleep so we are both well rested for tomorrow's journey."

Hunter stepped around Patience and went to his mum and gave her a kiss on the cheek. "Sleep well."

She nodded and smiled and ushered Beast inside the cottage, closing the door behind them.

Patience felt a rush of dread gripping her chest. She was alone with this man who was her husband of but a few hours. While she certainly did not fear him, she also did not know him. And how did she share intimacy with a stranger?

She was about to ask him where he intended they sleep since he had declined Edna's offer of her cottage when she recalled what Edna had said, "What nonsense is this that you told Edna that I stole your heart when you first looked upon me?"

"My heart near exploded when I first laid eyes on your beauty."

Patience laughed. "It was not your heart that was ready to explode."

"So your eyes were elsewhere that day."

"So was your attention, and it was not my beauty

keeping you stiff."

"But it will only be you keeping me stiff from now on." He reached out to take her arm and she winced and pulled it away.

Hunter's eyes narrowed and reached out again, though took hold of her arm far more gently this time. "Let me have look."

"It is nothing." She tried to free her arm and though he did not hold her tight, there was firmness to his grasp that she could not escape.

"It is *something* when you gasp in pain and refuse my touch," he said. "Now let me see it. I will not hurt you. I would never hurt you."

Gone was his usual cajoling tongue replaced with a tender strength that persuaded far more seductively. So much so that she surrendered her arm to him.

He pushed up her shirtsleeve and nearly winced himself, her arm was bruised so badly. "This has gotten worse. Have you been in pain the whole time?"

"I have noticed no pain."

"Or you ignored it."

"That is a distinct possibility with all that has gone on today," she confessed.

He stepped closer to her and with one fluid motion his arm slid around her waist and tugged her gently to rest against him. And she did not protest, since she found him quite comfortable to rest against, but then she was tired.

His fingers began to gently probe the bruise. "I want to make certain no bones are broken. You will let me know if I am hurting you."

There was some pain as his fingers moved along her arm, but it was his caring touch that she felt the most. His fingers stroked and probed, moving in a slow rhythm along her flesh, and her body relaxed more and more with each stroke.

She fought to keep her eyes from closing, though her head grew too heavy to keep it erect and she had no choice but to rest it on his chest. She pressed her face against his shirt, enjoying the scent. Too many men had pungent odors about them, not so Hunter. Pine and earth mixed with another scent she did not recognize, though favored greatly.

Feeling comfortable and safe, she allowed her eyes to close for a moment.

"You are exhausted," Hunter said, feeling her grow limp against his body.

She would not deny the truth. "I am."

"You are a wise warrior to admit it."

She liked that he not only acknowledged her warrior skills, but complimented her on them as well. It was nice that he thought her beautiful, but it touched her heart that he admitted and admired that she was a warrior.

Her eyes flew open when he scooped her up in his arms, and she raised her head to glare at him, a sharp retort on the tip of her tongue.

"Please allow me to be a gallant husband and see you bedded for the night."

While he sought permission from her, there was firmness to his tone that threatened that he would see it done no matter her response. Then she recalled that tonight was her wedding night and she had a duty to fulfill.

Patience sighed. "Of course you can bed me, after all, I must see to my wifely duty."

"I want you performing no wifely duty out of obligation," he said, carrying her through the village that had gone quiet for the night. "It is desire, fiery passion, hunger that I want to see in your eyes and feel in your body for me. And tonight you are too tired for us to share any of that."

"Are you telling me that we will not seal our vows tonight?"

"Do not sound so relieved," Hunter said with a laugh.

"You must admit this is a sudden and difficult situation."

"It is only as hard as you make it."

A smile tickled the corners of her mouth. "And you do turn hard so easily."

Hunter glanced down at her, a wicked smile highlighting his handsome face. "Instantly for you."

"I might have to make you prove that," she said surprised by her teasing words, but enjoying the banter with him.

"And I would prove it over and over and over again." He stopped by a small lean-to and lowered her slowly, keeping his arm around her waist until she stood on steady feet.

Patience glanced at the small three-sided structure. Fresh pine had been spread across the ground in the lean-to with blankets covering the pungent pine. She turned to Hunter.

"It is not much, but the blankets are clean, the pine fresh, and the night air perfect. It lacks privacy, but that does not matter for you are exhausted and need rest."

"You prepared this before you knew I was tired."

"I knew you were exhausted the moment I saw you dismount your horse. Besides, I heard not a protest from you once we arrived, another sign of your exhaustion." Hunter moved to the blanket and held out his hand to her. "Come, you need sleep."

She hesitated and again was surprised by her words. "I have only shared a bed with my sisters when I was young. Otherwise, I have slept alone."

"You will sleep alone no longer." He reached out and took her hand, gently tugging her to him. He lowered her down to sit, then joined her. "Get used to my arms, *mo chridhe*, for you will find them around you often." He took her in his arms and lowered them both to lie on the blanket.

Having rested her head on his chest and finding it to her liking, she laid her head there once again and settled comfortably against him.

"Patience."

She looked up and his lips came down on hers in a soft, tentative kiss, as if he was letting her get to know him and she favored the pleasant introduction, and instinctively returned his gentleness in kind. After a few moments, his kiss turned more ardent and she found she welcomed it. And as it grew, turned more urgent, his tongue slipped into her mouth and her own tongue greeted his eagerly.

Reluctantly, Hunter eased the kiss to an end. If he did not, he would not be able to stop himself from making love to her. He gave her lips one last gentle kiss. "I am going to kiss you good-night like that every night for the rest of our lives."

Patience stared at him, keeping her lips locked tight, for if she did not the words on her tongue would slip out. *Then we will never sleep and we will have a gaggle of children.* She blamed it all on her exhaustion. Tomorrow, after she was well-rested, she would not be so vulnerable to his charm. She would not ache for him to kiss her again. She would not find his arms so comfortable, his muscled chest so inviting. Tomorrow she would have her wits about her again.

She no soon as laid her head on his chest, then she was asleep.

Hunter, however, found sleep more elusive. He had taken advantage of her fatigue and kissed her, wanting her to become more comfortable with him, wanting her to see that she would enjoy his kisses. He had enjoyed every kiss he had ever shared with a woman and expected no difference with Patience. But it had been different... very different.

Naturally, he had grown aroused, though faster than he usually did, but never had he felt a jolt to his gut like he had with Patience or a grip to his heart that sent it pounding unmercifully. It was almost as if she had reached inside and claimed him, the feelings had been so intense. His heart still pounded madly and his gut was still recovering from the powerful jolt. And it was some time before he fell asleep, still thinking of Patience.

Chapter Nine

Patience woke when it was still dark and though comfortable in Hunter's arms, felt the need for distance. She was not used to sleeping or waking with another beside her. She was a restless sleeper, often waking throughout the night to sit by the fire in her bedchamber and think before returning to bed and a few more hours of sleep. It was her way, it suited her, and she had no want to change it. Now married, though, things would change and that unsettled her.

She maneuvered her way out of Hunter's arms without disturbing him and left him sleeping to go find Edward. She and Edward had discussed the possibility of sending two warriors home to fetch more warriors in case they would be needed and to bring much needed supplies for the McFarden village. It would take two weeks to reach home, though less if they kept a fast pace and another two weeks to return here. She hoped to be on her way home well before then, though if there was a possibility of discovering the Dark Dragon's lair, it might be even longer before she returned home.

Heather was foremost in her mind. She intended to rescue her sister even if it meant storming the Dark Dragon's lair, another reason to have more troops in the vicinity. Then, of course, they had to watch out for Greer. A man as angry as him could erupt at any time and do something very foolish.

There was much on her mind this morning, including the kiss, which she had been trying to ignore, but that was impossible. If she thought it would be different today when she woke, she was sadly mistaken. The memory stirred her flesh every time she recalled the feel of his lips on hers. She had never thought she would respond to him so easily, so willingly or that she would enjoy his kiss so immensely. There had been quick stolen kisses with lads when she was young that meant nothing and left her feeling nothing. Then there had been the son of a warrior her da had thought would make a good match for her and while he had seemed pleasing enough, he had made a fatal mistake. He had grabbed her when they were alone and kissed her, if it could be called a kiss after experiencing Hunter's kiss. She had stomped on his foot hard, kneed him in the groin, and delivered a blow to his jaw that had sent him reeling.

After he had told her da that they would not make a good match, he had left most hastily. Her da had said nothing to her and had not suggested another warrior as a possible husband, though she had later found out from one of her warriors that her da had questioned the warrior about the bruise on his face and after lies and accusations had been tossed about and a threat that her da would summon Patience to hear her side, the warrior confessed his folly. Her da had ordered the warrior gone and to never return or he would suffer far worse consequences than what Patience had bestowed upon him.

Her heart suddenly ached with the memory of her family. She missed her da and missed her sisters terribly. They had shared so much together and now with Emma married to Rogan, and she to Hunter, nothing would be the same again.

She pushed the troubling thought from her mind and hurried on her way, eager to speak with Edward and eager to take her leave.

~~~

Hunter watched his wife talking with two warriors and Edward. He had been surprised when he had woken to find her gone. How she had slipped away without him realizing it, puzzled him. Ever since he was young, he had learned to sleep lightly thanks to his brothers and their often painful pranks. He learned early on that Greer liked inflicting pain and Rab just went along with him, thinking it amusing. It was not until he got older, stronger, and wiser did it stop and that was because he had treated Greer to a taste of his own pranks and a few good beating afterwards. Greer and he had always been at odds, but then Greer was at odds with most everyone, and that included their father.

He chased the disturbing thought away and approached his wife. Memory of last night's kiss shot through his mind and he had to fight to control the arousal it brought with it. Naturally, some kisses proved better than others, but last night's kiss astounded him. No kiss had ever impacted him the way it had with Patience.

His wife waved him over when she saw that he approached, and he pushed the memory away and kept his thoughts clear so that his arousal would continue to fade.

"I am sending two warriors home to return with a larger troop and needed supplies for the village. I want them aware of our destination once we leave here. In case a problem should arise for us, they would know where to search. Can you detail where we are headed?"

Hunter nodded, crouched down, reached for a stick, breaking it in half, and began drawing in the dirt as he explained. The two warriors were quick to join him, pointing and asking questions. Once it was done, both warriors took their leave.

Hunter turned to Patience. "I would prefer to wake with you in my arms in the morning."

It was becoming a common occurrence for her to hold back her response to him and think on it. Her first thought had been to tell him that she would prefer to sleep alone, so how could they compromise. But another thought had quickly followed and that was that she actually enjoyed being wrapped in his arms and she also enjoyed the way his now familiar scent drifted around her.

Instead, she said, "I am restless when I wake."

He reached out and stroked her cheek gently. "I could ease that restlessness."

His tender touch instantly sent gooseflesh rushing over her. "I doubt that," she snapped annoyed that her body had sparked to his touch.

"A challenge," he said his smile spreading, "I love a challenge."

"I am sure you are good at them, but we have no time for this," she argued. "Your brother, no doubt, has plans for us and I would prefer not to make it easy for him to find us."

The mention of Greer melted Hunter's smile. "You are right. We need to be on our way and I would caution that we do not linger at the McCuil croft, for Greer has many eyes and ears about."

His warning set them both into action and within twenty minutes the small troop was taking their leave from the McFarden village.

It was a lovely spring day with a light breeze and a strong sun. The Macinnes warriors remained alert to their surroundings and a scout rode ahead and one rode behind to make certain no one surprised them.

Hunter rode up beside his wife after having ridden beside his mother for a few miles. Beast remained by Una, trotting alongside her horse, though taking his leave now and again to explore along the tail, and to happily return and resume his trot when done.

"Your mum does not tire, does she?" Patience asked with concern.

"No," he said with a smile, "she may be petite, but she is resilient."

Patience was eager for information, so she asked, "Does the Dark Dragon protect the McCuil croft?"

"Most believe so, which is why no one bothers or threatens them."

"Has he been seen there?"

"You do not know much about the Dark Dragon, do you?"

"Only his reputation as a ruthless warrior," Patience admitted, "though I would like to learn more."

"Do you know that few have seen his face? That he wears a helmet into battle, only his eyes and mouth revealed?"

"I did not know that. Why does he hide?"

"Some believe he is badly scarred and wants no one to look upon him. Others say his evil ways have turned him so ugly that no one could bear to look upon him. It is said the King, himself, has not laid eyes on him."

"And what do you think?"

"I think a lot of it is gossip and nonsense produced by fear."

"But gossip always has root somewhere," Patience argued.

"More like a single seed that sprouts and grows out of control until it completely devours the tiny speck that gave it birth."

Patience nodded, agreeing with him, though wondered if that pertained to Hunter as well. Had gossip run so rampant about his exploits with women that his true nature had been devoured by it? If that was so, who truly was he? The thought had her more curious than ever about her husband.

"Are you sure we will make it to the croft before nightfall?" she asked.

"Barring any surprises."

"You expect Greer to attempt an attack?"

"I cannot say, since there is, and never has been, any rhythm or reason to Greer's actions. When his anger sparks, there is no telling what he will do, which could prove deadly for all concerned."

Hunter was right, anger could turn a minor skirmish into a major war, and in the end both sides would lose, even though victory would be claimed. Patience wanted to avoid that, though she worried that with Greer's volatile temper that might prove impossible.

"I enjoyed the kiss we shared last night and look forward to kissing you often."

She found his tactic of suddenly changing subjects to catch her off guard, amusing. And she smiled, which she found she was doing more often since meeting Hunter. Smiles and laughter was something she had once shared frequently with her sisters... until Heather had been abducted. Guilt rose up to grip at her heart. How could she smile or even laugh when Heather was prisoner of the Dark Dragon?

While her heart ached for her sister, she would not let her sorrow show. She did not want it to be taken as weakness and used against her. She would remain a stalwart warrior, and she would rescue her sister, of that she was certain.

"You take time to answer me. You did not enjoy it?"

She kept her smile strong. "I was taking time to compare it."

"Good, for there is no one who kisses as well as I do, and you will realize how lucky you are to have me as a husband."

Patience laughed. "You are a boastful one."

He drew his head back as if affronted, though the teasing glint in his blue eyes told her otherwise. "I but tell the truth. And has not your comparison confirmed that?"

"I also speak the truth and admit that your kiss was more favorable than others."

"It is good we both speak the truth to each other, for it will make our marriage stronger. So, I will speak the truth again when I tell you that your kiss was more favorable to me than others."

"I am pleased to know that, especially since you have kissed scores of women."

"Have you not kissed many men?" he asked the question he had wanted an answer to since she had admitted that he had not been the first to kiss her.

"I am not sure if I should be insulted that you think me a woman who would be so free with her kisses or that you maneuvered me to the question you wanted to ask all along."

"You are much too perceptive. I will have to—"

"Be direct and say what you will to me, for I intend to do so with you."

"How many men have you kissed?" he asked irritated that his words were edged with annoyance.

Patience answered honestly. "I do not know if pecks on the lips could be considered kisses, but I experienced a few of those when I was young and the lads I would practice my sword fighting with began to look at me differently. The only other kiss I ever experienced..." She shook her head, and then went on to explain what happened with the warrior whose kiss had been anything but pleasant.

Hunter laughed, though anger stirred beneath his humor. Patience may not have known it, but that warrior had more in mind than just stealing a kiss.

"I must admit I was curious to see how a kiss would feel, but he had been a fool to even think I would let it go any further, or that he would be able to force me. Practicing on the sword field with the lads had given me a keen insight to a man's anatomy and what parts were most vulnerable."

He should have known she was aware of what the situation might have brought, but did she realize the same tactic might not always fit the situation? "You may not always be able to reach those parts."

"I am not a fool," Patience said with a tilt of her chin. "I have learned other ways to disarm a man and have had practice doing so."

"Other men have tried to force themselves on you?'

Patience was surprised by the sudden anger in his voice, but then he had always charmed women. There were some men who knew nothing of charm and others who only knew how to take.

"They learned their mistakes soon enough," she assured him.

After a moment of silence, and having turned his eyes on the road, he said, "Patience."

She turned to him and waited and almost jumped when he snapped his head around.

"No man will ever bother you now that you are married to me and if one dared to try, I would dispatch him to hell where he belongs."

Patience was taken aback by the fierce anger in his voice and the smoldering anger in his eyes. It was unexpected, though if his brothers possessed angry streaks, so then why not him? It seemed there was much she did not know about her husband, but it would be wise of her to find out.

Conversation ceased for a while between Patience and Hunter, each appearing lost in their individual thoughts. It was Hunter who finally broke the silence.

"How is your arm?" he asked.

She saw no reason to lie to him. "It pains now and

again and reminds me it is still healing when I brush against it. There is naught to be done for it except to give it time."

"You have healing skills too?" he asked surprised.

Patience laughed, shaking her head. "Not me, my sister Emma, though she taught me some fundamental care for injuries associated with battle."

"I recall hearing that one of the Macinnes sisters was well versed in healing ways."

"Emma is the knowledgeable one between the three of us. She learns all she can about whatever she can. She would worry me near to death when she would take off into the woods on her own. She would not return for hours and when she did it was with a basketful plus an armful of foliage. And then there is the way she senses the soil, knowing when it is lacking, hungry, or ripe for planting. She is amazing."

"You envy her?"

Patience laughed and shook her head. "There is no envy between my sisters and me, only admiration and love. We are the same, yet we are different, if you can understand that." She did not give him a chance to respond. She did what he had the habit of doing, she abruptly changed the subject. "With so few having seen the Dark Dragon that would mean he could visit the McCuil croft and no one would know it was him."

Hunter found Patience an interesting woman. She was intelligent, perceptive, a skilled warrior, and fiercely independent. She did what had to be done without much complaint, and she was not only loyal to her clan, she cared about them. She was, in many ways, unique.

"The question would be... why would he? Why risk exposing his identity?"

"To see those he cares about."

Hunter laughed. "The Dark Dragon care? Do you truly believe that a man who could do the horrendous things that has been said about him... would care?"

A knot twisted tight in Patience's stomach. "If I do not believe that, then there is no hope for my sister."

Hunter felt a punch to his gut and quickly reached out to her, laying is hand on her arm and giving it a gentle squeeze. "My tongue can be foolish at times. There is hope for your sister as long as you keep it strong in your heart. We will find her and all will be well."

His touch was not only comforting, but so were his words. That he made it known that he would join her in the search for her sister restored some hope in her. How was it that this man, a relative stranger, affected her so? She was never one to lose her thoughts over a man, but then perhaps she had never had one she wished to lose her thoughts over.

"We will see this done, Patience, you have my word on it."

One's word was not given lightly, at least not by an honorable man. Some men gave their word without ever having any intention of keeping it. And while she did not know Hunter well, the way he protected and cared for his mum said much about him.

He gave her arm another reassuring squeeze before removing his hand, and she caught a flare of determination in his blue eyes.

Patience sent him a nod. "That is most kind of you." She took firmer hold of her reins. "I need to go speak with Edward."

"I will be here waiting *impatiently* for you," he said with a flash of lust in his eyes and a brash grin.

Patience had to smile at his audacious manner, the man could titillate, charm, and coax. It was no wonder women were drawn to him. Still, she could not help but wonder if there was much more to her husband than he allowed others to see.

She was about to guide her horse away from his when she turned and said, "While your tongue can be foolish, it is also quite talented."

Hunter's grin grew. "Oh, *mo chridhe*, you have yet to taste its many talents."

Patience shook her head and rode off, though could not stop the images that flooded her mind of just what those other talents could be.

Chapter Ten

The sky had turned golden, the sun near to setting when they crested a small hill and spotted the McCuil farm. From the distance, Patience could see a small cottage, two pens, and fields that appeared ready for planting. There was nothing that distinguished it from any other farm, except that the inhabitants were protected by the Dark Dragon.

Patience was pulled out of her thoughts by Hunter's blatant reminder that she now had a husband.

"I am looking forward to bedding down with you tonight, wife," Hunter said, easing his horse alongside hers.

Patience wagged her finger at the farm in the distance. "I see no place for a private liaison tonight."

"A secluded spot can always be found."

"Impatient to have your way with me, are you?" she asked, tossing him a smile.

"Ever since I caught first sight of you."

"So you have said and now remind me yet again. It is whether I truly believe you or not."

"You wound me, wife," he said, slamming his hand against his chest.

"Your heart wounds so easily?" she teased.

"A man is no man, nor does he ever truly live if he refuses to open his heart and take the chance of having it broken or torn to pieces. And that goes for women as well."

"And have you ever had your heart broken or torn to pieces?" she asked.

He laughed. "Broken hearts are common, especially among the very young. I was but six years when I suffered my first."

"Six years? First?"

"I found women intriguing from an early age, but Liza wanted no part of me. She was, after all, an older woman of eight years."

Patience laughed.

"I was nothing more than an annoying little pest to her and she told me so, thus breaking my heart. But surely you have suffered a broken heart or two when you were young or have broken some."

Patience shook her head. "Swords and fighting interested me more than love and lads. While other young lassies were smiling at the lads, I was punching them."

His hand reached out to rest on her leg and she realized then how often he touched her, innocent touches, comforting touches. His hand was always there, becoming all too familiar.

He gave her leg a firm squeeze. "You are lucky then, for I will never break your heart or tear it to pieces."

"You are right," she said sadness in her voice. "You will never do either to me, for you cannot break a heart or tear one to pieces when no love exists." She rode ahead toward the cottage, fighting back tears that had suddenly threatened to consume her. She rarely cried and she would not start now. What did it matter that she had not gotten the chance to marry for love?

She had married for much more. She would rule her clan and she would keep her clansmen safe.

She realized then that she had been wrong... he had broken her heart. He broke it the day he wed her.

Patience swallowed back the tears that fought their way to her eyes. Never would she let him see her cry—never. She blinked several times to clear her eyes and as she did, she took note of how quiet the farm seemed. It was then she noticed that the pens were empty. There was not an animal in sight, nor was there movement about. She slowed her horse and brought her hand up for her men to ease their approach.

Hunter reached her before Edward did.

"It is too quiet," Hunter said his eyes attentive as he looked around.

Edward flanked her other side. "The place looks abandoned."

Patience turned to Hunter. "Would there be a reason for that?"

"I cannot think of what would make them take flight." Hunter rubbed his chin. "It makes no sense. They are well protected. Why would they leave their home?"

Patience had explained to her men the reason for their detour before returning home. Each and every one of them had expressed their support in helping to find Heather, though she had heard apprehension in their voices, and had seen it on their faces when the Dark Dragon had been mentioned.

She turned to Edward. "Take some warriors and check the surrounding area. I will see to the cottage, and see that a warrior stays by Una McLaud."

Edward nodded and rode off.

Hunter's hand shot out to grip her wrist with more strength than usual. "I will go with you, but first you will tell me why unshed tears linger in your eyes."

Patience yanked her wrist free, annoyed at his sharp eyes. She would have to remember that he saw more than she realized.

"And do not attempt to deny it. I know the glare of unshed tears when I see it."

"Is that because you caused the unshed tears?" she snapped her annoyance spiking, for though his tone was firm, as if he would not be denied an answer, concern was also there.

"I will not deny that I have caused a few, and I will not deny that I would be extremely angry with myself if I caused your unshed tears." He reached out once again, took hold of her hand and brought it to his lips for a gentle kiss. "Now tell me, *mo chridhe*, what I have done, so that I can make it right."

Damn him for making her heart flutter and damn him for having seen her unshed tears. She never showed weakness to anyone and that he should see it in her made her angry, though not at him... with herself. And at the moment anger would serve no purpose. She was on a mission and that came first.

She slipped her hand out of his and with a sharp, curt tongue said, "You cannot make it right." She tugged at her reins, but his hand was on hers quick to stop her and the strength of his grip was far stronger than before. More and more she was realizing that there was more to her husband than he allowed others to see.

"I can and I will."

"We have no time for this nonsense," she snapped. "Take your hand off me."

"Promise me we will discuss this later."

She tried to free her hand and found his grip impossible to budge. She turned blazing green eyes on him. "Do not make me tell you again to release me."

His hand moved off hers and his blue eyes suddenly blazed as brightly as hers. "We will discuss this later whether you wish to or not."

She rode off without answering him and he followed, taking a moment to calm his anger. He had somehow hurt her and it had not been his intention. His firm grip had not helped matters. He had to remember that she was a warrior, a woman of strength, though beneath was a woman yet to blossom and that was who, he was certain, he had hurt. He would find out and he would make it up to her.

Patience was dismounting when Hunter joined her. She looked over at him. "How many people reside here?"

"Five," he said once off his horse. "Noble McCuil, Ewan's oldest of four sons, Mary, Noble's wife, and their three children; Ella the eldest at ten years, Paul, eight years, and Trent the youngest at six years." Hunter glanced around. "There are usually other people about as well. Those from surrounding farms come to visit or offer Noble a hand, hoping it will help get them into the Dark Dragon's good graces."

Hunter stepped in front of Patience as she went to approach the door. "Let me. I am a friend."

She nodded and waited as he knocked before

opening the door and stepping inside. It was only a moment before he waved her in. A quick glance around the fair-sized room was all it took to see that it was empty. Uneaten food was left sitting on the table, though the fire had been doused in the hearth. On a closer look, Patience saw that all clothing, bedding, and personal items were gone.

"They left in a hurry," Patience said.

A shout from Edward had Patience and Hunter hurrying out of the cottage to see her warriors escorting an old man with long white hair toward them. His gait was slow and his shoulders hunched. That was until he turned his head and his eyes settled on something, and then suddenly it was as if he became a different man. He straightened to a height a head above Edward and his hunched shoulders turned broad, his chest wide, and his stance proud. No longer was he an old man who needed help or protection, but a seasoned warrior to deal with cautiously.

"Una?" the man said, squinting his eyes as if he could not believe it was her.

Beast took a protective stance in front of Una. His broad chest wide and his mouth raised in a snarl.

"Ewan," Una called out, her eyes squinting as well as if trying to confirm it was him and, when satisfied that it was, she patted Beast's head to let him know all was well and hurried over to the man.

The tall, white-haired warrior spread his arms and welcomed her with a tight embrace.

Watching them, Patience thought they appeared like long lost lovers, leaving her to wonder. She followed alongside Hunter as he approached the pair.

With an arm still around Una, the man extended

his hand to Hunter.

"It has been some time, Ewan," Hunter said, giving his hand a hardy shake.

"Too long," Ewan agreed and looked down at Una. "I am startled to see your mother here. Greer had told Noble that she had taken ill. I am pleased to see she has recovered."

Una shook her head. "I have not been ill."

Ewan's brow knitted and he looked to Hunter. "What goes on and why are you with a troop of Macinnes warriors?"

Hunter slipped his arm around Patience's waist. "Ewan McCuil, I am pleased and honored to introduce you to my wife Patience Macinnes."

Patience had to smile at the way Ewan's aged, though sharp eyes sprang so wide that she thought they would pop from his head.

"I do not know if I should congratulate you or give my condolences to the lass."

Una slapped his chest. "Mind your manners, Ewan McCuil."

Ewan took hold of her hand. "You have to admit, Una, it is shocking news to hear."

"But true nonetheless," she said, "and I am proud to call Patience my daughter."

Ewan nodded as if properly chastised. "Then I offer your son and his wife a long life and many children." He could not help but grin and chuckle. "Of that I have no doubt."

Una slapped him again. "You speak your mind as always, Ewan McCuil."

"And would you want it any other way, lass?" he asked bending his head down closer to hers.

"No," Una was quick to say. "I will take you as you are, just like I have always done."

Patience eyed the couple inquisitively. They appeared more than friends and naturally her curiosity about the pair grew.

Ewan raised his head and looked to Hunter and asked again, "What goes on here?"

"I could ask the same of you," Hunter said. "Where is everyone?"

Ewan took Una's hand. "Let us go inside and talk."

Beast took up guard beside the cottage door as the two couples entered, though Patience took a moment to talk with Edward before joining the others. She was quick to ask where Ewan had been found and if he had identified himself. What she discovered was what she had expected. The man had been vague, not admitting to his identity, even after Edward had identified himself.

She entered the cottage, keeping the information in mind.

The two couples sat around the table that occupied the center of the room. Patience was not surprised that Hunter reached out and took hold of her hand. She wondered if it was for support or was he attempting to show Ewan that their marriage was a firm one?

Ewan took the lead, his eyes settling on Una. "It has been heard that Greer is preparing for battle."

Una nodded. "It is true. He is much like his father, though more mean-spirited and much greedier. He hungers for power and he does not care how he achieves it."

"He had grown an army of cohorts who believe they can conquer other clans and expand their holdings," Ewan said. "When I learned that, I felt it was time to move my son and his family to safer territory."

"And where would that be?" Patience asked, hoping against hope that he sent them to the Dark Dragon.

"To my home in Gullie Loch," Ewan confirmed. "Noble and his family will be safe there and far from the fighting that will take place here."

Patience did not like the sound of an inevitable war with the McLauds, especially since she had wed Hunter to avoid it. She was quick to ask, "Why then are you here?"

"Ella, my only granddaughter out of eight grandchildren, cannot find the cherished cloth doll her mother made for her. She fears it is still here and as a grandfather who loves her beyond reason, I had to come rescue it for her."

Patience wondered over the truth of his words and the only way to find out was to see if the doll could be found and being the room was not overly large, it would not take long. "Let us help you look for it," she said and hurried off the chair.

Una joined her, forcing the two men to do the same.

"I found it," Una called out, pulling something from behind a basket near the door.

It appeared more a ragged piece of cloth, but on closer inspection, Patience saw that it was a worn doll that appeared to have been well-loved. And suddenly her heart ached for the young lass. Patience's own mother had not lived long enough to stitch dolls for her or Emma. Heather was the only one who possessed a doll their mother had made and she had been generous and had shared it with them. It sat in Heather's room, waiting for her return.

The memory sparked Patience's anger and she could not hold her tongue. She turned to Ewan McCuil and said, "You are the Dark Dragon's uncle. He has my sister and I want her back. "

Chapter Eleven

Ewan nodded, his expression solemn. "I am his uncle, but have seen little of him. I have heard rumors, though know nothing more that would confirm your suspicions."

"Suspicions?" Patience spit out. "They are not suspicions; they are fact. The Dark Dragon has my sister and I will not rest until I get her back. Tell me what you know of him."

Hunter walked over to her, ready to slip his arm around her waist, but she drew away.

"I will have my answers," Patience demanded and pointed to Ewan. "If you know anything at all, tell me."

Ewan pointed to the table for them to sit.

"Sit if you wish," Patience said, "but I will stand."

The three sat, Hunter keeping a concerned eye on his wife.

Patience paced in front of the door. She did not know Ewan and though he was friends with Hunter and Una, she could not forget that he was the Dark Dragon's uncle, which meant, she did not trust him.

"I have not seen the Dark Dragon in years. It is only when he feels that I or my family may be in danger, does he warn me and through a messenger, never in person."

Patience did not believe him, though she did not let her doubt show. If he had disguised himself as an old man in need of help to her warriors, then there was more to his story then he was admitting.

"I am sorry to hear about your sister and while I wish I could help you, I fear there is nothing I can offer that would be of any help. I can, however, suggest that we spend the night here so that you may rest before your return journey home."

He seemed eager for them to leave, which once again left her wondering if he was speaking the truth and how long it had truly been since he had last seen his nephew, the infamous Dark Dragon.

"You and Hunter," Una said with a nod to Ewan, "go have a nice talk and Patience and I will prepare a much needed repast."

Patience understood that Una was accustomed to men taking their leave to discuss important matters, she, however, was not... and as far as preparing a meal? She stood. "I do not prepare meals. I do not stitch. I do not tend a keep. I am a warrior and I lead my clan." She walked to the door and turned after opening it. "I do not believe what you say Ewan McCuil and when you are ready to be an honest man and speak the truth to me, I will be here to listen."

She closed the door behind her, leaving the three to think what they want. She had no time to waste in finding her sister; she had wasted enough already. Ewan knew more than he said and if he had no intentions of telling her, then she would find a way to find out what secrets he harbored.

Beast bounced up ready to follow Patience. She almost stopped him, then waved him on. "Come on, boy, I will be glad for the company of someone who will not demand anything of me."

With Beast keeping up with her hasty steps, the pair reached the warriors quickly and she explained to them why they had found the farm deserted. She instructed them to keep alert, her instincts telling her that Ewan McCuil did not travel here alone. And there was still Greer to worry about. It was not a question of if he would attack, but when.

Patience had ordered one of her warriors to keep a watchful, though inconspicuous eye on the cottage. She had expected Ewan and her husband to emerge and go off on their own to talk, but that had not happened. She had not thought that they would discuss certain matters in front of Una. She was, after all, a delicate woman or was she? Could she be like her son... more than she seemed?

With instructions to her men complete and the warriors set for the evening, she returned to the cottage. Beast once again took his stance by the door, while she entered to find the three around the table reminiscing over an adequate spread of food.

Una waved at the empty chair. "Come eat. You must be hungry."

"She must be since all she has eaten today is a small piece of bread," Hunter said and stood to hold her chair out for her.

His eyes were not only sharp, but watchful and just as inconspicuous as her warrior's had been. Another thing she had to keep in mind about her husband.

She sat, paying heed to her own advice that she made sure her warriors followed and her sisters in case something should ever happen to them... and it had. She only hoped they remembered, but then she had reminded them about it often enough.

Keep up your strength. Eat when you can and rest when you can. Rules her warriors were mindful of and made certain to follow, and she prayed Heather was doing the same. Before she dug into the light fare, she thought of Beast and his need to keep strong.

"Beast needs to eat," she said.

Una grabbed a small sack off the floor. "He was not outside when I went to feed him. I wondered if he had gone off with you. I will see to him now."

Patience ate, though sparingly compared to the others. When she finished a piece of bread and small hunk of cheese, her husband handed her another. She took it and ate slowly, finding the bread far too bland for her taste.

Una returned and talk resumed. Patience did enjoy hearing about Ewan and Una's younger days. And from their stories, Patience got the idea that somewhere along the way their friendship had turned to love. Unfortunately, as was the way with things, duty came first. Still, though, there seemed to be a sparkle in their eyes for each other.

Hunter offered her another piece of bread and cheese but she declined it. The bread already felt like a rock in her stomach and made her long for food from home.

Ewan yawned and stretched himself out of his chair. "Time to get some sleep."

Una stood as well. "I will walk with you and find a place to rest my head tonight."

"Nonsense," Patience said. "You will sleep here in the cottage."

Una shook her head. "No, the cottage is for you

and your husband. She went to Ewan's side and slipped her arm around his. "Ewan will make certain that I am settled well for the night and I will see to Beast."

Ewan patted her arm. "That I will." He looked to Patience. "Newly wed couples should have their time together."

Ewan snatched up Una's cloak, draped it over her shoulders, and ushered her to the door, sending a backward wave to them as the pair hurried out laughing.

Patience turned to her husband. "Were they once in love, for they seem so..." she wasn't quite sure how to explain what the couple shared.

"They are comfortable and familiar with each other," Hunter finished for her. "It would torment my da when Ewan came to visit, for he saw something in them that he never had with his wife... trust. My da would get angry after he left and treat my mum poorly, as if somehow she was at fault, never admitting that he was jealous. Then he would feel guilty and spend time making up for his meanness. It always surprised me how much he loved my mum. I used to wonder how such a hostile man even knew how to love. Then as I got older I understood. My da loved her as he would a possession."

"Are wives not considered possessions?"

Hunter learned about women from an early age out of complete necessity. He had grown tired of the endless fights with his brothers, so he had sought companionship elsewhere. His very first true friend had been a lassie who he had discovered would rather talk than fight. He had been devastated when her family returned to her mother's clan. But she had been the first to teach him about females, and he had continued to learn about them until he felt he knew them better than they knew themselves. That was why he understood that the question his wife had just asked was a trap waiting to be sprung, even if she did not realize it.

He smiled and walked over to her, his hand going to rest on her arm for a moment before slowly running it down to her wrist, and then lace his fingers with hers. He then brought her hand up to his mouth to press tender kisses on her fingers. He was pleased to see that she could not hide the shudder that ran through her.

"Need to think over your answer?" Patience quipped, trying to divert his attention away from her body's unexpected response to his innocent kisses or were they? Her body certainly had not thought so.

"I suppose it is common thought that a wife is a husband's possession, but I do not wish to own my wife as one does a slave. I want my wife to know that I cherish and admire her and wish for us to share a good life together and that we *choose* to belong to each other, and not out of necessity."

"If not necessity then what?" Patience asked curious.

"Friendship to start," he said, "and hopefully love will follow."

"And if it does not? Does the couple spend their lives indifferent to each other?"

"When a man or a woman first lay eyes on each other there is a moment when interest sparks or it does not. Those sparks can be the beginning of something if pursued. When I first laid eyes on you, I felt such a spark and I saw a similar one in your eyes." He lowered his mouth to hers and whispered, "Why not see if that spark can ignite into love?"

He did not wait for her to respond. He kissed her and not a simple kiss, but a complex one. It was as if he was demonstrating what they could have together, for Patience felt he kissed her as if he loved her.

The intensity of his kiss overwhelmed her, sending ripples throughout her body, turning her legs weak, and making her heart beat wildly. Could this be the prelude to love? Was it possible? Or was it nothing more than lust?

His arms slipped around her and drew her close ever so slowly, as though giving her a chance to reject him if she so chose to. That was not an option she gave thought to. Instead, she grew impatient to get closer to him and hurried to press her body against his.

His arms tightened around her and she welcomed their firm grip for it drew her even tighter against him. She did not know when she began returning his kiss with as much or perhaps more fervor than he did, she only knew that she could not get enough of him. She wanted more, so much more.

His hands roamed down over her backside and gave it a firm squeeze before they slipped beneath her plaid and squeezed her naked bottom. And damn if a bolt of delicious pleasure did not strike between her legs, turning her weak in the knees. If Hunter had not kept a tight hold of her, she feared she would have collapsed. He had in all essence, kissed her senseless.

The realization struck like a bolt of lightning,

alerting her to her vulnerability and possible consequences. Her training as a warrior had her pulling away from him and hurrying to place the table between them and to use the back of one of the chairs for support, her legs still trembling.

She was relieved that he did not approach her, but stayed where he was, though his blue eyes remained fixed on her. That in itself was unnerving, since his blue eyes stirred with such heated passion that her legs grew weaker and her hold on the chair tighter.

"What I make you feel frightens you," he said.

"Not frighten," —she searched for a more fitting word and could think of only one— "confused." She shook her head, as if the simple action would clear her troubled thoughts. "I understand duty and honor and doing what is best for my clan."

"And you thought to do your wifely duties with me and be done with it, but you have discovered it is not that simple."

"You stir things in me," she admitted, then quickly added, "though it is probably nothing more than lust."

"I suppose it is a possibility. Lust and love can often be confused, the difference being that one wanes fairly quickly whereas the other lingers in the heart and captures the soul, connecting the man and woman for life."

"And how do you come by this knowledge?"

"Observation."

"You have seen or perhaps experienced enough of both to reach this conclusion?"

"I have seen, and experienced, lust often enough to envy love when I see it. Love, thus far, has escaped me as I have already told you."

Her legs had regained their strength, to her relief and she stepped away from the chair, no longer needing its support. She did recall him telling her that, though for some foolish reason she seemed relieved to hear it again. This man—her husband—played havoc with her thoughts and feelings, and that would not do.

Patience raised her chin a notch. "Lust or love, what difference does it make. We are wed and nothing will change that."

"So we surrender to lust and be done with it?"

Why did his suggestion disturb her so? Would that not be the simplest solution?

Patience shook her head. "I cannot think on this anymore tonight." It was a poor excuse, but a truthful one. She was tired in mind and body, and she preferred a good rest before deciding anything.

Hunter walked over to her and slipped a gentle arm around her. "I do not wish to add to your burden and I do not wish to force anything upon you." He lifted her chin so that their eyes would meet. "When you are ready to make love, not just consummate our vows, then tell me and I will make love to you and show you what we can share together."

"But our vows—"

"Are sealed as far as anyone is concerned. We are wed and we will stay wed."

"Tonight—"

"We sleep together and every night from this night on, and when you are ready we will make love." He brushed his lips over hers. "But know one thing, *mo chridhe*, I will not—I cannot—stop kissing or touching you. I favor the taste of you and my hands instinctively reach out to touch and comfort you, and I cannot stop from doing so." He stepped back and took her hand. "Now come, we both need rest for tomorrow's journey and whatever my brother has waiting for us."

She went with him to the bed and after removing her boots and he doing the same, they settled beneath the blankets fully clothed. She turned on her side and he wrapped himself around her, kissed her cheek, and in a few minutes he was asleep.

Patience did not fare as well. She lay there thinking of what he had proposed and she wondered how long it would be before she gave into the passion that her husband had ignited in her.

Chapter Twelve

As usual, Patience woke during the early morning when light had yet to claim dominion over the land. Hunter lay wrapped around her and though his arms were a comfort, she also found them confining. She slipped away from him as gently as possible, needing distance, needing to be alone. She was glad she was clothed, allowing her to immediately take her leave, her boots in hand.

It was while she was slipping on her boots that she noticed a shadow rush by the pens that had once contained farm animals. She made her way quietly along the short distance and followed the shadow into the small cropping of woods. She kept her footfalls light and her breath shallow so as not to be detected.

When she heard a birdcall that sounded foreign, she halted her steps and listened. A rustle of branches caught her attention, and she ducked low to the ground, her ears alert and her eyes focused as much as possible in the dark just before dawn.

"He wants this settled," a voice said with authority.

"I am trying, but it did not go as expected."

Patience recognized Ewan's voice.

"He wants no war," the voice advised.

"I agree, but there are those who intend to prevail no matter what," Ewan said.

"He will intervene if necessary and it will not be

to anyone's liking," the voice informed.

"He may not have a choice," Ewan said.

"Unfortunate," the voice said.

"One thing," Ewan said. "This one sister is not to be ignored. I fear nothing will stop her."

"Time will," the voice confirmed.

With each word, Patience grew angrier. Ewan had lied. He was more involved with the Dark Dragon than he had claimed. She calmed her temper and gave thought to her options. She would be foolish to make herself known, for then she chanced being taken prisoner like her sister. If she kept Ewan in sight, then he may just lead her to the Dark Dragon.

She would assign one of her warriors to trail him. Ewan McCuil was not to be let out of sight. He was her connection to the Dark Dragon and the thought gave her hope that she would finally have a way of finding her sister.

When the meeting between the two men was over and they took their leave, Patience waited before she moved, not wanting anyone to know that she had been there and heard the men talk. Daylight was just peeking on the horizon when she returned to camp, staying close to the shadows so that no one knew she had been in the woods.

She quickly sought out Edward and explained that Ewan was to be watched and followed at all times. The warriors would take shifts so that Ewan did not suspect anything, and this was to be kept in strict confidence, shared with no one outside the troop.

Patience shared an early breakfast with her warriors, her mind on what had transpired in the woods. She could not help but wonder if Una knew of

Ewan's involvement with the Dark Dragon or if Una herself knew the infamous warrior. And then there was Hunter. Could he possibly be more familiar with the Dark Dragon than he had admitted?

Ever since her arrival in this region of the Highlands, it seemed that more truths than lies sprouted. She would need to remain attentive, and as far as war? She agreed with the Dark Dragon on that one... she wanted no war.

But how to stop it and rescue her sister were the answers that most eluded Patience.

~~~

Hunter woke, not surprised to find the spot beside him in the bed empty. What continued to surprise him was that she had been able to slip away without him knowing it. He was usually alert to movement and sound, and yet he had felt or heard nothing. She was quite a skilled warrior.

With a slow stretch, he got himself out of bed ready to find his wife. A smile touched his lips as he thought about last night and wondered if she had left before he woke because she was fearful she would surrender to the passion that he had seen burn so often in her eyes and felt ignite just as often in her body.

He may have given her a choice of when they would make love, but he would make certain to see it brought to fruition sooner rather than later.

With thoughts of making love to her growing him hard, he left the cottage, forcing his thoughts elsewhere. They fell on his brother Greer and he realized the possible consequences if he should discover that Patience and his wedding vows had not been sealed. On the other hand, it mattered little, since Greer no doubt had plans to see him killed and a war started.

He spotted Patience at a rain barrel, filling a bucket with rainwater. Her shirtsleeves were rolled up well passed her elbows, exposing her taut muscled arms and the bruise that was beginning to fade. She hefted the full bucket with ease and placed it on a bench. She then got busy scrubbing her face, neck, arms, and hands. He had noticed that she did everything with intense determination, even now while she scrubbed herself it was not with slow leisure enjoyment, but firm intense movement. She dried herself the same way, tucking the cloth she used at her waist.

Hunter crossed his arms over his chest and rested back against the corner of the cottage, continuing to watch her. She yanked off the stripe of leather that held her hair back and shook her head so that her long dark hair fell freely around her face.

His breath caught in his chest, his arms fell to his sides, and his eyes rounded wide. He could not believe how freeing her hair had changed his wife's appearance. He thought her a beautiful woman when he had first seen her, but with her dark hair released from its restraint to fall naturally over her shoulders and frame her face to perfection she was more than beautiful; she was stunning.

He winced for her, when she did not, as she roughly ran a comb through her long dark strands. She did it several times, then grabbed her hair and brought the silky strands to rest over one shoulder to comb, over and over again. Then she tossed her head so that her hair fell down her back and with deft hands restrained her lovely locks with the leather tie once again.

She set the comb on the bench and picked up a small crock that sat there and removed the top. She scooped something out with her fingers and began applying it to her face, neck, and then arms until she had rubbed it well into her skin.

Curious, Hunter finally walked over to her. The scent hit him when he was only a few feet from her and it stopped him, his nostrils flaring to drink in the pleasant aroma. It reminded him of a warm spring day when the wildflowers in the meadows were in full bloom.

He approached her with smile. "Do I smell wildflowers?"

She smiled while returning the top to the crock. "A salve my sister Heather created for me and Emma to keep our skin well-healed."

He reached out and took hold of her arm, running a single finger over it ever so lightly. "I would say it works well since your skin feels so very soft and so very appealing."

Patience eased her arm away from him reluctantly. She enjoyed the light feel of his finger stroking her arm, too much. It had sent ripples running through her that tingled her unmercifully, and she could not have that. She needed to remain focused at all times.

Hunter stepped closer, leaning down to sniff softly at her neck, then brought his lips to whisper in her ear, "Your delicious scent makes me want to touch and taste every inch of you."

Patience took an awkward step back and Hunter reached out to take hold of her arm so she would not fall. His remark stirred images in her head that caused her cheeks to rise with a soft heat.

She was unable to stop from scolding him. "You are wicked."

He laughed. "Oh, *mo chridhe*, I can be very wicked." He kissed her quick and whispered, "And I would love for you to be wicked with me."

She stared at him for a moment, giving it thought, then quickly stepped away. Whatever was the matter with her, letting his suggestion take root? She had to be careful around him, for he easily stirred her senseless.

"We have no time for this nonsense," she scolded again. "We need to be on our way and we need to keep an eye out for your brother."

"That we do," Hunter agreed, then with a whisper said, "But we will eventually be wicked together."

Patience's cheeks flushed hot and it annoyed her that he could cause her to be embarrassed over mere words when she had faced men larger than him with confidence. Anger and instinct took over, and she smiled as she reached down and slipped her hand beneath his plaid to grab hold of his balls. "Just wanting to make sure you had a big enough pair to see the job done."

"You might want to take hold of my manhood then to see if the size suits you as well."

He dared her, and she could not ignore it. She grabbed hold of him and felt him surge in her hand. He was large and thick and smooth to the touch and she found that she quite liked the feel of him, and so she explored, caressing every inch of him and wondering how it would feel to have such strength inside her.

"Keep it up and I will break that agreement we made," he whispered harshly.

Her hand fell away when she realized the possible consequences of her actions. She cast a quick eye around to see if anyone had seen their unseemly actions. But all were too busy with their duties to pay them heed and Una and Ewan were in deep conversation at the campfire a distance away.

Never had she allowed herself to become so lost in thought that she did not pay attention to her surroundings, and she would make sure it did not happen again.

Hunter stepped away, needing a bit of distance from her since her touch her turned him hard quicker than he had expected. He had always risen to the occasion easy enough, but the way he had surged to life in her hand had been unexpected, pleasantly so.

He smiled and had to ask, "He pleases you then?"

"That has yet to be determined," she said, scooping up her comb and crock and went to walk past him.

Hunter grabbed her arm and stopped her. "Say the word and it will be done."

She yanked her arm away and he watched her walk away, annoyance in her every step. He had to grin as he took a seat on the bench to wait for his arousal to fade. She was not only determined, she was feisty in action and words, and damn but he could not wait to make love to her. He could only imagine the intensity in which she would couple.

He shook his head, though his grin remained. He had to stop thinking about it or his arousal would only grow stronger instead of fading. He turned his thoughts toward his brother Greer. It was not a thought of would he attack, but when. Greer was vicious when it came to battle, but then he was vicious when it came to most things. And if Patience had left his wife Rona scarred in any way, Greer would be out for revenge. No one touched Greer's possessions without suffering for it, and he no doubt also planned on making Hunter suffer.

Hunter stood, his arousal gone and his thoughts on the battle to come. He had to make his wife aware of how cruel Greer could be, and he had every intention of protecting her, whether she wanted him to or not.

As Hunter approached, he heard Ewan say to Patience, "I will travel some with you and your troop, if you permit."

"You are more than welcome to join us, though I have no horse to spare," Patience said.

Una spoke up, Beast close at her side. "Ewan can ride with me. My horse barely feels my weight."

"If it is all right with you, Una, I have no objections," Patience said and turned to her men. "Everything has been seen to?" They all nodded and a strong chorus of ayes was heard. "Then let us be on our way."

Two by two they rode away from the farm and Patience knew that Hunter's keen eye would notice that two of her warriors were not with them, each having been sent to scout the area ahead and behind them. She only hoped that Ewan was not as observant as Hunter or that Una kept him too occupied with chatter for him to notice.

Hunter rode alongside Patience and was impressed with the way her troop remained aware, but then she did as well, her eyes continually scanning the surrounding area.

"I should warn you about Greer," Hunter said. "He is ferocious in battle, like a mighty animal intent on tearing his prey to pieces. He takes down all he can in his path and leaves some wounded to purposely suffer."

"Would you be upset if I killed him?" she asked with all seriousness.

"Aye, I would," he snapped. "That honor will be mine."

She nodded at him. "Then I leave him to you."

Hunter softened his tone. "I am grateful."

"I have posted one of my warriors to protect your mother when the attack comes, though if Ewan is still with us, I doubt his services will be necessary."

"Again I am grateful that you think of my mother's safety, but you will be surprised how well-versed my mum is when it comes to surviving a battle."

Patience turned concerned eyes on him. "Do you think Greer would truly take his own mum's life?"

"I believe there is nothing Greer would not do to achieve his goal of power and riches."

"Are his warriors well-trained?"

"I thought they were until I saw yours."

"You do have a keen observation, though my warriors have been taught not to think of themselves as superior to any warrior, for there are always warriors that could prove mightier than them. The truth of my words was proven when we faced the Dark Dragon's warriors."

Hunter stared at her, not certain he had heard her correctly, so he asked, "You and your men went against the Dark Dragon's warriors?"

"We did and lost, but then his warriors seem inhuman. I do not understand how they do what they do. They appear as if by magic and disappear the same way."

"There is much speculation about the Dark Dragon. It has been said that he trained with mystics in the misty mountains here in Scotland. Others argue that he dared to cross the great sea to learn from the barbarians in the north. I wonder if there is not a simpler explanation."

"If you had seen his warriors, you might think differently," Patience said, recalling the unexpected attack that had taken her sister.

"If his warriors are that skilled, and yours no match for them, how do you ever expect to rescue your sister?" Hunter shook his head. "A foolish question when I have seen for myself what you are capable of when determined. And I believe you are more determined than ever to find your sister and bring her home. So it is not a question of how or if, but when?"

This sharp observation of his pleased her and she was glad that he was aware that nothing would stop her from finding her sister and bringing her home. She was also pleased to hear in his voice the confidence he had in her.

"I will help you in any way I can."

"I am pleased and grateful for your offer," she said with a nod. Little by little, she was beginning to like her husband more and more. He was different then she had expected and she was glad for it since it gave her hope that perhaps they could share a good life together. Still, though, she had much to learn about him.

Hunter reached out and laid his hand on her thigh. "I will always be there when you need me." He grinned. "And even when you do not, for I find I favor your company." He gave her thigh a playful squeeze.

His touch, as usual, sent tiny yet potent ripples running through her. She decided it had to be lust that turned her this vulnerable; it was the only thing that made sense. But was she looking for logic where logic could not be found?

She tempered her annoyance at herself and said, "Your presence is not as bad as I expected."

"Then we are off to a good start."

Her own annoyance stung again when he withdrew his hand from her thigh. Never had she thought she would find such pleasure in the simple touch of a man's hand on her.

They did not lacked for conversation as the day wore on, and he noticed that though she was attentive, she also remained focused on her surroundings.

Just before they stopped for a brief rest, she turned to him. "I wonder what makes your brother think that he could kill you, leave me alive, and have everyone believe his word over mine." She shook her head.

"Are not lies sparks that ignite the flames of war?"

Observant and intelligent, could she be so lucky to find both in a husband? She nodded agreeing with his remark.

Patience rose up on her horse, her eyes wide and focused in the distance. A rider approached and it took her a moment to catch his signal. When she did, she shouted orders that an attack was imminent.

Hunter looked around for his mum and saw that Ewan was waving one of Patience's warriors off and hurrying with his mum and Beast to a nearby cropping of woods. He noticed that the warrior went straight to Patience. She certainly had trained her warriors well. He had not taken Ewan's word for it, but had confirmed that it was acceptable to leave Hunter's mum with the older warrior.

Her nod sent him off to join the others as some remained on the horses and others formed a cohesive formation with shields, bows, and swords.

Hunter reached his wife just as the scout warrior brought his horse to a halt in front of her. He was about to speak when he rose up, his eyes turning wide.

Patience and Hunter both turned to see what had caught his eye. The other Macinnes scout that had trailed behind them was riding fast toward them, signaling as the other scout had.

"They attack from both ends," Patience said and barked orders to her men. They shifted positions to cover both ends.

Patience turned to Hunter. "You stay by me."

"Where else would I be when my wife needs

protecting," he said with devilish grin.

"You will listen to me," she snapped, "for I will not become a widow before I am made a proper wife."

"And I'll not be dying before I have made love to you."

The sound of thundering hooves turned their attention in opposite directions. Armies of warriors, their swords drawn, their shouts echoing, charged at them from both ends.

Patience and Hunter's thoughts were the same... *we are outnumbered.*

Chapter Thirteen

"The McDolans join him," Hunter said as he recognized the colors of the plaid on the warriors approaching from behind. "Greer never did fight fair." He turned to Patience and voiced aloud what they had both thought. "We are outnumbered."

"We are," she agreed and shouted to her men, "to the woods."

Hunter followed and was surprised to see several of her men scale some of the trees in minutes. Their arrows poised at the approaching warriors still at a distance. Warriors on the ground formed a line with their shields and other warriors stood behind them, bows drawn and ready.

The woods would make it more difficult for the horde of warriors to attack, not to mention the arrows that would greet them from the trees. But the sheer number of attacking warriors would eventually prevail. Surprisingly, Patience's warriors did not appear concerned. They were ready to fight and obviously to win.

What Hunter did not understand was why Greer had McDolan join him. Did he fear he would not be able to conquer Patience and her warriors with his men alone?

Patience approached Hunter on her horse. "Go to your mum and stay with her, and if it looks as if we are being defeated take your mum and hurry to

Macinnes land. Someone must survive to tell my da what happened here."

Hunter's hand shot out and grabbed her wrist. "Listen well, wife, not now nor ever would I leave you to fight alone. We are one now and always. Ewan will see the truth gets out if need be."

Anger stirred in his blue eyes along with determination, and Patience saw the warrior within him. She nodded. "Then you will fight beside me."

A grin spread across his face. "Thinking to keep me safe, *mo chridhe*?"

She returned his grin. "Knowing I will keep you safe."

Their smiles faded at the same time.

"Do you hear that?" Patience asked.

Hunter nodded. "Silence."

They both turned and saw the Macinnes warriors staring out passed the trees and when Patience's eyes followed theirs, she was stunned to see that the horde of attacking warriors had come to a dead stop, their eyes transfixed on the woods as if frightened to approach.

What had stopped them? It certainly had not been her warriors.

She rode toward the edge of the woods, Hunter following. She would have preferred him to remain where he was safe, out of sight of his brother, but she would waste her breath telling him so, for he would not listen.

When she reached Edward, he fell in alongside Hunter and when they came to the edge of the woods, she saw what had stopped the attacking warriors. There on both sides of the woods, two deep, stood ghost warriors, their faces painted white and their weapons in hand, ready for battle. They stood as still as statues, not one making a single move.

Where had they come from? Had they been following them all along? She recalled following Ewan into the woods and wondered if he had brought them with him.

Patience guided her horse beyond the edge of the woods, out into the open, and Hunter and Edward followed, flanking her.

One of the ghost warriors stepped forward and shouted his words. "No blood will be spilled on the Dark Dragon's land or you will feel his wrath. Return now to your lands and you will live. Fight and you die." The ghost warrior stepped back in line and resumed his solid stance with the other warriors.

Dark Dragon land. The words repeated themselves in Patience's head. This land belonged to the Dark Dragon? Did that mean his home was nearby or was his land holdings vast? She had to find out. She could not leave here without knowing if her sister was being held close by.

She kept the thought in mind as Greer approached with his brother Rab at his side and they were joined by Hew McDolan, a short, man with a wide bulging middle.

Greer looked directly at the ghost warrior who had spoken and was about to speak when the ghost warrior raised his hand, stopping him.

"The Dark Dragon will hear no excuses. Do as he has ordered or suffer the consequences."

The first line of ghost warriors stepped forward and the second line moved up behind them and more warriors dropped out of trees to join them. And they all turned still as statues, staring straight ahead, waiting.

Greer attempted to speak once again when McDolan laid a hand on his arm and whispered something to him. Greer nodded, turned his eyes on Hunter, and said, "I wanted to make certain you were safe and that the Macinnes did not plan on making herself a widow when she had only become your wife." Greer sneered. "Good journey, brother, and I will see you soon."

Patience remained where she was watching both clans ride out of sight. The ghost warriors vanished into the woods as soon as the last retreating warrior disappeared from view. Patience was quick to gather her warriors and be on the way, the McLaud and McDolan clan heading back in the direction of McLaud land, but for how long she could not be sure.

Ewan appeared with Una, Beast at their side, and Patience could not help but wonder if it was because of him the ghost warriors had intervened.

Little was said as Patience ordered a faster pace and everyone obliged readily, the ghost warriors having intimidated all.

After Hunter had seen that his mother had survived the ordeal no worse for wear, he joined Patience.

She was quick to say, "Not for once do I believe that Greer will not attempt another attack."

"It would be foolish of him since he desperately wants the Dark Dragon to side with him in this conflict that he intends to escalate. He may have failed his mission to take my life, but Greer's message was clear. He wanted it known, false as it was, that he was worried for my life and so he had followed with enough warriors to see me safe. Of course the truth was that he planned to slaughter every one of us. Then he could have laid the blame where he wanted it... on the Clan Macinnes."

"Bloody hell," Patience mumbled. "So all he has to do now is send a small troop to see it done as soon as we are off the Dark Dragon's land."

"Or have McDolan send men to see it done."

"The Dark Dragon has only prevented the inevitable."

"It would seem so," Hunter agreed. "We will need to be on guard, though I believe the Dark Dragon's land extends far, so I do not think we will be seeing them anytime soon."

"How far?" Patience inquired, curious.

"I do not think anyone knows for sure and I have wondered if he has not purposely spread rumors so no one knows his exact location. Some say he has two or three castles, one supposedly holds those he imprisons, others disagree since it is said he never takes captives."

"He took my sister," she reminded.

"And why he did is a mystery. I doubt he has a problem attracting women since he is a man of immense power and wealth. There probably is not a chieftain in Scotland who would not trade a daughter in marriage to such a formidable warrior."

"My father would not," Patience said annoyed at the thought that fathers used their daughters to garner them more land, wealth, and power.

It was his turn to remind. "Sometimes a

proposition leaves no alternative, just like ours."

Patience shook her head vehemently. "My father would never be so callous. Besides, there would have been no reason to attack us and abduct Heather. She would have simply been turned over to the Dark Dragon if that was so."

"Simply turned over?" he asked, questionably. "You would not have objected?"

"Of course I would have," she argued, "but it is a ridiculous notion to even give thought to."

"I believe you are right, since your father is known to be an honorable man, but you must admit that when searching for an answer to a difficult question, all possibilities must be explored and eliminated so the truth can finally be revealed. Then perhaps a clearer trail can be followed."

He was right. So many things continued to mar her progress in finding her sister and if she did not begin to eliminate some issues, she would forever be stalled in her rescue attempt.

They rode until near sunset with limited conversation between them. When they finally stopped for the night, everyone was quick to set up camp. Sentinels were posted, food prepared, and the camp settled for the night.

Patient caught up with Ewan as he approached where Una sat with her son and a stretched out Beast by one of the three campfires. "A moment of your time, Ewan." Her firm tone let him know it was not a request.

He obliged her, slowing his step. "What can I do for you, Patience?"

"You can tell me why you lied to me?"

He turned a perplexed look on her.

She stopped, forcing him to do the same. "Spare me more lies. I followed you into the woods yesterday morn. The ghost warriors are not the only ones who know how to tread lightly on their feet so no one hears them."

Ewan seemed reluctant, but said, "I did what the Dark Dragon asked of me."

"And what was that?"

"Help prevent a clan war in this region of the north."

"Yet he abducts my sister and thinks nothing will come of it?"

He was quick to reply. "I know not of his plans and intentions when it comes to your sister."

Patience shook her head. "Why do I not believe you?"

"I can understand why you doubt me, but I speak the truth when I tell you that I know not why he took your sister or where he keeps her. I would dare not ask him, since he is not a man you want to anger."

Patience took a sudden step toward Ewan and he fell back a step or two. "Were you the reason the ghost warriors appeared today?"

Ewan shook his head. "The Dark Dragon has kept a keen eye on this region, knowing war has been imminent."

"How do you send news to him?"

"Through his warriors as you saw for yourself."

She took another step toward him, a slow, though determined one and brought her face close to his. "Next time you meet with one of his warriors, tell him I want a meeting with the Dark Dragon."

Ewan placed a gentle hand on Patience's shoulder. "I understand how difficult this must be for—"

Patience shoved his hand off her and turned furious eyes on him. "You understand nothing, old man. Is the Dark Dragon fool enough to believe that the Macinnes will not fight to get Heather back?"

"You cannot win against him."

"I will not leave my sister with that evil man."

"Do you truly have a choice?" Ewan asked.

"We all have choices, though most choices are not favorable ones," Hunter said.

Patience turned to her husband standing behind her. Once again he had been so light on his feet that she had not heard him approach.

"Your wife wants a meeting with the Dark Dragon," Ewan said as if it explained it all.

"You are his uncle," Hunter said as if her request made sense. "And with his warriors making an appearance today, I would say you are a favorite one."

"I was not the reason for their appearance. War in this region bodes well for no one, and the Dark Dragon knows it and does what he can to prevent it."

"Yet he abducts my sister and thinks the Macinnes clan will not go to war with him to have her returned home."

"I know not his reasoning behind his actions."

"Then get me a meeting," Patience demanded.

Ewan sighed in defeat. "I will try."

"Then you will stay with us until it is done," she said.

"It sounds as if I have no choice." Ewan turned to

Hunter. "Did you not say there is always a choice?"

"I did, though I also said that most choices are not favorable ones. Your choices being; remain here until you see the task done or be taken prisoner until you see the task done."

Patience smiled. Her husband understood her well and made her intention quite clear to Ewan.

Hunter placed a firm hand on Ewan's shoulder. "The Dark Dragon may prevent a war here, but if he does not answer for the abduction of Heather Macinnes and return her home, then he will chance a war with the Macinnes clan and their allies."

Her husband had not raised his voice or threatened, yet he had spoken with an authority that could not be denied.

"No one has seen victory against the Dark Dragon," Ewan reminded.

"Victory often comes with a steep price, which I am sure the Dark Dragon has paid many times over," Hunter said. "If he does not wish bloodshed spilled on his land, why would he want to spill it elsewhere?"

"Sound reasoning, though you forget one thing. The Dark Dragon is not a reasonable man. He is a fierce and fearless warrior who enjoys the taste of victory." Ewan gave a nod to Patience. "I will let him know you wish to meet with him, but I would not hold out hope that he will agree."

"All I ask is that you send the message," Patience said. "I expect nothing more from you."

Ewan walked off to join Una at the campfire, and Hunter turned to his wife. "And what do you plan to do if he gets a meeting for you with the Dark Dragon?"

"I will do whatever I must do to get my sister back."

Chapter Fourteen

Night fell on the camp, but Patience found no sleep. Her mind would not stay still. It jumped around with endless thoughts, not settling for a moment. Too much had happened since her arrival here, not the least being her marriage. She also was no longer upset with her father for having thrust this mission on her, not after having learned that this was the Dark Dragon's domain and meeting up with his uncle. It had been a lucky turn of events. Or had it?

A previous conversation with Hunter had placed a nagging thought in her head. What if Heather's abduction had been planned by someone she knew? It certainly would not be of her father's making, but if not him, then who? And more importantly why? Abductions were made to benefit someone. How could Heather's abduction benefit anyone? It made no sense and yet the idea had taken root and she could not let it go.

Patience sighed in frustration, though silently, as she walked the perimeter of the camp. It was best she remained quiet so that she could hear if anyone approached. That was why she was startled when her husband suddenly stepped out of the night shadows.

"Cannot sleep, wife?" he asked, walking over to her.

"You are light on your feet," she said, though sounded as if she accused.

"A skill that can prove useful."

She shook her head. "I am not going to ask how you acquired such skill."

"Good, for there are some things better left unspoken." He reached out and ran a gentle finger along her cheek. "Now tell me what troubles you so much that you cannot sleep."

His touch, though light, felt good. It was not at all intimate, but rather one of concern, and it touched her heart. She let herself enjoy his warm caress, feeling more relaxed with each tender stroke. She would answer him, though not just yet.

She did not know when she had rested against him or if he had eased her to rest against his solid body, but then what did it matter? All that mattered was that it felt good to be there, his one arm wrapped around her, while he continued to stroke her soft cheek.

"I would love to caress every naked inch of your beautiful body," he whispered near her ear before giving her cheek a gentle kiss.

His remark produced an image in her mind that sent a rush of ripples running through her.

"And kiss every inch of you as well," he whispered, following it with another kiss to her cheek, and an ever so gentle one to her lips. "Now tell me what troubles you, *mo chridhe*."

My love. Would she ever truly be his love? Did she want to? Too many questions. Too many thoughts. She would never rest this night. And as much as she enjoyed being in his arms, it left her with a sense of vulnerability. And that would not do.

She reluctantly stepped away from him, though he

tried to stop her, holding her around the waist a bit tighter.

Hunter loved having her in his arms. She nestled there perfectly and her body felt so good against his. He learned more and more about her with each touch and response, and by the time they made love he would know her well. That was why he had not wanted to let her go. He had felt a change in her just before she slipped away from him and he was not sure what had caused it. And he would not rest until he did.

"What is wrong?"

There wasn't much of a moon tonight, though the campfires cast a soft enough glow so that his face was somewhat visible. Concern was there in his blue eyes and even written in his knitted brow. How did the man care so much for her when he barely knew her? And how did she explain to him that he made her feel vulnerable and she could not allow that to happen?

"Your hesitance in answering me tells me that you are not sure what to say. The truth would be the easiest and wisest answer."

She was not ready to admit that he had made her feel defenseless. She did not know if she would ever be ready.

Before she could answer, he spoke. "I do not think you are ready to tell me the truth."

He was much too perceptive. It was no wonder why he could charm women so easily, charm them vulnerable so that they could not resist him.

"I see doubt in your lovely eyes, *mo chridhe*. Why?"

"I do not truly know you."

"And it frightens you that you can feel for someone you do not know."

How did he know he caused feelings to stir in her for him?

"Your response to my touch tells me much more than you know and your eyes are quite expressive also."

She shook her head. This man, her husband, was seeing things in her that no one ever had and it made her feel even more susceptible.

"Believe me, wife, when I tell you that you can trust me. I will not hurt you and I will always be there for you. I will repeat it as often as you need to hear it and my actions will confirm it as well." He reached out and took hold of her hand. "Come with me and let my chest cushion your head, my arms keep you warm, and my tender caresses lull you to sleep."

She almost surrendered to his tempting invitation, but instead took a step away from him, her hand falling from his. "I need to make sure of our safety."

"Our safety or yours?" he asked with a tilt of his head.

"Go sleep, I will join you later," she said annoyed that he sensed her unease.

"I will wait right here for you." With that he folded his arms across his chest and kept a firm stance.

Patience walked off, shaking her head at him or herself, she was not sure.

He was still there waiting when she made her first round of the camp and there again when she came around the second time. The third time she came upon him, he held his hand out to her.

"You need rest for tomorrow."

She could not argue with that. The day had finally caught up with her and weariness was creeping into her bones. And seeing him extend his hand to her, offering her comfort was something she could no longer resist. She reached out to him.

Hunter took hold of her hand and stepped close to her, his arm going around her waist. He was relieved that she had finally surrendered, not to him, at least not yet, but to the fatigue he had seen grow heavier on her with each step she had taken.

Once on the blankets he had spread out for them, he took her in his arms, and he was pleased that she snuggled close against him, her head resting on his chest. He stroked along her arm up over her shoulder and drew soft circles on her neck. In minutes, she was asleep and he followed soon after, pleased that his wife slept comfortably beside him.

~~~

Hunter woke from a restless dream to find the spot beside him empty. He rolled his eyes and shook his head. In his dream he had been frantic, unable to find his wife, and what did he find when he woke... his wife gone.

All women he had spent the night with had always woken beside him and, of course, they would make love again even after a long night of lovemaking. He wondered if it would be the same with his wife once they made love. Would she then be reluctant to leave their bed?

He stretched himself fully awake and sat up,

glancing around to see if he could catch sight of his wife. He spotted her talking with Edward and another warrior. The three were engrossed in conversation. Now was a good time to do something he had been planning to do.

After a good stretch of all his limbs, he got to his feet and went to find Ewan. He spotted him just coming out of the nearby cropping of woods.

"Did you pass on Patience's message?" Hunter asked when he got near.

"I have not had the opportunity as yet, but I will do as she asked when the chance presents itself." Ewan lowered his voice to a whisper. "It is a useless request. He will not meet with her."

"I feared so, though it is a foolish decision on his part."

Ewan looked at him oddly.

"My wife is relentless and will not give up. She will hunt the Dark Dragon down and find him and rescue her sister."

Ewan shook his head. "His skills and power far surpass hers."

"He forgets one thing."

Ewan once again looked at him oddly.

"The love Patience has for her sister. It is more powerful than any weapon."

Ewan stared at him a moment before he responded. "Love itself is a powerful weapon. It can topple kings and kingdoms. It can turn men weak and foolish." He paused a moment and cast a glance at Una. "Or it can be unselfish and prevent wars and make men stronger than they ever thought they could possibly be. Aye, love is the most powerful weapon in the world, but it depends on how one wields it."

"Is that a threat I hear?"

"More caution, and it would be wise to pay heed to it." Ewan stepped around Hunter, though paused a moment and placed a strong hand on his shoulder. "Especially since I see the love growing in your eyes for your wife."

Hunter grabbed Ewan's arm when he went to move away. "I will do whatever it takes to keep my wife safe and if any harm should befall her, I will seek revenge. Pass that message on to the Dark Dragon as well."

"He does not take well to threats," Ewan cautioned.

"Either do I." Hunter turned and walked off, annoyed that Ewan was not only much more involved with the Dark Dragon than he allowed anyone to believe, but that there was much more to Heather's abduction than anyone realized.

Hunter made his way toward his wife, his mum stopping him for a moment.

"Ewan is a good and honest man," she said with a gentle smile that quickly tempered his annoyance.

"A bit of a disagreement between us, nothing more," Hunter assured her, not wanting her to worry.

"He has been a good ally to our family through the years and will continue to be if you let him. He has kept me from harm on more than one occasion."

"I did not know that. How so?" Hunter asked concerned that his mother had been in harm's way and he had not known about it.

"Stories better left for another day," she said, patting his arm. "Just promise me that you will trust

Ewan, for he is a good man."

"As you wish, Mum," he said, though he would remain cautious when it came to Ewan. "Now are you well-rested and ready for another day's journey?"

"Aye, that I am and looking forward it to it as is Beast," she said, giving the dog a good rub behind his ears. He leaned against her, enjoying the attention.

"So, Beast, what do you say to a quick walk in the woods before we take our leave?" Patience called out as she approached.

The dog's head shot up and he looked to Una as if asking permission.

"Go on with you," Una said with a smile and Beast trotted over to Patience.

"I will go with you," Hunter said.

"It is privacy I want, not company," Patience said, coming up alongside him. She gave him a quick kiss on the cheek and walked off, Beast trotting eagerly beside her.

"She is strong-willed," Una said as if her son needed reminding.

Hunter leaned down and gave his mum a peck on the cheek, then smiled. "That she is, Mum, but if there is one thing I know best, it is how to handle women—all kinds."

Una laughed. "You may be in for a challenge with this one."

"Yea of little faith, Mum," he said with a laugh and followed after Patience.

~~~

Patience saw to her needs quickly, knowing her

husband would not be far behind her and because she wanted some time to scout the area. Something did not feel quite right to her. Her scouts had reported that they had spotted no signs of anyone following them, but for some reason Patience thought otherwise.

She looked around for any signs that might be present. It was the reason she had brought Beast with her. He just might be able to detect something.

The dog's head popped up from a spot he had been sniffing intensely and he stood perfectly still gazing straight ahead.

Patience hunched down and looked to where the dog had focused. Something had caught his attention. It could be a small animal roaming about or a creature out of its element.

Beast turned his head, his eyes searching the area behind Patience and she knew the animal had heard Hunter's approach. She kept her eyes straight ahead, concerned that Hunter's steps had interrupted Beast's attention to another's presence. But the animal quickly shifted his attention back, and Patience was quick to once again follow where his eyes went.

She caught the quick movement, then the glint, and she did not waste a minute, she ran toward Hunter, and Beast charged the intruder.

The arrow flew before Beast could reach the man and Patience flung herself at Hunter, knocking him to the ground with her one shoulder and her other shoulder feeling a searing pain as she went down on top of him, though not before another arrow barely missed her head.

An anguished cry echoed through the woods and

Patience was quick to get to her feet and after a brief glance to see that Hunter was all right, though a bit winded, she took off. She came upon Beast attempting to tear the assailant apart. She ordered him off the man and he obeyed without question, coming to stand by her side, though on alert if he should be needed.

The man writhed in pain, holding his arm that Beast had badly mangled. "Help me," he begged.

"Are you alone?" Patience demanded.

He nodded. "Please help me."

"You are one of Greer's men?"

He shook his head and winced. "Hew McDolan. Please... the pain."

"You cannot be the only man they sent."

"Please help me and I will tell you anything you want to know."

Her warriors would never beg an enemy if captured, their honor would never permit it. This man felt no honor to his laird and that told her something about Hew McDolan. He was not a man his men respected.

Rushing footfalls from behind her let her know that Hunter had recovered and was heading her way.

"I will see you tended, but first how many—"

"You have been injured," Hunter said, stepping in front of her, his hand going to her bloody shoulder.

She pushed it away, gave him a scathing look that had his brow rising, and pushed him to the side. She glared at the man on the ground, though the annoyed glare was meant for her husband. "How many men follow you?"

"As many as needed to see him dead," the man

said with a nod to Hunter.

Patience turned to Beast, pointed behind her, and ordered, "Go bring help."

The dog took off.

She turned her attention back to the man, but Hunter once again stepped in front of her. She went to shove him out of the way again, but this time he took firm hold of her arm and eased her a few feet away from the writhing man on the ground.

"I will not be put off this time," he said with a command that surprised her. "You have been wounded and I will see how badly."

"It is nothing," she insisted and went to yank her arm free. His grip was too firm and his expression determined, not to mention the spark of anger that flared in his eyes. Something she had never seen in him before.

Hunter kept tight rein on his anger. If he did not, he would have scooped her up in his arms by now and taken her back to camp to see to her wound. He could not believe how fast she had reacted or that she had taken him down with one forceful blow of her shoulder. It had taken several minutes for him to regain his breath and when he finally had, she had been nowhere to be seen. Fear had gripped him and it had turned to anger fast enough. The woman was fearless and that frightened the hell out of him.

"Tell me if I hurt you," he said his hands going to her bloody shoulder.

"Be done with it," she snapped, tilting her head to look past him at the groaning man on the ground. "Are others far behind you?"

"When I do not return to camp another will

come."

"What camp?" she demanded and went to move.

Hunter's hands went to her waist and held tight. "Listen well, wife, you will stay put until I see to your wound or I will snatch you off your feet and carry you back to camp."

Her brow knitted as her eyes narrowed. "You would not dare."

He planted his face so close to hers that their noses touched. "Do you truly wish to find out?"

His determined tone and stormy blue eyes warned her not to challenge him, so she said, "Hurry and be done with it."

"Wise choice," he said and gave her lips a quick kiss and for some reason she calmed.

Hunter worked as tenderly as possible, not wanting to cause her any pain. After spreading the tear in her shirt further apart, he was relieved to see that it was not serious. The arrow had grazed the surface of her skin and her shirt had soaked up the blood that had spilled, though spilled no more.

They heard Beast in the distance, his barking letting them know he would soon be there with help.

Patience lowered her voice. "I would prefer my warriors not see me so vulnerable."

He nodded. "It is nothing, though it still needs tending. I will help you with it when we return to camp." He stepped away from her, seeing Beast barreling through the woods, her warriors close behind.

He moved aside and waited as Patience praised a prancing Beast for his valor, then she issued orders to her warriors upon their arrival. He watched Edward give a nod to her wound as he followed her command. She shook her head and he nodded once more. She worried about showing weakness to her men, though he wondered if she also worried about feeling vulnerable.

He was glad for this time with his wife. It allowed him to catch glimpses of her, he doubted others ever saw. And with each glimpse, she became more intriguing to him.

Her men got the wounded man to his feet and assisted him back to camp while Edward remained behind speaking to Patience, and Hunter did not like what he heard.

He walked over to the pair, Beast trotting alongside him. "You cannot mean to join your men to attack the camp that idiot assassin spoke of?"

Patience turned a look on Edward that had him bobbing his head and heading back to camp. She then turned to Hunter. "Do not question me again in front of my men."

"Then do not make foolish decisions and I will not do so. You are wounded and what do you think will happen if you attack that camp and kill Greer's warriors? It will start a war we married to prevent."

"I attack those men to delay them, not kill them. Greer will find them trussed up, waiting for him." She held her hand up when he went to argue. "My warriors and I have done this before without an ounce of blood being shed. It will afford us extra time to reach Macinnes land."

"I will go with them," Hunter said as if it was done.

"No you will not." She turned and began walking

away and Hunter fell in step beside her. "You are not trained like my warriors and you will only get in our way. You and the others will take your leave and we will join you as soon as we are done."

Hunter did not say a word and when they entered camp, she was surprised that he walked away from her. She supposed he was angry, but she had made it clear before they wed that he was not to dictate to her. She shook her head. He would learn. He had no choice.

Chapter Fifteen

Hunter found Ewan talking with his mum by one of the three doused campfires.

"Is everything all right?" his mum asked anxiously when he joined them.

Hunter rested a gentle hand to her back. "Everything is fine, Mum, but Patience did suffer a minor wound. Could you tend to it for me?"

"Of course," his mum said and hurried to fetch her healing pouch.

"I will join you after I speak with Ewan," Hunter said.

His mum nodded and hurried off.

"A problem?" Ewan asked.

"A small one. No doubt the Dark Dragon is following our situation closely while we are on his land, but there is something he does not know and should be made aware of immediately."

Ewan bent his head forward to listen.

~~~

"You have a delicate and knowledgeable touch," Patience said as Una tended her shoulder. "My sister Emma would admire your skill and probably delight in talking with you."

"I have heard of your sister's exceptional knowledge. I would also enjoy talking with her and hopefully will be able to soon." Una finished wiping the blood away from the wound. "I have cleaned it well and it bleeds no more. It is a minor abrasion and should cause you no problem."

"I am glad to hear you confirm what I thought," Hunter said, joining them. "And now that you have finished and Patience's warriors stand in wait, we can all take our leave."

"Another day's journey." Una nodded and patted her son's arm before walking off.

Hunter stepped close to his wife, his fingers going to gently probe the wound through the tear in the shirt. "You are lucky."

Patience smiled. "I am skilled."

"Foolhardy as well. I can well defend myself."

"So you saw the arrow headed straight for you?" she asked her smile growing.

He took hold of her chin. "I would have rather suffered a wound than see you suffer in my stead."

She pulled her chin away. "And I would rather not become a widow before I was made a proper wife."

He slipped his arm around her waist and pressed his lower body against hers. "Just say the word and the deed will be done with much enthusiasm."

She laughed softly. ""You make it sound so romantic."

He slowly stroked her cheek with a single finger. "I will make certain that you never forget our first night together. It will live long in your heart and memory and some day when I am gone you will have that memory to keep you warm beside you in our bed."

Patience felt a wrench to her heart, followed by

one to her stomach. The thought that he would one day die, leaving her alone, left her with a loss that overwhelmed and also left her feeling more helpless than she ever had. Why did it trouble her so and why did she suddenly want to be as close to him as she could possibly get? She ignored the haunting thoughts and wrapped her arms around his waist and pressed her face against his chest. His shirt smelled of earth and pine and she inhaled deeply, as if she was breathing part of him into her.

He pressed his lips near her ear. "You will take care, wife, and come back safe to me."

That he was letting her go without any further argument surprised her. She had thought for sure he would once again strenuously voice his objection.

He eased her from his arms and kissed her lips softly. "Be safe."

When he turned and walked away, she felt a sense of emptiness pervade her. It went deep and it disturbed her. She was beginning to feel more and more for this man, her husband, this stranger. Or was he? He was becoming less a stranger to her and more a man she admired, and one that definitely made her smile more than any man ever had. And she liked that.

Heather had warned her numerous times about being too serious. She had cautioned her to smile and laugh more often, and when Patience had told her that there was not that much to laugh about, Heather had told her that that was her problem. She did not see enough joy in simple things. She, of course, had argued, but now that Hunter brought a smile to her face and made her laugh, she could see what her sister had meant.

She was growing attached to Hunter and she was not sure if that was wise or foolish.

Patience took one last look at her wound, stretching her shirt out to have a good look and saw that blood had run down over her breast. She would find a stream to camp by tonight and give herself a good washing and replace the bloody shirt with a clean one.

A smile tugged at her lips as she heard her sister Emma in her head. *Keep your wounds clean and yourself as well.* Her father had assured her that Emma was happy in her marriage to Rogan, but she wanted to see for herself. And she would upon her return home.

She joined her men and they took off on their mission, taking the wounded McLaud warrior with them.

~~~

Patience and her warriors watched from the bushes as ghost warriors saw to leaving every last one of Greer's warriors incapable of going after anyone. Some suffered wounds while others were trussed up like sheep ready for roasting.

Why had they struck now and not when Hunter had almost been killed? Had they not been around? If not, where had they gone off to? Could the Dark Dragon's home not be far from here? She hated not having answers, especially when it came to her sister Heather.

She watched as the ghost warriors finished their

chore. A sudden thought came to her and she did not stop to think about her actions. Why should she? Since the ghost warriors were so good at not being detected, it meant they kept themselves aware of their surroundings, which meant they had to know that she and her warriors where there this very minute.

She had nothing to lose; she stepped out from behind the bushes and trees and walked right into the middle of the camp. Her warriors followed, lining up behind her after two dumped the wounded warrior they had brought with them near his comrades.

The ghost warriors had turned still upon seeing them, though made no move to leave.

"I have a message for the Dark Dragon," Patience called out her voice full of strength. "Tell him I want to meet with him before I leave his land and to bring my sister with him. If he does not, I will hunt him down and cut out his black heart and feed it to the wolves."

None said a word.

She backed away with her men and disappeared into the woods, knowing the ghost warriors would not follow. If they had wanted to attack, they would have by now. And she had a nagging feeling she knew why the ghost warriors had suddenly appeared and solved their problem.

It did not take long for her and her men to reach the rest of her troop. Once she spotted them she urged her horse forward until she reached Hunter and Ewan riding alongside Una.

She eased her horse in front of the trio, forcing them to draw to a halt and looked from Hunter to Ewan. "I will speak with you both now."

They had all ridden for some time, so she ordered Edward to stop a few feet ahead for a rest while she turned and stopped at a small clearing and dismounted before her husband could help her.

Ewan dismounted, his expression serious, while Hunter grinned at her, his arms folded across his chest.

Without a word having yet been exchanged, she had an answer to her question. She marched over to her husband and jabbed him in the chest. "You advised Ewan of my plan and," —she turned and pointed at Ewan— "you supplied that information to whoever it is that connects you to the Dark Dragon."

"And Hunter was wise to do so," Ewan said. "You heard yourself that the Dark Dragon wants no blood spilled on his land."

Patience walked over to Ewan. "I do not care what the Dark Dragon wants and if he does not pay heed to my demand I will do exactly as promised... cut out his black heart and feed it to the wolves."

"You gave that message to the ghost warriors?" Ewan asked as if he could not believe her words.

"He meets with me, with my sister in tow, or so help me God I will see him dead," Patience confirmed.

"As I informed your husband, the Dark Dragon does not take well to threats," Ewan said, shaking his head.

Patience turned to her husband. "So you did speak to Ewan of my plans."

"He was right to do so," Ewan said. "There is no telling what the Dark Dragon would do if you had spilled blood. He wants no war."

"Then tell him to return my sister or it is a war he will get."

"Do not speak such nonsense," Ewan warned. "Your father would not be so foolish as to claim war against the Dark Dragon. I would think that he is already in negotiations to have this matter settled."

"The only way this matter can be settled is to have my sister returned home," Patience argued. "And there is no negotiating. The evil bastard releases my sister or he dies."

Ewan stuck his face close to hers. "Demands will get you nowhere and could harm your sister. Curb your anger and pay heed to your name, for you need to learn patience." He turned saying, "I hope I can undo the damage you have done."

Hunter grabbed her arm as she went to follow Ewan. "Think of your sister and let it be."

She glared at him, angry, though with whom she was not certain. She yanked her arm away from him and went to her horse, taking the reins. She turned heated eyes on him. "I thought I could trust you."

"And I thought you would listen to reason and not place yourself in harm's way when not necessary. It is not always wise to take everything upon yourself when there are easier solutions to a problem."

"So I should discuss it with you and have my husband approve my decision?"

"Your husband may provide insight to situations that could prove useful. You have made it explicitly clear that in the end the decision is yours. I would, however, advise that a wise leader does all she can before resorting to war, for though there is a victor, it comes with a heavy price."

"So I leave my sister in the hands of a monster?"

Hunter walked over to her, his horse trailing behind him. "Until it is prudent to do otherwise." He brushed a stray strand of hair off her face, tucking it behind her ear. She was a beautiful woman even when her temper flared. "I am sure that your sister harbors no doubt that you will come for her. And if she has only an ounce of your courage and strength, she will survive until then. Threats will not help her, patient action will."

She considered his words. Heather had always reminded her that patience was a skill she had yet to conquer, and one that was necessary if she was to lead the clan.

"You threatened?" she said curious to know what he had done.

"I advised that I protect what is mine just as the Dark Dragon does his."

"I do not need protecting," she reminded, though thought that she would not mind his arms around her or to rest her head on his chest and listen to the steady beating of his heart.

"Perhaps, but allow me to be a proper husband now and again," he said with a smile.

"Duty," she said not able to keep disappointment out of her voice that he did what he did out of duty and nothing more. "Aye, we have a duty to each other now that we are husband and wife."

"Duty has nothing to do with it," he said, taking her in his arms. "It is a good husband I want to be to you and a good husband protects his wife, sees that no harm comes to her, even if she is a skilled warrior."

How did he always manage to bring a smile to her face? "You are a good husband," she confirmed.

"I am forgiven for going to Ewan and telling him of your plan?" He tugged her closer.

It amazed her that she enjoyed being in his arms. More and more it was feeling as if she had come home when his arms wrapped around her. Her temper even lessened when he held her, and she found herself wanting to linger in his embrace.

Instead, she stepped away. "Do not do it again."

"Then promise me you will at least hear me out and consider my suggestions."

"Is that an or else I hear?"

"Aye, it is or otherwise you will drive me insane with worry and you will be stuck with a madman for a husband."

She laughed and realized how easily he brought laughter to her lips. "I would not want that."

He pressed a hand to his chest. "I am relieved to hear you say that."

"My word is final," she reminded.

"Of course," he agreed, stepping up beside her as they walked with their horses in tow to join the others.

He sounded as if he meant it, but she wondered if he actually did.

~~~

They stopped not far from a stream that evening and while a fine meal of fresh caught fish cooked over the campfires, Patience took herself off to clean herself up. She thought Hunter might follow, but he was in deep conversation with his mum, though it appeared more that he was attempting to soothe her. This ordeal had to be difficult for her with her eldest son wanting his youngest brother dead. She and her sisters might argue at times, but they loved one another and always came to one another's defense. Never would they harm one another.

She continued on to the stream glad to have a brief reprieve from everyone. She missed the times she could slip away, be on her own, and think of nothing but the quiet of the moment. She found a small secluded spot by the stream and placed her small bundle tucked under her arm on the ground behind her after kneeling at the water's edge.

With dusk not far off, she could not linger as she wished to, so she was quick to gather the piece of soap she kept with her when she traveled. It was scented with wild rose petals that Heather collected and dried, then added to the soap mixture. She loved the scent of it while Emma loved the heather-scented soap their sister made.

Thoughts of her sisters tugged at her heart and she wanted badly to be reunited with them again, hopefully soon. She shook her head, not wanting to linger in sorrow and placed the soap on the grassy bank, unwrapped the towel that held her clean shirt, and placed it on her lap. She then got busy lathering her hands with the soap and scrubbed her face until she felt it shine clean. After dabbing it dry with the towel, she gave a look at her wound. It was nothing more than a scratch, though the amount of blood that had caked along her breast and around her nipple would make one think differently.

"Can I help?"

Patience jumped startled by her husband's sudden appearance. "You have to stop treading so lightly when you approach me."

"Habit," he said and walked over to kneel beside her. His brow knitted and he leaned closer to her and sniffed. "Your scent entices."

She did not know what to say, so she held up the piece of soap.

He took a sniff. "How lucky am I to have a wife whose scent is so alluring. I may never let you leave our bed."

"You would have to chain me," she teased.

"Do not tempt me, for I could show you what pleasure chains can bring."

She shook her head, though the image his words evoked sent a tingle through her. "Be gone with you while I wash."

"Why? We are husband and wife. It is now permissible for me to see you naked," he said as if it required an explanation.

"And I you," she said without thinking.

"Aye," he said, stood and began to discard his garments.

She held her hand up. "It is not necessary to prove your point."

"But it is necessary that you are comfortable seeing me naked. Besides, I could use a washing myself, though I do not think I want to smell like roses." He laughed as he stripped naked.

She knelt there speechless as he stood a moment in front of her, his manhood not far from her face. He was an impressive size and he was only slightly aroused. How big would he be when he was completely hard? She might find out if she kept staring at it, since it was beginning to expand.

She turned her head away and she waited, expecting him to make a teasing remark. She was surprised when she heard splashing and turned around to see him in the stream up to his knees, splashing the cold water all over himself.

A smile surfaced and she could not chase it away no matter how hard she tried. Her husband had a magnificence body and a manhood that no doubt would bring her endless pleasure. At that thought, her smile faded.

He had left the choice to her when they would make love and while she could not deny the passion that flared in her for her husband, this was not the time or place to be thinking of such things. Heather still needed to be rescued and Hunter's life was still in danger, not to mention they were on the Dark Dragon's land.

She turned her attention away from him and did her best to clean off the blood without removing her shirt.

Sprinkles of water flew across her face and had her looking up to see Hunter dripping wet in front of her.

"Undress and join me, the blood will wash off much easier in the stream." He stood waiting as if she had already agreed.

She stared at him, rivulets of water running slowly down his body, hugging and licking his flesh as if it refused to let go. She envied the water clinging possessively to his naked body and marveled over the man standing before her. He was magnificent like an ancient mythical god who had just risen from the depths of the sea.

His presence suddenly overpowered her and she turned away from him and with an abruptness she did not mean said, "No!"

He hunched down in front of her and took her chin gently between his fingers to turn her head to look at him. "You are a warrior of immense skill, when are you going to allow yourself to simply be a woman?"

Chapter Sixteen

Hunter did not give her a chance to respond. He knew if he did not give her a little push, she could slip away from him as she had done too often since they had become husband and wife. He only had her plaid, shirt, and boots to contend with and with his experience in divesting women of their clothing, he would have her naked in no time.

Her hand grabbed his wrist when he slipped off the strip of plaid that ran over her shoulder. It fell to her waist while she kept a tight grip on his wrist. He waited a moment before laying a gentle hand on hers.

"I made a promise to you and I am a man of my word. Nothing will happen between us unless you want it to." He smiled and raised his hand to stroke her cheek. "You are not a warrior at this moment. You are a woman... let yourself be one."

She stared at him, her heart pounding heavily. She already felt partially naked without the leather ties that held her sword encased in a sheath to her back or her leather leggings that kept her legs protected. How would she feel completely striped of clothing?

Much too vulnerable.

"It will grow dark soon," Hunter reminded. "If you do not wish to completely disrobe then at least let me help you clean the blood off your breast."

Patience seemed to emerge from a haze and saw that dusk was not far off. If she was a wise warrior, she would strip, wash, and be done with it. If she was a shy woman, she would keep her clothes on until she had a more private moment to see things done.

The thought spurred her into action. She was comfortable and confident with being a warrior, and the woman side of her would just have to go along with it.

Hunter got to his feet as she yanked her boots off, then stood, and when he saw that she would disrobe, he said, "I can turn away if you wish."

She shook her head. "There is no need for that. You are my husband."

He kept his eyes on her, wondering what had given her the courage, then realized that her warrior side would never allow her to shrink from her duty. He wondered, though, if he could coax the woman within her to emerge or at least peek out.

His breath caught and damn if he did not harden like a rock at the sight of her naked. He loved all types of women, though he had preferred substantial women, ones you could sink your hands into or slam against without hitting bone. At first sight of Patience, he had thought her too slim but seeing her now her curvy body defined with taut muscles, he thought her perfect. Her breasts were high and full, her stomach and mid-section flat and taut. Her slender waist gave way to curved hips and her legs were slim and firm, and between them rested a forest of dark hair that his hands ached to explore.

Patience shivered not from the cool air, but from the way Hunter stared at her with hungry eyes. And she had to admit to herself that her own hands ached to explore his naked flesh, but now was not the time.

She hurried into the water, the crisp coolness startling her and making her rush to see to her task. She tensed when she felt water running over her wounded shoulder and down over her bloody breast.

Hunter stepped around in front of her and scooped up another handful and dropped it over her breast. His hand followed, rubbing away the remainder of the blood on her breast that still lingered. His thumb traced around her puckered nipple, wiping the last of the blood that remained there. And Patience almost groaned with the pleasure his touch brought her. She closed her eyes a moment, enjoying his caress and when his hands suddenly stopped, she opened her eyes to see him gone.

She startled once again when he suddenly appeared in front of her smiling and holding the bar of soap in his hand. She could not help but smile herself, though it turned to a groan she kept stifled when he proceeded to wash not only her one breast, but her other as well. He said not a word to her, he just kept rubbing the soap over her naked breasts. When his hands moved lower down her body, she realized he intended to wash all of her.

Hunter stepped closer to her, coiling his arm around her waist as he ran the soap down her stomach to just above the thatch of dark hair. He told himself not to do it, but when had he ever listened to reason when it came to women? He rubbed the soap over the dark triangle of hair, making certain his one finger was free to stimulate the tiny bud hidden there.

Patience gasped when a shot of passion ran through her so fast and furious that she thought her legs would buckle. She grabbed onto Hunter's arm for support and turned wide eyes on him. "You gave your word."

He teased the wet nub again as he said, "A sneak peek of the pleasure I can bring you, and a reminder that I did warn I would not stop kissing or touching you."

"Not fair," she whispered on a gasp when his finger tormented her again.

He ran his lips over hers in a faint kiss. "You are right. It is not fair to deny yourself pleasure."

A few intimate touches and she was ready to surrender to him. If he could bring her to this point so easily, how would she feel when he finally did make love to her?

Not love... lust. This was lust they felt, nothing more.

So why not enjoy it? He was her husband.

He saw the confusion in her eyes and that was not what he had intended. "It grows late and we both grow hungry," he said, though his hunger was for something far different than food and he had a feeling so was hers. "I will finish and we will return to camp and enjoy the fresh cooked fish."

He hunched down in front of her, soaping her legs and then rinsing them off with the cool water. He warned himself to behave, to be done with it and return to camp. But the thatch of dark hair beckoned and was just too tempting to ignore.

He warned himself again, but it did little good. His hands reached up and took firm hold of her backside, the muscles growing taut in his hands, then he buried his face in the triangle of dark hair.

It happened so fast that she had no time to think.

He held her tight; she could not move. Truthfully, she did not want to. She gasped when she felt his tongue skim over the bud that seemed to radiate with pleasure. When his tongue flicked, then licked it, she thought she would drop from the shot of desire that raced through her. When he did it again, she groaned and did not want him to stop, and he did not stop. He continued to torment her senseless, her passion soaring in leaps and bounds. Her legs grew weak, but his strong hands held her firm, keeping her on her feet.

She glanced down as he looked up and their eyes held and no words needed to be said, Hunter knew from the heated passion swirling in her eyes that she wanted him.

He stood and cupped her face in his hands. "Tell me, *mo chridhe*."

She was too consumed with desire to deny him or herself and just as she was about to insist he make love to her, Beast's loud bark echoed through the trees.

Patience took an abrupt step away from him and hurried to the grassy bank to quickly dry herself and just as she slipped a clean shirt on, Beast came barreling past the trees. He did not stop. He headed straight for the stream and plunged into the water, bouncing around as only a playful pup could.

Hunter splashed him and laughed as Beast barked and tried to catch the water in his mouth. He wanted to strangle the dog for interfering when he did, but it was for the best. Here and now was not the time for them to consummate their vows. But at least she had a taste of what to expect and so did he, and damn if he was not starving for her. Never had he wanted a woman so badly. He would need to keep a tight rein on his desire for her, something he had never had to worry about before. He had always found a willing woman when he was in need. Now he was in need but had to wait for the woman to be willing.

He laughed aloud at the ironic thought, tossing more water at the bouncing pup. When he looked over to his wife, he saw that she had dressed and gathered her things. She looked ready to speak, then shook her head, turned, and disappeared into the woods.

He smiled glad for their little escapade that left her wondering and her body wanting. She would want more now, and so did he. He turned his attention on the dog and the piece of soap sticking out of his mouth.

~~~

When Patience reached camp, she immediately went to Edward to make certain all her orders had been seen to, though having no doubt they had been. But she needed to feel... how? A warrior or a woman? She had surrendered too much of herself to Hunter and it had frightened her. She had always kept tight rein on things, although she did allow her temper to flare now and then, but that often served a purpose. But with Hunter, she had lost all control. She had been ready to surrender completely to him that was how badly she had wanted him to make love to her.

"Patience?"

She jumped feeling a hand on her shoulder and was startled to see Edward looking at her oddly.

"Are you all right? I have said your name three times," he said with concern.

"Tired, that is all," she assured him, which was partially the truth. She was tired of being concerned about these feelings that were growing more confusing yet stronger by the day for her husband. At first, she thought of coupling with him as a duty. Now she ached to share the intimacies of husband and wife with him.

"The fish is ready. Go eat and rest. I will see to everything."

It was not fair to leave it all on Edward to handle, but a good night's rest might be what she needed. She would have a clearer head tomorrow to deal with things and tomorrow night she would once again join her warriors in protecting the camp.

After seeing to spreading her towel on a branch to dry, she piled some fish on a piece of bread and found a spot to sit that allowed her a modicum of privacy. When she took herself off to find a solitary spot, her men knew well to leave her alone... not so her husband.

She was only sitting there a few minutes when Hunter and Beast joined her. Hunter had gotten himself some food while Beast stretched out beside her, his eyes closing as soon as he lowered his head to rest on his paws.

A whiff of rose petals drifted around Patience and she wrinkled her nose and sniffed the air, then bent over the sleeping Beast to take another sniff. She turned to her husband. "Did you wash the dog with my soap?"

"It was a small reward for him finding your soap that I had dropped, having been too occupied with a more important matter."

Her cheeks heated remembering the scene and she bent her head to scoop fish into her mouth, annoyed at herself for blushing like a young lass and not wanting her husband to see.

"Besides, it was either wash him with the soap or have him eat it, he so favored the scent," Hunter said with a laugh.

She could not help but laugh herself. "I will have to have Emma make some rose soap just for Beast."

"I think he would be most pleased with that."

They both laughed again and Patience felt her unease melt away. Her husband seemed to be able to do that to her... ease her worry with laughter. She was also relieved that he did not speak of the incident in the stream. He let it be and that was fine with her. She did not want to speak about it, though it plagued her thoughts.

"It has been a long, tiresome day. We should get rest, for tomorrow will come soon enough," Hunter said.

Patience brushed crumbs off her hands from the bread she had finished. "And we ride hard to put as much distance between us and your brother's warriors as possible."

He stood, dusting his hands of the last of his meal. He held his hand out to her. "Come, we sleep close by the fire. There is a chill in the air tonight and I want to make certain you stay warm."

Patience reached out to him and realizing how easily she followed his lead, she drew her hand back.

Hunter leaned over, his hand still stretched out to her. "I like the way your hand feels in mind, soft, yet strong. Do not deprive me of this simple pleasure."

She suddenly felt foolish. Whatever was the matter with her? Taking his hand did not designate surrender. It was a common gesture between husband and wife, nothing more. She reached her hand out to him.

He closed his hand around hers with a strong grip and pulled her slowly to her feet.

If holding hands with him was just a simple gesture, why did the strength of his grip send ripples racing over her flesh?

"Beast," he called and the pup shook himself awake and followed them.

Hunter saw to spreading a blanket for them a few feet from one of the campfires. He was not surprised when his wife did not wait for him to help lower her to the blanket. She sat herself down and stretched out on her side. Beast took up a spot on one side of her, which left Hunter to stretch out behind her. He threw a blanket over them before settling against her and draping his arm over her waist to tuck her closer against him.

He rested his lips close to her ear and as he went to speak, she interrupted him with a soft plea.

"Please let it be," she said annoyed that she sounded as if she begged. To be reminded of the incident at the stream would only serve to heighten her already passionate arousal. And if they were in a more private setting, she would probably beg her husband to make love to her.

"I will for now, but sooner or later..."

He let his words trail off and they resonated in her head like a bell that forever tolled. She felt a coward and that was not like her. But she realized how easily she had lost control to him at the stream and loss of control left one vulnerable and she could not allow herself to do that, at least not now.

"What disturbs you?" he whispered, his warm breath tickling the tip of her ear. "And do not bother to tell me nothing, since I can feel the disquiet in you."

"Too many thoughts, always too many thoughts," she said with a sigh. "There are times I wish that just for a moment, a sheer moment, my thoughts would drift away."

"I suppose it is a warrior's lot," he said his hand slipping over hers to take hold.

Was she growing accustomed to him constantly reaching out and touching her with an innocent intimacy? She had to admit that she did not mind at all when he held her hand. It might be a simple gesture, but it was a pleasant one. Strangely enough, it somehow made her feel connected to him, as if they belonged to each other.

She sighed again, her thoughts having been so busy she had not realized that his thumb had begun to massage the palm of her hand. His finger dug deep in her flesh and she realized why she continued to sigh—it felt so very good.

She tucked her head back into the crook of his arm and let her eyes drift closed, not that she could keep them open. The warmth of his body wrapped around her like a loving hug and she cuddled into it, enjoying the comfort.

His thumb turned slow and easy on her palm and she shivered at the faint touch while soft ripples washed over her. Never had she felt so at peace. One last sigh drifted from her lips as she fell asleep.

Hunter nestled closer around her when he felt sleep claim her body, though sleep avoided him. He had made love to more women than he could remember and though he had enjoyed some more than others, he had found pleasure with them all, just as he assumed he would with his wife. But there was something different about Patience and they had yet to make love, something he was extremely eager to do, though not until she was ready.

A smile tickled his lips. He did hope she would be ready soon.

She stirred in his arms and he whispered, "Easy, *mo chridhe*, I have you; you are safe."

His reassuring words worked, for she settled quietly in his arms and he realized he felt an overpowering need to protect her and keep her safe. Not that she needed him to since she was a powerful warrior in her own right, yet the need to see her safe overwhelmed him. And the thought that anyone would hurt her angered him beyond belief.

She was his wife and he would let no harm befall her. He would keep her safe and still her thoughts so that she could have a moment's peace and he would make love to her and bring her endless pleasure.

As Hunter fell asleep a strange thought came to him... he was falling in love with his wife.

Chapter Seventeen

They kept a good pace when they started out the next morning, though Patience's eagerness to return home had waned. While it was imperative that she get Hunter and his mother safely home, it was also important that she see if she could make contact with the Dark Dragon and find out about her sister. Or if that proved impossible, she would at least want to attempt to find out the location of the dragon's lair.

"Deep in thought again?" Hunter asked, riding up alongside her.

"There is much for me to consider."

"Why not take a respite from your troubling thoughts and think on more pleasant things?" he suggested.

She thought she knew what he would suggest that she think about, so his remark that followed caught her off guard.

"You will make a good mother to our children. You will teach them how to defend themselves whether lad or lassie. And once you grow accustomed to returning my constant hugs or holding hands you will give more freely of both, yourself."

"Warriors do not hug," she said, as if needing to defend herself.

"But women do."

Her head snapped to the side and she sent him a scathing look. "Does my being a warrior threaten you so much that you must remind yourself that I am a woman?"

"It is not me who needs reminding that you are a woman."

She grinned. "I see the problem. I am the only woman who has not fallen so eagerly into your bed."

He returned her grin. "I suppose my pride is wounded some, though it is more so that I want to know the whole of my wife, not just part of her."

"I keep nothing from you. You see clearly who I am."

"I see what you let everyone see. I want to see what you have not shown others. I want to see the woman who hides within you."

"You talk nonsense," she said, though wondered over his words. The only ones who truly knew her were her sisters. There were no secrets between them, even if some things had been left unspoken. They shared a special bond and always would.

"Think what you will, but one day I will coax her out of you and, I daresay, she may never return inside again."

"And what of you?" Patience asked. "What is it that lurks inside of you that you have yet to show me?" She was surprised to see his smile fade for a moment and it made her wonder if there was a side of him she had yet to see.

"I can be grumpy," he said with a laugh.

Her brow arched. "Somehow I do not see you as grumpy."

"We have many years ahead to learn about each other." He reached over to rest his hand on hers for a moment. "And I look forward to every one of them."

Patience laughed. "You may think differently after spending a few years or maybe months, possibly weeks with me."

Hunter shook his head, his smile remaining strong. "You are an intriguing woman. I will never grow tired of being with you. And when you finally let loose of that passion you so strongly try to deny, I believe you will ravish me every chance you get."

Patience laughed harder this time. "Do not count on it." Though, she did wonder if his words would prove true. His touches, kisses, and even his thoughtfulness stirred passion in her. And the incident at the stream had made her realize just how pleasing intimacy with him could be.

She turned away from her husband for a moment not wanting him to see the heated passion that no doubt was reflected in her eyes. It faded quickly enough when she caught sight of Edward's quick approach.

"We are being followed," Edward said as he drew his horse up alongside hers. "They wear no paint on their faces and they do not hide themselves well."

"Then it would seem likely that they want us to know they follow us," Patience said and hoped it was the ghost warriors with a response to the message she had sent to the Dark Dragon.

"Should we approach them?" Edward asked.

Patience shook her head. "No, we will wait for one of the ghost warriors to make contact, though keep close watch on them."

Once Edward rode off, Hunter turned to his wife. "You assume it is the Dark Dragon. How do you know it is not Greer's men following us, waiting until we leave the Dark Dragon's land before attacking?"

"Greer wants the Dark Dragon as an ally. With the failed attempt on your life and the ghost warriors attacking his warriors, he will do nothing until we are no longer on the Dark Dragon's land. Besides, he is a foolish leader. He lets his anger rule."

Her clear perception of situations continued to amaze him and concerned him. Would she eventually see that he was not that different from his brothers that anger lurked in him as well?

"Now that I think about it, I recall my da never allowing me to accompany him the rare few times he met with your father. He would tell me that he would take me another time, but another time never came."

"Then he must have warned you before coming here about the lot of us."

"He did," she said with a nod, recalling the conversation with her da.

"And what did he have to say about me?"

She laughed softly, tilting her head slightly as if she was about to shake it while the sun reflected off her face, leaving him stunned and slightly aroused by her beauty. He had been with many women but not a one compared to her. And at that moment he felt something sneak into his heart and squeeze it. Could he truly be falling in love with his wife? That was the second time the thought had come unbidden to him and he doubted it would be the last.

"He told me that I would not need to worry about you." She laughed again. "He was wrong about that, though he was right that you kept yourself entertained with the lassies."

"Not any longer," Hunter said. "You are the only

lassie in my life now and forever."

How was it that he could reach out and touch her simply with words? He sent her whole body tingling and heart thumping much too rapidly. And now was not the time or place to be distracted.

She recalled what else her da had told her and curiosity had her saying, "My da also mentioned that your father did not speak very highly of you and that you had come to blows with him a few times."

"Sadly, that is true. My father was mean-tempered, stubborn beyond reason and though the truth could stare him right in the face, he ignored it and did as he pleased. However, he could not ignore me, for I was as stubborn as he. And so we disagreed and a few times our discussions ended in brawls."

"That you let him win of course."

"How did you know?"

She shrugged. "I did the same. My da would sometimes challenge me on the practice field. I always thought he did it for amusement, never truly believing I could ever best him. Then one day as we fought I realized he had made a deadly error and that with one swing of my sword I could take him down. And I saw that he had realized the same. It was not even a thought, I reacted, shifting and leaving myself vulnerable to his sword. He praised my efforts, but it was the last time he ever challenged me on the practice field."

"No man wants to be bested by his daughter."

"Though I did not need to be told that, Emma and Heather made sure to remind me."

"My brothers encouraged me to speak my mind to my da. They enjoyed watching me take a beating."

"Surely, they must have taken a few themselves," Patience said.

"Rab took a good hit now and then, but was wise enough to avoid any confrontation with our father. Greer, on the other hand, welcomed a brawl with our da, knowing the day would come when he could best him. But as you remarked, Greer lets his anger rule and because of that he was never able to best our father, which is something I believe he regrets to this day."

"And do you have regrets when it comes to your da?"

Hunter nodded as he stared off in the distance. "I do. I regret not being there when he needed me."

Patience said no more about it. She saw how much the question had disturbed him and she did not wish to see him reminded of sorrowful memories. And so she asked with a smile, "What will you teach our children?"

His grin returned and Patience almost gasped. He was a handsome one, but when he grinned, it turned him wickedly handsome. Or was it now that she knew how wicked he could be that she was seeing him differently?

"Since you will teach our sons to be great warriors, I will teach them how to attract and please the lassies."

"And our daughters?"

"I will keep them locked away until we can find suitable husbands for them," he said with a laugh that faded as he looked to his wife. "I will pray they are like their mum, brave and wise warriors, who will bow to no man, yet love with all the passion they possess."

She felt a catch in her chest. "Aye, our daughters will have what we never had, a chance at... finding love."

Hunter leaned over and gave her a quick kiss on the cheek. "Love plays tricks on our poor souls, showing up in unlikely places between unlikely people and once it settles in, there is no denying it. Be careful, *mo chridhe*, it may have already played a trick on us."

He rode off, leaving Patience speechless. She had to shake her head, he so confused her. Was he actually suggesting that love brought them together and they had yet to realize it? Impossible. Or was it?

She groaned. She had no time for love right now. Hunter and she had wed out of necessity and that was all there was to it. Or was it?

"Damn," she mumbled. She did not need more questions haunting her. There was too much at stake. Too much that needed to be seen to. Far too much time since her sister had been abducted. Heather had to come first. Love would simply have to wait.

~~~

Patience sent men to hunt so that when they settled camp, food could be set to cook as soon as the campfires were lit. And it was with relief that they finally stopped for the night, having traveled at a good pace throughout the day.

Rabbits were set on spits over campfire flames and blankets were spread in anticipation of a sound night's sleep. Sentries walked the perimeter and Beast made his round passed each one, as if giving his approval.

Una and Ewan sat beside each other before one of the campfires as usual. They never seemed to leave each other's side, except of course when Ewan disappeared into the woods. Beast usually settled by them or by Hunter. Tonight the animal seemed content to stretch out by Una.

Patience did not need to concern herself with preparing a pallet for bed. Hunter saw to it each time. And that was where she took herself off to after speaking with Edward in regards to the night's watch. Her warriors had covered her watch last night, but not tonight. Tonight she would take her turn.

She stretched her arms up, her hands reaching out as if she was trying to touch the sky, then she rolled her shoulders back a couple of times before dropping down to the blanket. She would rest until the food was ready, and then sleep until she took the last watch before morning.

"Let me take your watch for you," Hunter said, lowering himself down beside her.

She smiled, pleased that he asked and not ordered. "I appreciate the offer, but this is my duty."

He leaned closer to her. "And your duty to your husband?"

She did not know what made her do it, or perhaps it was that his lips looked so inviting, but whatever it was, she kissed him, though hesitantly and briefly too her regret.

His hand cupped her jaw, holding it firm. "Do you temper your kiss for fear of what the consequences could bring?"

She gazed into his blue eyes and realized just how intoxicating they could be. They were as brilliant as a beautiful summer sky, shifting in hues of blue that mesmerized. She shook her head, not wanting to succumb to their power.

"If not that, then what?"

She looked at him oddly, her brow scrunching, not understanding what he asked, but then at the moment she found her mind too fuzzy to focus.

His hand moved slowly off her jaw to stroke her neck. "Your lovely eyes speak for you." He brought his mouth down on hers and kissed her with a strength that had her responding instinctively.

Her eagerness fired his loins and he would be in trouble soon enough if he did not ease the kiss to an end, but she was too tasty and too hungry, as was he. His tongue delved into her mouth and she zealously met his thrusts with her own. And of course the image of him thrusting deep inside her flared in his mind and turned him rock-hard.

He told himself to end the kiss and move a safe distance away from her, but he was beginning to realize that there was no safe distance from his wife. She was forever in his thoughts, haunting him like no woman had ever done. So without thought to consequences, his hands went to her waist and he lifted and shifted her onto his lap right over his bulging manhood.

She drew her head back with a gasp and stared at him with wide eyes.

He waited for a scolding or staunch objection from her, but it never came. Instead, she wiggled her bottom against his aching manhood and the urge to climax hit him so hard that he barely had time to control it. *Never*. Never had he come that close to losing control.

He hurried her off his lap and stood, not trusting himself to cart her off into the woods and make love to her. He pointed a finger at her. "Be aware, wife, that you are making it nearly impossible for me to keep my word." He turned and rushed off, the utter innocent look on her face, making him want her all the more.

Patience stared after him stunned, though not by his remark, but by her disappointment that he had left her. Her body raged with a need for him that had her wanting to go after him and demand he make love to her.

"You will not," she ordered sternly to herself.

She actually had to fight the feeling, it was so strong.

"The time will come, but not now," she reminded herself in a soft whisper.

Though her words were true enough, they did not help calm her need. She wanted him now and her body refused to relinquish its ache. She dropped down on the blanket, turning on her side. She forced herself to think of something else and was relieved when thoughts of Heather entered her mind. Soon, she was thinking of various ways that could prove helpful in locating her sister and what could be done once she did. The busy thoughts tired her even more and before she realized it she was sound asleep.

Hunter found her curled on her side and he placed a blanket over her and left her undisturbed. He had thought to wake her so that she could eat, but she needed rest. He would see that she got food in the morning before they started out for the day's journey.

He did not trust himself to join her, so instead he took himself off to eat with her warriors and to take her watch.

~~~

Patience did not know what startled her awake. The camp was quiet, nothing seemed to stir. Then she heard it... her sister Heather's voice, calling out to her. She sounded frightened and desperate, and Patience's stomach clenched. In her fear, Heather was reaching out to her. Her sisters had always had a strong bound. When Emma was young and they thought her lost, Heather had heard her in her thoughts and they soon found Emma foraging in the woods.

That Heather should attempt to reach out to Patience now made her realize how desperate Heather must feel, and her heart ached for her sister, while her anger soared. She was about to sit up, too overwrought to sleep when she caught a shadowy movement out of the corner of her eye. She watched the figure creep into the woods and from his shape and size, she realized it was Ewan. She did not hesitate. She got up and followed him.

It was not easy to follow Ewan in the dark, but Patience managed to keep his shadowy figure in sight while keeping a safe distance. She came to a halt when she saw him stop between two trees and look as if he waited. It was only a moment later that a man dropped from one of the trees giving Ewan and herself a start, though she made no sound.

She wanted to creep closer, but feared they would hear her, especially the ghost warrior. Though he wore no paint on his face, he was obviously one of the Dark Dragon's men and she was curious to know what news he had brought Ewan.

Frustrated that she caught only a word here or there, she took a chance and crept silently as possible, closer to them.

"What do I tell her?" Ewan said, sounding as frustrated as she felt.

"Whatever you must to make certain she returns home," the warrior advised. "All is set and will be done soon enough, then there will be nothing she can do."

Ewan laughed. "Underestimating Patience would be a huge mistake."

"Thinking the Dark Dragon has done so would be an even larger mistake," the warrior warned. "Do what you must and you will hear from him soon."

Ewan nodded and the warrior disappeared into the darkness, Patience following after him.

Chapter Eighteen

Sunrise was just peeking over the horizon as Hunter stretched his arms up and out. He had slept beside his wife for a few hours, then woke and went to inform Edward that he would take Patience's watch. Edward had first denied that his help was needed, but Hunter could be persuasive and with a few well-chosen words, a grin, and a laugh he had Edward finally agreeing. Though, Hunter had noticed that the other warriors on watch had checked on him more than was necessary. Still, he had given his wife another good night's rest.

Besides, it was time he got to know her warriors and for them to know him. They had to see for themselves that he presented no threat to Patience or to them and that he was pleased and honored to be part of the Macinnes clan. And that he would fight with his life to protect it just as they did.

Once the next warrior on duty arrived, Hunter entered the camp, not surprised to see everyone up and about, preparing for another day's journey. He looked about for his wife and when he did not spot her, he went and asked his mum and Ewan if they had seen her. After the two of them had informed him that they had not, he went and asked Edward.

"I have not seen her, though I noticed her sleeping pallet was empty when I woke," Edward said and scrunched his brow.

"What is wrong?" Hunter asked.

"Patience insists that all our whereabouts must be known at all times. It is very odd that she should go off without telling anyone, unless it was unavoidable."

Hunter did not like what Edward implied. It would mean that Patience had to make a quick decision and had no time to inform anyone of what she was about to do.

"She could have been in the woods and saw something that she felt she had to pursue. Patience is no fool. She would leave tracks for us to follow."

"And what if others came upon her without her notice and simply snatched her up?" Hunter asked annoyed that the man was not more worried about her.

"If it were not for the ghost warriors, I would find that an unlikely possibility and I still do since they have made no effort to truly hide the fact that they follow us."

That reminder only worried Hunter more. What could have happened to her? Could she have simply had an accident and was unable to return? Had a band of renegades come across her? Hunter ran his fingers through his hair more frustrated and frightened than ever. She was his wife. It was his duty to protect her whether she wanted him to or not. And Patience was far from invincible, though she did not think so.

Edward suddenly smiled and pointed. "There she is."

Hunter turned and saw her step out of the woods and head his way. He was never so relieved in his life and that startled him all the more. He truly cared for this woman and his feelings for her were growing stronger by the day.

He was ready to reach out and grab her, when she stepped around him and went to Edward. He held his arms firm at his sides as he turned to face her.

"Warriors will arrive momentarily," she said and Edward nodded and left her side with haste.

Hunter went to speak and Patience quickly said, "Not now."

Her dismissal infuriated him and he fisted his hands so tightly that his knuckles turned white.

Beast's loud bark had Hunter turning to see the dog take a protective stance in front of his mum, and Ewan moved to stand directly at her side. He turned to do the same to his wife, but she was already stepping around him to take a stand several feet in front of him. Her stance was firm and her hand rested on the hilt of her dagger tucked at her waist.

A few of her warriors hurried to spread out behind her while her other warriors formed a half circle to the rear of the camp.

The ghost warriors stepped out of the woods in unison, forming a line directly across from Patience and her warriors.

One warrior stepped forward. "There will be a meeting. You are to go home and the Dark Dragon will send word when and where it will take place."

"Not good enough," Patience said her tone strong and confident. "I want my sister brought to me before I leave his land and I will not leave his land until he does. Remind him that he has no right to keep my sister against her will. And remind him again that I will cut out his bloody, evil heart if he harms her in any way."

"No one commands the Dark Dragon," the ghost warrior warned.

Patience took several quick steps forward and jabbed her finger in the air at the warrior. "And no one, not even the infamous Dark Dragon himself, abducts my sister and thinks my family will do nothing about it. He is dead, do you hear me," she shouted. "Dead, if he does not bring my sister to me."

"I will take your message to him, and you will return home," the warrior said.

Patience took another step toward him and pointed her finger at him. "I listened to you and your men talk before I let you discover that I was there watching and hearing all you had to say. So, now I know where the Dark Dragon's land ends and it is there I will wait until he brings me my sister."

"You are a fool-headed woman," the warrior said.

"Remember that, for there is nothing I will not do to get my sister back."

The warrior stared at her a moment, then raised his arm and all the ghost warriors stepped back and disappeared into the woods.

Patience turned to her warriors. "Break camp. We leave soon." She waved Edward over to her. "Send a warrior ahead to let my father know what goes on here and that my return will be delayed."

Edward nodded and took himself off to do as she had instructed.

When she finally turned her attention on her husband, Hunter stepped forward with a smile, grabbed her arm, and hurried her along to a more private spot.

"You go off without letting anyone know where you go?" he said, fighting to keep the anger out of his voice.

Patience yanked her arm free. "I do not have to explain myself to you."

"Aye, you do. You are my wife and your well-being is my concern."

"It is a duty you need not concern yourself with."

He shook his head, his smile fading. "You cannot be serious. You think that it is out of duty that I say this and that I would not care what happened to you or if you were in danger or God forbid had an accident and were unable to return home? You think I would not go out of my mind with worry? That I would simply sit idle and wait? Think again, wife, for that will never happen."

It took a moment for his words to penetrate. Was he saying that he cared for her?

While he had not raised his voice, it did soften as he said, "We are one now, *mo chridhe*. Anything that harms you harms me as well. Any danger to you is danger to me. There is no separating us; we are bound together."

"Out of duty," she said and felt a stab of regret.

"Unless we allow otherwise."

She opened her mouth to respond, but he captured it in a potent kiss. His arm went around her waist and he drew her up against him, squeezing her tightly. She did not mind. It felt good to be in his arms, to feel his lips on her, and to feel as if he truly loved her.

When he ended the kiss, he whispered near her ear, "Do not frighten me like that again, *mo chridhe*, or you will drive me mad with worry."

She felt a rush through her body and a catch to her heart. How was it that this man could affect her so? She had trained herself to show no emotion, but when he took her in his arms that seemed all but impossible. She felt things like never before. It was as if he had sparked something to life that had been missing. And now she never wanted to let it go.

Could he be right? Could they allow otherwise? Could they possibly fall in love?

Voices distracted her and she sighed, remembering that they were not alone, though wishing they were. She peered beyond the slim trees where they stood to see her warriors busy carrying out her orders. It brought her back to the situation at hand.

She did not want to, but she had no choice but to say, "We need to go"

There was much more that Hunter wanted to say to his wife and questions he wanted to ask, but there was no time for either now. Once on the road for the day, there would be time for both.

He nodded and they both reluctantly returned to camp.

Patience went immediately to the warrior who was readying his horse for the swift journey home to take news to Donald Macinnes. She gave him further instructions, then spoke with Edward again and, shortly after, they were all mounted and ready to leave.

Hunter made certain to ride alongside her. He had questions that needed answers and he did not wait to ask them. "We plod along today. You are no longer eager to return home?"

"Not with my sister in the area, and knowing that the Dark Dragon's men keep watch over us while on his land I worry less that your brother will attack us, though I do not discount him attempting something."

A few strands of hair fell loose cupping her face and Hunter recalled how she had looked with her dark hair set free—more beautiful—if that was possible. Its silky softness often tickled his nose at night when she lay snuggled in his arms. He had itched to set the long strands free, thinking perhaps it would also free the woman within.

He reached out and tucked one strand behind her ear as he asked, "And what if the Dark Dragon does not take lightly to your harsh demands and attack?"

"He will not attack," Patience said with certainty. "If he wished us gone, he could have easily disposed of us by now. And he made it clear he wanted no blood spilled on his land. No, something else is afoot here and has been since Heather was abducted. I only wish I knew what."

"Do you truly believe he will meet with you and bring Heather with him?"

"One thing I feel certain of," she said, "and that is that he will not want me camped on his land indefinitely. That means he will need to do something."

"He could have his ghost warriors chase you away," Hunter argued.

Patience laughed. "And what do you think I would do?"

Hunter smiled. "Return again and again."

"You know me well, husband."

"Nay, your stubbornness is well known."

"And that is a good thing," she said proudly, "for the Dark Dragon will know he cannot ignore me."

"You cannot honestly believe that the Dark Dragon will simply release your sister out of the kindness of his heart."

"That would depend on why he abducted her to begin with. At least if I get a chance to speak with Heather, I might learn his intentions and discover where exactly he is keeping her."

"You cannot mean to attempt a rescue?" he asked incredulously.

"Anything is possible when it comes to freeing my sister."

His usual pleasant countenance turned stern along with his tone. "You cannot be that foolish and if you dare try, it is one time you will find me forbidding you to do something."

Patience looked at him as if he had suddenly turned into a complete stranger and her green eyes brightened with anger. "Fair warning, husband, like the Dark Dragon I do not take well to threats."

"It is not a threat, but a promise." And not wanting his temper flaring any further, Hunter rode off, leaving her staring after him.

It took all her willpower to stop herself from going after him and making it clear that not now or ever would she be dictated to by him. Other women might be able to tolerate such nonsense, but she would not.

After a few moments Una rode up beside her, Beast keeping pace next to her until something caught his interest and off he would go.

"He is a good dog," Patience said while staring at Hunter's back as he rode beside Edward who he had engaged in a humorous conversation, since both men laughed often. Why that should annoy her, she did not know, which annoyed her all the more.

"Marriage is not an easy lot," Una said with a pleasant smile.

"Especially a marriage you had not planned on."

"A planned one is just as much of a challenge, but then how can it not be when two strangers are thrown together and forced to wed?"

"Did you know Hunter's father before marrying him?" Patience asked, curiosity poking at her.

"I met him the day we exchanged our vows and I cried during the whole ceremony, for I loved another and foolishly believed my father would let me wed him." Una shook her head. "It was not a pleasant day. I was young and so terribly naïve. When I was finally alone with my new husband, I told him that I would never love him for I loved another, thinking he would not want me and release me from my vows."

"What happened?"

She smiled, though it was with sadness. "Kevin told me he knew of my love for another, but marriage was not about love for those who must sacrifice for their clan. He told me he would treat me well and always keep me safe and all he asked of me was to be an obedient wife and give him sons and perhaps a daughter." She wiped a tear from her eye. "He touched my heart with his patience and tenderness that night. Though he had a temper, he never raged against me. He kept his word and treated me well and kept me safe and after many years I realized that I loved him in my own way." She smiled, this time happily. "I told him one night that I loved him. He wrapped me in his huge thick arms and told me he was happy that I finally did, for he had loved me on first sight. We had a good marriage and I was sad when he died."

"But your heart always belonged to another?"

"My love for Ewan never faded and I believe his love for me remained just as strong, but we both knew it would never be and so we lived our lives with courage and did the only thing we could... we remained friends."

"And now that you are both free?" Patience asked.

Una's smile grew and a faint flush tinged her cheeks. "Who knows?"

Patience could not help but smile along with her. "Perhaps true love will prevail after all."

Ewan rode up to them then and after a quick nod to Patience he turned to Una. "Beast is off foraging and I thought you would like to join him."

Una's face lit with delight. "I would," she said eagerly and just before she urged her horse to join Ewan, she turned to Patience. "Beast learned his foraging from Saundra and no doubt he misses it and her as well."

"Hopefully, he will be able to return to her soon," Patience said.

Una's face lost its joy. "He is much safer here and Saundra would want him safe." She rode off with Ewan, her smile returning and his growing stronger.

Patience watched them and hoped that they would finally have their time together.

The day wore on and Patience's growling stomach made her decide that they would camp early for the evening so that the warriors could hunt. She was surprised when Hunter decided to join them.

It was when she finished speaking with Edward and turned to leave that she stopped and wondered where to take herself. She had grown accustomed to Hunter arranging their sleeping pallet and glancing around the campsite, she saw that everyone was occupied with something. She did not wish to disturb Una and Ewan who appeared engrossed in a private conversation. Beast was stretched out by their fire, sound asleep and her warriors had their tasks to do before settling for the evening.

This was nonsense, she told herself. She did fine before Hunter came along and she would continue to so, then why did she feel so terribly alone? She shook off the empty feeling that pervaded her every thought and got busy fixing her bedding for the night.

With nothing to keep her occupied and her yawns coming much too frequently, she stretched out on the blanket for a nap.

A delicious scent woke her as did her growling stomach. She sat up with a broad stretch and a yawn. Her mouth remained open, actually dropped open, and her arms slowly fell to her side as her wide eyes settled on her husband's naked back.

He was about an arm's length away from her, crouched down by the fire, tending the meat on the spit. The scent of roses drifted off his wet hair and his skin glimmered from a fresh scrubbing, and her body tingled, sending a shiver through her.

She startled when he turned, and he reached out,

his arm going around her back to stop her from falling. He held her effortlessly and she gazed into his gorgeous blue eyes that seemed to hold her captive, though it was more like she surrendered. The thought startled her even more and tinged her cheeks with heat.

Hunter's mouth curved slowly into a smile and he lowered his head to whisper, "How much longer will you torture yourself and me? I am as hungry for you as you are for me, why not appease our hunger?"

"Aye, why not appease it and be done with it?" she said, thinking of how many times he must have so easily appeased his lust with a woman.

His smile grew. "Oh, *mo chridhe*, one time with you will only whet my appetite for more."

She could not stop the shudder that racked her body, but then she also could not stop but think that she felt the same way. She would never get enough of him. She would always hunger for him and that made her wonder once again about love. Was this about appeasing hunger or was this about the feelings growing inside of her?

Chapter Nineteen

Hunter was not surprised to find himself alone when he woke the next morning. Last night had not been easy for either of them. Passion had remained high and fear that once he touched her he would not stop, had him keeping his distance from his wife. He also blamed his lusty state on not having been with a woman in almost a week, but then he was finding that he did not want just any woman... he wanted his wife.

He once again wished that he had never left it up to her to decide when they would consummate their vows. But the deed had been done and he would have to wait—he smiled—though he could help the inevitable along.

He joined his mum and Ewan, sharing the dwindling supply of bread and cheese. He was pleased to see her smiling so often. Life had not been easy for her after his father had died, and he could only imagine the fury his da would have unleashed on Greer for treating their mum so badly. The time would come when he would see his brother pay for it and other evil deeds he had done.

"Will you be leaving us when you reach Gullie Loch and let Noble know it is not yet safe to return home?" Hunter asked Ewan and saw that his mum tensed at the question.

"No, I have sent word to him to stay put. I think it is best I remain with your mum." Ewan reached out and took her hand, then quickly turned to Hunter. "And you, until you both reach the safe haven of your new home."

"That is kind of you, Ewan, but not necessary. I have and will continue to protect my mum."

Hunter waited for the sharp-eyed, annoyed look his mother would turn on him and his brothers whenever she did not approve of something they had said or done. Greer had been a constant recipient of it and as usual it had been lost on him. Not so much Rab and Hunter.

The look came swiftly as did a response to his remark. "Nonsense, Hunter. Ewan has kindly offered his help and we should generously accept it."

"If you insist, Mum," Hunter said, smiling and proving to himself that his mum and Ewan did not want to be parted just yet.

Word circulated to break camp and be ready to leave soon.

With everyone busy, Hunter went to find his wife.

~~~

Last night crept into Patience's thoughts far too often and was the reason she had had a restless night. Of course, it had not helped sleeping in such close proximity to Hunter. And damn, damn, damn if she did not think of him bent over the fire half naked and what followed every time she caught the scent of roses, which of course meant every time she washed.

She shook her head and mumbled.

"Talking to yourself, wife?"

Patience rolled her eyes and groaned, though not loud enough for him to hear. She looked up and she felt her stomach catch at the sight of him. His features were much too alluring as was his body, and then there was the way he exuded confidence and charm, as if it came naturally to him.

The thought came so sudden that it shot out of her mouth before she could grab hold of it. "If you ever cheat on me, I will make sure it is the last time you ever enjoy any woman."

Her angry threat brought him to an abrupt halt and a smile to his face. "You are jealous and that pleases me since it means that you are beginning to care for me, perhaps even more than you realize."

"I have no time for such nonsense," she said tersely and went to walk past him.

He grabbed her around the waist and yanked her up against him. "There is always time for such nonsense." He kissed her and she squirmed in protest, though not for long.

She could not deny his kiss. She craved it, though her body craved much more. It would not be long before she surrendered, not to him, but to her own desires. And the thought sent gooseflesh running over her and a shiver running through her.

Her tingle rippled along his body, teasing his already alert manhood. He wisely ended their kiss and rested his brow against hers. "You are the only woman I want to make love to."

"You will be satisfied with merely one, when you have had such a variety?"

He drew his head back, his brow scrunching. "Do you worry you will not satisfy me?"

"Can any one woman satisfy you?"

"Aye, my wife."

"Why me?"

He leaned close and whispered, "Make love with me and find out."

She patted his cheek, smiled, and before walking away said, "In time."

~~~

"You set a slower pace today," Hunter said, riding alongside her.

"I am not anxious to leave the Dark Dragon's land just yet. Besides, it provides us with a modicum of safety from your brother."

"Do not completely disregard Greer," Hunter warned.

"I am not that foolish. With the anger that rages in that man, there is no telling what he is capable of doing."

"He is capable of anything."

Patience detected a hint of anger in his voice and she could only wonder at the cause.

"I would not be surprised if his men lay in wait for us beyond the Dark Dragon's border." "I thought the same myself so I ordered more men to be brought to meet us, hopefully in time, once we leave his land." She shook her head. "Though, I cannot help but feel your brother will not wait that long. I would not, for it would bring me too close to my enemy's land."

"What would you do?" Hunter asked curious, for never had he known a woman with such excellent instinct for people and battle.

"It is not what I would do that matters. Knowing what your enemy would do is what makes the difference. And what little I know of Greer, I believe he would stop at nothing to see you dead."

"With my marriage to you, he has more of an excuse to see it done now than ever before."

"He will not take my husband from me," Patience said adamantly.

Hunter grinned. "You worry over me that much, do you?"

She returned his grin and said, "As much as you do for me."

Edward rode up then, ending their conversation.

~~~

The day wore on and clouds captured the sun. With hours to go before they camped for the night, Patience ordered a respite. Her warriors remained on alert, keeping a keen eye on their surroundings. Edward had informed her that ghost warriors continued to trail them and when she saw that Ewan was nowhere in sight, she wondered if he went to meet with them. Hunter sat with his mother since she was alone, even Beast had deserted her.

She walked over to join them and was sitting only a few minutes with them when Ewan rushed out of the woods, Beast at his side, and hurried over to them.

"We have a problem," Ewan said and Hunter and Patience got to their feet. "There is a large troop of mercenaries that are about to descend on us from the north. We are greatly outnumbered. It will be a bloodbath."

"What of the Dark Dragon?" Hunter said. "He wants no blood spilled on his land. Will he not stop it?"

"Word has gone out to the Dark Dragon, but there is not enough time to get more warriors here. I would give him a day or two, at the most, before he could clear the mercenaries from his land," Ewan explained.

"Edward," Patience called out and the warrior hurried to her side. "An army of mercenaries are about to attack, we need to divide. Send two warriors in all directions, except north, with instructions to meet in two days' time at Eddleston Abbey and one to my father to let him know what goes on. You know the orders. If by the next morning—the third day—not all have arrived at the abbey, then those who are there are to leave and head home."

Edward nodded. "I will see you at the abbey. Keep safe." He hurried off and within seconds pairs of warriors began mounting their horses and riding off in different directions.

Hunter turned to Ewan. "I would prefer you took my mum and Beast to your son's home in Gullie Loch and keep them there until you hear from me. Greer would not dare attack there."

Una did not protest, she threw her arms around her son, hugged him tight, and told him that she loved him.

Hunter hunched down and took Beast's face in his hands. "You stay with Una and protect her."

The big dog licked his face and went to Una's side.

Hunter helped his mum mount her horse as Ewan

got on his, and then they were gone, Beast following alongside them.

Patience had already mounted and as soon as he did, she said, "I know of Eddleston Abbey because we stopped there on our way here, but I know of little else in the area. Do you know of a place we could take refuge until the Dark Dragon sees to the mercenaries?"

"I know a place where no one will follow," he said with a nod. "Stay close."

They took off and Patience was grateful that they had maintained a slow pace when they had set out this morning, for the horses were not tired and flew like the wind. They traveled west, never slowing down or daring to stop.

The mercenaries would find their tracks, all going in different directions and not know which ones to follow. They would probably divide as Patience and her warriors had done and that would be good, for it would make it easier for the ghost warriors to dispose of them.

Still though, this reminded her that she needed more men. Greer would not stop until Hunter was dead, the Macinnes clan blamed, and a war started.

After a few hours of grueling travel, Hunter slowed his horse and Patience followed along, doing the same. They came to a stop at the edge of thick woods, a small mountain rising behind it. The trees were so dense that barely any light could be seen among the branches and for some reason Patience shivered at the thought of entering it. Then she spotted the numerous objects hanging in the trees and knew why—they were charms to keep evil at bay.

She looked to Hunter. "Evil resides here."

"Not so," Hunter said and turned and guided his horse through the dense trees and foliage.

Patience followed, realizing her husband knew the way... he had been here before.

It took some time and maneuvering through areas that had no path yet Hunter seemed to find one and it brought them to a cottage sitting in a small clearing. The place appeared as if it had not been occupied in years, though the thatched roof remained intact as did the closed shutters on the one window. Beneath, a broken bench leaned lopsided against the cottage wall. The woods had reclaimed what once must have been a large garden. At one time it must have been a lovely place, though lonely tucked away in such a dense forest.

"You are familiar with this place," Patience said as Hunter approached the front door.

"Aye, I am," he said and opened the door.

Patience followed him in and stood staring at the rather large room that appeared as if it had been left waiting for someone to return. In the meantime, cobwebs and dust occupied it.

Hunter pushed the shutters open, letting in some light.

Patience looked around and knew a woman had to have lived here. Though the blanket on the bed looked to have been repaired several times, it had been done so with skilled hands. A shawl, also repaired several times, hung on a peg near the door, and baskets and crocks were plentiful.

"You knew her well?" Patience asked curious and though she hated to admit it to herself, a bit of jealousy.

"She knew me better," he said, his glance going to the dust-covered shawl with sadness.

"You cared for her?" A stronger pang of envy struck her then.

Hunter nodded. "Very much, she saved my life in so many ways." He reached for one of the chairs and smashed it to the floor, the aged wood splintering. He continued to break the chair apart as he spoke. "Her name was Elspet and people thought her a witch. She was no more a witch than you and I. What she was—was a knowledgeable and plain-featured woman. And that could be a curse in itself for any woman."

Patience thought of her sister Emma. She was knowledgeable and plain and had suffered for it, men wanting nothing to do with her. It had broken her heart to see her sister treated so poorly and she had made anyone who treated Emma poorly pay dearly for it.

Hunter placed the broken chair pieces in the fireplace and as he worked to get a fire started, he continued. "One day my father did not like what I had to say and gave me a good beating. Greer came upon me before I had a chance to recover and finished what my father had started, beating me senseless. I vaguely recall him dumping me someplace. When I woke, I found myself here." Elspet eventually told me that she had found me outside her cottage."

"When was this?"

"About eight years ago when I was ten and six years. Elspet healed my wounds and helped me understand much about evil. She had suffered more than her fair share of it. I visited her often after that, though I let no one know that I did. I knew none would understand. They believed her a witch and fear kept them from hurting her, though there were many women who came to her for her healing knowledge, never letting their husbands know." He stilled, staring at the flames greedily licking the broken chair pieces. "We would talk endlessly when I visited and I would see that she had what she needed. One day she took ill and she told me that her time here would soon be done. I was heartbroken and spent much time with her. I did not want her to die alone and was glad I was here with her when she took her last breath. I still miss her."

Patience felt her heart break for him and hurriedly wiped a tear from her eye before he turned around.

"She did tell me that after some turmoil I would find happiness and have a loving family of six children."

"Six?" she repeated startled.

"Aye," he said with a firm nod, and I look forward to having every one of them.

"It would not be you having them."

"I told you once that whatever you suffer I suffer."

Patience laughed, shaking her head. "I do not think you would suffer the same pain that I would while delivering our child."

Hunter walked over to her and ran the back of his hand gently down her cheek. "Believe me, *mo chridhe*, my pain will be as great as yours, for I cannot stand the thought of being so helpless in preventing you from suffering such pain."

He bent his head, to take a kiss when a swirl of

wind rushed through the door sweeping up the dust around them. He went to shut the door and stopped, casting a glance at the heavy gray clouds.

"A storm brews," he said turning to her. "I need to settle the horses and hunt for food."

Patience looked around the room, then at Hunter. "I know nothing about tending a keep, let alone a single room, that was Heather's responsibility. Besides, I would feel as if I intruded upon Elspet's home, touching anything of hers. I will hunt for food."

"Do not go beyond the woods," Hunter cautioned, not surprised by her decision.

Patience stopped at the door and turned with a smile and a sting to her words. "Thank you so much, I truly needed that reminding."

Hunter walked over and grabbed her arm before she could get out the door. He stepped close to her, lowering his face only a few inches from hers. "It is best you get accustomed to me reminding you, worrying about you, warning you when necessary." He held up his hand as soon as she attempted to protest. "I will always look after you, always take care of you, always be there for you and I will always—" His blue eyes scorched with a sudden passion, and then he kissed her.

It was a potent and abrupt kiss and Patience stumbled when he released her and turned away. She hurried off, not wanting to stay there, not wanting to hear what he was about to say to her before he stopped himself and kissed her, not wanting to hear those words that would change everything between them... *I will always love you.*

Chapter Twenty

Patience stilled after entering the woods. Could it be possible? Could he truly love her? Could she be falling in love with him? Surprisingly, she no longer felt him a stranger. Was she growing that accustomed to him? She also found that she enjoyed his company. Conversation came easily with him. Then there was the way he touched her, a gentle touch to the arm, his hand at her cheek, his arm around her waist, so innocent and yet her body sparked to life with each tender touch. And now that they were alone... she shook her head. What was she doing wasting time thinking on such things now? There was hunting to be done, warriors to avoid, and they needed to get to the abbey to meet the others. There was no time for this nonsense.

She made her way further into the woods, marking the trail as she went. She had grabbed her cache of arrows and her bow off her horse and readied one, then with light footfalls she combed the woods.

Stopping a moment to listen, she heard a rustle. She turned slowly and there just a few feet ahead was a doe, her eyes wide, standing as still as Patience. She was a beauty and would provide them with more meat than they needed, but they did have to eat. She raised her bow ever so slowly when suddenly a gust of wind swirled up around her, sending dust to sting her eyes.

Then she heard the sharp voice in her head. *Do not harm my family!*

Patience dropped her bow to her side and when the wind settled, she saw that the doe had remained where she was, though she was now busy munching on leaves. She was no longer fearful of Patience; she felt safe and protected.

Patience felt otherwise. Elspet was obviously protecting her forest family. Tales of ghosts were often shared in the Highlands and the storytellers would warn against upsetting spirits. So Patience took heed and decided to see what else she could scavenge from the woods.

With her arrow returned to the cache and her bow draped over it, she started foraging. Many plants still needed maturing, while some young plants could be tasty. Wild onions were tasty at any time and would flavor a weed stew as Heather liked to refer to it. She had shown Patience and Emma how to easily cook one if it should ever prove necessary and Patience wished she could hug her right now for having taught them.

She circled around to make her way back to the cottage with enough plants to make a filling stew, when a voice called out in her head.

He comes!

Patience dropped the armful of plants and grabbed for her bow, but before she could reach for an arrow a voice echoed through the woods.

"Do not dare draw a weapon against me!"

Patience turned slowly, knowing who she was about to face, though she wondered if he was half beast for he spoke with a growl. She almost gasped when she laid eyes on him, and she was relieved that he stood a distance away from her, for there was no doubting that it was the Dark Dragon.

He wore a black metal helmet etched with symbols unknown to Patience. The helmet covered all but his eyes and the tip of his chin, making him appear all the more fearsome. Black leather armor covered his entire body, defining his thick-muscled frame, while hardened leather spikes ran along his shoulders and down his upper arms, warning all to keep their distance.

Patience had never liked the taste of fear and had always fought against it, but seeing this giant of a warrior encased in black made her tremble, for it was as if pure evil stood in front of her. And that evil had her sister.

With quivering limbs, she took a step forward. "When do I see my sister Heather?"

His voice rang with authority. "When I so choose."

Patience held her tongue and her temper, though she wanted to lash out at him and scream that he had no right to keep her sister. But her warrior side warned against such a foolish response.

"Two days and you and your husband are to leave this place," he commanded.

She did not bother to ask or else, for she knew if they did not obey his ghost warriors would see that they did.

"Do not dare defy me, Patience." He turned and walked off, consuming the shadows that embraced him.

Patience stood staring after him, her body

trembling more than before. He had said little, but had spoken volumes. His visit had one purpose... to warn her against disobeying him. The problem was that she was never good at being obedient, but then she had never met a warrior that made her quiver with fear.

With shaking hands, she gathered up the plants she had dropped and made her way back to the cottage, her mind on her sister. How was sweet, kind Heather dealing with such a menacing man? She could only imagine the fear Heather must feel. She had to see her. She had to know that she had not been harmed. Once she saw that for herself, then she could concentrate on the obvious... how to combat such a formidable warrior?

She reached the cottage as the first drop of rain splashed on the ground. The door sat open and she entered, though paid little attention to the fine job Hunter had done of making the place habitable. She dropped the plants on the table and stared at her husband.

"What is wrong?" he asked concerned by how pale his wife was.

"I met the Dark Dragon."

Thunder rolled over the land with her announcement and Hunter hurried to close and latch the door against the arriving storm, then went to his wife, taking her in his arms.

Patience latched onto her husband's strong arms. "He is more than I imagined."

"So I have heard."

"He came to warn me not to defy him," she said his snarling voice ringing in her head. "He sounds more like a beast than a man." She turned sorrowful eyes on him. "How do I rescue my sister from a beast?"

"With great patience and care."

Patience stepped away from him, shaking her head. "How can I be patient when my sister remains the captive of that monster?" She shook her head again and answered her own question. "I have no choice just as the Dark Dragon said, and he made sure to let me know that."

"The more you know of your enemy, the more power you amass against him. You will be ready when the time comes."

Hunter was right and that thought calmed her some. The Dark Dragon may have had a message for her, but in return he had given her a glimpse of the man—and he was just a man—the one she would battle to get her sister back.

"He also warned that we were to stay here no more than two days."

Hunter rubbed his chin. "I wonder why two days. Will it take him that long to rid his land of the mercenaries?" Hunter shook his head. "That does not seem likely. It is known that he is quick and deadly in his pursuit of those who wrong him." The corners of his mouth turned up some as he pointed to the plants on the table. "This is what you hunted?"

"I was warned against hurting Elspet's forest family," she said, slipping off her bow and cache of arrows to hang on the peg. Her sword followed. "It is called weed stew."

"Sounds pleasant enough," he said with a laugh.

"Do not be so quick to judge," she scolded

playfully, glad for the diversion from her troubled thoughts, and then told him of the origin of the stew.

As usual conversation flowed smoothly between them, while the storm outside raged.

Once the plants were ready to cook, Patience looked around the room for a crock or cauldron.

Hunter found one tucked in with the baskets. "I will take it out to clean and fill with rainwater."

Patience shook her head, grabbed the cauldron, and snickered, though with a smile. "Let me. I would not want to tire you after all the cleaning you have done."

"True, after all, you will want me well-rested when you beg me to make love to you tonight."

That wiped the smile off her face and had her hurrying out the door. They were alone. They could make love. Why had she not given that a thought? Was she afraid to? Or was she afraid once she made love with him, she would hunger for more?

The pelting rain reminded her of her task and she hurried to clean the cauldron with some of the discarded leaves from the plants.

The attack came quickly, knocking her off her feet. She reached for the dagger at her waist, but it was not there. She had left it on the table in the cottage. She was grabbed before she could scramble to her feet, but she managed to give her attacker enough of a punch to send him flying away from her, but not keep him from returning. At least, she was on her feet when he did and she bent and swerved to stay out of his reach until she could get in a good position to take him down permanently.

The rain slashed viciously at them and the

darkening sky did not help and was probably the reason she did not see the second attacker coming. In the next instant, she was grabbed and a knife put at her throat. Just then, the cottage door flew open and Hunter stepped out.

Rage turned his blue eyes molten blue as he took in the scene in front of him.

"Your brother says it is time he finished what he started," screamed the one who held her. "Then it is your wife's turn. Of course, we will have fun with her before we kill her. Greer wants to take no chance that your randy ways has already taken root in her belly."

With more calm than his blazing eyes betrayed, Hunter said, "Let her go, Bruin, and I will kill you fast."

Bruin laughed. "Give him a good beating, Leith, and then I will slice his throat and watch him die slowly as Greer has instructed."

Leith did not hesitate, he charged Hunter.

Patience did not hesitate either. With Bruin distracted by the two men fighting, it gave her an advantage and she took it. She threw her head back with force, connecting with his nose. He howled and released her abruptly.

Blood poured like an overflowing river from his nose and Patience did not wait, she continued her attack.

Not waiting for Leith to reach him, Hunter let out an angry roar and launched himself at him. One solid blow from Hunter and Leith hit the ground, though he was back on his feet fast enough. Fists flew, though Leith landed not one blow. Blood not only poured from his mouth but his nose as well and his eye was beginning to swell.

Leith stumbled back from another vicious blow and spit blood from his mouth. "And here I thought the only thing you were good at was poking a woman."

"And here I thought you could fight," Hunter shot back.

Leith snarled with fury and shouted, "Bruin, it is time for this bastard to die."

"Then leave him to me and you see to the woman and make sure she's ready for me to have a go at her while her husband lies dying. I want it to be the last thing he sees before the devil claims him," Bruin said, laughing as he walked over to Leith.

Hunter shot a glance to his wife and saw how exhausted she was from defending herself, yet she stood strong and proud, letting him know she would continue to fight, and his rage soared. He released a roar that shook the forest trees and sent a tremble through Patience.

She froze, shocked as she watched Hunter advance on the two men with such speed and such rage that neither saw him until it was too late. With a vicious kick to the knee and a snap of the other's neck, Patience watched Bruin drop in agony to the ground and Leith fall over dead.

Hunter then grabbed Bruin by the throat, his fingers digging deep and, with malice so strong in his tone it made her shiver, he said, "You dare threaten my wife and think you will not suffer for it?"

Bruin's eyes bulged from his face. "You are more like your brother than I thought."

"Then you know this will not end well for you,"

Hunter said.

"Hunter," Patience said, approaching him.

He snapped his head to the side, his blue eyes heated with such fury that she took several steps back away from him.

"Go into the cottage," Hunter ordered sternly.

"He may have information that could be useful."

"NOW!" he shouted and Patience went to argue. "I will not tell you again. GO!"

Fury gripped Patience like never before and if she did not put distance between them, she would lash out at him, and now was not the time. Bruin had to be dealt with and permanently. With fiery anger raging through her, she stomped past him and into the cottage.

Bruin choked on his words as he glared at Hunter. "Greer will see you dead."

"Not if I see him dead first." Hunter punched Bruin so hard that his head bounced to the side, stunning him and giving Hunter enough time to snatch the man's dirk from the ground and place the blade snugly against his neck. "Give me the answers I seek and I will kill you fast, otherwise—I will enjoy making you suffer."

Bruin laughed, blood spilling from the side of his mouth and the rain washing it away. "You are just like your brother—heartless."

Hunter pressed the dirk hard enough to his throat that blood oozed from the edge of the blade, but rainwater did not wash it away since Hunter hovered over him, the raindrops splattering against his back. "Then you know I will do as I say... the choice is yours."

Chapter Twenty-one

Patience stalked the front of the fireplace, a sizzle being heard now and again as the rainwater dripped off her and hit the stones lining the hearth. She was angry with herself. Why had she obeyed his demand that she retreat to the cottage? This was his fight; his family. She shook her head. She was his family now and family did not desert in time of need.

She groaned, annoyed, and kept up her quick pacing. This was something that involved his brother and he needed to see to it, just as she wanted no interference when it came to rescuing Heather. And that was what made her wait, though impatiently.

Her breath caught as the door flung open and Hunter entered, the rain following him in, lashing out at him as he shoved the door closed against it and secured the latch. When he turned, she almost gasped at the scowl that marred his usual handsome features. This was not the husband she had grown accustomed to and as he came around the table toward her, she braced herself, her shoulders squaring and her chin turning up.

"Are you hurt?" he asked, his hand going to a slight bruise on her cheek, his finger skimming it so faintly that it sent a quiver through her body. He mumbled several oaths before resting his brow to hers and slipping his arm around her waist. "I am sorry you had to suffer at Bruin's hands."

Concern was heavy in his voice and though his touch was light and caring, she could see his controlled rage in his taut muscles. His wet shirt clung to them, refusing to let go, and she suddenly got the same urge. She threw her arms around him, pressing her body so hard against his that water dripped down between them.

His arms tightened around her, relieved to have her in them. His heart had crashed against his chest when he had seen Bruin holding the dirk to her throat. The thought of losing her when he had just found her, just discovered he was falling in love with her had a rage like none other rise up in him. He knew then and there he would kill both men, nothing would stop him... and it hadn't.

Her shiver rippled over him and he silently cursed before easing her away from him most reluctantly. "You need to get out of those wet garments." He did not wait for her response. He simply began unwrapping her plaid.

"As do you," she said, her hands going to divest him of his clothes.

He tried to keep his thoughts focused. He needed to see that she got dry and make certain neither man had hurt her, but his loins had another idea. With every inch of her exposed flesh, he grew harder and harder and when she was fully naked he knew it would be almost impossible to keep his hands off her.

Their first joining should not be fueled by the rage of battle and yet the need to touch her, taste her, drive deep inside her was all but impossible to ignore or contain.

Patience was too busy trying to control the

passion that suddenly took root in her and grew with every piece of garment she practically tore off him. She told herself they had to talk. She wanted to find out what, if anything, Bruin had told him, though it became less important the more garments she stripped off her husband.

It took all the willpower he possessed to step away from her. "Dry yourself and get in bed and get warm."

Patience stared at him, her mouth agape, then her temper took hold. "Truly, that is what you say to me when I stand in front of you naked?"

"You are wet."

"In more ways than one."

"You play with fire and will get burned if not careful," he warned.

"One can only hope."

Hunter held on to his mounting passion by a thread. "You are bruised from the beating you took and need to rest."

"From what I see you appear to be up for the job." She gave a nod to his manhood that jutted out from a patch of dark hair, hard and thick. "Though, your stamina is no match for mine."

Hunter smiled and walked over to her, though he did not touch her. "Are you begging me to make love to you?"

"Never would I beg you to make love to me."

"Never say never, *mo chridhe*," he warned with a husky whisper.

"I do not beg," she reiterated.

He laughed softly. "Do not make me prove you wrong."

"Are you challenging me?"

"Are you asking me to make love to you?"

Her chin went up another notch. "Our vows do need consummating."

"So you join with me out of duty."

"Duty, curiosity..." She shrugged.

He kept his eyes on her as he brought his hand up to rest one finger at the bottom of her neck, then slowly ran it down her chest and around one breast, circling round and round, drawing ever closer to her nipple that had already hardened to a tight nub.

"You forgot hunger, urge, craving," —he lowered his lips close to hers— "passion." His finger circled her nipple lightly, then gave it a gentle squeeze.

She gasped, not only at his touch, but at the startling sensation that settled between her legs and refused to let go.

"Do you want me to make love to you?"

She wanted to scream, *aye, and hurry before I come without knowing the joy of you inside me*, but something stopped her. She quickly turned her back to him, that sense of vulnerability rearing its head and causing her to hesitate.

She may have only taken a step away from him, but Hunter sensed it a far greater distance and he did not hesitate. He stepped behind her, slipping his arm around her waist and moving to rest his naked body against hers.

He pressed his lips to her ear and whispered, "It is not out of duty or curiosity or even lust that I want to make love to you." He turned her around slowly, his arm remaining around her waist. He brushed his lips over hers, then said, "It is because I have fallen in love with you."

Her gasp stuck in her throat this time and for a moment she felt robbed of breath.

"And I hope in time, you will come to love me as well."

She stared speechless at him, her heart pounding madly in her chest and while in her mind she shouted *I do love you*, she could not bring herself to say it... not yet. Instead, she said, "Make love to me, husband."

"You will be saying that to me often, *mo chridhe*, once I do," he said and scooped her up in his arms and carried her to the bed.

Hunter lay on his side beside her, the bed barely big enough for them both, but then he wanted no distance between them, not now, not ever.

He ran his hand down along her body, loving the feel of her. She was slimmer than most women he had been with and her muscles taut in spots where other women were soft. Her hips had a luscious curve to them and her backside rounded nicely, the flesh firm. And her skin was the smoothest he had ever touched.

Ever since that day in the stream, he had ached to touch all of her, to explore to his and to her pleasure. And that was what he intended to do, take his time and explore.

Patience loved when he touched her, but even more so now that she was naked. His fingers faintly traced over every part of her like a feather lightly skimming her body. She wanted to linger in every delicious moment, never having felt anything so pleasurable. And while she had the urge to touch him, she was much too mesmerized by his loving touch to move.

"You are beautiful, wife, every inch of you," he whispered and claimed a tender kiss that soon turned more demanding.

She had enjoyed every kiss she had shared with him, but this kiss was different. This kiss was from a man who loved her, and she let herself get lost in it. She never felt anything so freeing. No vulnerability, no doubt separated them. It was as if love joined them as one, never, ever to be separated... never wanting to be.

He eased his mouth away from hers and whispered, "I have ached to taste every inch of you."

"Do I get to do the same to you?" she asked with a wicked smile.

"Most definitely," he said and settled his mouth over her nipple, his teeth catching hold to tease it.

Patience was soon lost in a haze of pleasure, his tongue and lips doing unspeakably wonderful things to her. She did not want him to stop; she wanted him to go on forever. And when he paused, she urged him to continue. It was when his tongue settled on the tiny nub between her legs and sent a rush of tingles through her that she begged him not to stop. And when she felt as if she was about to explode and have those tingles rain down upon her, she still begged him not to stop.

When he did stop, she was ready to beg him again, but then he got to his knees, grabbed her backside and pressed his bulging manhood between her legs and slipped slowly into her.

Patience proved she was nothing like her name when she pleaded, "Hurry, I cannot wait any longer."

"Either can I," Hunter said, surprising himself, since he feared he would not be able to stop himself from climaxing, something he had never had a problem doing. He had always been able to hold back and bring a woman pleasure more than once, then come at will. Not so with his wife. His need to climax was much too strong. He would never be able to stop it.

He eased into her, not wanting to cause her any pain. She arched up, forcing him further into her and that proved his undoing.

He drove into her deep and hard and she cried out. He almost stopped, thinking he had hurt her when he realized her cries were passionate ones. He rode her hard and fast, knowing they both wanted and needed it.

Her cries of pleasure increased with his rhythm and try as he might he could not contain the climax that hovered all to near. He would come soon and he would be damned if he would come before her. He kept up his furious rhythm, but reached to tease the little nub he had so enjoyed feasting on. She tossed her head back and screamed out his name as she burst in climax.

He could hold back no more, he joined her, tossing his head back and groaning at the intense pleasure that gripped him like never before and seemed to go on forever.

Patience felt as if her body had been shocked in the most pleasurable way and when she thought it had ebbed, she felt it build again. She screamed out, "Do not stop!"

Hunter was pleased that she would climax again,

and he teased her nub once again to bring her as much pleasure as possible.

Patience let out another scream, thinking the sensation much too satisfying and she would surely die from such exquisite pleasure, and she would not care.

Hunter did not ease out of her until he was sure she was spent, then he gently turned her on her side and slipped behind her so that they could fit on the bed together. He wrapped his arm around her and tucked his leg over hers, drawing her snug against him.

Patience sighed, then laughed softly. "You have definitely proven your prowess."

"Nowhere near, have I proven my prowess."

Her soft laughter drifted over her shoulder and brushed his face like a soft kiss. "Then I very much look forward to you doing so."

"I shall not disappoint you, wife," he boasted playfully.

She wiggled her way around to face him. "I do not believe you will ever disappoint me, husband."

He tucked a soft strand of hair behind her ear, then ran his finger along her jaw to faintly trace over her lips. "You have my word on that." He kissed her softly.

She shivered from his touch, his kiss, and the slight chill that filled the room.

"A moment," he said and gave the tip of her nose a quick kiss before getting out of bed and hurried to break another chair and add the pieces to the fire. He returned and pulled the blanket at the end of the bed up and over Patience and climbed beneath to take her in his arms once again.

Patience never felt so content and never felt so lucky then at that moment. Though her marriage had been forged out of necessity, her husband loved her. And she did not quite understand how she had managed to fall in love with him, but she had. She was not yet ready to confide her love to him, though she could not say why. Perhaps she felt it was because she had no right to feel such joy when her sister suffered at the hands of the Dark Dragon.

What right did she have to be happy when Heather was being held prisoner? It was not fair that she and Emma had found love. Heather should have been the first, but she truly had been. She had been barely ten and four years when her heart had been broken, never to heal again.

"You are quiet, troubling thoughts?" Hunter asked, running his hand soothingly down her arm.

"Haunting ones that are better left unspoken for now." Patience was glad he did not insist that she confide in him. He was a patient one.

Hunter confirmed it when he said, "When you are ready."

They lay quiet for a few minutes before Patience asked, "Do you truly love me?"

He slipped his hand under her chin to raise it so that her eyes met his when he said, "I would not say it if I did not mean it."

Her brow scrunched in question. "How?"

"That is an age-old question that has no answer. I could not tell you how it happened, when, or where. I only know that I felt myself falling in love with you and there was nothing I could do to stop it, nor would

I if I could have. I quite like being in love with my wife and I wait for the day she discovers that she loves me."

"So sure, are you?"

He turned a playful grin on her. "How could she not love me? I have fine features and I am an excellent lover and I do not dictate to her," —his humorous grin faded— "unless it is to keep her from harm."

Patience saw it as an apology of sorts for ordering her into the cottage, which had her asking, "Did you learn anything from Bruin, like how he knew we were here?"

"He was quite willing to talk, after I convinced him it would be wise of him to do so. Greer had him and Leith join the mercenaries with strict orders that you and I were to be left to him and Leith to deal with. They rode ahead and laid in wait for the mercenaries to attack when they saw your troop divide. They followed us. Leith feared entering the woods because of the charms in the trees, and it took time for Bruin to convince him, the fear of what Greer would do to him if he failed their mission being greater than the fear of the evil woods."

"So, Greer wants us both dead now?"

"He wants no child of mine laying a future claim to McLaud land."

"But how now then does he intend to start a war between our clans?"

"Bruin and Leith were to claim that they watched us fight and that we both succumbed to our wounds, you slicing my throat before dying. Make no mistake, Patience, my brother is intent on making certain a war is started between our clans. He is hungry for power and wealth. He has been planning this since before my father died, and he will see it done."

"You know there is only one way to stop him."

Hunter nodded. "My brother must die."

Chapter Twenty-two

"This is good," Hunter said, scooping up the greens along with the broth with one of the large shells that Elspet had kept for such a purpose.

Patience sipped from the wooden bowl before saying, "The one and only thing I have ever cooked." After placing the bowl on the table in front of her, she hoisted her naked legs up on the chair to sit cross-legged. She tucked the long shirt over her legs as best she could to keep the chill off them. She was glad she had not discarded the shirt torn by the arrow that had left her with a shoulder wound, well-healed now.

Hunter had done the same, finding a dry shirt among his meager belongings, though she had to admit she preferred looking at his naked chest. Actually, she preferred him entirely naked, but it was better they were at least partially covered or else she might just be after him to...

She pushed the thought of begging him to make love to her out of her head. She did not beg, though she certainly had sounded as if she had when he had made love to her.

"Do you stitch?" he asked with the hint of a tease in his blue eyes.

"Wounds. I stitch wounds and I do a good job of it," —she shook her head— "Embroidery not so much. I was forbidden to sew with my sisters, both banning me from the chore. Though, Heather was the one who saw to it that both Emma and I learned how to stitch a wound. And my warriors are pleased that she did, though they would much prefer to have Emma tend them since her hands are more skilled and tender with a needle."

"It appears that you and your sisters are accomplished women. I am impressed and proud to be part of such a knowledgeable family."

"Much is due to Heather. The day our mum passed, she took her place and she was barely six years. I do not think that my da realizes how much Heather sacrificed for us all. She cared for me and Emma like only a loving mum could. I remember one day, when I was about ten years, I came upon Heather several times throughout the day busy with chores and after having watched her, I realized that she had more duties to tend to than the whole of our servants combined. There was not a moment of rest for her. And in the evening, she would spend time with Emma and me, tending to our needs and listening to our complaints. And it was not only Emma and me who brought our complaints to her or needed soothing. The clan sought her out often and she settled disputes, leaving Father to believe that since so little of his clan complained to him that he was a wise laird."

Her heart grew heavy with memories of her sister.

Hunter reached out taking hold of her hand. "We will bring Heather home."

"I know, but I worry if she will be the kind and loving sister I once knew." She shook her head, chasing away the troubling thought.

Seeing how much it had upset his wife, Hunter moved the conversation away from the subject. "I look forward to seeing my new home."

Patience smiled and began telling him all about it.

Hunter stretched out of his chair two hours later and went to the door and opened it. A fine mist of rain was all that was left of the thunderstorm.

"Elspet will not stop me from hunting, I will go find us supper before it grows dark." He turned around to Patience. "Keep the door latched and a weapon close."

"Do you think there are others who know where we are?" she asked, slipping off her chair and walking over to him. His arm went around her waist as it always did, though this time she drifted close to rest against him of her own accord. She loved the way his strong arm settled around her, possessively and lovingly, and she loved the way the gentle whiff of his natural scent wrapped around her and sent her body tingling.

"There are few as foolish as Bruin and Leith to enter woods believed to be touched by evil. Besides, the mercenaries were given orders to leave our fate to the two fools. They will not bother to see if it was done, that will be Greer's problem."

"What of ghost warriors?" she asked uneasy that he was going off on his own when she had been protecting him since leaving his home.

Hunter kissed her gently. "You worry for my safety, wife?"

"I do, husband," she said with a curt nod, then kissed him not so gently.

He rested his brow to hers when the kiss ended. "I do not think I will ever get enough of you, *mo chridhe*."

"I was thinking the same of you," she admitted. "I have this need for you that never fades, it only grows stronger." She took a deep breath. "I had hoped that through the years I would come to care for you. Never had I thought to feel so much so soon."

"Love is sneaky."

"Love is... far different than I ever imagined."

A crack of thunder startled them both.

"I best see to getting us supper before the rain starts again," Hunter said and reluctantly stepped away from her to dress quickly and was out the door just as quickly, making sure to remind her once again to latch the door behind him.

Patience braced her back against the door after doing as her husband reminded, and smiled. He was not even there with her and he brought a smile to her face. She chased her smile away and shook her head. She was not some young lassie falling in love with a lad. She was a woman and a warrior one at that, and she had a mission to accomplish and foes who wished her and her husband dead.

This was no time to fancy herself in love and lose all sense and reason, which she had seen too many young lassies do. She had to keep her wits about her and not be caught off guard. But with her thoughts her only company, they wandered off on their own, constantly settling on Hunter. She finally realized the futility of fighting against it and let her mind have its way. And for the first time since her sister had been abducted, she felt her worries fade and a smile linger on her face.

~~~

Hunter found her on the bed, lying on her side sleeping. Her bare backside was partially exposed and with her knees bent up to her waist, the tempting view turned him rock hard. He shook his head and hurried to set the rabbit he had caught and cleaned to cook on the spit in the fireplace. With more hasty steps, he grabbed a bucket, went outside, and filled it with rainwater from the rain barrel, then quickly scrubbed his hands.

The rain had started again just as he had returned to the cottage, though not as badly as before. Once inside, he slipped out of his clothes, placed them by the hearth to dry, and went to join his wife in bed.

He had not been able to get her off his mind since leaving the cottage, and damn if it had not been difficult leaving her. All he wanted to do was spend the rest of the day with her, preferably naked in bed. And it appeared that he was about to get his way.

He snuggled against her, pressing his manhood against her warm nest that grew moist with each gentle stroke. He ran his hand up under her shirt to cup her breast. He stilled as a yawn took hold of him.

She pressed herself back against him, wiggling until she fit to him perfectly and sighed contentedly.

He had thought she had woken, but when he heard a gentle snore he realized she was asleep. The ride here had been a hard one, and then there was the bruising she had taken fighting off Bruin and Leith, and the most pleasant, though still strenuous part of the day, making love. She had every right to be tired.

Of course, it did not stop him from wanting to wake her, most lovingly, but he fought the urge. He would not disturb her; she needed rest.

A scent of roses drifted off her silky hair to tickle his nose and tempt him. He told himself it would be far wiser to leave her in the bed alone, but he could not bring himself to move away from her. He loved being wrapped around her. He had had many women, but never had he felt the immense need to keep one close and never let her go.

He was so comfortable and content that he never realized that his eyes were growing heavy and his body relaxed. In minutes, he joined his wife in a sound sleep.

~~~

A delicious scent had Patience sniffing the air and her stomach rumbling. She opened her eyes to find herself wrapped in her husband's arms. She smiled, content and ready to make love again. She was about to wake him when she decided that this was the perfect opportunity to explore. She would get to know his body as he had gotten to know hers, though she was sure it would take much more exploring for both of them to learn all they could about each other. At least, she hoped it would.

With a faintly devilish smile, she set to work and what delightful work it was. Her hand roamed over his chest ever so lightly and though his muscles were hard, his skin was smooth and so terribly tempting to touch. Eager to touch that part of him that some women had warned her would bring more distress than pleasure, her hand dipped down further, her fingers running gently through the thatch of hair that nestled his manhood that was just beginning to rouse.

Her hand took hold of him, curious to know how it felt... silky smooth. And as she repeatedly ran her hand over it, squeezing it now and again, it began to grow. Thinking back on how much pleasure she had gotten when he had tasted her, she thought to do the same for him. Though, she had to admit that she was deriving pleasure from just the thought of it. How much pleasure would it bring her when she was actually engaged in it?

It did not take long for her to discover how much she liked it and she soon lost herself in the enjoyable task.

Hunter did not want to wake from the dream, but his own moans roused him and it took a moment for him to realize he was not dreaming. When he finally was able to think somewhat clearly, he glanced down, his eyes turning wide. "Patience?"

She lifted her head and slipped her mouth off him, to his chagrin, and grinned. "I am busy." She returned to her task with a determination that soon had him groaning and coming harder than he thought possible.

It took him a moment to gather his wits about him so that he could return the pleasure, but she was up and climbing off him and out of bed before he could stop her.

"I am starving and that meat smells as if it is done." She reached out with a thick stick to disengage the spit.

Hunter, still recovering from his explosive climax, turned his head to enjoy the view of her naked backside. He smiled, thinking what a lucky man he was to have such a beautiful wife and one that was not timid about exploring intimacy.

"Damn it," Patience yelped, dropping the stick in her hand.

Hunter was out of bed and at her side in an instant. "What is wrong?"

"A spark from the fire got me." She held up the back of her hand, showing him the blistery spot.

He grabbed a bucket by the door and stepped outside to fill it, then returned and gently immersed her hand in the cool water.

She chuckled. "You do recall that you are naked?"

"The perfect way to confront the rain," he said with a playful wink. "Now sit while I see to getting our meal."

She pulled her hand out of the bucket and he grabbed her wrist. "Keep your hand in the water."

"I want to get my shirt first."

He circled her one breast with his finger before giving the hard nipple a squeeze. "I prefer you naked."

"I am chilled."

"I could keep you warm."

She looked past him at the meat on the spit. "After we eat, you can warm me as much as you please."

He frowned, though with a laugh said, "You prefer food over me making love to you."

She nibbled at her lower lip for a moment, then said, "Aye, at the present moment I do."

He pressed his hand to his chest and staggered back as if struck. "You wound me, wife."

She grinned. "But not fatally."

He walked to the bed and retrieved her shirt,

returning with it to slip over her head and gently guide her arm through the sleeves. Then he gave her a quick kiss. "It was, however, a near fatal climax I lovingly endured." He placed her hand back in the bucket of water.

Her grin grew. "You enjoyed it."

"Immensely, but what of you? Did you enjoy it?"

"I loved the taste of you and look forward to feasting on you often."

Hunter groaned. "Damn it, Patience, you will grow me hard again."

"Good, then you will be ready to satisfy this wet ache between my legs after we eat."

His fist came down on the table. "If you continue to talk wickedly to me, you will be eating later rather than sooner."

Patience clamped her lips tight, though only for a moment. "I like being wicked with you."

Passion sparked Hunter's blue eyes and he placed his hands flat on the table, then leaned close to Patience's face. "You have yet to taste wickedness, though you have my word that you will and soon."

She was glad he turned away from her to see to the meat so that he did not see how his remark made her whole body quiver with anticipation. She decided it would be wise to temper her remarks concerning intimacy, at least until they had eaten.

They were soon enjoying the tasty meat done to perfection.

"I have been thinking," Patience said.

His brow knitted and his look was one of caution.

Patience shook her head. "I do not only think of—" She shook her head again, knowing it was futile to deny that since being intimate with him she thought of little else. So, she continued proving to herself that she could think of something else, while refusing to admit that the thought of making love with him again intruded on her every thought. "The Dark Dragon did not fear entering the woods."

"I doubt the Dark Dragon fears anything."

"Everyone fears something, whether they will admit it or not. And then there was Elspet's warning in my head, '*he comes*' as if she spoke of someone she knew. Do you think it is possible that Elspet knew the Dark Dragon?"

"She never mentioned him, though anything is possible."

"He walked with knowledge of the land and the shadows themselves seemed to embrace him. I would say he is no foreigner to this place, which would mean he spent a good amount of time here to know it so well."

"I imagine he knows a good portion of Scotland well with all the fighting he has done for the King."

"I suppose, but if Elspet was truly a witch perhaps she—"

Hunter shook his hand at her. "You cannot possibly be suggesting that she taught him magic and that is why his ghost warriors are so skilled?"

Her eyes turned wide with excitement. "See you have thought it yourself."

"I have not," he insisted. "The thought is ridiculous. Elspet was no witch. She was a learned woman like your sister Emma. And because she was wiser than most, she was claimed a witch."

"Then where did the ghost warriors get their

skills?"

"That is a question many would love to know, though seeing them myself I would tend to believe that it is speed and precision that set them apart from other warriors. With their faces painted white and their infamous reputation, they instill fear on first sight and fear alone can immobilize. They are nothing more than highly skilled warriors."

"Who possess a touch of magic, and do not scoff at me," she warned as his brow arched. "We both know the old myths and the magic within them. So, do not easily dismiss the possibility."

"I do not dismiss it. Many believe in magic, I simply do not and that is due to Elspet. She taught me to keep my eyes open and my ears attuned to all around me, and that I would learn the truth of things. And she was right."

"And you never saw her perform any magic the whole time you knew her?"

"Every day."

Her eyes turned wide.

"Every day she would smile and speak kindly, whether to animals or people and such unfettered kindness is true magic."

He spoke with such reverence of the woman that it touched her heart. "Elspet sounded like a remarkable woman."

"She was, and if she had given the Dark Dragon the gift of her friendship, then you can be sure that there is some goodness in the man."

"I truly hope that is so."

It was some time later that Patience went outside to see to her nightly need. Hunter had objected to her going alone and a brief debate had ensued. She had assured him that she would remain close to the cottage, since the woods were foreign to her and with it being dark she could easily get lost. Besides, she took her sword with her.

Wearing only her shirt and boots, and with sword in hand, she left the cottage. She intended to be quick about it, since she was eager to go to bed with her husband, though not to sleep.

Night had fallen hours ago, making the dense woods more difficult to navigate. But she kept the cottage in sight and found a quick spot to see to her needs. She was done in no time and when she turned to return to the cottage she halted and stared at the trees that lined the side of the cottage. There were several white carvings in all of them and she stepped closer to take a look.

They symbols seemed familiar, but where had she seen them? She ran her fingers over the straight and angled lines carved smoothly into the bark and highlighted in white and the more she did, the more her mind worked to recall where she had seen them.

She shook her head and walked around the tree, making her way back to the cottage. She halted again a few feet from the door and swerved around, her wide eyes settling on the trees.

She remembered where she had seen them. They were similar to the symbols that had been on the Dark Dragon's helmet.

Chapter Twenty-three

Patience hurried into the cottage, grabbed Hunter's hand, and hurried him outside and over to the trees. "What are these?"

Hunter stood naked, staring at the carvings as his mind drifted back to the day he had first seen them and asked Elspet the same thing. And he said what she had told him. "They keep evil at bay."

"Similar symbols were on the Dark Dragon's helmet. Where do they come from and if the symbols can be used to fight evil, then there must be symbols that can be used to engage evil's help."

"You are talking magic again."

"What else am I to believe?"

"That the Dark Dragon is a man of great skills, one of those skills, putting the fear of the devil into his opponents."

"A fear that is all too real for all too many and for good reason."

Hunter started them back to the cottage, his hand strong in hers. "Granted, but it has nothing to do with magic or Elspet. If the Dark Dragon practices the dark arts, then he learned them elsewhere, not here."

Once inside, Patience walked away from him to place her sword against the wall with her other weapons. She turned to her husband. "What if those symbols that ward off people from this place were not meant for Elspet? What if evil came here and Elspet knew it and that was why she carved the protective symbols in the trees and perhaps she herself hung those charms in the trees to protect herself?"

"What is truly troubling you?" he asked, approaching her slowly.

Patience sighed and stepped toward him, relieved when his arm went around her waist and she eagerly rested against him. "The more I learn about the Dark Dragon the more he seems a myth to me rather than a man. And so I find myself looking for a way to make sense of him."

"Or is it that you fear you will not find a way to defeat him and thus fail your sister?"

Her eyes glistened with tears that she refused to allow to fall. "I cannot leave her with such a monster."

"You sound as if you are ready to give your life for her."

"If I must; I will without hesitation."

He took hold of her chin. "Hear me well, *mo chridhe*, I will not allow that, but even more so, Heather would never forgive you. Do not be discouraged. We will find a way to best the dragon." He kissed her lightly as if sealing a pact.

She should be annoyed that he dared to dictate to her, but instead his caring remark had touched her heart as did the fact that though he did not know her sister, he understood how she would feel. He also reaffirmed as he had done many times that he would stand beside her in her efforts to rescue her sister.

"You are a good husband," she said, laying a tender hand on his cheek.

"Then you do not regret marrying me?"

"No, you have proven to be more of an asset, rather than the hindrance I had expected," she said with a soft chuckle as her hand fell away from his face.

He kissed her quick. "And you have proven to be—the woman who has stolen my heart."

Her heart quickened at his words.

"I have a question for you, wife," he whispered. "You remarked that everyone, men and women, fear something. What is it that you fear?"

She touched her lips faintly to his, then whispered, "You not making love to me tonight."

"Then you truly have nothing to fear." He hastily slipped her out of her shirt, then scooped her up and carried her to the bed.

He intended to take his time, but Patience, as usual, did not live up to her name.

He barely stroked her and teased her hard nipples, when she pushed him off her onto his back and climbed on top of him.

"I cannot wait," she said and let out a gratifying yelp when she impaled herself on him. "That feels so good." She began to move. "And that feels even better."

Her actions, the passion in her eyes and in her every movement pushed him to the edge of climax. He feared he would lose control at any moment and that he could not do.

She bounced up and down on him with the abandonment of a child just discovering the thrill of a new game. And when she grabbed his hand and plastered it against her breast, he thought for sure that was the end.

Sweat broke out on his brow as he fought against the climax that was so close to consuming him. He had to make her come and fast. He would not come before her. He never came before a woman. He had always seen to their pleasure first.

He teased her nipples with his fingers and her lingering groan and the way she tossed her head back only made it worse for him. Good lord, but she was so snug and the way she squeezed him.

Damn, he was going to come. He could not stop it.

"Patience, if you do not," —he groaned as her movement turned more frantic— "I'm going to come if you do not slow down."

She moaned deep and long, her finger going to her mouth to bite on it.

That was all he needed.

"Good Christ, Patience," he cried out as the climax claimed him in an explosion that sent him tumbling through a void of never-ending pleasure. And the more she rode him, the longer his climax lasted.

He did not know when his hands had gripped her hips, but her hands where now on top of his squeezing as she screamed out his name over and over and joined him in a blinding climax.

When he was finally able to focus on her, she gasped and rode him even harder, screaming out, "Good God, I am going to come again."

He shuddered as a strong tremor rocked her body and she finally collapsed on top of him. She laid so motionless that he feared something had happened to her. Then she spoke, though he could not understand her, since her lips were plastered to his chest.

Gently, he eased her off him, tucking her body along his side. "What was that you said?"

She dropped her arm across his chest, as if she had not the strength to hold it. "I want to do that often."

He had to chuckle for that had been his first thought when he had first been with a woman. "We can do it as often as you like."

Her head shot up to look at him. "I will not tire you out, will I?"

He chuckled again. "Never."

She rested her head on his chest. "Good." Her head shot up once again. "Once we reunite with my troop there will be no privacy for us to be so intimate. We cannot even sneak into the woods for ghost warriors or your brother's men may be lurking nearby." She sighed as she lowered her head to his chest once again. "You have given me a good reason to return home sooner rather than later."

"I will make sure that we always find a private place no matter where we are," he said, stroking her arm.

"I will think on it myself, for I do not think I can go a day without making love with you." She yawned, reached for the blanket to toss across them, and then snuggled close to him.

Hunter lay listening to his wife's even breathing. She had fallen asleep so quickly and he had hoped to do the same, but he found that he was not as tired as he had thought. The day had certainly been exhausting in more ways than one and had given him much to think about.

That he loved his wife had been a shock to discover, but to realize that his love for her could grow ever stronger was even more of a surprise. She was a remarkable woman. She was not afraid to defend herself or him and she embraced intimacy with an overwhelming passion. And that she should even think of giving her life to save her sister... he felt a stab to his heart.

He was familiar with the pain of losing a loved one, but this pain he felt with the thought of losing Patience was beyond anything he had ever experienced. He would do anything to keep her safe. And now that he knew Greer intended her dead as well as him, it added even more to the score he needed to settle with his brother.

He lay there, his thoughts hopping from one thought to another until sleep finally intruded and he drifted off.

~~~

Patience woke suddenly from a dream, her heart beating madly. She had been in a dark forest and Heather was calling out to her for help, but no matter how hard she tried she could not find her sister. It was when her sister's voice faded that she woke. Thinking on it now, she wondered if she was being shown that she would never find Heather. She was lost to her forever.

The thought unsettled her and she eased herself out of her husband's arms and carefully left the bed so as not to disturb him. She scooped up her shirt and slipped it on. She added more logs to the fire, then paced in front of it. She could not get her sister's voice out of her head or the thought that she would never find her. Heather had to know that she would never give up, not ever. But the longer it took Patience to find her, the more Heather suffered at the hands of the Dark Dragon.

Her chest felt heavy with the pain of her sister's suffering and with the need for a fresh breath, she hurried out of the cottage.

Hunter stirred, thinking he heard a sound, though he much preferred not to be disturbed, feeling much to content in bed wrapped around his wife. That was until he realized he was the only one in bed. His eyes sprung open and when he saw that the cottage was empty, he did not even bother to grab his shirt, he rushed naked out into the night.

Relief soared in his heart when he saw her standing only a few feet away, staring into the woods. He approached her with quick steps.

Patience heard the cottage door creak open and his swift footfalls approach and at that moment she wanted nothing more than to get lost in her husband's arms and not think another thought on how she was failing her sister.

She turned and spread her arms wide.

Hunter saw the need in her glistening green eyes. She never let her tears fall. She battled them as intensely as she would a foe and from what he had seen, she always won, though it was far from a victory.

He did not hesitate. He had her up in his arms in an instant and just as fast he had her in the cottage.

After he shut the door with a shove of his

shoulder, she said, "I do not want to think anymore tonight."

He lowered her to the ground, latched the door, striped her of her shirt, then hoisted her up by her waist to plant her against him. Her legs tightened around him. "As you wish, wife."

He kissed her with a hunger that surprised him. You would think that he had not had a woman in weeks the way he fed on her and how hard he grew. He ached for her, but he also ached to free her of her troubling thoughts. And for that she needed more than a gentle loving. She needed a driving, relentless loving.

He was glad nothing was on the table, for he dropped her bottom down on it and took her face in his hands. "I am going to make you come again and again and again."

"Promise."

He kissed her again, tugging along her bottom lip with his teeth as he ended it, and she whimpered. He took hold of her chin. "I hurt you?"

She took his hand and pressed it to her cheek. "No, it is that I fear I will never get enough of you."

He ran his thumb tenderly over her lower lip that had plumped from his loving bites. "I share your fear, for the more we make love the more my need for you grows."

She rested her brow to his and with her mouth nearly on top of his, whispered, "Then do as you said and make me come again and again and again."

Hunter slipped his fingers between her legs.

"I am already wet and aching for you."

He growled like an angry beast and grew so hard

that his manhood throbbed viciously. He wrapped his arm around her waist and hefted her up to bring her bottom down on the edge of the table. Then he grabbed her legs, spreading them, forcing her to lie back and with a hard thrust, he entered her.

She cried out with such pleasure that it brought a smile to his face. He grabbed her taut bottom, held it firm and helped her meet his every potent thrust.

It did not take long before she was crying out his name as she exploded in a tremendous climax that she felt down to her bones and back again.

Hunter did not stop. He had promised her more and she would get what he had promised, even though he was straining not to come.

Her second climax came close on her first one, shattering her to pieces, turning her body limp.

Hunter slowed his pace some, delaying his own satisfaction while he methodically teased the dwindling pulses of her last climax to life once again. "Once more," he ordered and turned his rhythm hard and fast.

Patience shook her head, thinking she would never survive another climax, but not caring. She welcomed the enormous wave when it hit her, drowning in its glorious pleasure until she had no breath left and felt faint.

Hunter exploded in a blinding climax that had him groaning like never before. When he was spent and left standing unmoving between her legs, his body trembled with the last vestiges, and he dropped his head back and let out one final groan that shivered his body again.

It took him a moment to realize that Patience was

not moving or speaking and that her body was limp. "Patience," he nearly shouted. When she did not answer, he pulled out of her and grew far more upset when he lifted her in his arms and felt how lifeless she was.

He shouted this time as he carried her to the bed. "Patience!"

She cringed and was barely able to whisper, "I am not deaf."

"What is wrong?" he asked roughly as he placed her on the bed and hunched down beside it.

"It would seem," —she paused, needing to take a breath— "that your sword is a mightier weapon than I had first thought." She paused a moment again, though smiled. "It has done me in."

Hunter laughed with relief, then went and grabbed the bucket of water and a cloth and returned to hunch down beside the bed again. After wetting and rinsing the cloth, he gently wiped her face with it.

Patience sighed. "You are a most pleasing husband, I will definitely keep you."

Hunter laughed again. "I am glad to know that, for I intend to keep you as well." He rinsed the cloth again and wiped her neck.

She shivered.

"You grow chilled," he said, reaching for the blanket.

She rested her hand on his arm. "I would prefer that you keep me warm."

Hunter got in bed with her, settling her to rest her back to his front, then he slipped the blanket over them and laid his arm across her.

She pulled it tight against her chest, snuggled

back against him, mumbled something, and fell fast asleep.

Hunter expected sleep to elude him again, but not so. Sleep crept over him as fast as it had his wife and his last thought before drifting off was that he could have sworn that Patience had told him that she loved him.

Chapter Twenty-four

Patience sat on her horse staring forlornly at the cottage. When they had first arrived here two days ago, she had been anxious to have the time pass quickly so she could meet up with her warriors and continue on their mission. Now she wished for more time alone here with her husband. It had been the most wonderful two days of her life. She had hoped to come to love Hunter one day as his mother had come to love his father. Never had she expected to fall in love with him so hard and fast. She could not think of life without him. It was as if he had suddenly become part of her, an essential part, she could not live without.

"Are you ready?" Hunter asked, riding up beside her.

"It is more difficult than I thought to leave this place."

He reached out, resting his hand over hers. "We take with us what we shared here. As long as we are together, that is all that matters. Besides, we have things that need tending if we are to ever enjoy our life together. Heather must be brought home and Greer must be seen to."

She leaned over and gave him a quick kiss. "You are proving to be a worthy husband more and more each day," —she grinned— "and an exceptional lover."

"I told you I would be a good husband," he said, turning his horse to lead the way out of the woods. "As for my skills as a lover... I believe I will continue to prove them to you."

Patience followed him. "I think that once we are home you should prove them at least twice a day."

"Why wait until we reach home?"

"There is little privacy left to us on this journey," she reminded.

He laughed. "You misjudge my many talents."

A shiver of anticipation ran through her at the thought of making love with him in places other than the cottage. They had made love endlessly there. Every time she believed herself spent, her body satiated, he would touch her and her body would spark to life, though it was more a fire now than a spark.

She sighed with the memories. "I truly love your talents and you displayed them most wonderfully when I straddled you on the chair this morning."

"You are welcome to straddle me any time, wife."

"Be careful," she warned, "you may grow tired of me."

"That will never happen," he said with a laugh that rang through the forest, though stopped suddenly.

Patience's hand instantly went to the hilt of her sword at her side.

"We are being followed or perhaps the Dark Dragon feels we need an escort."

"Or does he protect us from what waits beyond the woods?" Patience pushed all thoughts from her mind and let the warrior in her reign. She had her warriors to see to, Hunter's mother returned to them, and the both of them kept protected from Greer, and then there was Heather.

There was not time to think about falling in love with her husband or making love with him. She needed to concern herself with more important things.

"We need to hurry the pace," she called out to Hunter.

It was hard to ignore the distinct command in her voice. She was once again a warrior, the woman in her pushed aside and locked away. He had thought she was free, but not yet. In time, she would be, and then the warrior and the woman would finally become one.

Patience halted her horse when she reached the edge of the woods and Hunter followed suit. Her stallion pawed the ground, anxious to be on his way, but she held him firm.

She turned to Hunter. "Anything could be waiting for us."

"At least we are not alone," he reminded.

"Aye, and he wants no blood shed on his land."

"Though, he will spill it if necessary."

"And so will I," she said with a fire in her eyes as she urged her stallion forward.

"I know," he whispered as he rode after her, "and it frightens the bloody hell out of me."

~~~

They stopped a few hours later to give the horses and themselves a brief rest.

Hunter disappeared for a short time in the nearby woods and returned with news. "The ghost warriors have left us."

Patience wrinkled her brow. "That seems odd. Why leave us now when we still have a distance to go?"

"Perhaps they believe we are no longer in harm's way."

"Or something more urgent calls them away."

"Whatever the reason, we need to be more watchful," he cautioned.

"Is that concern I hear, husband?"

"Aye, it is and you should be feeling it yourself. It is not only the unknown reason the warriors departed that worries me, but my brother as well. I have repeatedly warned you that Greer will stop at nothing to get what he wants and you have seen that for yourself. If one plan fails, it will be followed by another, then another. He is relentless."

"And the Dark Dragon's threat means little to him since he will make our attack appear as if he had no hand in it." She shook her head. "The ghost warriors saw Greer's men attack us and possibly heard what they said. They will inform the Dark Dragon."

"Greer will claim he gave no such order," Hunter said.

"I cannot believe that the Dark Dragon would believe him."

"He probably would not, but if distracted elsewhere..."

"The Dark Dragon is much too skilled a warrior to be so easily deceived."

"You do not truly know the extent of my brother's deviousness," Hunter said. "He will kill, without remorse, anyone who stands in his way."

It struck Patience then. "Greer killed your father."

Though Hunter remained silent, the burning rage in his blue eyes answered for him.

It was not curiosity, but concern for her husband that had her asking, "What happened?"

A rustle close by had them both drawing their swords and turning. The two squirrels at play froze a moment, then scurried up a tree.

"Time to be on our way," Hunter said, sounding as if he commanded.

She walked over to him. "You will tell me." Her voice rang with authority, though her hand went to gently rest on his shoulder. "When you are ready."

Hunter's arm shot around her waist and his lips came down on hers, brisk and potent.

The brief, intense kiss shivered her down to her bones and turned her limbs so weak that she held onto his arms for a moment.

"We ride fast and hard," he said and swiftly lifted her onto her horse.

It was not her horse that she wanted to ride hard and fast and annoyed at the distracted thoughts, she chased them away with a few silent oaths. However, a few lingered in the corners of her mind, taunting her.

Hunter set a faster pace. He wanted to make certain that his wife was safely ensconced within the abbey before nightfall so that she would have the added protection of her skilled warriors.

A roll of thunder was heard and a storm cloud hovered in the distance. Patience hoped it would leave them in peace and travel opposite of their direction. Another sound of thunder had her turning to see if the cloud had moved closer.

"Riders!" she shouted to Hunter, catching sight of four men not far from them.

Hunter turned and let loose with a sharp oath upon seeing the warriors bearing down on them. They were still too far from the abbey to try an outrun them. They would have a better chance of surviving if they stopped and battled them.

Patience voiced the same. "We cannot outrun them."

"A clear field ahead," Hunter said with a quick nod for her to take a look.

She did and nodded in agreement.

They were off their horses as soon as they reached the field. Patience did not waste a moment, she grabbed her bow and cache of arrows and positioned herself for a shot.

Hunter was about to tell her it was too far of a distance, but never got the chance.

Her arrow hit one man in the chest and he went flying off his horse.

Hunter stood speechless as he watched Patience grab another arrow and with a quick draw of her bow sent it flying in the distance. It caught another warrior in the shoulder and knocked him off his horse. He took a hard fall, his head hitting a large rock.

"To pests left," she said as if talking of nothing more than a couple of annoying insects.

The last two warriors slowed their approach and their pace, while talking between each other.

"Get on your horse," Hunter ordered and when she did not move, he yelled, "Now Patience!"

"More warriors are coming, are they not?" she asked. "That is why they slow and no longer wish to engage us. They will follow and leave a good trail for others to do the same."

"Aye, now get on your horse," he ordered again.

Patience paid him no heed. She readied another bow, but when the two warriors saw what she was doing, they soon had their horses taking several steps back. The arrow missed its mark and she got angry and mounted her horse.

"Now you obey me," he said frustrated and mounted his horse.

"They cannot be allowed to follow us," she said and urged her stallion straight for the two warriors.

Hunter froze, her action shocking him. He swore and took off after her, fearful that he would not reach her in time, but then she was a skilled warrior. But she was also his wife and that mattered more than anything. His worry surged. Once this was over and he got his hands on her he would—he shook his head—he would hug her tight and be grateful that they had survived.

The two warriors wore big grins and rode directly at her.

"Idiots," she said to herself, giving her horse rein, as she had taught him to do, while she readied her bow.

The two idiot warriors laughed and kept coming at her.

"Perfect, you fools," she said and let an arrow fly.

It went straight through one man's neck and blood flew everywhere. The warrior barely had time to grab his neck before he fell from his horse dead.

The other warrior looked on in horror and abruptly brought his horse to a halt. Then his face exploded with bright red rage and he advanced on her with a horrific battle cry.

Hunter's blood ran cold and he reached for his sword as he watched his wife release another arrow.

It pierced the man's chest, going straight through his back and he toppled off his horse.

Patience hurried and turned her horse, and Hunter was about to do the same when Patience called out for him to halt.

She came up alongside him, her stallion snorting and stumping, annoyed over being reined in. "We need to separate."

She once again stunned him silent, though he did not take long to recover and with a jab of his finger in her direction said, "Absolutely not."

"We have no choice and no time to argue about it. Others will come and discover our tracks. We need to separate."

"And what stops them from dividing and following us?"

"Nothing, but separating will not give them what they want... a scene where it appears that you and I died battling one another. And that could very well save our lives."

"I cannot let you go off on your own," he insisted, even though she made sense.

"We have no choice," she reiterated, "and no time to argue. You know full well I can take care of myself and you have shown you are capable of the same. We separate and meet at the abbey."

"I am not leaving you on your own," he said fiercely, reaching out to grab her reins.

She yanked her horse away from him. "If you

love me you will, for if you do not do as I say we both surely will die."

Her point was too valid to argue with, though he certainly was not pleased by it. As much as he hated to admit it, separating would spoil Greer's plan, together they would not survive. "You better make it to the abbey, wife."

"Give me reason to," she demanded with a smile.

"I can give you many," he said, his tone suggestive.

Her smile softened. "I will give you one good reason to make it to the abbey."

"And what would that be?"

"I want to make love with my husband tonight...the man I love with all my heart and then some. So hurry and do not keep me waiting." She rode off, knowing if she did not they would wind up in each other's arms and there was no time for that.

After entering the woods that ran parallel to the field, she turned to look for him, hoping he was gone. She sighed when she saw that he was nowhere in sight and sent a quick prayer to the heavens that he be kept safe. Then she did what she did best, she called on her warrior skills to survive.

~~~

Hunter took off and in minutes laid tracks that any idiot could follow. Then he dismounted and followed backwards behind his horse, erasing their tracks. He ended at a stream where he mounted his stallion and took off... after his wife.

He never had any intentions of leaving her whether her plan held merit or not. She had sealed his decision when she had told him she loved him. He had wanted to reach out, grab her, and never let her go. And when he caught up with her, he intended to do just that... never let her out of his sight.

For now he had to create the illusion that they had separated and remained so. He followed the stream down for quite a ways, then crossed it. It was not long before he picked up her trail, though he halted his horse, realizing that there was not one rider but many. He dismounted and quickly examined the tracks, determining that they were fresh ones. One rider was light in weight while the others were heavy. Could Greer's men have caught up with his wife so soon? He was about to find out since the riders were not too far ahead of him.

Hunter mounted his horse once again and proceeded slowly and cautiously. It did not take long before he saw riders a few feet ahead and he eased his horse to a halt.

"If you had not been so busy entertaining the lassies, you would remember what you were taught about tracking. One warrior always lags behind to catch fools like you."

Hunter shook his head and turned, relieved to see Ewan's oldest son, Noble sitting astride his horse. "But just think of all the fun I would have missed."

Noble approached him and Hunter could see that he was a younger version of his father, fine featured and solidly built.

Noble looked around. "Where is your wife? My father speaks highly of her and I want to meet the woman who has the unfortunate task of being wed to you."

"I am going after her now."

"Ran out on you already, did she?"

"Running from Greer's men," Hunter said.

Noble's smile faded. "Come, we will talk with my father. My brother Ross and I insisted on accompanying him and your mum to the abbey."

Hunter was relieved to see that his mum was fine and that she now had the added protection of Ewan's two sons. Beast circled his horse, his tail wagging rapidly, happy to see him. Once he explained to Ewan what happened, he ordered his sons to go with Hunter to find Patience. He would see that Una got safely to the abbey.

Before Hunter took off, Ewan took him aside. "No ghost warriors followed you?"

"They did, though they suddenly disappeared. It was one time I wished they had stayed."

"That is odd."

"Patience and I thought the same. They have trailed us for almost the entire journey and they knew we had been in danger. So, why did they leave us so abruptly?"

"A question we need answered," Ewan said. "Now hurry and be on your way."

Hunter nodded and joined Ross and Noble to lead the way.

It took more time then Hunter cared for to finally pick up Patience's trail and not long after that to discover she was skilled at misleading which both annoyed and pleased him. If he was having difficulty finding her, then so would Greer's men.

"I am eager to meet this woman who has the talent to avoid her husband," Noble said.

Ross' thoughts more mirrored Hunter's. "And avoid those who chase after her."

"I see that your brother is still the most intelligent of the lot of you," Hunter said with a look to Noble.

"And not an ounce of humor," Noble said as if it was the gravest affliction of all.

"Quiet and concentrate before we miss her tracks," Ross ordered, his glance fixed on the ground.

"Patience would commend your vigilance," Hunter said.

"Good, then perhaps she will let me join her elite warriors so I do not have to put up with the likes of him." Ross gave a nod to his brother.

"Go on and give him more reason to think more highly of himself," Noble teased.

"Not think—know," Ross said with an increasing smile.

Hunter listened to the brothers' banter as Ross kept his attention focused on the ground and Noble on their surroundings. The two may sound like they argued, but it was nothing more than brotherly banter. Hunter wished that he had had the solid and caring camaraderie the two had with his brothers. Unfortunately, any and all banter with his brothers had always ended in a fight, particularly with Greer. Hunter often thought that Greer must have been born angry, for it was his constant nature. When a wedding contract had been announced, Hunter had felt pity for the poor woman forced to wed Greer, then he met Rona. They made a perfect match, for she was just as angry as Greer and the both were also selfish. They both felt that whatever they wanted should be theirs. And Rona had gotten it in her head that she wanted Hunter to please her in bed since her husband had failed to do so.

Hunter wanted no part of her and besides, knowing how his brother thought, he probably suggested it to his wife so that he would have a good excuse to see Hunter dead for such a betrayal.

"A clear track," Ross said, bending down to examine it more closely. He turned his head as if following it and said, "That way."

An hour or so later, the three men were exasperated.

"I cannot believe we lost her tracks," Ross said, slamming a stick he carried down on the ground.

"At least we have seen no other tracks," Noble said.

"We keep looking," Hunter ordered frustrated that he could not find his wife.

"Of course," both men said in unison and the three continued searching.

Hours later Ross spoke up. "We have barely an hour's worth of daylight left. We should head to the abbey. I would not be surprised if your wife is there waiting for you."

Noble agreed. "Aye, Ross is right. It will do no good searching in the dark, and since your wife has avoided us so easily, I would daresay she avoided Greer's men as well."

Hunter hated to admit that it was a strong possibility that Patience was already at the abbey. But his fear was that she might not be there, and then what?

He knew what he had to do. What Patience expected him to do. "The abbey it is," he said with more confidence than he felt.

Dusk was fading into night when they reached the walled abbey. Monks greeted them and took their horses while a sole monk led them to the communal room.

Hunter's eyes immediately searched the room. Every one of Patience's warriors occupied two of the trestle tables and benches as well as Ewan and his mum, though Beast was nowhere to be seen. They all looked at Hunter, and then glanced expectantly past him. He knew then that they were waiting for Patience to appear.

His wife was not there.

Chapter Twenty-five

The six of them would be on her soon enough and Patience made the only decision she could. She leaned down and whispered in her horse's ear, instructing the stallion to race to the abbey. She had taught him the names of many places they had been, so that if a situation like this one should arrive he would go where she directed.

"Do not let them catch you," she commanded and flung herself from the horse. She took a good hit to her side and allowed herself to roll a few feet before she got up, and scurried behind a thick set of bushes, scrunching low to the ground.

It was only a matter of minutes until she heard the thunder of horses' hooves. She stilled her breath and waited, praying for them to pass. After a several minutes of silence, she sighed quietly and slowly. Now it was just a matter of avoiding them until she reached the abbey, which would be well after nightfall.

She pulled her dirk from its sheath at her waist, adjusted her sword strapped to her back, and cautiously proceeded to get herself safely to the abbey.

Patience did not know how long she had walked, having stopped a few times when she thought she heard horses or footfalls. It was almost dusk and soon it would be harder to see where she was going in the dense forest. Even if she came across a much traveled path, she could not take it for fear of running into Greer's men. It would be an arduous journey and one she was hoping would soon come to an end.

She walked for several more hours, her steps cautious and her ears alert. The sound came suddenly and she was grateful she had kept her dirk in her hand. She swung with full force as she turned and caught her assailant across the stomach. He yelled out in pain and, pressing his hand to his gut, collapsed to the ground.

Two more warriors were upon her in no time. She slashed out and caught one on the face, her blade tearing at his cheek clear down to his chin. He stumbled back, screaming out in fury. The other one swung at her and she dodged his fist, though not completely. The end of it caught her chin and sent her stumbling. It was all the time he needed to grab her with a force that sent both of them reeling to the ground.

He landed on top of her, the sword sheathed to her back slamming hard against her. She fought to catch her breath while fighting to get him off her.

"Hold her good," the warrior she had scarred ordered as he came to stand over them. His hand was plastered against his face, blood spilling from between his fingers. "I am going to give her a scar prettier than the one she gave me."

"Not before I have some fun with her first," the one on top warned, grabbing her shirt and ripping it, then catching her hands in one of his big meaty ones.

Her one breast lay partially exposed, the leather straps that crisscrossed her chest holding the torn material in place. She felt her strength wane, not only from fighting him, but the weight of him on her growing ever heavier.

"Get them damn straps out of the way so I can give her some pretty scars," the wounded one ordered.

"Greer will not like that. It will make it seem that Hunter went at her good and she had to defend herself," the one on top said and with his free hand used his dagger to cut the leather straps.

Patience was actually glad he did. It meant if she could somehow dislodge him, she could go for her sword and have a fighting chance against them.

The scarred one moved to stand just past the top of her head and grabbed for her arms. "I'll keep good hold of her while you give her a hard poke."

Patience could not let him get a hold of her. If she did, she was finished. They would have their way with her and she could not let that happen. She struggled against the two large men and when the one slapped her hard across the face, leaving her flesh stinging and blood seeping into her mouth, she lost control.

She let out a furious roar, bucked against him and yanked the scarred one's hand down to give it a hard bite. He howled and raised his hand, tightening it into a fist that he swung at her face with such force that she knew it would knock her out.

Out of nowhere Beast appeared, clamping down on the man's fist.

Patience took advantage of the moment and gave a hard twist to her body, sending her assailant flying off her. She got to her feet as fast as possible and pulled her sword from its sheath. She turned just in time to slice it across the warrior's gut. He went down hard and she turned and saw that the scarred warrior was laying on the ground dead, Beast having torn at his throat.

She dropped to the ground exhausted and relieved and hugged Beast to her when he came over and began licking her face. "I owe you, my friend."

Beast wagged his tail and continued licking her.

"We need to get out of here fast. There may be more of them." She stood still for a moment, feeling herself sway. This was no time for weakness. She had to get to the abbey. "Stay with me, Beast." And the dog stood at her side. "Good boy, now we go join Hunter." Silently, she prayed that he had made it to the abbey and she kept praying as she set a quick pace for herself.

~~~

Hunter stood, his arms braced on the top of the stone wall that surrounded the abbey, staring out into the night. He had been overjoyed when he had caught a glance of Patience's horse coming out of the forest until he had seen she was not on it. He wanted to mount his horse and go search for her, but everyone had stopped him.

It was a moonless night and barely a hand could be seen in front of him. It would have been foolish to try, and Edward had insisted that Patience probably sent the horse ahead to draw the enemy away from her. He had also insisted that she would arrive at the abbey sometime tonight.

Hunter had not been so confident.

"We leave at first light," Edward said, approaching him. "Those are her orders and I will follow them."

"Go if you must, but I intend to find my wife," Hunter said his heart heavy, feeling as if the life was being squeezed from it, so worried was he for what might have happened to her.

"Patience would want you safe," Edward reminded.

"And I want the same for her."

"Patience is a determined and skilled woman. I am sure she will make it to the abbey," Una said as she approached the two men.

"That she is," Edward agreed. "She will arrive here soon enough."

"I hope that Beast does as well. Why he never returned after wandering into the woods, I do not know. Saundra will be so upset if something has happened to him."

"How odd of him to do that," Hunter said. "He is a devoted dog and it makes no sense that he would leave your side, Mum."

"I thought the same," Ewan said, joining them.

"Did you hear that?" Edward said and turned to look out over the wall.

They all quieted and the sound came again.

"Is that a bark?" Ewan asked and turned silent to listen.

The bark grew louder and more frantic.

"Beast returns" Una said joyfully and with relief.

His barking continued until Edward called out, "There he is."

They all looked and saw two bright eyes glowing in the dark.

"What is he doing?" Hunter said and strained to see, the heavy darkness making it difficult. "He comes no further."

"He turns and runs back," Ewan said, squinting as he tried to see the animal better.

"Oh my God," Una cried, her small height barely allowing her to see over the wall. "He looks as if he is dragging something."

Hunter ran to the gate, throwing it open. His heart pounded against his chest as he ran toward Beast, hoping against hope that the animal had found his wife—alive. He flew across the field and his heart stopped when he reached Beast and looked to see his wife lying face down on the ground. He hunched down and reached out to turn her over gently, dread filling him and silent prays on his lips.

Patience felt someone turn her and, though her body ached terribly, she reacted instinctively. She swung her arm around, her hand fisted, ready to land a solid punch, only to have it caught in a strong grip.

"It is me, *mo chridhe*," Hunter said.

"Hunter," she cried and opened her hand to grasp his.

He had her up in his arms in seconds, tucking her close against his chest, swearing silently that never—never—would he let her out of his sight again.

"Beast?" she questioned.

"He is here. He dragged you out of the forest," Hunter said, hurrying her inside the abbey walls.

"I love that dog," she whispered against his chest.

He was thinking the same himself, but had no

time to agree with her. He looked to Edward. "Post more warriors at the wall."

"Has she been wounded?" Edward asked anxiously.

"I do not know. I will inform you of her condition as soon as I find out," Hunter said, praying she suffered no irreparable harm. He turned to his mum as Edward hurried off.

"Bring her to my room," Una urged and Hunter followed his mum, prayers remaining on his lips as they walked along the narrow stone corridors of the abbey.

Hunter entered the small, stark room that contained a bed and a small table with one chair. A single candle barely cast any light in the room and there was no hearth to chase away the chill and dampness of the stone walls.

He laid her gently on the bed.

"We need more candles, a bucket of water, and cloths," his mum said.

"I will not leave her," Hunter said firmly. "I will not leave her ever again."

Una patted her son's shoulder. "I will have someone help me get them."

"I will help you," Ewan said from the open doorway.

Hunter left his wife's side a moment to fetch the lone candle and bring it closer to the bed so that he could see her better and when he caught sight of her bruised and bloodied face and her torn shirt, his fury soared.

He placed the candle holder on the chest next to the bed and fisted his hands to try and stop them from shaking, he was so angry.

"Patience," he said more calmly than he thought possible, "have you been wounded?"

"Aye," she said and turned a smile on him that soon changed to a wince of pain, "my pride has suffered greatly."

That she could find humor in her horrific ordeal brought a smile to his face and eased his anger as well, though only a little.

His mum returned carrying a basket filled with the needed items, and she was followed in the room by Ewan who toted two buckets of water.

Patience pulled her torn shirt together, covering her breasts. Though appreciative of the pair's help, she was accustomed to tending to herself. Not realizing it, she reached out and laid her hand on Hunter's arm, squeezing it.

Hunter saw the unease in his wife's eyes and felt it in the way she gripped his arm. While she had responded humorously to his question, it did not mean she was not upset. Besides, he wanted to talk with her alone. There were questions he wanted to ask her that no one else needed to hear.

"I will tend to her, Mum," Hunter said, turning to his mother.

Una handed him a candle. "I had no doubt you would. There are more candles in the basket along with the other items you will need. I will go see about getting Patience some food." She looked to Patience. "If you need anything, my dear, I am here for you." She laid a gentle hand on her son's shoulder. "You are in good hands."

"Glad you made it here," Ewan said as he

followed Una out the door.

"Ewan," Patience said and he stopped just outside the door and turned and poked his head in. "Find out why the ghost warriors left us."

He gave a nod and shut the door behind him.

The more candles Hunter lit, the angrier he grew, seeing the extent of her injuries. Once finished, he said, "Tell me what happened while I get you out of these garments."

"I can do it myself," she said, though she felt so battered, she wondered if she truly could.

He leaned over her, brushing stray hairs gently off her face. "I know you can, *mo chridhe*, but this time I am going to do it, and you are going to tell me *everything* that happened to you."

Patience did not object or grant her consent, she simply lay silent as her husband began to remove her garments. And at that moment she was relieved to be here with him.

Hunter eased her out of her clothes, carefully examining every inch of her. He winced when he saw the dark bruise on her back and surmised it was from her sword that she always wore strapped to it, which would mean that she took a hard fall on her back. Her wrists were bruised, as if someone held them in a tight grip and her hands were smeared with blood, but he was thankful to find no serious wounds on her body.

He covered her to her waist with a soft wool blanket and rinsed a cloth to begin wiping her hands clean of the blood.

A shiver racked her body, and she said, "I killed two of the three men who came upon me. Beast killed the other one. I heard them approach too late. I do not know why I did not hear them." She shook her head. "They were large men, I should have heard them."

Hunter listened quietly, a hundred questions hanging on his lips, but letting none fall. He wanted to hear it all, whether he liked what he heard or not.

"I dispatched the first one fast, but the other was upon me before I knew it and," —she shut her eyes for a moment, the memory not an easy one, then she continued— "I cut the one on his face good, and he promised to do the same to me, though not just to my face."

Hunter's anger mounted with every word she spoke, hating what she had gone through and hating that he had asked her to relive the nightmare.

She seemed to drift off a moment, her eyes on him, though not truly looking at him.

He dropped the wet, dirty cloth in the one bucket, laid a tender hand over her clean hands that rested on her stomach, and waited impatiently.

It was when he saw her eyes glisten with the first sign of tears that he reacted. He lifted her up onto his lap and throwing the blanket over her shivering body pressed her tightly against him.

He should have been there for her. He should have been the one to kill the bastards that had harmed her. He pressed his cheek to the top of her head, the scent of earth stinging his nostrils, evoking an image in his mind of her on the ground fighting the large warriors as they tried to force themselves on her. He wanted to roar with rage. "Never again will I ever leave you. Never again will I obey such a command."

She raised her head off his chest to look at him.

"Never again do I want you to." And then she did something she had never done in front of any man, not even her da... she let her tears fall.

Hunter was stunned when one tear after another rolled down her cheeks. He had comforted many a woman when they cried, but never had any of their tears pierced his heart as his wife's tears did. Then suddenly it dawned on him, she loved and trusted him enough to cry in front of him...something she had done with no other man.

"I love you so very much, husband," she said through tears. "And I want no other man's hands on me. I belong to you and you alone and you are mine and mine alone."

"Aye, I am yours now and always, and it is glad I am that you finally admit you belong to me." He wiped away her tears, though he could not still the tide.

"It hit me suddenly when the two attempted to take from me what I had given to you, what belongs to you and only you—my husband. The thought that they would defile me angered me beyond belief, and the thought of never seeing you again," —she shook her head— "I could not bear the pain. So, I fought with all my strength to return to you, though I doubt I would have been successful if Beast had not helped me."

He had planned on killing Greer and being done with it. Not anymore. Now he would be sure to make him suffer.

"Beast assisted you, but it was your warrior skills that kept you alive and brought you back to me." He reached down and rinsed the cloth in the bucket, then began cleaning the blood from the corner of her mouth. She had suffered a hard blow, but he did not want to remark on it. It was time for her to rest and to heal.

She eased the cloth away from her mouth. "It was returning to you that kept me going, though it was a startling revelation that nothing in the world mattered but getting back to you. All I could think of was you and how much I wanted to be in your arms, taste your kisses once again, feel your touch, and make love." She rested her hand to his chest. "I want to feel your heart pound against mine, feel you spill into me as you come, and hear you groan with pleasure. I need you to wash away the bad memories and replace them with ones that will last forever. I need you to make love to me."

Chapter Twenty-six

A knock at the door prevented Hunter from responding. He hastily pulled the blanket up over his wife's breasts before opening the door.

His mum stood there with a pitcher and two tankards in hand and Ewan stood behind her, holding a wooden tray covered with a cloth.

"How is Patience doing?" Una asked her son, handing the pitcher to him, though remaining just outside the door.

Hunter took them from her and sat them on the chest. "She needs rest."

She turned and took the tray from Ewan, then handed it to her son. "We will not disturb her. Make certain she eats something. We will see you both in the morning."

"Where will you sleep?" Hunter asked. "This was to be your room for the night."

"Worry not," his mum said, "Ewan has already seen to it."

"Wait," he said to the both and took a moment to place the tray on the small table, then stepped out into the narrow hall to speak with them. "Inform Edward that Patience is too battered and bruised to leave tomorrow. We will give her a day to rest and see then what she wishes to do. Tell him I will speak with him as soon as I can."

Ewan nodded. "Take good care of her. She is a

strong warrior who continues to earn the respect of her clan and admiration from all who meet her. Donald Macinnes would be wise to make her laird of the Clan Macinnes."

"I wish my father felt the same about me being laird," Patience said after Hunter closed the door.

"I think you underestimate your father," Hunter said. "He is known for his fairness and wise leadership skills. Surely, he sees that his daughter is much like him."

"The problem is that I am his daughter and not a son."

"And glad I am for it," he said with a teasing glint.

She laughed softly. "We were not separated long and yet I missed your humorous tongue."

"It is also a very talented tongue."

"Show me," she said with an inviting smile and stretched her hand out to him, only to wince in pain.

"Do not move," Hunter ordered, returning to sit on the bed beside her and taking her hand in his. Her hand felt chilled and he rubbed some warmth into it with his two hands. "You have been through a terrible ordeal and you need to rest and heal," —he raised his hand when she tried to interrupt him— "at least for tonight, rest. There is always tomorrow."

She pulled her hand out of his two and struggled to sit up, annoyed at herself for letting her need for her husband interfere with her duties. "I must speak with Edward."

Hunter took hold of her shoulders gently, though firmly. "Lie down. I have spoken with Edward."

That got her ire up. "What did you tell him? You

should have spoken to me first and—"

Hunter pressed his fingers to her mouth, stilling her words. "You were—still are—in no shape to do anything but heal, if you hope to finish out this mission. I instructed Edward to do what I assumed would be your orders, to post more guards along the wall and remain alert and that I would speak to him about your condition as soon as I could. I also had him informed that we would not be leaving in the morning as planned—" He pressed more firmly against her lips when she tried to speak. "That you are too battered and bruised to travel and once rested, we would see what you wished to do."

Patience glared at him, her anger obvious in her bold green eyes.

Hunter brought his face close to hers. "Be angry all you want. I am your husband and I will make decisions that are best for you when you are unable to or when you are too stubborn to admit what is best for you." He kissed her softly, her lips rigid against his. "I respect your position as leader of your warriors and will not interfere unless necessary, like now. And I do so, not to usurp your authority, but because I love you and would find life without you quite unbearable."

Patience lifted her head just enough for their lips to meet and she kissed him as softly as he had kissed her. "At least we agree on one thing," —she grinned— "life would be unbearable without each other, though I never would have thought, at least not so soon, but then I had not expected to fall in love with you so suddenly and so deeply." It was her turn to press her fingers to his lips to prevent him from responding. "It is not so much that you gave Edward orders, though it does rankle me some, but more so that upon my return I gave no thought to my warriors and instructing them. My thoughts rested solely on you, and that is not good for a wise leader to do."

"Is it not better to know that there is someone there who knows you, understands you, and will lead in your stead if you are unable to? Is it not more comforting to know that you are never alone, but that someone will always be there for you to help, to guide, to listen, but most of all to love you?" Hunter smiled. "And did you not instruct Ewan about the ghost warriors? Do not be so hard on yourself, Patience. You are an exceptionally skilled warrior and should be proud of all you have achieved, that includes being wise enough to have married me."

"How is it that you can make me smile, even when I am angry?" she asked, losing her fight, along with her will, not to smile.

"Love, *mo chridhe*, love," he said with a chuckle. "Now, you need some food and rest."

"I need you more," she said, sitting up with a wince that had Hunter immediately reaching out to help her.

She winced again when he braced her back against wall, the abrasive stones painful to her bruise and his annoyance flared that she continued to suffer and would until her bruises faded.

"Lean forward, while I fetch something to put behind your back." He retrieved his mum's blanket that she had left draped over the lone chair. He wondered if she would need it, then knowing his mum as he did, he knew she left it there for Patience to use. He folded it and placed it behind her back as he eased her to rest against it.

"Much better," she said with a sigh.

He handed her a tankard of wine and a piece of cheese. "Eat, so you regain your strength."

"I would regain it faster if you would make love to me," she said, then took a bite of the cheese.

"You need—"

"You," she said, tossing the remaining piece of cheese at him. "I need you. How do you not understand that?" She shook her head. "I can still feel the grip of the one warrior's hands on my wrists and the other one straddling me and tearing my shirt," — she shut her eyes— "I fear I will never rid myself of the horrid memory." She opened her eyes, tears lingering in them, though this time she refused to shed them. "So, please—please—make love to me."

Hunter stood and striped off his garments. He tenderly lifted her off the bed and sat again, straddling her across his lap. He would not cause her more pain by letting her lie on her injured back, nor would he straddle her like her attacker did. He kissed her lips gently. "Tonight we make new memories."

She tightened her arms around his neck and pressed her cheek to his, "Promise."

"Promise," he whispered his hand going to her breast to gently cup it while his lips settled on hers.

His kiss was tender and teasing and she soon was lost in it and the sensations it was awakening in her. His hand was equally as gentle and teasing with her breast, his thumb doing wonderful things to her nipple.

She moaned in disappointment when his lips left her mouth, though she cried out in pleasure when they settled on her nipple. And when she felt him grow hard beneath her, she wiggled her bottom against him, eager to have him inside her.

When his hand moved to stroke her sensitive spot, she cried out, feeling as if she would come there and then, and she let him know it. "I will not last long."

His lips moved from her breast to brush across her lips. "Then come now and I will see that you come again."

He slipped a finger into her while his thumb teased her tight nub and it was not long before she screamed his name, though he caught the scream in a kiss. Passion rippled through her like never-ending waves crushing along the shore and it felt so wonderful that she wished it would never end.

"Hunter," she whispered.

"Not finished yet," he said and lifted her just enough to ease her down on his rock-hard manhood.

She dropped her head back and groaned with the feel of him deep inside her. This was what she had wanted, needed, pleaded for from him. And he had not denied her. She lowered her mouth to his and said, softly, "Thank you."

"I am not finished yet," he teased and with his hands at her hips, he moved her up and down and after a short while he felt her limbs weaken and he shifted positions. He cupped her backside, swung her down on the bed, staying inside her, and then lifted her legs over his shoulders as he knelt between her legs and hurried to finish, knowing exhaustion was about to claim her.

Patience shut her eyes tight and moaned with satisfaction so deep, she swore it touched her soul.

And when she burst in another climax, it rocked her body so hard that she felt herself grow faint.

Hunter came along with his wife, hard, fast, and explosive. The last of it was just fading away when he felt his wife's limbs go limp, much too limp. "Patience?" he said, looking down at her. When she did not answer, he pulled out of her and his worry grew when her legs slipped off his shoulders. He leaned over her. "Patience," he snapped and patted her cheek.

She did not answer and he hurried off the bed, cursing himself for giving into her instead of making her rest. But she had to go and plead with him. How could he deny her when she begged him?

He dumped a clean cloth in the unused bucket of water and rinsed it, then ran it over her face. "Damn it, Patience, answer me."

His sharp voice had her eyes springing open. "Why are you shouting?"

Hunter released a heavy sigh before saying, "I was worried I had hurt you and you had fainted."

She smiled and raised a weak hand to drop against his cheek. "A slight faint, I believe, though it was from the fantastic climax you gave me. I am such a lucky wife."

He shook his head and smiled, thinking he was the lucky one. "You need to rest." He tried to sound stern, but his smile betrayed him.

"But not alone," she said and tugged at his arm.

"It is a narrow bed and—"

"Perfect, for we will have to snuggle close to fit."

He thought then that perhaps she did not want to be alone, but then he had no intentions of leaving her alone. He wanted her where he could see her at all times or he would lose his mind with worry. At least until the problem of his brother was put to rest.

Hunter eased the blanket out from under her and stretched out beside her, tossing it over them as she turned and rested back against him.

She took hold of his hand after he draped his arm over her waist, and threaded her fingers with his then rested them between her breasts. "I made it home, Hunter. I made it home." And with a contented sigh, she fell asleep.

He threw his leg over hers, tucked her a bit closer and whispered, "Aye, and never again will I let you leave me, for my heart would break."

Chapter Twenty-seven

Patience woke, her body aching as she stretched herself awake. She was alone in bed, though she heard hushed voices outside the door. She sat up and stretched again, wincing as she did. The sooner she got herself moving the less her body would complain. She had learned that through experience. Besides, this cell-like room was much too confining, though last night with her husband it had been just the right size. However, it was morning and she did not intend to stay abed any longer.

She got out of bed with another wince and spotted her garments folded on the table. Her plaid had been shaken out and the dirt and debris brushed off and her shirt had been repaired, the stitches so neat they were barely visible. Patience smiled, grateful to Una and reminding herself to thank the thoughtful woman. Once she had donned her garments, she slipped on her boots, and then added the leather coverings. Her weapons where nowhere to be seen, but she was not worried, Hunter or her men would have seen to their care, though she would not feel fully dressed until she had them on. Of course, she no longer had her leather straps, but she would make do.

The door opened and Hunter entered with a surprised look upon his face. "You are up and dressed."

"I will not lie abed. I want to be on our way," she said, adjusting her plaid at her waist.

Hunter walked over to her and brushed her hands aside, tucking the strip of plaid that ran over her shoulder tightly at her waist. "First, we eat, and then we will see how you feel."

"The decision is mine," she said, stepping away from him.

His arm shot out to wrap around her waist and pull her toward him. "Unless you are too stubborn to make the right one."

Her eyes narrowed and she looked ready to argue.

Hunter kissed her quickly and thoroughly, then rested his brow to hers, his arms remaining firm around her waist so she could not pull away. "I love you, *mo chridhe*, and I want you safe and well."

Why did he have to melt her heart like that? Now she could not be angry with him. "Very well," she said irritated that she could surrender so easily to him. "We eat first, and then decide."

He released her to her disappointment since she was ready to jump back in bed with him, but she warned herself there was no time for that right now. And it gave her all the more reason to get home as quickly as possible. At least there they would not only have time to themselves, but a bedchamber as well.

He took her hand. "Come—"

"I wish," she mumbled.

"Do not tempt me," he said, hurrying her to the door. "Your men wait to see you and know that you have suffered no harm."

She felt chastened, thinking only of herself, though it was more an unrelenting need for him that haunted her thoughts or was it her body it haunted? She would push her husband out of her thoughts for today and be done with it. She had much more important matters to worry about.

Her warriors cheered when she entered the communal room and she smiled, as pleased to see them as they were to see her. She was also pleased when Hunter released her hand and walked over to join his mum and others at a table, leaving her in the middle of the room to address her men.

She raised her hand to quiet them and they stilled instantly. "I am well, a few bruises no more, thanks to Beast," she said with a nod toward the dog, busy gnawing on a large bone. "He saved me and I am indebted to him. After we finish enjoying the generous meal the monks have provided, I will speak about our plans for the day."

The warriors wore smiles as they eagerly turned to the meal.

Hunter stood when Patience approached the table where his mum, Ewan, Edward and Ewan's sons were seated. Before he could introduce the men, Ewan spoke up.

"It is good to see you looking so well and it is my pleasure to introduce you to two of my four fine sons who accompanied Una and me here." He gave a nod to the one at the end of the table; "Noble, my oldest son and Ross my youngest."

"It is an honor to meet you," Ross said. "We have heard much about your fine warrior skills and even more an honor to see it is more truth than tale."

"The fool wants to join your warriors," Noble said with a laugh. "He is a McCuil and always will be."

"Ross is a fine man, is he not?" Patience asked.

"Aye, he is for sure," Noble said with a firm nod confirming it.

Patience shrugged and reached for the pitcher. "Then it is his decision, not yours."

Hunter smiled as Noble stared at Patience with his mouths open, though not a word spilled from it.

Patience turned to Una. "Thank you for tending to my garments and repairing my shirt. I only wish I could sew as fine a stitch as you."

"But you do sew a fine stitch, Edward and many of your warriors will attest to it."

"I do better on wounds than I do on cloth," Patience said.

"That is because you are a warrior and have no time for womanly things," Ross said.

Patience smiled. "You will tell that to my father when we return home."

"We leave today then?" Edward asked anxiously.

Patience felt her husband tense beside her and she realized she was about to answer without considering him. The decision was hers to make, though she had agreed to wait until after their meal to do so.

"Let us enjoy the meal and then we will discuss the day's plan," she said and felt Hunter's hand rest on her thigh and give it a squeeze, as if letting her know her response pleased him. And that he acknowledged it, pleased her. Marriage took more effort than she expected, but then perhaps it was not marriage but love that had her making the effort to not only acknowledge her husband but please him, for he had certainly pleased her many times.

Damn. There she was thinking about making love

with him. Would she ever stop thinking about it or wanting him?

She turned her concentration on her meal and laughed along with the others as Noble regaled them with tales of the four McCuil brothers. She was glad, though, that when the meal was finished the two brothers excused themselves, leaving the rest of them to talk.

Patience placed her hand on top of her husband's where it rested on the table. "I feel fit to travel and with Greer McLaud so determined to see Hunter and me not survive the journey home, I think it is wise if we return home as soon as possible."

"I could not agree more," Edward said, looking pleased. "Should I see to readying everything for departure?"

"Aye, we will leave shortly."

Edward nodded and hurried off, gathering the men with him as he went.

Patience looked to Ewan. "Any word on the ghost warriors?"

"Until we leave here I cannot say for sure, though there has been no sign of them for a while," Ewan said. "As soon as we leave here, I will see what I can discover."

"Any thought on why they would simply vanish like that, especially after we had been informed that the Dark Dragon wanted no blood spilled on his land? Having his warriors follow us and offer their protection is evidence that he does not trust Greer to keep the peace, so why leave us vulnerable to him?"

Ewan shook his head. "It puzzles me."

"There would be only one reason," Una said as if

it was obvious. "To have summoned all his warriors, something of extreme importance must have interfered with his plans."

"Perhaps the King called on him for help," Hunter said.

Ewan shook his head again. "He keeps a contingent of warriors ready at all times if the King should require help."

"Then what could possibly have him summoning his men?" Hunter said.

"Oh my God," Una cried and turned to Patience beside her, grabbing hold of her arm. "Your sister escaped and he sends his men to find her."

A shiver so strong ran through Patience that she was certain it touched her soul. Could it be possible? Could Heather have escaped the Dark Dragon?

"Nonsense," Ewan said, dismissing her claim. "How could one lone lass escape his highly-skilled warriors?"

"By watching them," Patience said, growing more confident at the possibility. "I had always wondered how Heather knew so much about our clansmen and even more so how she understood them. I asked her one day and she said it was simple; she watched and listened."

"So you are saying that she watched the ghost warriors and learned—"

"How to avoid them," Patience finished for her husband. "And if she did, then she would be making her way home. We could very well come upon her along the way." She hurried to stand, wanting now more than ever to get home.

Hunter tugged on her arm for her to sit, and she

did so reluctantly.

"How do we know this for sure?" Hunter asked, not wanting his wife to be disappointed if it was proven false.

Patience looked to Ewan. "Would you be able to find out?"

Ewan shook his head. "He would never admit it, for if it was learned, it would leave your sister vulnerable to those who want revenge against him."

Patience grew upset with herself for not having given that thought. "Then it is more important than ever that we leave and hopefully find her along the way."

"And what if this is just a derision to distract you?" Hunter said. "Is it not better that we try to find out for sure if your sister has escaped?"

"But how?" Patience asked, not wanting to lose faith in the idea that Heather was free of the evil man.

"That should not be difficult," Una said once again as if they should understand. "You demanded to see your sister or you would remain on his land until he did. If he no longer has your sister, then I imagine he will find a way to make you leave so that he can continue his search without worrying that you will linger and discover the truth."

Patience turned a scowl on Ewan. "You will not let them know what we think or plan, my sister's life could depend on it."

"I want no harm to come to Heather," Ewan said.

"And if this proves to be true, I certainly do not want Greer to learn about it," Hunter said. "There is no telling what he would do if he came across her."

"He would return her to the Dark Dragon, so that

he would feel indebted to Greer," Ewan said.

"You do not know my brother," Hunter said. "He might return her to the Dark Dragon, her body that is, and then he will lay blame on her own clan, infuriating the Dark Dragon which would have him retaliating with a vengeance."

"I need to find out for sure if Heather is still with the Dark Dragon or if she has escaped," Patience said her worry for her sister mounting. She stood and she was pleased that her husband stood along with her. "Time to leave."

~~~

Hunter rode alongside his mum, Ewan having gone off to see if he could find out anything about the ghost warriors while Patience was busy riding among her warriors.

"She is a wise warrior, talking with each of her men, listening to their opinions and complaints, knowing them well. They will stay true to her," Una said. "Your father never realized that. To him, his warriors had a duty and they had better adhered to that duty or suffer the consequences. Unfortunately, Greer is even worse. He has little regard for his warriors and cares naught if they die. He thinks there will always be another to take one's place, another one to die for him."

"Da realized too late how little regard Greer had for anyone's life but his own," Hunter said.

Una glanced at her son, a tear in her eye. "You

tried to warn him."

"And got a beating for it."

"Your father was blind when it came to Greer and no one could tell him otherwise. You cannot continue to blame yourself for what happened."

"I try, in time perhaps..." Hunter said no more. He had to keep the truth from his mum. He did not want her to know that until he revenged his father's death he would have no peace. To do that, Greer had to die and he did not want his mum to know that he planned to take his brother's life.

"Your wife keeps glancing your way, I think she misses you."

He had noticed her frequent glances and from the spark in her bright green eyes, he had an idea of what was on her mind, but then it was on his as well. "I miss her as well, though we are only a few feet apart."

"When you are in love, a few feet can seem like a chasm. Go to her," Una urged and gave her son's shoulder a loving push.

"Stay close to the warriors, Mum," he said.

"Worry not about me, the McCuil lads keep a good eye on me and I have Beast to protect me and Ewan when he returns. Now go," she ordered with another gentle push.

As he moved away from his mum, he saw that his wife moved away from her warriors. They had the same thought in mind and soon they were riding alongside each other.

"Your mum does well?" Patience asked having grown fund of Una.

"Aye, and you should know that she is as

observant as you are, for she could see how much you missed me, though you were not that far from me."

His playful grin tickled at her heart and brought a smile to her face. "And did she see how much you missed me?"

"She did," Hunter said proudly. "She knows her son well."

Patience lowered her voice. "I think I know you better."

"I think she would agree on that," Hunter whispered.

Her smile faded. "I wish we were home and had time to spend alone as we did at the cottage. I would love uninterrupted days with you where we could..." She sighed and shook her head. "My desire for you is simply outrageous."

He laughed. "And glad I am for that."

"Talk to me of something else or I fear I will drag you into the woods and have my way with you."

"Do not tempt me, wife," he warned. "I would love to do the same to you, but it would be unwise of us both."

"I know," she sighed with resignation, "but the temptation remains."

Hunter did what she had asked, knowing it was the wisest thing to do. "How long until we leave the Dark Dragon's land?"

"A day and a half ride and we will reach the Dark Dragon's border. Once we cross it, I fear what your brother may do, and there has not been sufficient time for my message to have reached my father, which means extra men are yet on the way."

"I do not care for the odds," Hunter said. "Do you

know what clan borders the Dark Dragon's land?"

"Clan MacTavish, though I doubt the clan is aware of its infamous neighbor."

"Do you call the MacTavish clan friend?"

"There have been sparks between us over the years, but my da has always managed to make certain they never ignited," she said.

"Would they aid us if need be?"

"I suppose that would depend on if Greer has struck a bargain with them or not," she said, the thought setting a worry in her. "The Clan MacThore sits next to the MacTavishes and also borders Macinnes land. They have always been an ally of our clan and my da has been there for them whenever needed. Clan MacThore we can count on."

"Then perhaps you should send a message to them and ask them to meet us at their border," Hunter suggested.

She smiled. "We do think alike. I had Edward send a man out shortly after we departed the abbey."

They continued discussing different scenarios they might face along the way and various ways to avoid them or confront them while they traveled with caution to their surroundings. A quick rest mid-day saw Ewan returning to them.

Patience was eager to hear his news, though one look at his face told her she was not going to like what she heard.

"I saw not a trace of the ghost warriors," Ewan informed her and Hunter when they joined Ewan and Una.

Una broke the silence that followed. "That is good news, for it means they continue to hunt for Heather."

Patience threw her arms around the woman and hugged her. She wanted to believe that Heather was free of the Dark Dragon and that she was safe and on her way home. She had to believe it, for to believe anything else would mean that Heather was worse off than when she was with the Dark Dragon, and that thought tore at Patience's heart.

Chapter Twenty-eight

"I am not going to argue this with you, Patience," Hunter said, adding more broken branches to the campfire. The camp was finally settling down for the night, warriors getting ready to change posts. "You have given yourself little time to rest and heal. Tonight you will rest. Your warriors will see to guarding the camp. You do not need to take a turn."

Patience was ready to protest when a yawn hit her hard.

"And there you have proof of my words," Hunter said, walking over to her to wrap his arms gently around her. "You do not need me to tell you what you already know, but I have no trouble reminding you of it. You will be of no help to anyone, especially your sister if you let your strength wane. And your warriors do not expect you to share in the duties tonight just as you would not expect it if one of them had suffered an injury. So do what you must and rest."

She thought to ask him if he would rest with her, but that would be much too tempting and to be truthful she was much too tired and her body much too sore.

With a look of surrender in her green eyes, she said, "I am tired."

"And no doubt your body is feeling the effects of your ordeal. Lie down," he said, though there was a hint of command to his tone. With an arm around her waist, he helped her down on the blanket he had arranged near the campfire, then he joined her, stretching out beside her. He covered them with another blanket.

Patience cuddled close to her husband, wanting the comfort of his arms around her and the warmth of his body against hers. Content, her eyes closed and in minutes she was asleep.

~~~

Patience did not know what woke her, perhaps it had been the hiss and spit of the campfire, or the stillness in the air. Whatever it was had disturbed her sleep and brought her fully awake. She realized then that her husband was not beside her and wondered if that was what had woken her. She was used to having him close and when he was not there, she felt the loss.

She sat up and looked around. The camp was quiet, everyone asleep, except for the guards posted at various spots. She could not tell how long she had slept, though if she went by how rested she felt, then it had to have been several hours.

Hunter was probably at his post, and she decided to go find him and see if she could relieve him so that he could rest. She kept her footfalls light so as not to disturb those sleeping and went to find her husband.

She knew where Edward would post the guards and found Hunter at the third post she checked. She stopped a few feet from him, admiring his silhouette. Even the shadows could not hide his handsome features or distinct muscled body. It was easy to see why women favored him, but he belonged to her now and that brought a smile to her face.

"Are you going to just stand there or come over here and give me a kiss?"

"That would distract you," she said, walking over to him.

"I will leave one eye open." He reached out and snatched her arm to tug her against him. "You should still be sleeping." He gave her a quick kiss.

While she would have liked a more lingering kiss, she was pleased that he took his duty seriously and kept his focus on what was most important... guarding the camp.

"I woke and felt well-rested and came to relieve you so that you could get more sleep."

"I am pleased that you got a good night's sleep, and I got enough myself. Sunrise is only about an hour away."

"Then we can watch it together," she said and slipped out of his arms, though took his hand and walked to rest against a nearby boulder.

Hunter came to rest beside her. "You winced now and then in your sleep. Are you sure you feel well?"

"An ache and pain now and then, nothing more," she assured him.

"Some aches never fade, and some grow with time."

She slipped her hand in his. "Never healing. I think my sister Heather suffers from such a wound, though she bears no scar to show it." She squeezed his hand. "I think you bear a wound that shows no scar also, though I believe it continues to fester. It might do well to clean it out and let it heal."

Patience waited, hoping her husband would confide in her about Greer and his father. She had told herself to be patient, a near impossible thing for her, that he would tell her when he was ready. Though she had remained silent, curiosity continued to plague her. Now she hoped he would talk with her about it.

After a long silence, he finally said, "How can a son possibly kill his father?"

Patience knew he sought no answer from her, so she remained silent and listened.

"I tried endlessly to tell my father what type of man Greer was becoming, but he refused to listen. He claimed I was jealous of Greer because he was the firstborn son and would one day lead the clan and inherit the land. And of course Greer continued to feed my father's misgivings about me. I was appalled at my father's denial of the obvious. How could he not see the power-hungry man Greer was becoming?" Hunter shook his head and grew quiet a moment. "It was when my mum spoke her own thoughts on the matter to my father that things grew worse.

"My father felt that my mum favored me and that I had convinced her that Greer was not to be trusted. I do not know if my father ever realized how much it took for my mum to speak out against her own son. I believe she did so because she realized her husband's life was in danger.

"Greer saw what was happening and was careful in all he did and only ingratiated himself even more with our father. Until it seemed that he trusted no one as much as he did Greer." Hunter stopped, lost in memories.

"What of Rab at this time?"

"Rab always looked up to Greer and never found any fault with him. His foolish devotion to our brother is what made my father believe that my concern for his life and the future of the clan was nothing more than petty jealousy. He discovered too late how very wrong he was."

"What happened?"

"A day of hunting was planned so that the storehouse could be stacked for the coming winter. I did not know that Greer and my father went on ahead of the others and when I found out I went after them." He took in a deep breath. "I got there too late. Greer was nowhere to be seen and my father lay in a pool of blood dying. When I got to him, blood was running from his mouth and oozing from his chest and I could not stop it."

He held up their joined hands and stared at them as he spoke. "I took his hand and he grabbed mine, with what strength was he had left, and clung to it as if it would somehow keep death from taking him. He had difficulty speaking but managed to tell me he was sorry. That I was right about Greer and that I was to protect my mum and let her know he loved her. He wanted my word on it and I gave it. His last words were garbled, but he fought to get them out. He claimed me the rightful heir and laird of the Clan McLaud. But there would never be any way for me to prove it."

"I am so sorry," Patience said, stunned by the terrible injustice he had suffered at the hands of his own brother. It was unimaginable to her that a brother could do that to another brother. But she had seen many in the Highlands who had allowed the desire for power to corrupt their morals. She was grateful her father had not been one of them.

"So am I," Hunter said, anger punctuating his every word. "Greer took my father from me long before he killed him and for that I will never forgive him. As my father lay dying, unable to speak any longer, I swore to him I would revenge his death. With what little strength he had left, he squeezed my hand and barely nodded his approval, and then he died."

"How horrible for both of you," she said, tears clouding her eyes. "But at least he died a proud man, knowing his son had not spoken falsely or that he was jealous and that his son was a man of his word and would honor him."

Hunter brought her hand to his lips and kissed the back of it. "I do not think I will ever stop feeling as lucky or blessed as I do to have you as my wife."

She smiled. "Give it time, you might change your mind."

Instead of returning her smile with one of his infamous grins, his expression turned serious. "Never. I will always feel lucky and blessed that you are my wife and even more blessed that you love me."

Damn, there he went again tugging at her heart. She went to step away from him for their own good, but he refused to let go of her hand, refused to let her move too far from him. And with one strong tug, he brought her up against him.

She pressed her hands against his chest to keep him at a distance. "I cannot trust myself to be this close to you, since I have an overwhelming urge to devour you. And now is not the time or place for such a wicked thought."

He took hold of her wrist and yanked her arms, spreading them to her sides, so that her chest fell against his. "You tempt me to shirk my duties far too much, wife, but my respect for you as a leader has me holding fast and thinking how I will make it up to you later."

She smiled again. "Promise?"

"Believe me, *mo chridhe*, you have my word on it." He kissed her quick and released her with a slight shove, not trusting himself to keep her close.

Patience was relieved when he released her at a distance. If she remained in his arms, she feared she would make him surrender, not that it would take much to do so, and that had her smile growing.

She forced her smile away, and asked, "No sign of the ghost warriors?"

"None, which makes me wonder if your sister truly has escaped the Dark Dragon and he and his men are now busy hunting for her."

Patience paced in front of her husband. "The more I give it thought, the more plausible it seems."

"You would know better than anyone if Heather was capable of such a feat."

"I think that is what would have helped my sister the most, the ghost warriors thinking my sister too frightened and incapable of escape. Heather may look sweet and kind, but there is a strength to her none see. I sometimes think my father is unfamiliar with the depths of his daughter's strength. The Dark Dragon probably assumes my sister too fearful to do anything but comply with his demands."

"Even in fear there is strength."

Patience stopped pacing. "My sister said the same to Emma and me one day. She told us that we were never to be ashamed of being afraid, for in fear there was strength and knowledge to be learned."

"Your sister is as wise as me. I look forward to meeting her."

Patience's smile returned and she nodded. "I believe Heather will like you."

His infamous grin surfaced. "Of course she will, all women do."

Patience approached him and with a quick jab to his chest said, "Remember one thing, you are now my husband. You belong to me and only me and if you so much as dare look at another woman I," —she jabbed him in the chest again—"why are you laughing? I am serious."

"I know," he said, trying to contain his laughter, "and I love that you are jealous, though believe me when I tell you that you demand enough of me to keep me from wanting any woman but you. Besides, all women pale next to you. I want you and only you and I love you and only you."

Patience planted her hands on her hips. "How is it you always know the right thing to say?"

He straightened up away from the boulder, his shoulders going back, his chest wide, and his chin up. "It is easy when you speak the truth."

"See," she said, wagging her finger at him, "you did it again."

He laughed again. "And I always will, for I will always speak the truth to you." He stepped forward, took hold of her waist and turned her away from him, though kept her in his arms. "The sun rises."

Patience leaned back against her husband and watched as light began to inch its way up past the trees to illuminate the sky in an orangey glow before the sun blazed across the land.

Patience sighed. "Sunrises are beautiful."

"More beautiful when you share it with someone you love," Hunter whispered near her ear and gave her cheek a kiss.

Patience squeezed his hand that rested at her waist.

After basking in the sunlight for a few moments, Hunter said, "We best get the camp moving."

"My thoughts exactly," Patience said and it was not long before everyone was ready to leave. Patience let it be known that they would reach the border of the Dark Dragon's land by sunset if they kept a consistent pace and stopped to rest just once. Their nods and smiles told Patience that they were just as eager as she to get one step closer to home.

Eyes remained alert and hands were never far from their weapons as the troop's pace remained steady throughout the day.

Patience sat by Una under the covering of a large pine when they stopped for a brief rest and to grab whatever food was left available to them. Ewan had taken himself off, probably to see if any of the ghost warriors would contact him and Hunter had gone off for a few moments of privacy, though Patience wondered if he intended to follow Ewan.

Beast came over to her after she sat and plopped down beside her, resting his head on her leg. She rubbed behind his ear and said, "I never properly thanked you for saving my life." The dog moaned and turned his head as if letting her know he wanted another spot rubbed. Patience smiled. "You are a good dog, Beast. Your master will be proud of you."

"He is a good dog," Una agreed. "It took a strong love to send him away so that he would be safe, but then Saundra is a strong woman stuck in a loveless union like far too many women. I feel for my son Rab as well, since he has always loved another and had hoped his father would have approved of the union, but he did not. So, Rab married the woman my husband chose for him. The only difference is that Rab continues to practically live with the woman he loves," —Una shook her head— "I have often wondered if Rab has ever consummated his wedding vows, always hoping that one day he could have the marriage annulled."

"At least they both would be free to live as they please," Patience said, thinking how horrible it would be to be stuck in such a terrible union. She truly was lucky to have wed and fallen in love with Hunter. She could not imagine sharing the intimacy they share with someone she cared naught for or who cared nothing for her.

"Unfortunately, Greer will never allow it. Saundra's marriage to Rab sealed the ties between the McLaud and McDolan clans. Greer made it clear to Rab that he expected the marriage to prevail, though would prefer he delayed any children until Rona got with child. And if she fails to conceive soon, I fear he will find himself another wife."

Patience scrunched her brow. "Are you saying he will—"

"Aye, he will rid himself of his wife with one swift blow and think nothing of it," Una clarified. "Greer is ruthless in his pursuit of power and wealth, and I fear if he is unable to stop you and Hunter from returning home safely that he will devise an excuse to start a war with your clan."

"He will not care that our clans are united?" Patience felt a chill run through her, for she feared Una might be right.

"Not in the least. He will see that the Macinnes clan is blamed for some vicious act against the McLauds, an act that will require retaliation, an act that will begin a war."

Chapter Twenty-nine

Clouds moved in overhead blotting out the sun and turning the day as gray as Patience's thoughts as her horse plodded along the rutted path. Una's words kept repeating in her head, bringing with them the distinct possibility of war for the Clan Macinnes and its allies. Unless, of course, Greer succeeded in killing her and Hunter before they returned home. Then there was Ewan, having informed her upon his return from the woods that the ghost warriors were nowhere to be seen. What truly was happening to her sister?

"There is more than one thing troubling you," Hunter said, riding alongside her. "You did not take note when I rode up beside you several minutes ago. Tell me what so disturbs you that you pay your handsome husband no heed." Hunter grew worried when he saw that his usual teasing did not bring a smile to her face. He reached out and placed a hand on her arm. "Your troubles are heavy, share them with me."

Patience did not hesitate. She told him of her conversation with his mum, and voiced a thought that had nagged her ever since. "You know your brother well. You must have known that our union would delay, but not stop him from doing what seemed to be his plan all along... wage war against the Macinnes clan. So why wed me?"

"To save you."

She shook her head. "Save me?"

"I was not about to let a beautiful woman die."

"Are you telling me that Greer had plans to kill me?"

"He had plans to kill whoever your father sent here to aid the McFarden and make it seem like the Macinnes troop started the war. I had hoped to find some way to prevent the massacre he had planned. When I saw it was you, Donald Macinnes's daughter, I knew there was only one way to save your life and delay my brother's plans, and that was to wed you."

"You were dishonest with me," Patience accused. "You should have told me of your brother's plans."

"Would you have wed me, knowing my brother intended to wage war regardless of our union?"

She was about to shout no, when she stopped and gave it thought.

"When you think about it as you are doing now, you see that there was truly no alternative. Greer would have killed you and your men and plunged your clan into war. This way you had a chance to survive and perhaps somehow still prevent a full scale war."

"And what plans did your brother have for you if we never wed?"

"An accident similar to my father's, I imagine," Hunter said. "No matter what way we view it, joining in marriage was the best thing we could have down to delay and hopefully prevent a war."

"Now I fear even more for the MacFarden safety," she said, thinking of the small, vulnerable clan.

"Do not worry about them. They hold no power, so they are insignificant to Greer. He believes they will soon belong to him and does not worry over them. It is you that became the major pawn in the game when you arrived on his land. He believed his plan would be even more successful than ever, claiming that the daughter of Donald Macinnes started the war."

"Until you announced that we would wed."

"It infuriated him, for the power suddenly shifted to me."

"And you ruined what had become a perfect plan for him with my unexpected presence."

"He is out for blood and will not stop until he gets it," Hunter said.

"I have to get home and warn my father," Patience said, knowing preparations had to be made and allies engaged.

"You do realize that you must delay your search for Heather or chance losing your own life if Greer should find you and use you as a pawn that would start the war between the clans."

"And what of my sister?" she snapped annoyed that he was right. "If she has escaped the Dark Dragon and is on her own, Greer's men could possibly find her. Then what?"

"Greer wants to keep favor with the Dark Dragon. I do not believe he would take the chance and harm her if he found her. And from what you tell me of Heather, would she not be the first to tell you to protect the clan? Besides, we cannot be certain that Heather has escaped the Dark Dragon."

"But I can hope it is so and with Ewan not seeing

a ghost warrior in sight, it is a likely chance. Unless something else goes on that we do not know about. We should reach the border before sunset and we shall see if the Dark Dragon has a message for me then."

"You do realize that my brother most likely has a contingent of men waiting to attack once we leave the Dark Dragon's land."

"I do and I am thinking on what can be done to prevent it."

Hunter grinned. "If you find a solution, then you truly do deserve to be laird of the Clan Macinnes."

"Make certain you tell my father that when you meet him." Patience rose up some on her horse to cast a glance around her. "Our pace has slowed and that will not do." She sat her horse once again and turned to her husband. "That promise you made me earlier might need to hold until we get home. We need to keep focused on the dangers at hand."

"Aye, you are a distraction, thoughts of making love to you come unbidden to me far too often as well as places where we could sneak off to, to share a fast, hard poke."

A sharp tingle hit her between the legs and she had to ask, "And where would that be?"

He nodded to her left. "Just beyond there, behind the trunk of that wide tree. A quick lift off the ground, your legs around my waist, the tree truck to balance against, and a quick slip in, since you are probably already wet and I am already hard and with my mouth on yours to stop you from screaming out in pleasure, I would have you coming in no time, maybe even twice."

"Enough," she snapped. "You are purposely tormenting me."

"And myself as well, though it is one of the ways I will have you when we reach home. You do have sturdy, wide trees, do you not?" he teased.

"Many, and I may just have you try all of them."

He grinned. "Promise?"

"Only if you promise that our first night home we make love in my bed all night long."

"I will not be restricted to only your bed, so I promise we will make love in your bedchamber all night long."

The intensity of his blue eyes, the boldness of his words had her nearly reaching out and dragging him over to the tree.

"You best ride away, *mo chridhe*, or I will satisfy that burning passion in your eyes and the hell to the danger it may bring."

Patience froze for a moment, ready to surrender to him and the danger, then she shook her head and without saying a word rode away.

He fought against the overpowering desire to go after her, yank her off her horse, and take her behind the tree and satisfy both their heated passions. He kept reminding himself it would not be a wise thing to do, though his hard manhood argued otherwise.

Patience had her troop pick up the pace and for the remainder of the ride she kept her distance from her husband. She needed to let her passion ebb and being near him would not allow her to do that. She cursed her attraction to him, feeling it out of control, something a wise warrior did not allow to happen.

At the moment, her thoughts were her enemy,

constantly drifting to her husband and the wickedly wonderful things he did to her body that made her feel... she almost groaned aloud.

It stops. It stops now, she warned herself silently. There were far too many important matters to think about than getting a fast, hard poke from her husband. The thought the image evoked worsened her aching desire and she silently cursed her husband, then herself, then his brother and anyone else who popped into her head.

It was when Heather entered her thoughts that they finally changed. Emma joined in her thoughts as well and she realized just how much she missed her sisters. She would love to talk with them about Hunter and how she felt about him and how he made her feel. She wondered if Emma felt the same way about her husband. Did she enjoy making love with Rogan? Father had said that they loved each other and that Emma was happy. She prayed it was so. Heather and she had always worried that Emma would never find anyone who would accept her and her vast knowledge and penchant to learn, that came along with her. Now, though, it was Heather who was left alone, in more ways than one.

Was she out there now walking through the forest alone, frightened for her safety, worried she would never find her way home? Patience was never more grateful for having forced Heather and Emma to learn how to navigate woods if they should ever get lost. If Heather remained calm, there was a chance she could find her way home.

Patience felt a grip to her heart. With the Dark Dragon and his ghost warriors going after her, not to mention Greer's men and allies searching for her and Hunter, Heather's chance at succeeding was dismal. Still, she had to have hope. It was the only help she could give her sister right now.

The path soon opened to clear, soft rolling hills, and they left the forest to further quicken their pace. It would not be long now before they reached their destination and with thoughts of her sister clearing her mind, she began to devise a plan.

~~~

When they once again came upon woods, they stopped for the night, the sun near to setting. They did not enter it, for if they did they would leave the Dark Dragon's land. They set up camp and settled for the evening and waited for the rabbits, a couple of warriors had hunted, to cook.

Guards were posted as usual and apprehension settled over the men. They all knew that once they entered the woods, there was nothing to prevent the McLauds from attacking. A battle was inevitable and they would be outnumbered.

Hunter sat beside his mum, watching the men cast glances at Patience, sitting speaking with Edward.

"You look worried," Una said, resting a hand on her son's arm.

"They expect a miracle from her," Hunter said angry and turned to his mum. "I want you to leave here with Ewan and his sons in the morning. They will keep you safe. This is not their fight. Greer will not bother to go after you. He will be too busy with us."

"We shall see," his mum said.

"I mean it, Mum," he insisted.

"Look," his mum said, smiling and pointing.

Hunter saw Ewan step out of the woods and hurry over to Patience. He got up and walked over to join them, Beast trotting alongside him and caught his wife's words as he approached.

"The ghost warriors have returned but they make no contact with you?" Patience repeated as if she had not heard Ewan correctly.

"They make their presence known."

"What good does that do me? I want answers."

"They are not ready to give them," Ewan said.

"I do not care," she said and pushed past him.

Ewan took hold of her arm. "You do not mean to confront them, do you?"

Patience yanked her arm free. "I will accept no more excuses or delays. I will have answers now."

Her warriors stood when she positioned herself in the middle of the camp.

"I cross the land border alone," she called out. "Not that I think warriors lie in wait for us, not here, not so close to the Dark Dragon's land. Mind the camp well. I will return shortly."

Hunter fell in step with her, and she stopped. "Did you not hear me?"

"Do you not remember what I told you? I will never again be separated from you? And before you waste a breath arguing with me, know that nothing—absolutely nothing—will stop me from going with you."

Ewan stepped forward. "I go too."

Beast barked as if letting them know he would go as well.

"Very well, but do not get in my way," Patience said, striding forward.

"She is a determined one," Ewan said to Hunter as the two men followed her.

"You mean foolhardy, stubborn, impulsive—"

"Do not forget beautiful," Patience called out over her shoulder.

"I was getting to that," Hunter said.

"It should be first on your list," she corrected.

Ewan laughed. "Just like a woman."

"Not *just* a woman," Hunter said, "a *warrior* woman."

Patience smiled, not that the two men could see it, and said, "You are forgiven."

"And here I was prepared to truly make it up to you," he said teasingly.

"Believe me, husband, you will."

Ewan laughed aloud. "You two are perfect for each other."

"That we are," Patience and Hunter said in unison, and Ewan laughed again.

It did not take long to return to the spot where the ghost warriors had made themselves known, but this time they did not show themselves.

"With their message delivered, I suppose there is nothing else left for them to say," Ewan said.

"What message?" Patience asked annoyed. "That they let us know they are here and yet say nothing? That is no message." She stepped away from the two men and shouted, "I know you can hear me. I want to speak with my sister and know she is safe and unless the Dark Dragon wants blood spilled on his land, he better bring her to me. You have until tomorrow morning." She turned and started walking away.

Ewan caught up with her while Hunter remained a few steps behind to protect her should anyone surprise them. Beast walked beside him, his senses alert and his eyes roaming the land around him.

"You cannot threaten the Dark Dragon," Ewan said.

"Why not? He threatens me." Patience halted abruptly, thinking she saw a shadow pass by. "I know you are watching us." Her shout echoed in the woods. "Blood will spill if you do not give the Dark Dragon my message."

They returned to camp without any further incident and Beast went to Una as did Ewan.

Hunter grabbed his wife by the arm when she went to walk away. "What did you hope to gain by that threat?"

"To turn an enemy into an ally, if only for a short time."

Chapter Thirty

Heavy gray clouds dawned with the day and reflected the somber mood of the camp. All knew that a battle was inevitable and all knew that the small troop would be outnumbered, leaving death on everyone's mind.

Patience sensed her warriors' unease and called them all together. She stood in the middle and spoke with confidence. "You are honorable warriors every one of you and, know now and without doubt, that I will do whatever is necessary to see that you get home safely. You have my word on it."

Nods and smiles circled the camp and the sun peeked through the clouds as if confirming her promise.

As the warriors drifted off, their moods lightened and Hunter approached her. "How can you promise that?"

Patience wrapped her arm around his and walked him away from the camp to a more secluded area. She took a step away from him. "It occurred to me that for some unknown reason the Dark Dragon wants my sister." She shuddered. "I cannot imagine why, nor do I want to, but if Heather has escaped him, then he would be concerned as to her whereabouts, which would mean he would not want war waged in any areas she might be hiding." She turned a smile on him. "So I intend to turn a foe into an ally for the time being and ask for his protection in returning home."

"And if he does not agree?" Hunter asked, though had no doubt his wife would make it so.

"Then I know that he stills holds Heather captive and we wait on his land until reinforcements arrive."

Hunter stepped toward her, his arm reaching out to snag her around her waist and pull her against him. "Your leadership skills amaze me." Her frown disturbed him. "I compliment you and you frown?"

"My father advised me once that most men would not appreciate my exceptional warrior skills and it might be difficult to find me a husband."

Hunter brushed her lips with a kiss. "If you have not noticed, I am not most men."

She chuckled. "That you are not."

"And I am glad that your father had yet to find you a husband, since I am the perfect husband for you." He tucked her closer against him.

"I cannot argue with that," she admitted, resting comfortably against him.

"It takes a wise warrior to know when an argument is futile."

"Or when the truth has been spoken," she said, laying her head on his chest.

Hunter rubbed her back. "You are tied."

"I have no time to be tired, there is much I must see to."

"Your husband being one of them," he teased.

"I will always look after you," she said, slipping her hand inside his shirt to stroke his warm, naked chest.

Hunter braced himself, her gentle strokes arousing him. He warned himself to push her away or soon he would not be able to. But he did not listen to his warnings, her touch felt much too good.

Patience wished they were home, locked away in her bedchamber where no one would disturb them. "I cannot wait to return home."

"My thoughts as well," he said, thinking how he would keep her locked away in her bedchamber for a day or two or more. "We may never leave your bedchamber."

She looked up at him. "I would not mind."

"We think much the same."

"Then you know I ache terribly for you right now," she whispered.

"Not as bad as I do for you."

"I would not wager on that," she said with a laugh.

"Patience!"

She jumped away from her husband the sharp sound of her name and turned to see Ewan waving her over.

Hunter followed along with her.

Patience's eyes followed Ewan's nod to the edge of the woods, where stood a line of ghost warriors, their faces painted white.

Her warriors were in formation, ready to fight and she ordered, "Stay as you are." She walked toward the ghost warriors and one stepped forward. She stopped a few feet from him.

"You will return home. You will be contacted with the time and place to meet with your sister."

She knew then that Heather had escaped the Dark Dragon. She fought to keep the joy from her voice and the thrill from her green eyes. She took a quick step forward, jabbing her finger in the air at the warrior who remained frozen in place. "I warned him blood would be spilled if I could not see my sister and it will be if I am forced to return home. There are those who wish to see me, my husband, and my entire troop dead. They will hunt us down like animals and see us slaughtered. The blood spilled whether on his land or not is still on his hands." She straightened her shoulders and held her head high. "If the Dark Dragon wants me to return home, then I demand his warriors escort us." She let her remarks settle in for a moment, then took a step back. "I will wait for his answer."

The line of warriors retreated into the woods, Patience watching them merge with the shadows.

She heard the men mumbling behind her and as she turned, Edward approached.

"You embrace the enemy, something I would have never imagined doing," Edward said with admiration. "The men are impressed and relieved. They now feel they have a good chance of surviving our return home."

"And so they shall."

"You are that confident that the Dark Dragon will agree?" Edward asked.

"I have no doubt he will," she said with a firm nod. "Have the men hunt for food and settle in for the day. We can all use a day of rest."

Edward smiled, "Aye, that we can, though it will be good to get home."

"You amaze me," Hunter said after Edward walked away.

"And here I thought you were amazing me."

Hunter laughed. "Is your mind forever on coupling?"

She felt her cheeks heat red and she turned away.

Hunter grabbed her arm and turned her to face him. "I did not mean to embarrass you. I love how hungry you are for me, for I feel the same for you."

She drifted closer to him and kept her voice low. "Is it right for me to feel this way or am I being sinful?"

"I love how sinful you can be," he teased and kissed her cheek.

She gave him a playful punch to the arm. He winced, though it was she who should be wincing, since her fist had hit hard muscle and stung.

"And we are going to continue being sinful for as long as we live."

"Promise?" she whispered her lips close to his.

"You have my word, wife."

"Patience!"

She turned, annoyed at being interrupted again and was surprised to see Ewan, nodding once again at the edge of the woods. There stood a lone ghost warrior and Patience walked over to him, her hand pressing against her husband's chest before she did to let him know she would do this alone.

Hunter let her go, but remained close enough to follow quickly if necessary. He would never take the chance again of letting her out of his sight. He watched and waited, prepared to do whatever was necessary to keep his wife safe.

"We will see you home," the warrior said.

And before he turned to disappear once again into the forest, Patience asked, "My sister?"

"In time."

"I have his word on it?" she asked.

"You will see your sister again," the warrior said as if he had just decreed it and turned, the forest swallowing him up.

Patience stood there, not sure what to make of his response. The warrior seemed confident that she would see Heather again. Had his confidence been renewed because Heather had been found? If so why would the Dark Dragon have his men follow her troop home? Could he want her as far away from her sister as possible?

Frustrated at her chaotic thoughts, she swerved around and walked right into her husband.

He grabbed her shoulders to stop her from toppling over. "Disturbing news or thoughts?"

She shook her head. "I cannot be sure, though the ghost warriors will follow us home. It is my sister's situation that worries me. I cannot be sure if she has escaped, and I fear more than ever for her safety."

"She will do well."

"You cannot know that."

"I know that there is a part of you in her and that is all she needs to survive."

She hugged him, then stepped back. "I do love you." Then she walked off and called her men together. "We have the added protection of the ghost warriors on our way home. We rest today and leave at first light tomorrow." Patience surprised Hunter when she turned to him and said, "Is there anything you would like to add."

Hunter stepped forward. "My brother and his cohorts do not fight fair, be prepared for anything."

"Now rest for the day, for we will travel hard and fast starting tomorrow and God willing, we will be home in four days' time."

The men wandered off smiling to sit around the various campfires, while some prepared to go hunting and others saw to caring for their weapons.

"Why wait the day? Why not leave now?" Hunter asked as they walked off together.

"I am hoping that word was received of our plight and that Macinnes warriors are on their way or the MacThore clan and that we will meet up with them. I will rest easier having more warriors around."

"And will you rest today as you instruct your warriors to do?" Hunter asked.

"Your grin tells me that you already know the answer."

His grin grew. "I am shocked that you do not pay heed to your own advice."

"Tease me all you want, but it is what makes me worthy of being laird."

"Your father must recognize your exceptional skills," he said and took her hand to walk her over to a fallen branch where they could sit.

Patience had to laugh as she sat beside him. "It would be impossible for him not to since they were evident from the moment I took hold of a weapon."

"And when was that?" Hunter asked curious to learn anything he could about his wife.

"According to my da, it was when I was four years and I picked up a stick and brandished it at someone who was teasing me. After that my da says he could not keep anything out of my hands that could be used as a weapon. He finally relented and had a small wooden sword fashioned for me." She laughed again. "My father's warriors were forever chasing me away from the practice field. They told me repeatedly that lassies do not belong there, it was not proper, and I was to stay away."

"And, of course, you did not listen," Hunter said, thinking that when they had a daughter he wanted her to be as brave, resilient, and beautiful as her mum.

She laughed again. "I haunted them. My father was so upset with me that when I was about ten years he told me that if I could best his best warrior in a sword fight, then I could train with his warriors."

Hunter looked at her skeptical. "A ten year old lass could never best a warrior."

Patience grinned with pride. "I did."

"How?"

"I knew the warrior my da would choose and I knew his weakness and used it against him."

Hunter scrunched his brow. "This I must hear."

"My father chose his best friend and best warrior James. I knew at first he would tease me and let me think I might best him, and then he would knock my sword from my hand with one easy blow and stand over me as if about to deliver the final blow, teaching me a lesson and proving I was not fit to train as a warrior."

Hunter waited anxiously to hear the outcome.

"When he did as I expected, I fell to my knees, my head bowed as if in defeat. I heard the warriors that circled us laughing and snickering amongst themselves, not a one of them paying attention to me while they reveled in their humor. James moved to stand in front of me and raised his sword and as he did I swiftly placed the dagger I had slipped from my boot and stuck it between his legs and told him that I would cut off his balls if he did not drop the sword and surrender to me."

Hunter stared at her speechless, his mouth hanging open.

"He looked at me the same way you are looking at me right now," she said with a laugh.

"What did your father do?"

"He was furious, but James came to my defense. He told my da that if I had enough courage to do as I did that I deserved to train with his warriors, and so my training began."

"I am curious as to what was James's weakness?" Hunter asked.

"Me," she said with a thump to her chest. "He made the mistake of thinking of me as the lass that was like a daughter to him, instead of a foe that was out for the kill."

"You are more than worthy of being laird of your clan... you deserve the title and all that goes with it," Hunter said. "And I will make that clear to your father."

"I do appreciate that, but it will be my father's decision as to who becomes the next laird of the Clan Macinnes."

"But if not you, who?"

Patience shrugged. "Possibly you or whoever weds Heather, since I think my father would put more stock into the laird being a man rather than a woman."

"My father spoke highly of your father, insisting he was a fair and good man. And since he sent you to settle this dispute, I would say he has confidence in you and respects your abilities. I would not be so quick to judge that he would deny you what you have earned."

Patience smiled and took hold of her husband's hand. "No matter the circumstances, I am truly glad I wed you."

Hunter leaned in close. "As I have repeatedly said, wife, "We think much alike." He kissed her slow and easy and she melted against him.

A shout of her name brought them apart.

"I will be so glad when we are finally home," Patience said, annoyed at being interrupted again.

"Again we think alike, wife," Hunter said with the same annoyance.

She stood, releasing his hand reluctantly. "Later we will spend time together?"

"Aye, we will and I will kill anyone who interrupts us."

Patience laughed. "I think your threatening look alone will frighten them off."

"Then I will wear it the rest of the day, so all stay clear."

Patience's soft laughter continued as she shook her head. "You are far too congenial to wear a scowl all day."

Hunter stood and wrapped his arm around her waist. "Are you telling me that I am not a feared warrior?"

"You are not the common warrior," she said, laying a hand to his chest. "You do more damage with words than you do with weapons and that in itself is a remarkable talent."

He grinned. "My tongue is talented."

She punched him softly in the chest. "There you go tempting me again."

"It does not take much to tempt you. I sometimes think that I only need look at you and you become aroused."

"You know me well."

"I intend to get to know you even better," he said, nuzzling her neck with tender kisses.

Her name was shouted again and she cursed softly.

"My sentiments exactly," he agreed and stepped away from her, fearing if he lingered he would not let her go.

"Later, husband," she said as if declaring a declaration and hurried off before she changed her mind or before he stopped her.

Hunter watched her go, wishing that tomorrow was here and they were on their way home. He intended to make certain that they kept a fast pace, for once home they would have privacy and she would be all his. At least that was his hope, though he feared that somehow his brother might find a way to interfere.

Chapter Thirty-one

The small troop left the Dark Dragon's land at sunrise the next morning, each and every one of them, including Beast, keeping keen eyes on the changing landscape around them. Few exchanged words, most too intent on what might lurk beyond the bend or over the small rise to be occupied with idle chatter.

Ewan had agreed with Hunter that Una should leave with his sons and return to his home where she would be safe until this matter was finally settled. Una had not been the only one to disagree, Ewan's sons did as well and so it was settled that they would stay and lend their swords should it prove necessary.

Hunter had no doubt it would prove necessary. His brother would not allow this opportunity to pass, though when the ghost warriors made themselves known Greer would have second thoughts, and that worried him even more.

"Your silence and scowl tells me it is you who is now having troubling thoughts," Patience said, breaking the silence that hung heavily around them.

"I am concerned over Greer's response when he discovers that the Dark Dragon's warriors will come to our defense."

"If he wishes to stay in good graces with the infamous warrior, he will have no recourse but to retreat."

"Then his anger will spark and ignite into a fiery

rage, and there is no telling what he will do to see his plan reach fruition."

"One thing at a time," Patience cautioned. "Once home, we can seek my father's council on the situation. After all, with the both of us safely home, what could Greer possibly do that would be serious enough to plunge us into war?"

"That is what concerns me most... what would he do?"

They continued traveling, though mostly in silence and when they camped that night, neither slept well. The next day was more of the same and by the third day, only a day away from reaching home, anxiousness and determination prevailed thanks to the speech Patience had given her men at sunrise.

She had not dwelled on an impending battle, but rather on how good it would be to get home and see loved ones again and finally have tasty food to eat, which had brought laughter. She talked about how the crops would be sprouting, gardens flourishing, animals giving birth and a clan that would be overjoyed to welcome them home. She had given them a taste of home and the determination to get there.

It was when they approached a forest, thick with foliage, that everyone grew apprehensive, for it was a good place for an attack.

Hunter turned to his wife riding beside him. "Stay close."

Patience smiled. "Do not worry, I will protect you."

"I have no doubt you will, wife, since we have only one day before your bedchamber welcomes us for a full day, perhaps two."

Patience was about to respond when Edward approached them.

"Ghost warriors have been spotted, many of them," Edward said.

Patience was not surprised. "They want not only us to know they are about, but they want Greer's men to know as well. Hopefully, their presence will ward off an attack."

They day passed without incident and by the time the group was camped for the night apprehension had dissipated and excitement was high that they would arrive home tomorrow.

Patience and Hunter joined Una, Ewan, and his sons to enjoy fish caught in a nearby stream. They talked and laughed at Noble's humorous tales and just as Patience and Hunter were ready to seek their blanket for the night, Beast started whining and pacing. Before anyone could discover what bothered him, he took off into the woods as if the hounds of hell were on his tail.

Una went to go after him, but Hunter stopped her. "Leave him, Mum, we do not know what he senses out there in the dark. It would be dangerous for any of us to go after him."

Suddenly vicious barking ripped through the air.

Hunter saw the look on his wife's face and knew what she was about to do, so he blazed ahead of her into the woods. Ewan and his sons followed.

Patience was already on the move, silently berating her husband for being faster than her to react, as she summoned a few warriors and headed in after them.

They all followed the dog's continuous barking. He sounded as if he was trying to keep a foe at bay. It hit Patience then, could he have sensed her sister and was keeping the ghost warriors away from her? She picked up her speed and she was glad her warriors had had the good sense to light torches, the darkness suddenly pierced by the glowing flames.

Her heart slammed against her chest when she saw her husband bent over the body of a woman and Beast continuing to bark and warn off the ghost warriors who attempted to approach the prone woman, as if they also were anxious to learn her identity.

Patience hurried to her husband's side as he turned the woman over.

"Saundra?" Hunter said shocked, and gently brushed her hair away from her pale face.

Once again Patience felt her heart slam against her chest only this time in disappointment.

Beast's barking halted abruptly and when Patience looked up, she saw the ghost warriors receding into the darkness. They had been curious as to her identity, which lead Patience to believe that they did continue to search for Heather.

Hunter lifted Saundra into his arms. "We need to get her back to camp."

Beast trotted protectively beside Hunter, growling now and again if anyone else got too close to him and his master.

Una hurried over to them once they entered camp to see to Saundra's care and directed her son to place the unconscious woman on the blanket by the campfire. Beast lay beside his master, daring anyone with a snarl to move him.

With some tender ministrations by Una and Beast licking her face, Saundra's eyes began to flutter open.

A gentle smile crossed her face as her hands reached out to grab the large dog around the neck and pull him to her to bury her face in his fur. "Please do not let this be a dream," she murmured.

"It is not a dream; you are safe now," Una said.

Saundra's eyes opened and tears gathered in them. "Una, I am so relieved to see you."

"What are you doing here and however did you get here?" Una asked perplexed.

"Aye, we are all curious to know what happened to you," Patience said, dropping down beside Una.

Hunter hunched down by Beast. "We are all pleased to see that you are well, Saundra, and are eager to learn of your ordeal."

Patience looked at her husband and realized it was not only charm he possessed, but a caring heart.

Saundra stretched her hand out to Una and the woman took firm hold of it. "About a day after you all left, Greer summoned me and wanted to know why he had not seen Beast around. I got the impression that he was looking to harm him and I was so relieved that I had sent him with you."

"What did you tell him?" Hunter asked.

She turned tear-filled eyes on him. "I told him that Beast had taken off and had not returned." She shivered. "He smiled as if I had given him a wonderful gift, and then he told me that I was to go with a group of warriors and find him and not come home until I did."

"Rab never objected to Greer sending me away

and I knew why. My husband knew I would never return home. It was when I heard the warriors talking one night when they thought I was asleep that the deed could not be done until they reached Macinnes land." She quieted a moment, then continued. "They talked about the fun they would have with me and that night I made my escape. My only choice was to seek refuge with the Macinnes clan."

"And you have it," Patience said. "You are now under the protection of the Macinnes clan."

A tear fell from the corner of her eye and Beast was quick to lick it away.

"Oh, how I have missed you, Beast," Saundra said and hugged the dog again. He whined and licked her face some more, letting her know he felt the same.

"You rest," Patience said. "We reach my home, now your new home, tomorrow."

"Thank you," Saundra said her arms firm around the big dog, his head resting on her chest. She would be going nowhere without him.

Patience stood and asked before leaving, "How did you ever avoid the ghost warriors?"

"I traveled at night after having observed that they traveled mostly during the day."

"You did not meet up with anyone else along the way, a blond woman perhaps?"

Saundra shook her head. "I saw no one; I did not want to. I felt safer that no one could see me at night, especially with there being no full moon yet."

"Sleep well," Patience said. "I will see you in the morning." Patience gave a nod to her husband to let him know she wanted to talk with him.

Hunter exchanged a few words with Saundra, and

then bid her good-night and joined his wife.

"Your brother was not taking any chances. Besides having us killed, he would also make it seem as if his brother's wife had been abused and killed by the Macinnes clan. He is intent on declaring war on my clan."

"And it makes one wonder what he will do when he discovers that both plans failed."

~~~

The Macinnes warriors woke with smiles and an eagerness to be on their way. Today they would arrive home and the sooner the better.

Patience approached Ross McCuil. "You are a fine warrior Ross McCuil."

"I thank you, Patience Macinnes, and I am honored by the compliment from such a skilled and honorable warrior."

Patience acknowledged his tribute with a nod. "I need a favor of you."

"Anything."

Patience smiled. "Your response proves you are not only a superior warrior but a confident one."

"He only lacks confidence with the lassies," Noble said, walking up to his brother and giving Ross's shoulder a firm squeeze.

Ross shook his head and yanked free of his brother's grasp. "Go away, Noble, this does not concern you."

"Anything that concerns my little brother concerns me."

"Not this," Patience said. "Now leave us."

Noble's brow went up and he was about to speak when Patience held her hand up. "Do not waste your words or time on me. This matter is between me and your brother. Take your leave now."

Noble looked to Ross as if waiting for him to come to his defense. Ross folded his arms across his chest and glared at him. Noble walked off mumbling.

Ross turned to Patience with a smile. "How may I help you?"

"Saundra has suffered a terrible ordeal and she needs to feel safe and protected. I would like you to see to keeping her safe and also to let her ride with you on your horse for the remainder of the journey home."

"I would be pleased to help her in any way I can."

Patience held her hand out to him. "I am indebted to you."

Ross gave her hand a shake, surprised by the strength of it. "Then perhaps when the time is right we can talk about me joining your elite warriors."

Patience nodded. "That we can."

"One other thing," Ross said, "I do not lack confidence with the lassies. It is that I show no interest in the lassies Noble tries to force on me that leaves him believing his own foolish words."

Patience laughed. "Come, I will introduce you to Saundra and let her know that you will look after her as long as necessary."

Hunter caught up with them, his arm catching his wife around her waist. "What did you do to Noble? He tells his father that you have turned Ross a trader."

"He is upset because he has come to realize that his little brother is not his little brother any longer, but a grown man," Patience said.

Ross stopped for a moment, his eyes wide, then hurried along with them. "I never thought of that."

"I am guilty of the same myself," she admitted.

"You are?" Hunter and Ross said in unison.

"I am," Patience repeated. "I was overly protective of Emma, my youngest sister, and when I found out she married, I was furious. I feared she was stuck in a forced marriage. My father told me she was very happy and loved her husband, but at first I did not believe him. It took me a while to realize that it was not my father I did not believe, for Emma would never lie to him about a thing as important as her marriage. It was the fact that I had lost my little sister. She was a married woman now with a husband who loved her. I will miss her greatly, for she has been, and will continue to be, my loving sister." She sighed. "Life changes whether we want it to or not."

Hunter hugged her close. "You have me now."

"Not the same as a sister," —she grinned— "though there are some advantages." Patience eased out of his arm to walk ahead and speak with Saundra.

"You are a lucky man, Hunter," Ross said with envy. "She is a fine woman."

"Aye, I am and one day you will meet a fine woman as well."

The two men joined Patience and she turned to Ross. "Ross, I would like to introduce you to Saundra McLaud."

"It is a pleasure," Ross said with a bow of his head.

"It is kind of you to take on the unfortunate task of protecting me," Saundra said.

Ross stepped forward, closer to Saundra. "It is not unfortunate and not a task, but an honor to help such a lovely lady in distress."

Patience stepped back, tugging her husband along with her. When they were a few feet away, she said, "He charms a woman almost as skillfully as you do."

"I always knew I liked Ross the best," Hunter said with a laugh. "Now I know why."

~~~

Anticipation grew as the day wore on and they got closer and closer to home. Patience could not wait and it was not only because she would have her husband alone to her in her bedchamber, but also because she missed home and her clan.

She was surprised that they had not come upon warriors from the MacTavish clan or that they had not met up with Macinnes warriors, but time had been limited.

By late afternoon the village and keep came into sight and relief and joy spread throughout the group. Their pace was quickened without an order from Patience.

Patience felt her heart swell as soon as she passed through the gates.

"Finally home," Hunter said, seeing her face light with joy.

She stretched her hand out to him and he grabbed it. "All is well now."

Hunter nodded, though did not feel as confident as she was. Greer had not gotten the chance to successfully attack them, but he was not finished with them yet.

Chapter Thirty-two

It was the usual chaotic scene when warriors returned home after a long absence. Loved ones rushed to greet the warriors and tears of joy that all returned safely flowed freely.

Patience had duties to see to before she went to see her father. While she was looking forward to seeing him, she also had the task of introducing her new husband to him, and she was not sure how he would react to that, especially since she had married Hunter out of duty to her clan, something she had been adamant about not doing. She had told her father repeatedly that she would wed who and when she wanted to.

She instructed servants to prepare rooms for the guest and more permanent quarters for Saundra and to let them know that Beast was welcome in the keep at all times. But first and foremost, a good, tasty meal needed preparing since most would come to the Great Hall to celebrate the warriors' return.

After orders were given and guests settled, Patience found her husband sitting at the table by the large hearth in the Great Hall with Ewan and his sons.

"It is time for you to meet my da," she said.

"A good man," Ewan said, raising his tankard of ale and his sons joining in the salute.

Hunter raised his as well, took a swallow, and stood. "Then it is best we do not keep him waiting."

He went to his wife's side and, with hands clasped, they left the room.

"I am not sure how my father is fairing, so—"

"We will take it slow," Hunter said and knocked on the door they had stopped at.

Maura opened the door and greeted them with a smile. Patience quickly introduced her to Hunter, then asked, "How is my da feeling?"

"He is feeling well and has been eager to see you since learning of your arrival," Maura said and stepped aside for them to enter.

"Finally," her father called out from a chair by the hearth and stretched his arms out to her.

She hurried over to him and threw her arms around his neck and was so happy when he hugged her tight. It meant his strength was returning and it also reminded her of when she was young and how tight he used to hug her and make her feel so safe and protected. And it was wonderful to feel like that little lass again, if only for a moment, and have all her troubles melt away.

A tear tickled at the corner of her one eye, but she refused to let it fall. She reluctantly left his arms and stood tall, her shoulders drawn back. "Da, there is someone I want you to meet." She held her hand out to Hunter.

He stepped forward, taking his wife's hand and gripping it firmly.

"Da, this is Hunter McLaud—"

"Kevin McLaud's youngest son," her father said his brow knitting slowly as he looked to his daughter.

"And my husband," she said.

Her father looked back and forth from her to

Hunter. "What has happened to bring this marriage about?"

"Possible war with the Clan McLaud," Patience said.

Her father looked to Hunter. "Please leave us while I speak with my daughter."

Hunter was about to do as he asked when Patience said, "Hunter is a good husband and an honorable man, and surprisingly I have fallen in love with him. So whatever is to be said, will be said with him by my side."

Hunter was shocked speechless. His wife loved him even more than he imagined she did. He quickly found his voice and said, "It is the same for me, sir. Your daughter stole my heart and I love her more than words could say, and I would give my life to keep her safe."

Patience turned to him. "Did I not tell you I would protect you? I do not need you giving your life for me—as gallant as the gesture is—I am more than capable of taking care of myself and further more—"

Hunter grabbed her around the waist and swung her around in front of him to kiss her soundly. He was pleased when he heard her father chuckle.

Patience was not as amused, though his kiss had aroused her. "That is not proper—"

"Proper or not," Hunter said interrupting her, "I wanted to show your father that I could silence you when necessary."

She was about to explode at him when his teasing grin surfaced. She smiled herself and stepped to his side, his arm remaining around the back of her waist. "As you can see, Da, he makes not only a good husband, but a wise one."

Her father laughed. "He does at that and I am pleased you are happy with him." He extended his hand to Hunter. "And I am pleased to welcome you to the clan and call you son."

Hunter took the man's hand and was surprised by the strength of it as they shook. With her father having been so ill, Hunter had not expected him to be so strong. "Thank you, sir."

"Donald," her father offered and Hunter nodded.

"There are important matters we need to discuss, Da," Patience said.

"Can they not wait until you have eaten and rested?" her father asked.

"I am afraid not," Patience said. "One matter concerns Heather."

Her father's hand went to his chest. "Do not tell me—"

"No, Da, it is not what you think," Patience assured him quickly. "The news is good. We believe Heather has escaped the Dark Dragon and hopefully she is making her way home."

"What?" he said, bolting out of his chair.

Patience stepped back, forgetting what an impressive size her father once was and still was.

"Are you telling me that Heather is out there all on her own?" he shouted.

"I believe she is, though I cannot be sure," Patience said, staring at her father and seeing the strong, imposing man she remembered he once was, then suddenly he faded before her eyes, his face growing pale and his body slumping.

Hunter got to him before he could collapse and

helped him to sit in his chair.

Her father shook his head. "Heather will never survive on her own."

That had been Patience's fear and while she still feared for her sister's safety, Hunter had made her see that Heather possessed the same unwavering strength as Patience and Emma.

"I am confident that Heather can survive on her own," Patience said, "though I intend to search for her after a day's rest."

"You are not going anywhere," her father ordered sharply.

She was startled by his adamant response.

"You have much to tell me. Why you wed Hunter? Why a guest has been given permanent quarters in the keep along with her dog? Why Hunter's mother is also here? And why Ewan McCuil and his two sons are with you."

Patience was not surprised that her father knew all that was going on in the keep since her return. His eyes and ears had always been everywhere and that had not changed.

She went to speak, but her father silenced her with a raised hand. "I have not the strength or desire to speak any longer. I would worry, but I would have no doubt that you or Emma would survive if either of you were out there on your own. But my heart is heavy with concern for Heather. Now leave me to rest. We will speak in the morning."

Patience felt as if she had disappointed her father, but then she had disappointed herself by not finding her sister. It was her fault that Heather was out there somewhere on her own, confronting danger with no one to help her. At the moment, there was not much she could do to make it up to her father, but she did feel the need to ask, "Is there anything I can do for you, Da?"

Her father shook his head. "Maura will see to my care."

His response stung Patience's heart, for she would have done anything for him. "I will see you in the morning."

Hunter took his wife's hand and walked with her to the door.

"Patience," her father called out and she turned eagerly. "Make certain you see to the care of our warriors and make certain to offer a salute to their service while I speak with Hunter privately for a moment." He scowled when she looked about to speak. "Do not argue with me on this."

Patience's green eyes blazed with fury and she left the room, slamming the door shut behind her.

Hunter went over to her father.

"Make certain that she does not leave here tonight and begin searching for her sister."

"I would never let her put herself in such danger," Hunter said.

"Good."

"I would go with her if she chose to go." Hunter held up his hand to ward off any response. "Patience has sacrificed much for you and her clan, so heed me well, sir, when I say not now or ever will you again speak to my wife as if she was a child. She is a strong warrior deserving of your respect. Now I will take my leave and join my wife who should be the one deserving of the recognition you expect her to give your warriors, though it was not necessary to tell her so, she would have honored them with a toast anyway."

Hunter turned and left her father staring after him.

Hunter fought back the fury stirring inside him. How dare her father speak to his wife that way, if the man had not been so ill he would have called him to task for it. He made his way downstairs and into the Great Hall, entering just as Patience finished her speech to the packed room and raised her tankard high.

Cheers rang out, and then she ordered everyone to enjoy the delicious food they had sorely missed while away. Not a one of them hesitated, they dug into the numerous platters with gusto.

Patience walked over to her husband as soon as she caught his eye, wrapped her arm around his and walked with him to the dais. Once they were seated, their tankards filled, she turned and looked at him.

They had come a long way in a short time in trusting each other. His wife knew without asking that he would tell her what her father had to say to him, just as she knew he would not stop her from searching for her sister, though he would join her.

"You father wanted me to make certain you would not go off this evening in search of your sister. I informed him that I would never let you do that."

A fire sparked in Patience's green eyes, then she smiled. "Of course not, you would go with me."

Hunter laughed. "You know me too well, wife."

"Well enough to know you will share with me what more was said."

He took her hand. "Know that I will defend you

whether it is your father, sisters, or warriors who dare treat you wrongly." He shook his finger at her when she went to argue. "Do not ask me to hold my tongue when it comes to your family, for I will not do so. I will speak my piece whenever necessary."

"Why was it necessary?" she asked with resignation.

"Your father spoke to you as a child when he should have addressed you with the respect a true warrior deserves. I let him know that I would not tolerate him speaking to you like that ever again. I think he understands now how devoted we are to each other."

"I appreciate and admire your courage in defending me against my father," —she smiled—"but you may find yourself doing it often since I often do as I please and deal with the consequences later."

"Then your father's bluster serves little purpose."

"I think that is what angers him the most. He knows his threats and orders will wound me, but only for a short time. Then I will do as I please." Her brow narrowed. "What truly surprised me was that he ordered me not to search for my sister. I simply cannot understand why, when he appeared so upset by the news."

"I do agree with you on that."

"It is almost as if he knows something we do not," she said, shaking her head. "It makes no sense."

"And probably makes even less sense being you are tired from our long journey." Hunter leaned closer to his wife. "You need to seek your bedchamber as soon as possible."

She laughed softly. "That *we* do."

A rough cough broke them apart and Patience smiled at Ross standing in front of the dais, his arm wrapped around Saundra. She looked much improved, having scrubbed the dirt from her face, and brushed the debris out of her hair and off her garments, most of all though, she wore a smile, something Patience had never seen on her.

"I have brought Lady McLaud to sup with you," Ross said.

Hunter stood. "You both must join us."

Ross escorted Saundra to her seat next to Hunter and he took a seat next to Patience. Ewan and Una also joined them with Una sitting next to Ross and Ewan taking the seat beside Saundra.

Conversation flowed easily as did wine and ale. Food was replenished often, Hunter, Ewan and Ross continually extolling the delicious fare. What was most interesting to Patience though, was how Ross and Saundra could not stop looking and smiling at each other.

So, it was no surprise when Ross said, "I will remain here, with your permission of course," —he bobbed his head at Patience— "and be Saundra's protector as long as necessary."

"I am sure Patience has a warrior that can see to Saundra," Ewan said, reaching for another piece of the tasty dark bread.

All but Ewan saw how Saundra's smile vanished instantly.

"True enough," Patience said, "though I think the decision should be Saundra's, not mine. What say you, Saundra?"

A slight blush tinged Saundra's cheeks and she

lowered her head for a moment. "If it is permissible, I would prefer Ross was the one to see to my protection. Though, it has only been a brief time that he has taken on the chore, he has made me feel safer than I have ever felt."

"And I will continue to make certain you remain safe," Ross said.

Ewan went to speak, but Una was quick to ask, "Could you come over by me a moment, Ewan, there is something I wish to ask you?"

He was out of the chair quickly and Ross stood just as quickly, saying, "Take my seat, and I will take yours." He did not wait for his father to agree. He hurried past him and eagerly took the empty chair beside Saundra.

Una and Ewan were soon huddled in conversation and when Ewan's head jerked around to stare at Saundra and Ross smiling and talking, their heads closer than they realized, Ewan shook his head.

Hunter leaned his head down to whisper in his wife's ear. "This can prove to be a troublesome situation. Saundra is Rab's wife and he can demand her return."

"One thing at a time," Patience said with a sigh that quickly turned to a yawn.

"You are exhausted," Hunter said loud enough for all at the dais to hear.

"You need rest and a good night's sleep," Una said like a mother concerned for her child.

"Una is right," Saundra said, "You have neglected your own needs for others. It is time you see to your own care."

Hunter smiled. Saundra always had a generous

heart and he was pleased that she was free of his family, though he feared it would not be for long.

Hunter stood and held his hand out to his wife. She took it and after everyone at the dais bid her good night, she and Hunter walked to the staircase. The pounding of fists on the tables had them both turning around and when they did every one of her warriors rose to their feet and raised their tankards high.

Patience held her head high and laid her fisted hand to her chest, then bobbed her head, thanking them for the recognition they bestowed on her.

The warriors let out a resounding roar that followed Hunter and her all the way up the stairs.

Once in her bedchamber, Patience collapsed back on the bed, her arms spread wide, her legs dangling off the edge. She had not realized how truly exhausted this ordeal had left her. She had never felt so depleted of strength or felt her body ache so badly. It was as if by entering the sanctity of her bedchamber that she felt free enough to collapse under the weight of her responsibilities and give herself a reprieve from them.

Hunter stood by the side of the bed glancing down at her, thinking how the unrelenting ache in his loins had him wanting to tear both their garments off and make love to her. But the concerned husband warned him against it, and so he found himself saying, "You need sleep."

"I need you." She stretched her hand out to him and she fought back the yawn trying to surface, but lost the battle.

"You prove my point," Hunter said annoyed that his growing arousal was urging him otherwise.

"You promised," she said and hated that she sounded like a petulant child.

Hunter hunched down beside the bed, taking her hand and kissing it. "I ached to make love to you, but it is not what you need right now. You need sleep."

"I need you," she said on another yawn.

"As you wish," Hunter said, seeing her fighting to keep her eyes open. "Let me get you out of your garments."

"You first."

"Very well," he said and took his time removing every piece of his clothing so that by the time he was completely naked, her eyes were closed.

He smiled and reached down to ease her out of her garments and was surprised when her eyes popped open.

"I fear it will have to be a quick one tonight," she mumbled. "So tired."

She tried to help get her clothes off and he had to smile at her laughable efforts, though he admired her attempts to make certain she had her way... with him.

He settled her in his arms beneath the soft blanket when he finished and when she woke again, he stroked her breasts and teased her nipples and she sighed with satisfaction, and her eyes closed once again.

It was not long before she was sound asleep, while he lay wide awake.

"Tomorrow," he mumbled. "Tomorrow they would not leave this room."

Chapter Thirty-three

Patience woke to find herself alone in bed. She bolted up, looking around the room and seeing that she truly was alone. Where was her husband? How long had she slept? And why hadn't he woken her? And mostly importantly why had he not kept his promise to her and made love to her all night? She shook her head, knowing the answer. She had been too tired to simply disrobe, how then would she have ever been strong enough to make love.

Annoyed at the myriad of questions plaguing her, she got out of bed. She was glad to find the usual bucket of water, left daily by a servant, being warmed by the hearth. She quickly scrubbed herself and donned clean clothes, having seen that her other garments had already been removed for washing.

With her hair tied back and feeling refreshed, she made her way to her father's room. Maura was just coming out and when the woman placed a finger to her lips, she knew her father was either sleeping or was not feeling well.

"He had a difficult night," Maura whispered as she drew near.

Guilt washed over Patience, feeling she had been the cause of it.

"I will let you know when he feels well enough to talk with you. Right now, sleep is the best thing for him."

Patience nodded. Disappointed, she went to the Great Hall. Finding it empty, she realized that she had slept much later than she had realized. She had always been an early riser, greeting the dawn more times than not. It annoyed her that she had wasted the morning in sleep.

Servants in the Great Hall hurried to get her food, but she ordered them to remain at their tasks and went to the kitchen. She grabbed a piece of bread and cheese, to the dismay of the cook who argued that she should sit and eat a solid breakfast as the woman had scolded since Patience had been young.

She gave Balia, the cook, a kiss and a hug as she had always done after snatching food from the kitchen and told her how she looked forward to the noon meal.

"And it is something special and filling I will be making you," Balia shouted with a smile as Patience scurried out of the kitchen.

She found her husband by accident or perhaps it was more by like minds. He was in the stable seeing to his horse and Patience had gone there to see to her stallion.

Hunter grinned when he saw her. "I thought for sure you would sleep until noon, you slept so soundly, though I did fear your snoring might wake you."

"I do not snore," she said.

"You do, though not loud, softly."

He wore his plaid and boots, nothing more and a fine sweat had broken out across his skin, accenting his muscles with a fine sheen. He was much too appealing and she found herself growing aroused.

"Why did you not wake me this morning?" she demanded.

He laid the pitchfork he held to the side, away from the freshly cleaned stall and ran his forearm across his brow, the muscles in his arm growing taut. "You needed sleep."

"I needed you," she said, biting at her lips for sounding as if she begged him.

"It appears you still do," he said and walked over to her, grabbed her around the waist, and hefted her up against him.

Her arms went around his neck, her lips went to his, and between her legs turned damp.

He held her firm, turning and carrying her into the stall to press her back against the far wall. While he would have liked to take his time making love to her, there was no telling how long they had to themselves. It would be a fast joining, though he would make certain it was a satisfying one.

"Hurry, I cannot wait. I have been too long without you." There she was pleading with him again. Would she never stop begging him to satisfy her?

Never, she thought, *never*.

He hoisted her up so that he could easily plunge into her, and he was not surprised that she was wet and ready for him. He kept her braced against the wall so that his one hand was free to tease her nub as he pounded into her repeatedly.

She came in a flash and he knew he could make her come again. But first he had to capture her scream with his mouth, before someone came running, thinking someone was in dire need of help. And when he made her come again, he caught her scream in his mouth for a second time as she tightened around him and that was all he needed to climax.

He rested his brow against hers after he was sure she was too spent to scream or moan any longer. He did not want to let her go. He did not want to pull out of her. He wanted to remain inside her, joined with her, reveling in the exquisite aftermath of their lovemaking. Even though it was quick, it was more satisfying than some long lovemaking sessions he had experienced. He credited the difference to being madly in love with his wife.

"You know this is not the end of it," she said through labored breath. "I have things to see to but after the noon meal we are going to my bedchamber and not leaving until morning."

"You will keep me prisoner?" he asked with a laugh and a soft nuzzle to her neck.

She moaned. "If I must, I will tie you to the bed."

"If you would like, though I would much rather tie you."

She shuddered at the thought.

"And do you know what I would do to you?"

She was barely able to whisper, "What?"

He murmured in her ear, "Every wicked thing imaginable."

She shuddered again, thinking she would not make it until noon, and then thought about her duties and attempted to shake some sense into her herself. Having him inside her did not help, especially when she felt him stir.

"The thought of making you my prisoner of love stirs me to life," he said and brushed his lips over hers before kissing her with a tenderness that sent a shiver through her and sent her tiny nub tingling.

"Stay inside me," she whispered and nibbled at his earlobe.

Hunter shuddered. "God, I cannot get enough of you."

"Then take what you want, for I want all you can give me."

To his surprise, his manhood shot to life and he started moving inside her once again, slow at first, for this time he wanted to take his time.

Voices drawing near tore them apart, but they passed by and Hunter was quick to grab her, lift her, and enter her, though this time he did not take his time.

Patience locked her lips as he slammed into her repeatedly, exciting her with every thrust and when his fingers teased that spot that brought her so much pleasure her mouth found his so that she could cry out in climax without being heard once again.

Never had she felt anything so good, and she ran her hands up under his plaid and over his naked backside to squeeze it tight and shove him harder against her, forcing him to climax as well.

It was not voices passing by that tore them apart this time, it was voices shouting out her name and they were quick to disengage and after a hasty check to see that they were presentable, they hurried out of the stable.

Bruce, her most trusted warrior approached her as soon as he spotted her. "The sentries on the far west border have found a body. They are bringing it here now."

"Male or female?" Patience asked, fear prickling

her skin.

"I do not know."

Hunter wanted to take her hand and reassure her that it was not Heather, but what if it was? He remained by her side, not touching her, though he wanted to, but she stood a warrior in front of her men and it would not do for her to show that she sought solace from another, even if he was her husband.

Hunter walked with her and Bruce to the entrance of the village and waited. The two warriors approaching were not that far away, though it seemed like the time dragged on forever before they reached the village gates.

When they did, Patience's heart slammed against her chest. The body draped over the one warrior's horse was distinctly female.

"We do not know who she is," the warrior said.

Hunter came up behind his wife when he saw her body go limp from relief that it had not been her sister. He coiled his arm around her waist to support her and moved her forward so none could see that her limbs had gone weak.

"Let us see if we recognize her," Hunter said, giving his wife enough time to regain her senses.

It was Hunter who took a sharp step back when he saw the bruised and bloodied face of Rona, Greer's wife.

"Is that Rona?" Patience asked, taking a closer look and seeing the missing thatch of hair on the top of the woman's head, confirming her suspicion.

"Aye, it is," Hunter confirmed his stomach tightening.

Patience paled and ordered the body to be taken to

the empty storehouse. She also ordered Bruce to make certain that the identity of the woman was kept secret for now.

He looked at her, knowing her well and whispered, "War brews, does it not?"

"Aye, it does," she said and turned to her husband. "We need to speak with my father."

By the time she and Hunter reached the keep, news had already spread that a body had been found, though no identity made and that led to speculation.

Patience had to reach her father before he worried that it was Heather who had been found beaten to death. She rushed up the stairs, Hunter close behind her and found Maura coming out of her father's room.

"Tell me it is not Heather," she said with tears in her eyes.

"It is not, and I must let my father know." Patience entered to find her da fully dressed and looking as if he was ready to leave the room.

"Tell me," he ordered.

Patience shook her head. "It is not Heather."

Her father sat with a thud in the chair, his legs no longer able to support him. "Who?" he asked his breathing heavy.

Hunter stepped forward. "Greer's wife, Rona. She was beaten badly, her face almost unrecognizable."

"You are sure it is her?" Patience's father asked.

Hunter nodded. "I am sure, and I am sure you realize why my brother had his wife beaten to death and left on Macinnes land."

Donald Macinnes nodded. "He will claim a Macinnes killed her, giving him the perfect excuse to declare war on the Macinnes clan."

Patience waited, hoping her father, in his infinite wisdom would find a way to avoid a war and as the minutes passed in silence she feared that war was inevitable.

Hunter broke the silence. "Rab will demand his wife's return once he discovers she is here, claiming the Macinnes took her captive. And I would not be surprised if Saundra met the same fate as Rona with Rab also laying blame on the Macinnes and sealing the claim for war."

"Is there not a way out of this, Da?" Patience asked her worry growing.

"I need to think," her father said. "Leave me and we will talk later." He shook his head. "I almost forgot. Emma and her husband are on their way here. I am sure Rogan has a strong enough force with him since I sent word of the situation to him. But send some warriors out to meet them. They should arrive by evening. Now go and enjoy what time you can together and send Maura to me."

Patience did not have to go far to find the woman, she was pacing outside the door. "He wants you."

She nodded and hurried into the room, closing the door behind her.

Patience did not like the sound of the latch being locked. It felt as if her father was keeping her at a distance while entrusting a stranger. She silently scolded herself for thoughts that had no place in her head. She and her sisters had been lucky to have Maura enter their lives. She had helped take much of the burden of caring for her father and running the keep off Heather's already heavily weighted shoulders, allowing her some time to herself. And furthermore, she should be thrilled that she and Emma were finally going to be reunited.

"It will be good for you to see your sister," Hunter said, taking her hand.

"Aye, I am pleased."

"Yet you do not smile."

"How do I smile when Heather is still missing and war looms large on the horizon?"

Chapter Thirty-four

Patience paced the steps of the keep. Word was received that Emma and her husband Rogan were only minutes away. Patience had a difficult time knowing that her sister was so close and yet protocol dictated that she wait patiently to receive her. She would much rather ride out and greet her. And where had her husband gone? He was there on the steps watching her pace only moments ago and now he was nowhere to be seen.

Her pacing increased, though when she turned for the umpteenth time and caught sight of her husband on his horse, her stallion following behind him, she grinned from ear to ear.

As soon as he stopped, she mounted her horse, then leaned over and kissed his cheek. "I do so love you."

They took off together and as they rode out of the village and across the land memories flooded her mind and brought tears to her eyes. She and her sisters would run to greet their father when he returned home after a long journey and when they would see him reach the rise they would squeal with joy. As they got older Heather would admonish such unseemly actions, but Patience had always managed to talk her into running to greet him.

Now it was just her greeting her married sister, her father ill, and Heather still missing. A tear fell from her eye and she wiped it roughly away with the back of her hand. She did not want to cry, but she could feel the tears welling up in her and she knew there would be no stopping them.

When they finally spotted the troop, and she and Emma's eyes met, they urged their horses into a gallop toward each other.

Hunter increased his pace, though kept a distance to give his wife time with her sister. He noticed that the man who followed after Emma, presumably her husband, did the same as he.

Once the sisters were near on top of each other they drew their mounts to a halt and dismounted, Patience quickly, Emma with a bit more caution. They ran straight at each other, embracing when they finally came together.

Tears spilled liberally down their cheeks and they hugged tight, each one talking over the other until they finally erupted into laughter and more tears.

Hunter dismounted a few feet from them and walked around them to introduce himself, to Emma's husband, though he would leave it to his wife to let the couple know they were married.

"Hunter McLaud," he said, offering his hand.

"Rogan MacClennan," the man said and accepted Hunter's hand, giving it a firm shake.

"You must meet my husband," Emma said, wiping tears off her wet, flushed cheeks.

Patience followed Emma over to the two men and with one glance she could see why Rogan MacClennan had first wanted Heather as his wife. He was as handsome as Heather was beautiful, long dark hair, dark eyes, fine features and a tad taller than

Hunter. He and Heather would have made a fine pair, yet seeing the way Rogan looked with such love at Emma made them truly a perfect match.

"Rogan my sister Patience," Emma said proudly.

Rogan slipped his arm around his wife and bobbed his head at Patience. "It is a pleasure to finally meet you. Emma speaks highly of you and your skills as a warrior."

"I can vouch for them," Hunter said with a smile, slipping his arm around his wife's waist.

Emma looked from Hunter to her sister.

Patience grinned. "My husband... Hunter McLaud."

~~~

Patience and Emma chatted on their way to the keep, both filling in what had happened to each of them since Heather's abduction and their separation.

Emma shocked Patience when she said, "Heather was so frightened when I saw her."

"You saw our sister? Where? When?"

"I foolishly followed a ghost warrior, hoping he would lead me to Heather, until I realized it was what the warrior expected me to do. He wanted me to find their camp and see that Heather was there. I went to her and again foolishly believed I could help her escape."

"Where was Rogan?"

"He arrived with his warriors, but as skilled as they are, they were no match for the ghost warriors. Besides, Heather and I were hugging each other tight. I was determined not to let go of her, but the ghost warriors ripped her from my arms so quickly that I could not believe she was gone."

"It was not your fault," Patience said, hearing the guilt in her sister's voice.

A tear ran down Emma's cheek. "And how would you have felt if she had been ripped out of your arms?" She shook her head. "Especially after seeing the intense fear in her eyes when she learned that it was the Dark Dragon who had her abducted."

"Heather did not know?" Patience asked perplexed. "He had not made himself known to her?"

"She had seen no inkling of him. She told me that she had been moved around and believed her captors were waiting for a ransom to be paid."

"Perhaps it was the fear of learning that the Dark Dragon was her captor that gave her the courage to escape him."

Emma's eyes turned wide. "Heather escaped?"

"All signs point to it being so," Patience confirmed. "I thought you knew. Father said he sent a message apprizing you of the situation."

"There was no mention of Heather at all, only that you had returned and that war with the McLaud clan was possible. He warned us to be cautious. He also said nothing of you being wed, though I suppose he felt it was your news to share. But if Heather escaped where is she?"

"Hopefully, she is making her way home. I intended to rest for one day and then search for her, but father forbid it."

Emma's brow scrunched. "Why? He must be worried about her."

"More than anyone realizes, but with the

McLaud's hungry for war, he has even a bigger problem. Greer has men in the area, so our land is not as safe as it once was."

"What of Heather? What if the McLauds find her?"

Patience explained how Greer hoped to have the Dark Dragon side with him.

Emma paled. "If that happened..." She shook her head. "We would be defeated."

"So, you see how dire the situation all around."

"Father will think of something," Emma said hopeful.

The sisters turned quiet, both knowing that this was one time their father may not find a way to prevent the inevitable.

When they reached the steps of the keep both women hurried off their horses and up the steps, eager to speak with their da.

The men followed, joining them in the Great Hall.

The women stopped abruptly, their husbands doing the same behind them, when they saw their father standing in the middle of the Great Hall, looking fitter than he had in years. He threw his arms out wide and his daughters ran into them.

He hugged them to him, holding them tight. "Thank God, you are both safe and home."

"You are out of bed, Da," Emma asked, looking up at him. "You must feel better."

"It is time I see to my duties and time to celebrate my daughters' return home."

"We cannot celebrate until Heather has returned home safely," Emma said.

Donald hugged his daughters again. "Let us eat

and drink and put a plan together to bring our Heather home."

Instead of sitting at the dais, he took his daughters to the table in front of the large hearth and they smiled. There were many a day they had sat there with their da talking and laughing and feeling more loved than ever.

Their husbands joined them and soon Una and Saundra did as well. Ewan and his sons wandered in and Donald welcomed them. Rogan's warriors wandered in after setting up camp and all the tables were soon occupied and piled high with food and drink.

Conversation flowed easily, missing blanks were filled in as the sisters shared their stories, and the skills of the ghost warriors were discussed.

"It is truly remarkable that you avoided being captured by the ghost warriors," Emma said to Saundra.

"What was remarkable was watching them," Saundra said. "They are precise and focused in their movements, almost as if every step is measured. And they are patient, sitting for hours in a tree simply waiting."

"For what?" Ross asked.

Saundra shrugged. "I do not know."

"You never saw the Dark Dragon?" Hunter asked.

Saundra shivered. "No, and I would not want to. Many speak of what a frightening sight it is to set eyes on him."

"The sight of him can disturb, since he is covered almost entirely in black," Patience said.

"You saw him?" her father asked surprised.

"I did, and I warned him that I would not leave his land until I spoke with Heather, which is what eventually led me to believe that he no longer had Heather."

"We need to find her," Donald Macinnes said firmly. "And we need to do it before the McLauds start a war."

Rogan and Emma looked to Hunter, but it was Donald who explained the situation.

Rogan nodded at Hunter after Donald finished. "How do we know we can trust him?"

"Because I say we can," Patience snapped.

Hunter rested his hand on his wife's arm to calm her. "Rogan has a right to doubt a man he does not know and one whose family wishes to wage war against the Macinnes."

"Hunter is not like his brothers," Saundra said. "He is a good, honorable man and did what he thought was best to save his clan from war as did Patience."

"She is right," Una said. "Hunter is nothing like his two brothers, but be warned for Greer cares for nothing but himself and will kill anyone who stands in his way."

Hunter thought of Rona's beaten body in the storehouse. He had not informed his mum about her death, for though there was no love between Rona and his mum, it would upset her to know what the poor woman had suffered.

"Greer will play his hand when the time is right," Una said. "He learned that from his father, though nothing more."

Ross walked over to Saundra and placed a hand

on her shoulder. "They will surely demand Saundra's return."

"Without a doubt," Una said, patting the young woman's trembling hand.

"Saundra must stay here under our protection," Ross declared as if he decreed it.

"You cannot keep another man's wife," Ewan said what everyone feared. "It would give Greer the excuse he needed to start a war. And it will give Hew McDolan an even greater reason to join Greer in battle."

"I will not have a war started over me," Saundra said more bravely than she felt.

"And it has not come to that yet," Donald Macinnes said. "For now we eat, drink, and enjoy my two daughters return home." With that he raised his tankard and all joined in.

~~~

Patience lay naked in her husband's arms, having made love with him twice and feeling more wonderful than she had a right to, especially with Heather plaguing her thoughts.

"There is something I do not understand," Patience said.

"I will be glad to provide, in full detail, any further lessons you need," Hunter said with a pat to her bare bottom.

She jabbed him in the chest. "I am not talking about our lovemaking." She raised her head off his chest and looked up at him. "Though, lessons are always welcomed."

Hunter grabbed her chin and kissed her quick. "Careful, wife, or you will find me inside you fast enough."

"You are welcomed there even more."

He had her flat on her back in an instant and her hands pinned above her head. "Before I do more wicked things to you, tell me what it is you do not understand."

Her brow furrowed.

"You do not remember?" he teased with a smile.

Her eyes shot wide, recalling what had been on her mind. "Ghost warriors. They are exceptionally skilled warriors who I believe would rarely make a mistake. So how were two women able to avoid them?"

"Luck?"

"One perhaps, but two?" she said shaking her head. "That does not seem feasible."

"What are you thinking?"

"I do not know, but the thought has troubled me and when a thought troubles there is usually a good reason behind it."

"In time, you will find it," Hunter assured her.

"But will I find it *in time*?"

Hunter saw the worry in her eyes and his response was to change the worry there to passion and he did. He kept his promise and made love to her throughout the night and in between sleep."

Surprisingly, they both were up by sunrise the next day, feeling more rested than ever. They hurried to the Great Hall hoping to have breakfast alone and were surprised to see Emma at the table by the hearth, her head resting on it.

Patience approached her with anxious steps and when her head came up and Patience saw how pale she was, she hurried to her side.

"What is wrong?" Patience demanded.

"I am not feeling well that is all," Emma said.

Maura suddenly appeared with a wet cloth in hand and pressed it against the back of Emma's neck. "This will help."

A servant appeared and placed a wooden board with sliced bread on it in front of Emma and sent her a sympathetic smile as she said, "It will pass."

"She is right," Maura said. "Take the bread it will help."

"I cannot. It will make me more ill," Emma complained.

Hunter tore a small piece off a slice and placed it in her hand. "Eat. It will help."

"How do you know?" Patience asked perplexed that her husband understood what was wrong with her sister while she knew absolutely nothing about it.

"I have seen it with sisters and friends of the women I have known," he said.

"It is something that spreads easily?" Patience asked concerned.

"Hopefully," he said with a smile, "you will catch it soon."

"How lovely it would be for both of us to be with child at the same time," Emma said.

"You carry a babe!" Patience said with joy.

"You what?" Rogan's roar echoed through the Great Hall as all eyes turned to see him entering the room.

Hunter took his wife's hand and tugged her away

from her sister and Maura stepped away as well.

Rogan strode up to the table and slapped his hands down on it in front of his wife. "Why did you not tell me?" He shook his head and answered his own query. "You feared I would not let you travel to see your sister."

"Would you have?" she asked, rising her chin.

"No," he shouted and pointed at her, "and this proves why. The babe has you ill and you need to rest."

"Do not yell at my sister," Patience said and tried to step forward, but Hunter stopped her.

"Keep a hold on your wife's tongue, Hunter," Rogan yelled.

Hunter laughed. "God himself could not perform that feat."

Emma laughed. "Your husband knows you well, unlike mine." She got quickly to her feet, too quickly. Her head spun and her stomach revolted. She moaned and dropped back down on the bench.

Hunter's arm hurried around his wife's waist when she went to move and whispered, "You would not want anyone interfering with us." His words stilled her, though her body remained tense as if ready for battle.

Rogan shook his head as he hurried to his wife's side, hunching down in front of her. "Forgive me, I am a fool."

"No one will argue with that," Patience said.

Emma smiled and rested her brow to her husband's. "My sister is accustomed to defending me."

"And glad I am for it," Rogan said.

"Perhaps he is not so bad," Patience said begrudgingly.

"He is not bad at all," Emma said, resting a gentle hand to his cheek. "He is a most wonderful husband and I love him dearly. I should have told him of the babe, but I feared he would have restricted my activities, out of concern for me, and that could have stopped me from searching for Heather if the chance presented itself."

Rogan took her hand and kissed her palm. "I would go search for Heather if you could not. I will do whatever is necessary to see her brought home as I promised you."

"He just redeemed himself," Patience said.

"Thank you," Rogan said with a nod to Patience, "but I much rather my wife forgive me for reacting so badly to news that fills my heart with joy."

"There is nothing to forgive, for I share a fault in this," Emma said and kissed her husband.

Handshakes and hugs were shared in congratulating the couple and soon they were all seated at the table enjoying breakfast. Even Emma managed a few bites, her stomach calming.

Donald Macinnes joined them and got tears in his eyes when Emma told him of the impending birth.

"My first among many grandchildren," he said, raising his tankard.

Emma's smile faded, her face turning pale again.

Rogan kept his arm firm around her. "What is wrong?"

Emma looked to Patience and reached across the table to her.

Patience took her hand and gripped it firmly.

"Heather should be here to share this special moment with us," Emma said. "It is not right that we are so happy and she..." Tears stung her eyes and choked away her words.

The door to the Great Hall swung open and a hooded, cloaked figure stumbled in with the slashing rain. Servants hurried to shut the large doors and the figure stumbled forward, a hand going to rest on the edge of a table to steady itself.

Patience stood, thinking perhaps it was a messenger who had braved the weather, but from whom?

It took the figure a moment for limbs to regain strength, and then with hands that trembled, pushed back the hood.

Gasps echoed around the Great Hall.

"I made it," Heather called out as if she did not quite believe it. "Thank God, I made it home."

Patience and Emma were out of their chairs in an instant and made it just as fast to their sister's side. They threw their arms around her and hugged her tight. Tears fell rapidly, and the sisters refused to let go of one another. Noting would separate them again. Nothing.

It took their father's love and need to take his oldest daughter in his arms, to tear the sisters apart. Rogan took his weeping wife in his arms and Patience turned to fling herself in Hunter's arms.

"All is well now," she said after hugging him tight. "My sister is home and she is finally safe. Whatever the future holds, we face it together as a family once more."

Donna Fletcher

THE END

Coming winter 2015...
Highlander: The Dark Dragon,
Heather's story and the final book in the Macinnes Sisters trilogy.

Donna Fletcher

Titles by Donna Fletcher

Single Titles

San Francisco Surrender
Rebellious Bride
The Buccaneer
Tame My Wild Touch
Playing Cupid
Whispers on the Wind

Series Books

Wyrrd Witch Series

The Wedding Spell
Magical Moments
Magical Memories
Remember the Magic

The Irish Devil
Irish Hope

Isle of Lies
Love Me Forever

Dark Warrior
Legendary Warrior

The Daring Twin
The Bewitching Twin

Taken By Storm
The Highlander's Bride

Sinclare Brothers' Series

Donna Fletcher

Return of the Rogue
Under the Highlander's Spell
The Angel & The Highlander
Highlander's Forbidden Bride

Warrior King Series

Bound To A Warrior
Loved By A Warrior
A Warrior's Promise
Wed To A Highland Warrior

Highlander Trilogy

Highlander Unchained
Forbidden Highlander
Highlander's Captive

Rancheros Trilogy

Untamed Fire
Renegade Love
Third book yet to be titled

Sexual Appetites of Unearthly Creatures Novella Series

Sexual Appetites of Vampires

Macinnes Sisters Trilogy

The Highlander's Stolen Heart
Highlander's Rebellious Love
Highlander: The Dark Dragon, Winter 2015

About the Author

Donna Fletcher is a *USA Today* bestselling author of historical and paranormal romances. Her books are sold worldwide. She started her career selling short stories and winning reader contests. She soon expanded her writing to her love of romance novels and sold her first book SAN FRANCISCO SURRENDER the year she became president of New Jersey Romance Writers.

Drop by Donna's website www.donnafletcher.com where you can learn more about her, get a printable Book List, and read her blog.

Printed in Poland
by Amazon Fulfillment
Poland Sp. z o.o., Wrocław